THE COFFIN MAKER'S GARDEN

Stuart MacBride is the No.1 *Sunday Times* bestselling author of the Logan McRae and Ash Henderson novels. He's also published standalones, novellas and short stories, as well as a children's picture book.

Stuart lives in the northeast of Scotland with his wife Fiona, cats Grendel, Gherkin, Onion, and Beetroot, some hens, horses, and a vast collection of assorted weeds.

For more information visit StuartMacBride.com
🅕 /StuartMacBrideBooks
🅣 @StuartMacBride

D0470361

By Stuart MacBride

The Logan McRae Novels
Cold Granite
Dying Light
Broken Skin
Flesh House
Blind Eye
Dark Blood
Shatter the Bones
Close to the Bone
22 Dead Little Bodies
The Missing and the Dead
In the Cold Dark Ground
Now We Are Dead
The Blood Road
All That's Dead

The Oldcastle Novels
Birthdays for the Dead
A Song for the Dying
A Dark so Deadly
The Coffinmaker's Garden

Other Works
Sawbones (a novella)
Twelve Days of Winter (short stories)
Partners in Crime (two Logan and Steel short stories)
The 45% Hangover (a Logan and Steel novella)
The Completely Wholesome Adventures of Skeleton Bob
(a picture book)

Writing as Stuart B. MacBride
Halfhead

STUART MACBRIDE

THE COFFIN MAKER'S GARDEN

HarperCollins*Publishers*

The quotation 'Sauf', und würg' dich zu todt!' is from the opera *Siegfried* by Richard Wagner, first performed at the Bayreuth Festival Theatre, Germany, on 16 August 1876.

HarperCollins*Publishers* Ltd
1 London Bridge Street,
London SE1 9GF

www.harpercollins.co.uk

Published by HarperCollins*Publishers* 2021
1

A catalogue record for this book
is available from the British Library

ISBN: 978-0-00-820831-8 (HB)
ISBN: 978-0-00-820832-5 (TPB)

Set in Meridien by Palimpsest Book Production Limited,
Falkirk, Stirlingshire

Printed and bound in Great Britain by
CPI Group (UK) Ltd, Croydon, CR0 4YY

MIX
Paper from
responsible sources
FSC C007454

This book is produced from independently certified FSC™ paper
to ensure responsible forest management.

For more information visit: www.harpercollins.co.uk/green

In memory of Marion Chesney
(AKA: M.C. Beaton)

a firebrand, force of nature, and excellent writer
whose books brought happiness to millions

including me

Without Whom

As always I've received a lot of help from many, many people while I was writing this book, so I'd like to take this opportunity to thank: Sergeant Bruce Crawford, star of Skye and screen, who answers *far* more daft questions than anyone should ever have to, as do my forensic gurus Professor Dave Barclay, Professor James Grieve, and her most excellent Dameness Professor Sue Black; then there's Julia Wisdom, Jane Johnson, Kathryn Cheshire, Jaime Frost, Ann Bissell, Linda Joyce, Anna Derkacz, Isabel Coburn, Alice Gomer, Charlie Redmayne, Roger Cazalet, Kate Elton, Hannah O'Brien, Sarah Shea, Abbie Salter, Adam Humphrey, Charlotte Cross, Ben Wright, Anne O'Brien, Marie Goldie, the DC Bishopbriggs Naughty Book Brigade, and everyone at HarperCollins, for all things publishy; Phil Patterson and the team at Marjacq Scripts, for keeping my numerous cats in cat food; Craig Robertson, Alexandra Sokoloff and everyone at Bute Noir for their hospitality; and Allan Guthrie for being an excellent pre-reader yet again.

While I'm doling out 'thank-you's, here's one for all the librarians and booksellers whose enthusiasm and dedication inspire us all to try something new. And let's not forget you: the person reading this book! The world seems to get dumber and nastier by the day, but it's people who *read* that keep the world that teeny bit brighter and saner than it would otherwise be. I salute you, my friend.

I've saved the best for last – as is my wont – Fiona and Grendel (with a nod to Onion, Beetroot, and Gherkin who weren't that much help, but haven't interfered too much [except for Beetroot]).

— stormfront rising —

1

'...*after the New Aryan Crusade claimed responsibility for the bombing. The American Vice President described it as a cowardly and disgusting attack...*'

How come there was never any *nice* news on the radio?

Margaret chopped a crunchy orange carrot and tossed it into the bubbling brown cauldron of mince, as rain rattled the fogged-up kitchen window. 'You know what I think, Alfie? I think people are poopheads.'

No response, but then there never was. Once Alfie got himself into a colouring-in book, that was it. You'd get more response from a garden gnome.

'...*ongoing operation to rescue the crew of the* Ocean-Gold Harvester, *run aground against the cliffs at Clachmara. We spoke to Sophie O'Brien at the Coastguard...*'

'Ooh, did you hear that, Alfie? Clachmara! We got a mention on the radio, isn't that exciting?'

Still nothing.

Honestly, might as well be on her own, here. Oh, it'd seemed *so* romantic on the website: 'An unmissable opportunity to rent a delightful, period, seaside cottage, with traditional fixtures and decor, in a much sought-after location!' Which meant a leaky roof, wood-panelled walls that hadn't seen a paintbrush since Fred and Rose West were doing up their patio, and single glazing that fogged up if you so much as looked at it. The wind whistled right through the frames if you didn't stuff all the gaps with scrunched-up newspaper, too.

Still, at least it was cheap.

Another carrot snapped and crackled into random-shaped chunks, because, let's face it, *rounds* of carrot were revolting.

'*…extremely challenging conditions, but we're doing everything we can.*'

The warm brown scent of mince filled the room, comforting and familiar as a favourite jumper. Hiding the more usual dusty whiff of mice-and-mildew. Keeping the darkness at bay.

'Well, *I* think it's exciting, even if you don't.'

'*Police, today, announced the discovery of a child's body in woodland south of the city. The remains haven't been formally identified yet, but are suspected to be those of Lewis Talbot – the four-year-old, missing since the fourteenth of October…*'

'Poor wee tyke.' Margaret dumped the last carrot bits into the pot. 'That's why you should never get into a car with strange men, Alfie. Or take sweeties from them.'

'*…third victim, after Oscar Harris and Andrew Brennan's bodies were discovered earlier this year.*'

'Actually, you know what? Stay away from men, full-stop.' She rubbed at her swollen belly and puffed out a heartburn breath. 'Wouldn't be in *this* condition if I had. No, I'd be grad-uating tomorrow with a degree in forensic anthropology, and your granny and grandad would still be talking to me.' Sounding kinda bitter, there, Margaret. And whose fault was it you got yourself knocked up?

Sigh.

'Never mind, Alfie, at least we've got each other, right?'

Still nothing.

Seriously: a garden gnome.

'*Now here's Doug with the weather.*'

'*Thanks, Colin. Better batten down the hatches, folks, because it's going to get a lot worse before it gets better as Storm Trevor moves in from Scandinavia…*'

'Oh, that's just fffff…' Margaret pinched her lips together and bit down on a word that Alfie was definitely not meant to have

4

in his vocabulary. Because knowing *him*, he'd parrot it at the top of his voice at playschool tomorrow and she'd have to go in for another 'chat' with that pudding-faced harridan Mrs Gillespie. Try again: 'So, my teeny monster, how about you help Mummy and fetch some of those tatties from under the sink?'

She turned, speed-peeler in hand, holding it like a fairy wand about to grant Alfie's fondest wish – as long as it was for mashed potatoes.

Then stopped. Mouth open.

'…all down to this massive area of low pressure moving in from the east…'

'Alfie?'

The scarred wooden table was home to a scattered rainbow of felt-tip pens, a partially coloured Tyrannosaurus Rex in garish shades of purple and green roaring out of the colouring-in book. A glass of milk and a bourbon biscuit, sitting next to them. But Alfie's chair was empty.

'Alfie?' Margaret dumped the peeler on the worktop, wiping her hands on her pinny as she walked over and poked her head out into the hall. More so-called period wood panelling. 'Alfie?'

The bathroom door hung ajar, but there was no light on in there. Nothing but the darkness of a stormy November evening.

'Alfie, did you go for a wee-wee?'

No: the bathroom was empty.

'Alfie?' Getting louder now as she hurried through the two tiny bedrooms, the dining room – stacked high with all the boxes she still hadn't got around to unpacking yet – and the living room with its gaping fireplace and water-stained ceiling. 'ALFIE!'

Into the kitchen again.

Table. Pens. Colouring book…

Where were his wellies? His wellies should've been sitting next to hers, by the back door, but Alfie's red wellington boots were gone. His yellow anorak and sou'wester too.

Her eyes widened as she stared at the fogged-up window and rain rattled the single glazing. At the grey-blackness on the other side.

5

Oh no.

Margaret wrenched open the door and stumbled out into the darkness, losing one of her slippers on the way. Rain slashing at her face with frozen, sharp little knives. 'ALFIE!'

She hurried around the side of the house. Only a handful of streetlights were still working – trembling in the downpour, buffeted by the wind howling in from the North Sea, casting their sickly yellow glow out onto the cracked tarmac. The lampposts stopped a dozen yards past her house, leaving everything from there on – not that there was much of it – wreathed in gloom. Hiding the end of the world.

'ALFIE!'

Into the middle of the road, turning, hauling in a deep breath and making a loudhailer of her hands. 'ALFIE!'

Wait … there was a noise. Something hiding in the bellowing storm. A clattering growling noise. A hard mechanical *whomp-whomp-whomp* that stuttered and yowled. Then a light, bright and sharp, rose in the distance, bringing with it winking eyes of red and green as a helicopter rose over the cliffs, the whining engines and thrumming blades louder now. Clearer.

And Alfie loved helicopters.

'ALFIE!'

Margaret stumbled past blacked-out houses towards it, ducking under the line of 'No Entry' tape that *frrrrrrrred* in the wind. Temporary metal fencing cut straight across the road, eight-foot high, blocking off the last 'habitable' house on either side from the 'uninhabitable' ones beyond. A faded sign, bolted to the chain-link: 'WARNING! ~ COASTAL EROSION ZONE ~ NO ENTRY ~ DANGER OF DEATH'

They never maintained the fence, did they? Just moved it one house further inland every time some poor sod's home disappeared into the North Sea. The thing was probably riddled with holes big enough for a five-year-old to wriggle through.

She hauled one end of the fence out of its concrete footplate, dragging it as far as the chain holding it to the next segment would allow, then squeezed between the cold metal uprights and into the darkness beyond. 'ALFIE!'

Above her, the helicopter turned and its spotlight slid across the rain-slicked grass. A flash of yellow burst in the night, 'ALFIE!' then the light moved on and he was swallowed by darkness again.

Margaret stumbled forward into the wind, staggering in the helicopter's downdraught. Moving from the tattered tarmac into someone long-gone's garden. Feeling her way along what was probably a picket fence. Heaving herself over to the other side with a tugging rip of fabric. Losing the other slipper in the process.

'ALFIE?'

He was standing there, at the edge of the cliff, staring down into the water.

Oh God.

The cliff. The one all the warning signs were about.

What if it collapsed underneath him?

What if *he* was light enough, but *she* was too heavy and trying to save him caused it all to fall into the sea?

Her bare feet slithered through the wet grass as she crept closer, arms held out to him. Trying to hide the tremble in her voice, bottling it down. 'Come on, baby, come to Mummy. It's OK, it's OK. Come to Mummy.'

He looked over his shoulder at her and smiled a gap-toothed smile, one finger pointing up at the red-and-white machine hammering the air above them. 'Hellingcopter!'

'Please come to Mummy, Alfie. Come on, you can do it.' Reaching for him. Inching closer.

Alfie's finger pointed downwards. 'Boaty!'

She dropped to her hands and knees, crawling towards him.

Swear to God, if she could get Alfie home alive she'd never duck her mother's calls again. She'd give up drinking. She'd do volunteer work for a homeless charity, or a foodbank or something.

Closer.

Alfie stuck his thumb in his mouth.

She'd even stop calling Gary a child-support-dodging barmaid-shagging wanker, as long as she GOT ALFIE HOME ALIVE.

Margaret's fingertips snatched at the wet hem of his bright-yellow anorak, and she hauled him off his feet and into her arms. Knelt there, on the clifftop, holding him tight, squeezing, breathing in the rubbery scent of his waterproof. 'Don't *ever* do that again!'

'Look, Mummy, a boaty and a hellingcopter!'

'Let's get you home.' Tucking an arm under his bottom, she scooped him up, stood, and turned.

The Coastguard helicopter shone above them, its spotlight pointing straight down at a dumpy fishing boat – about as long as a double-decker bus, but twice as wide. As if it were nearly as pregnant as she was. The *Ocean-Gold Harvester*'s blue-and-white livery was pristine on this side, but its other side was pushed up against the brown-grey cliffs that towered above it. One of its fishing booms lay twisted along its deck, the other poking out to sea, still fixed to a ballooning swell of net as the waves slammed the boat against the wall of earth and rock.

Five men clustered by the wheelhouse, all in fluorescent-orange survival suits and life jackets, clutching at the boat's handrails, staring up at the helicopter, as one of their number was winched into the air.

The boat slid into a trough, the hull screeching down the cliff face, then the next wave battered it into the headland again.

'Want to see, want to see!'

'No, Alfie, we have to get home before...'

A dark, rumbling noise cut through the wind and the rain and the helicopter's thrumming blades.

It was too late.

The cliffs were giving way.

Margaret swallowed. Pulled Alfie's head against her chest. 'Close your eyes, darling. Mummy loves you!'

Then the headland slumped, the sound of cracking rock building to a deafening bellow as a huge wall of earth and stone curled forwards and crashed down on top of the *Ocean-Gold Harvester*. Burying it. Sending up a massive gout of spray as it forced the crushed boat beneath the churning waves, taking everyone with it.

Five men, dead, just like that...

Above, the Coastguard helicopter wobbled, as if trying to catch its balance.

And Margaret *stared*. Not at the mound of rubble where a boat and five men used to be, but at the cliff face, caught in the helicopter's spotlight. The newly exposed soil was darker than the cliff had been, and that made it easier to see what poked out of it.

Bones.

Dozens of them.

Human bones.

— thoughts and prayers —

2

Bloody potholes.

The car lurched from one to the next, sending gouts of water splashing up from the wheel arches as the windscreen wipers squeak-thunked their way back and forth, fighting a losing battle against the pummelling rain. Streetlights made septic halos in the downpour, doing almost nothing to hold back the darkness. Half a dozen of them, then nothing but the angry coal-black sweep of the North Sea.

I grabbed the handle above the passenger door as the wee Suzuki jeep thumped through yet another pothole. 'Are you aiming for these things?'

Alice hunched closer to the steering wheel, squinting out through the greasy arc of semi-clear glass. 'Should be *somewhere* around here...' She'd bundled herself up in a black padded jacket, a pair of rainbow-coloured fingerless gloves poking out of the too-long sleeves. Curly brown hair pulled back in a bun that jiggled and bounced in time with the jeep's potholing adventures.

Thump. Lurch. Bump.

'Only, it's OK if you don't hit every single one of them.'

'Is that it down there?' She freed a hand for long enough to point at yet another post-war semi in unappealing shades of beige and brown. The only thing that distinguished it from its neighbours was every single light in the place seemed to

13

be on, and it had an a snot-green rattletrap Fiat Panda parked outside.

'Still say this is a waste of time.'

'But we—'

'Supposed to be catching a child-killer, not sodding about with some half-baked Misfit Mob is-it-or-isn't-it case.' I stretched my right leg out, rotating the ankle, setting it clicking. Always the same when the weather turned – scar tissue throbbed right the way through my foot, like some sadist was jabbing a soldering iron into the bones. 'What's the point of *having* uniform officers if you don't give them all the pointless jobs?'

Alice parked behind the Panda. Killed the engine. Sat there as the storm rocked our jeep on its springs. 'It's only temporary.' A shrug. 'Besides, it was this or attend the post mortem, and I *really* don't want to watch another wee boy getting eviscerated.'

Fair point.

'Ash?' She cast a sideways glance across the car at me. 'Have you thought about what you want to do tomorrow? You know, as it's—'

'Can we not talk about this right now?'

'It's perfectly natural to feel—'

'I'm fine.' Which was a lie. 'And we've got a job to do.' I clicked off my seatbelt and turned, reaching into the back of the car. Ruffled the fur between Henry's ears. 'You look after the jeep, OK?' He gazed up at me with his gob hanging open, wee pink tongue lolling out, nose all shiny and black like a fruit pastille. 'Bite anyone who tries to steal it.'

Alice groaned. 'Stop changing the subject. Tomorrow's a—'

'Don't interrupt: I'm arming the Scottie Dog Vehicle Defence System.' Henry's head got another pat, his grin widened. 'Who's a vicious little monster? You are. *Yes*, you are.'

'But—'

'For a forensic psychologist, you're really bad at picking up on the subtle signals people give out, aren't you?'

A bright smile. 'Oh, I pick them up fine, I'm just choosing to ignore them. For your own good.'

'Lucky me.' I grabbed my walking stick from the footwell. 'Come on: we'll do our civic duty then go grab a pizza or something.' The wind tried to rip the door from my hand as I opened it – stinging needles of rain jabbing into my face.

Alice clambered out the other side, head buried in the periscope hood of her coat. 'Can we have a sitty-inny instead of takeaway for a change?'

'Got a child-killer to catch, remember?' Hurpling up the puddled driveway to the front door, where a small wooden overhang offered almost no shelter from the rain. The guttering was broken on one side, letting loose a waterfall to splash down the grubby harling.

Her voice took on a distinct whiny tone. 'I'm tired of everything we eat coming out of greasy cardboard boxes. Or plastic tubs.'

'Stop moaning and ring the bell.'

She did, leaning on the button till a harsh *drrrrrrrrrrrrrrinnnnnnnnnnnnnnng* sounded on the other side of the wasp-eaten door. 'Forgotten what plates and cutlery look like.'

'I think we should take another look at Steven Kirk. Haul him in and rattle his dentures till something falls out.'

'And it's not exactly healthy, is it? When did we last have a salad?'

'I'm not buying his whole, "I was caring for my dying mother at the time" shtick. Once a nonce, always a nonce.'

'Or broccoli!' Alice made a thin keening squeaky sound from deep within her hood. 'I miss broccoli.'

'Not as if he couldn't...'

The door swung open and a greasy-looking bloke with floppy brown hair, a cheap suit, and ginger-pube beard scowled out at me. 'Took your time.' One of his eyes didn't quite point in the same direction as the other, as if he'd put it in squint.

'DC Watt. Nice to see your winning personality hasn't deserted you.'

A grunt, then he turned on his heel and marched down the hallway. The move showed off a palm-sized bald patch at the back of his head, complete with thick U-shaped scar, the skin

15

dented inward around it, as if a section of his skull was recessed. 'Mother's in the kitchen.'

Alice followed me inside and unzipped her padded jacket, revealing yet another exhibit from her black-and-white-stripy-top collection, teeny red Converse trainers squeaking against the damp linoleum as we made our way into a steamed-up room at the back of the house, redolent with the welcoming scent of mince and tatties.

A heavily pregnant woman sat at the table, with a small boy on her knee, holding him close as he made a pig's arse of colouring a triceratops in horrible shades of puce and turquoise.

Mother's wide back was turned towards us, frizzy Irn-Bru hair spilling across the shoulders of her black police-issue fleece. She'd pulled the sleeves up, exposing two large pale forearms clarted with tattoos of roses and thistles. 'And you're *sure* they weren't animal bones, or something like that?'

The pregnant woman rolled her eyes. 'I should be graduating with a degree in forensic anthropology tomorrow, but I drank too much prosecco at my birthday party and here we are.' Pointing at her swollen belly. 'I *know* human anatomy, and those bones were definitely human.'

DC Watt cleared his throat. 'Sorry, Guv, but that's the LIRU lot here.' Pronouncing 'LIRU' as if it were a venereal disease.

Mother turned and raised an eyebrow at us. 'Well, well, well, if it isn't Ash Henderson. Returned to the land of the living?'

I nodded back. 'Detective Inspector. You know Dr McDonald?'

Alice scampered forward like an excitable spaniel, hand out for the shaking. 'Actually, we haven't met, DI Malcolmson, but please call me "Alice" – I've heard a lot about you, it's a pleasure, and don't worry, we're not here to take over your case, we've only come because you said you needed our help, well, probably not *our* help, but Ash's help anyway and I came along because he can't really drive, what with his foot and everything.' All delivered in one long machinegun breath. 'And I was wondering about your nickname, why do people call you "Mother", is that because you're a nurturing influence, which I know is a repressive societal stereotype imposed on the female psyche by the

16

repressive forces of a dictatorial patriarchy, "oh women are so nurturing and soft, they can't possibly compete with men," but sometimes that really is the case, isn't it, well the nurturing bit, not the competition thing, and is that a pot of tea, I'd love a cuppa if there's one going spare?'

Mother's eyebrow went up even further. 'Is she always like this?'

'More than you could possibly believe.' I stuck my hands in my pockets. 'Now, can we get this over with? Alice and I have a child-murdering ...' my eyes flitted to the small boy, staring up at me from his badly coloured dinosaur, 'naughty man to catch.'

'I dare say you do.' Mother waved at Watt. 'John, be a dear and stay with Miss Compton. Mr Henderson and I need to go check something.' And with that, she was squeezing her way past me and out into the hall. Hauling on a large wax Barbour jacket. Pausing at the front door. 'You don't mind making a wee detour before we get down to it, do you?' She didn't bother giving me time to answer that. 'No? Good. Come on then.'

She flipped her hood up and stepped out into the howling gale. Round shoulders hunched against the wind as she picked her way down the path, between the puddles.

Alice pouted at me. 'Do you think I made a bad first impression there, because I think I made a bad first impression and I really didn't want—'

'No point us both getting soaked. You stay here with DC Watt and the witness. Maybe, if you're lucky, she'll give you some mince and tatties. On proper plates. With cutlery.'

'Be careful, OK?'

'Promise.' The horrible weather wrapped itself around me like a fist as I limped after Mother. Down the path and out onto the pockmarked tarmac. Struggling to keep up. 'Where are we going?'

'Well, we can hardly take a civilian's word for it, can we? Even one who *almost* has a degree in forensic anthropology.' She pulled out a torch, sending its beam sweeping across the gardens to either side as we made our way towards the end of the road. Raising her voice over the howling wind. 'We used to come here when I was a wee girl. Every Easter, Mum and Dad would take a cottage down by the beach and we'd play in the dunes and build sandcastles and chase other people's dogs.' She stepped over a small picket fence and scuffed her way through wind-whipped clumps of yellowing grass. 'I remember Clachmara was really pretty, till the old part fell in the sea. Still, that's climate change for you, isn't it?'

She came to a halt at a line of chain-link fencing panels. Pursed her lips as she frowned at the gap between two of the segments – pulled tight against a padlocked chain – then down at herself, then back at the gap again. 'Somehow, I don't think this is going to work.'

'A *pregnant* woman managed to squeeze through, remember?'

'Not this bit, she didn't. And besides, you're in a rush to get back to catching your child-murdering naughty man, remember?'

For God's sake…

'Fine: give me the torch.'

I forced my way through to the other side, following the circle of white as it writhed through the long grass, leaving her in darkness.

'Take photographs, we need evidence!'

Rain soaked through my trouser legs, making the cold wet fabric stick to my skin. Seeped through the shoulders of my jacket. Ran down my face and the back of my neck. '"Oh, it'll be a quick job," he said, "a simple hand-holding exercise," he said, "in and out in a jiffy," he said.'

And on I went, following the torchlight. Limping and stumbling through the tussocky remains of someone's garden, grass dragging at my walking stick with pale wet tentacles. The house itself was reduced to a single gable end, the rest of it had been ripped away, leaving a jagged line of cliff face with the North Sea roaring beyond.

Jesus, this was bleak.

A gust of wind shoved me back a couple of paces. Punched another fistful of rain into my face.

Sod this for a game of police officers.

The torch's beam slithered along the boundary between here and oblivion. Off to the left, the near-vertical cliff had given way: a thick spill of rock and earth that ran down into the battering black waves. That would be where the fishing boat had disappeared.

Poor sods.

Waves crashed against the ramp of fallen headland, tearing it away with foaming teeth.

Its upper slopes reached down from the garden opposite. The house sat about a dozen feet back from the edge: a detached bungalow in sagging greys and manky browns. They'd tacked a wooden garage on the side closest to the sea, its up-and-over door hanging squint.

I slid the light across the exposed slab of earth. Faint glimmers of white shone back at me. Yup, those definitely looked like bones.

First couple of snaps on my phone came out as nothing but wobbly blurs, its flash nowhere near strong enough to illuminate anything, even with the torch's help. The video setting was slightly better, zoomed in full, footage jerking about as wind tore at my back.

Looked as if our heavily pregnant friend was right – what loomed out of the black soil was definitely human. A pair of empty eye sockets stared at me from a skull, tilted to one side, the jaw missing. Then another thumping from the North Sea sent a chunk of dark earth peeling off, taking the skull with it, tumbling and bouncing down into the crashing waves.

A small rumble sounded beneath me, and the garden I was standing in lost another foot of mud and grass.

Yeah, maybe not the *best* of ideas to hang about here any longer.

Hurry back to the fence line and through to the relative safety of the storm-battered road.

Mother peered out at me from her hood. 'Well?'

'One hundred percent human.'

Her shoulders dipped. 'Sod. Why couldn't it have been a tasteless hoax? Or a stupid misunderstanding? Maybe a buried pet, or something?'

'Never mind, leave it a couple of hours and it'll all have fallen into the sea anyway.'

'I knew this one was a poisoned chalice soon as I saw it. But I couldn't go home early when everyone else did, could I? Couldn't leave it for the nightshift to deal with. No, *I* had to be all stoic and dedicated.' She sagged. Huffed out a long sad breath. 'Take it from me, Mr Henderson, never *ever* answer the office phone two minutes before your shift ends. It's always a disaster.' Deep breath. Then a nod. 'Suppose we'd better get Scene Examination Branch down here. Pathologist, Procurator Fiscal, search teams...'

Wind howled through the chain-link, sending us lurching sideways until we leaned into it.

'Good luck with that.' I gave her the torch back. 'Now, any chance we can get on with the reason I'm actually here, while there's still some of me that's not drenched?'

'Sure you don't want to hang around and help?' Pointing the beam at the crappy green Fiat Panda parked outside the pregnant not-quite-qualified forensic anthropologist's house. 'I've got biscuits in the car.'

'*Still* got a child-killer to catch.' No one ever listened, did they?

'Can't blame a girl for trying.' Mother swung the torch around, shining it across the street at the last house on this side of the fence, the one next door to where the body was buried. A semi-detached with sagging guttering and a lichen-acned roof. An old blue Renault rusting away by the kerb and a filthy caravan in the driveway. A light in the living room window. 'Shall we?'

'Still don't see why you couldn't have done this without me.'

'Because Helen MacNeil won't talk to me. And she won't talk to John. And when I sent a uniform round to try, she came this close,' holding up two fingers, millimetres apart, 'to making him cry. Control says you and Helen have history, so maybe she'll talk to you. What with your overabundance of charm and everything.'

Sarcastic sod.

Besides, the kind of history Helen MacNeil and I had wasn't exactly the *good* kind.

I followed Mother over to the house. The caravan acted as a windbreak, groaning on its springs as the storm pushed and shoved into the other side.

She leaned on the bell for a second or five, then squatted down and levered the letterbox open. 'Helen? Helen, it's Flora, can you come to the door please?'

No reply.

She tried again. 'Helen? Hello, can you hear me?'

'Can we stop pussyfooting about?' I whacked the head of my walking stick against the door, three times, nice and hard. Hauled in a deep breath. 'HELEN MACNEIL, POLICE! OPEN UP OR I'M KICKING THIS BLOODY DOOR IN!'

A tut from Mother. 'The epitome of diplomacy, as ever.'

Three more whacks. 'I'M NOT KIDDING, HELEN, OPEN THIS DOOR OR IT'S—'

The door swung open and a middle-aged woman scowled out at us. 'All right, all right.' The years hadn't been kind to Helen MacNeil, each one of them carved into her heart-shaped face in deep spidery wrinkles. She hadn't lost any of her bulk, though: broad of shoulder and thick of bicep, wearing a black muscle shirt with a pentagram and goat's head on it. Short cropped grey hair. A long sharp nose that had been broken two or three times since we'd last met.

Helen clearly didn't like me staring. 'What the hell are *you* looking at?'

Mother shuffled closer, trying on her big dimply smile. 'I know you weren't keen on talking to us before, Helen, but it's really important we—'

'Wasn't asking you. Him.' Pointing. 'The lump with the limp.' Her chin came up. 'Think I don't know who you are?'

I nodded. 'Helen, you're looking well.'

Her eyes narrowed, the wrinkles around them deepening. 'Eleven years in HMP Bastarding Oldcastle – I missed my grand-daughter's birth because of you!'

'No, Helen, you missed your granddaughter's birth because

21

you battered Neil Stringer's head in with a pickaxe handle. And you'd have been out after eight years, if you hadn't chibbed Ruth Anderson in the prison library too.'

'Hmmph… Bitch was asking for it.'

'Sure she was.' I jerked my head towards next door, on the other side of the chain-link fencing. 'You heard about the body?'

'*Alleged* body.' Helen folded her thick arms, muscles bulging through the freckled skin. 'Fat Girl here said it was—'

'Who are you calling fat?' Mother pulled herself up to her full height, shoulders back, considerable chest out. 'I'll have you know—'

'—don't see what it's got to do with me, and—'

'—because big bones are nothing to be ashamed of! It's—'

I thumped my cane on the door again. 'ALL RIGHT, THAT'S ENOUGH! *Both* of you.'

Mother shuffled her feet. Turned her reddened face away. 'Not fat.'

Helen shrugged. Looked at the ground. Cleared her throat. Didn't say anything.

Better.

'There's nothing "alleged" about the body, it's real.'

'Still don't see what it's got to do with me.'

'With *your* reputation? A dead body miraculously turns up next door: you really think we're not going to connect the dots?'

The chin came up again. 'No comment.'

'Just like old times.' I took a step back and made a show of examining the roof, then the walls on either side. 'Place looks ready to fall down round your ears. Crime really didn't pay for you, did it? What, they didn't have a retirement package waiting when you got out of prison? A nice golden handshake to say thank you for keeping your mouth shut?'

'No comment.'

'Dropped you like a radioactive jobbie, didn't they? And I thought loyalty was supposed to go *both* ways?'

Her eyes hardened. 'No comment.'

'There you are, sent down for killing Neil Stringer, on *their*

22

orders, and I bet they didn't even bother picking you up from prison when you finally got released. Bet they stopped taking your calls. Bet they ghosted you. Like you were nothing to them.'

'No – comment!' Both words squeezed out through gritted teeth.

'Stuck out here, waiting for your craphole house to fall into the sea. An irrelevant, useless old lady.'

Helen stiffened, as if she was about to take a swing ... then licked her lips. Blinked. Let her shoulders drop. 'I know what you're doing.'

Mother huffed out a breath. 'I'm glad someone does.'

'You think if I kick off, you can do me for assaulting a police officer. Drag me down the nick and fit me up for whoever got buried over there.' Pointing in the vague direction of next door's garden. 'Well I'm not stupid and you can bugger right off. Go on, and take your fat bitch with you.'

Mother's eyes bulged. 'There's no need to be so rude!' Fists curled, trembling.

A voice peeped up at my shoulder: 'Hello?' And there was Alice, slipping into the gap between Mother and Helen MacNeil, the hood on her jacket thrown back, nose a Rudolf-shade of pink. She had Henry's lead in one hand, the other held out for Helen to shake. 'I'm Dr McDonald, but you can call me Alice if you like, because it's easier when everyone's not standing on ceremony, isn't it, and I like your T-shirt – is that Crowley's Ghost, I used to listen to them all the time, there's a lovely urgency to *proper* death metal, isn't there – anyway I was taking Henry for a walk and I heard raised voices and thought maybe I could help?'

Helen MacNeil stared at her.

Alice handed Henry's leash to me. 'Excellent, right, now: Ash, DI Malcolmson, could you give me and ... Helen, isn't it? Yes, so if you can give us a moment – if that's OK with you, Helen – and we can have a chat, you and me, two girls together, and see if we can't find a way to be all friendly about things and really work as a team, right?' She turned a full-strength

23

smile on all of us. 'Great, let's do it!' Clapping her hands as she advanced on the door.

Helen's face went a bit pale as she backed away, looking as if an articulated lorry was bearing down on her, but Alice followed her in anyway.

Thunk, the door closed behind them, leaving Mother, Henry, and me outside in the rain.

A shuffle of feet, then Mother cleared her throat. 'Are you sure your wee friend's safe in there? Like you said, Helen MacNeil's reputation isn't exactly—'

'You mean the organised crime, loan-sharking, enforcement beatings, general mob violence, and involvement in *at least* three murders, two of which we couldn't pin on her?'

'That kind of thing, yes.'

I shook my head. 'It's not Alice I'm worried about. Helen MacNeil doesn't stand a chance.'

3

'Well, this is nice, isn't it?' Alice patted the arm of the saggy couch she was sitting in, smiling around at a living room that had all the warmth and charm of a decomposing corpse.

In addition to the two horrible couches; horrible armchair; horrible painting of a wee girl holding a balloon, above the horrible china dogs on the mantelpiece; horrible Anaglypta wallpaper; and horrible brown carpet; a large multigym took up a good third of the space. But unlike any normal person, the stainless-steel bars and weights weren't draped with washing and furred with dust. The thing *shone*, the scent of metal and WD40 almost strong enough to mask an underlying grubby taint of mildew.

God knew how she'd done it, but Alice hadn't just managed to get us all invited inside, she'd even talked Helen MacNeil into producing four mugs of tea. And a couple of biscuits for Henry, too.

The wee lad sat at my feet, crunching away on his Hobnobs, tail thumping against the armchair's side, as Helen wriggled backwards along a black leather bench until her head and shoulders were under the metal rod of a loaded barbell. Hissing as she lifted it off its metal pegs and bench-pressed what had to be about sixty kilos.

'So, Helen,' Mother had a sip of tea, grimaced, then put the mug back on the coffee table, 'if you had nothing to do with the body buried next door, who did?'

25

'See, the trouble with most people is they bulk up in prison for protection.' The weights went up and down again. 'No one messes with you when you're solid muscle.' Another rep. 'Then they get out and it all turns to flab.'

'Tell us about your next-door neighbour...' She checked her notebook. 'Mr Gordon Smith?'

Another rep. 'No comment.'

Alice leaned forward. 'Please, Helen, I know it can't be easy, helping the police after everything that's happened, but if—'

'You useless buggers didn't help me when our Leah went missing, so why should I?' The barbell made another trip. 'My granddaughter disappears and you tossers didn't even bother your arses sending someone round.'

I looked at Mother; she just shrugged.

OK.

Good to see Oldcastle Division was every bit as useless as it'd always been. You'd think any competent police officer would have run a PNC search on someone before trying to interview them.

'How long ago was this?'

Helen clunked the barbell back on its support pegs. 'Don't pretend you care. None of you police bastards ever do.'

'We're not police. Well, DI Malcolmson is. Alice and I work for the Lateral Investigative and Review Unit: think the *A-Team* meets *New Tricks*, only with civilian experts bailing the local cops out when they cock stuff up. Like this.'

That got me a slightly outraged stare from Mother.

Tough. Truth hurts.

'So when did Leah go missing?'

'Friday, ninth of October. Walked out of here to go shopping, never came back.'

What was that ... five weeks ago? So too recent to be our skeletonised remains. Well, unless he boiled her down, of course.

'How old was she?'

Helen wriggled out from under the bar and sat up, wiping the sweat from her face with a holey tea towel. 'Eighteen. Which means your lot did bugger all.'

'Eighteen's old enough to make her own decisions.'

'Leah wouldn't run away! She wouldn't do that to me. Not after her mother…' A deep breath. Silence settled into the room as Helen wiped the tea towel across her eyes again. 'She wouldn't.'

That was the thing about missing people, though – no one they left behind ever believed their loved one was unhappy enough to disappear without a word.

'OK.' Trying to sound like I actually cared. 'You give me her details and I'll see what I can do.'

Alice sat forward. 'You should get a tracker app on Leah's phone. For peace of mind. I've got one on Ash's, haven't I, Ash?'

'Can we not do this, right now?' I turned back to Helen. 'I promise I'll chase up whoever's looking for your granddaughter, OK?'

A nod. Another breath. 'Gordon Smith was the best neighbour you could ever have. Him and his wife, Caroline, were like grandparents to my Sophie. Then when she… After that, they looked after Leah for me, while I was inside.' Helen picked at the holes in her tea towel. 'Broke her heart when Caroline died. Bowel cancer, four years ago. Took eighteen months.'

'And where is he now?'

'Gordon? End of September, the council come round and condemn his house. Poor old sod's been living there for fifty-six years and some spotty Herbert with a clipboard tells him he's got three weeks to get out. Oh, and not only does he get bugger-all compensation, he's got to pay for their contractors to tear down his home and ship it off to landfill somewhere? How's that fair?'

'Yes, but where *is* he?'

She draped the tea towel over the pull-up bar. 'Gordon wouldn't hurt a fly. Everybody loved him and Caroline. And how do you know your dead body wasn't there when they moved in? Got nothing to do with him.'

'Indulge me, Helen: where's your sainted next-door neighbour?'

A pause as she frowned at me.

'And before you try "no comment" again, I'm tired, I'm soaked through, and I'm in no mood to fanny about. Where – is – he?'

'His brother's got a croft on the Black Isle. Gordon said something about staying there till he figured out what to do.'

'There we go, that wasn't difficult, was it?' I stood. Nodded at Mother. 'And that concludes our hand-holding duties. You can take it from here.'

'Actually,' Alice put her hand up, 'if he had to pay the council to tear his house down, why is it still...?' Pointing at the wall nearest next door.

'He told them to stuff their landfill charge. Sixteen grand? They try getting sixteen grand out of me, I'll break every bone in their bodies.'

Another grimace, then Mother levered herself to her feet. 'Helen, if Gordon Smith was like a grandad to your girls, any chance you've still got the keys to his house?' Frown. 'And you wouldn't happen to have a pair of bolt cutters, would you?'

'Are we certain this is a good idea?' Alice turned on the spot, breath making a trail of white that glowed in the light of her phone's torch app. 'I mean a hundred percent, definitely, shaky-boots, cast-iron certain, because it feels like a really risky thing to be *inside* a condemned house on the edge of a crumbling cliff during a massive storm...'

Mother's real torch drifted across the pile of furniture heaped up in the living room. Didn't look as if Gordon Smith had bothered taking any of his stuff with him. When he left, he heaved it all in here and left it in a big mound of sofas, sideboards, a double bed, a Welsh dresser, dining table and chairs, medicine cabinet, spare bed, wardrobes, what looked like a wicker laundry basket. All piled up, higgledy-piggledy, as if he'd been planning an indoor bonfire but forgotten to set fire to it.

Rain crackled against the window, no sign of anything through the dirty glass but blackness. As dark outside as it was in.

'What if the house falls down while we're here?' Alice

huddled closer as wind screeched across the roof. 'Or the whole thing ends up in the sea?'

'You're right. Here,' I held out Henry's lead, 'take the wee lad and go wait in the car.'

That got me a pout. 'Bit sexist. Just because I'm a woman, I have to go wait in the car?'

'It's not because you're a woman, it's because you're a *whinge*. And DI Malcolmson's a woman, aren't you, DI Malcolmson?'

'Last time I checked…' She opened one of the wardrobes – a heavy mahogany job that lay at forty-five degrees, propped up on the back of a dusty floral sofa – and peered inside. 'Women's clothes. The dead wife's?'

'And I'm serious: go wait in the car.'

Alice shook her head. 'If it's safe enough for you, it's safe enough for me.' Then raised her fist. 'Smash the patriarchy.' And followed Mother out into the hall again.

Why did every single woman in my life have to be a card-carrying nutjob?

Ah well, can't say I didn't try.

My walking stick made hollow thunking noises as we did a quick sweep of the house.

Bathroom: empty, a darker square of wallpaper where that medicine cabinet had sat above the avocado-coloured toilet. Master bedroom: nothing left but the carpet. Spare bedroom: same again. Dining room: more nothing. Kitchen: empty, all the doors hanging open on the units, exposing bare shelves. A small utility room led off it: either the washing machine and chest freezer were too heavy to shift, or Gordon Smith didn't think they'd be flammable enough for his bonfire that never got lit.

I levered the lid up on the freezer: better safe than sorry…

Nothing but a thin layer of rancid greasy water. No dead bodies in sight.

Mother pointed her torch down the far end of the dog-legged corridor. 'You want to try that one?'

Alice crept over, turned the handle – the howling wind got a lot louder. She stuck her head and her phone arm in through the gap for a moment, then shoved the door shut again. 'Garage. Nothing in there, either.'

'Hmph.'

So, that was all the doors taken care of, but there had to be an attic, right?

My phone's torch wasn't half as good as Alice's but I played it around the hall ceiling anyway. 'There we go.' A hatch, set into the plasterboard, about six foot in from the front door. 'Alice, can you grab a chair from the living room?'

'Urgh… You know the only thing that'll be up there is spiders, don't you? Spiders and dust and fibreglass insulation, all itchy and sneezy and creepy-crawly, so *bags* I don't have to be the one who goes up there.'

'What, you expect the man with a walking stick and buggered foot to do it?'

Mother shrugged. 'Don't look at me: they never make these hatches big enough for normal-sized people.'

Alice slumped. Groaned. Then scuffed her way into the lounge and sulked back out again dragging one of the wooden dining-room chairs behind her. Thumped it down beneath the hatch. 'It's because I'm a girl, isn't it?'

'Up you go, Monkey Girl.'

'Should've gone and waited in the car.' She clambered up onto the seat, wobbled a bit, then shoved at the hatch, forcing it up on squealing hinges. 'If I get spiders in my hair, I'm suing Police Scotland for mental cruelty, PTSD, and punitive damages.'

'Stop milking it.'

Another slump, then Alice grabbed the edges of the hatch and pulled herself up into the attic. Sat there, black jeans and red shoes dangling in the mildewed air over our heads.

'Anything?'

Her muffled voice filtered down from above. *'Filthy up here. And cold! And… Aaaahhh… Aaaaaahhh…'* A high-pitched squeaky sneeze. *'Dusty! Horribly dusty.'*

'What about boxes, or suitcases, anything like that?'

'No, it's all dust and fibreglass insulation and SPIDERS! OH GOD, THEY'RE SODDING HUGE!' Her legs kicked and squirmed, then

she dropped from the hatch, arms at full stretch, hands clinging to the edges, feet swinging as the chair clattered over onto its back. 'AAAARGH!' Alice let go and crashed to the hall carpet in a tangle of limbs and chair legs. Then lay there, making spitting noises as she wiped at her face.

'Well, that was dignified.'

'I hate you both.'

Mother's face soured. 'That's that, then. No further forward than we were half an hour ago.'

Alice accepted my hand, scrambling to her feet and scowling. 'Honestly, they were *this* big!' Holding her hands about a foot apart. 'Now can we get out of this spider-infested horror show before the house falls down?'

Might as well.

'Come on then.' I chucked the chair back into the living room where it bounced off the pile, setting loose a little mahogany avalanche of furniture. That medicine cabinet crashed into the floor, the doors flying open as the mirrors shattered; a wardrobe keeled over, jammed against the double bed; and a coat stand timbered down, the curled crown snapping off as it battered into the rug. *BOOOM...*

Henry jumped about two feet in the air, scuttling away from the living room, hackles up. Barking at the pile of furniture.

The echoes faded away, but the pall of dust – kicked up by the falling pieces – lingered in the cold dark air.

Hmm...

Mother wafted a hand in front of her face, spluttering the dust away. 'We'll get a lookout request sorted, see if N Division can find the brother's croft and get Gordon Smith picked up.' She opened the front door and a scream of wind shoved its way into the house, bringing with it the hissing roar of the sea as it gnawed on the headland only thirty or forty feet away.

Alice followed her out, muttering about spiders and lawsuits.

Leaving Henry and me alone in the darkness, with nothing but the weakening light from my phone for company.

I raised the rubber tip of my walking stick and jabbed it down again, into the hall carpet. It made the same hollow thumping noise it had when we'd searched the place. Henry barked at that too.

Might be nothing, but still…

The hallway was completely carpeted, as were both bedrooms and dining room. Linoleum down in the bathroom, kitchen, and utility room. Which left two options.

Down to the end of the corridor – shouldering open the door through to the garage. A row of empty shelves ran along the rear wall, a pegboard opposite the door, with black marker outlines where tools were meant to be. Spattered spray paint making a crime-scene outline of a workbench that wasn't there any more. A concrete floor, littered with leaves blown in through the sagging up-and-over door. With the front door open, the wind whipped straight through the house, sparking the fallen leaves up into an angry ballet of whirling greys.

Hard not to picture the waves crashing against the cliff, less than a dozen feet away. Eating them.

Henry looked up at me, a whine rattling at the back of his throat.

Yeah. Good point.

I got out of there fast and shoved the door shut again, killing the wind tunnel.

One place left.

By the time I'd returned to the living room, Alice was standing in the hall, arms folded, crease between her eyebrows, mouth turned down. 'Can we *please* go now? Before the house falls into the sea?'

'Give me a minute.'

She took the proffered lead and frowned down at the wee man. 'Your dad's got a death wish.'

The daft hairy sod sat on his bum, tail wagging as he gazed at her with his gob hanging open.

'See, I've been wondering: why pile all the furniture up like this? There's only two reasons I can think of.' I clunked my walking stick down on the windowsill and grabbed the wardrobe that had nearly fallen over. Helped it all the way. 'One: you're planning to burn the place down and maybe claim on the insurance. Assuming you *can* insure a house somewhere like this.' The double bed's legs juddered across the carpet as I dragged it into the corner. The armchair went on top of it.

'What's reason number two?'

Foot was beginning to ache now. Every step sending another burning needle slicing all the way through to the sole.

The broken medicine cabinet got picked up and tossed onto the bed.

'Ash?'

I did the same with a pair of dining room chairs. 'Who do you think our victim is?'

Then a bedside cabinet joined them.

'What's the second reason?'

'Someone he knew, or a complete stranger?' A standard lamp got javelined into the corner. 'And how long does it take for a body to rot down to a skeleton? Twenty years?'

'Eight to twelve. Assuming it's not been embalmed, and you've not buried it in a coffin, or sand, or peat.' The light from her phone cast shadows on the wall as I heaved another wardrobe off the pile. 'I'd really like to go now, so if you can stop messing about, we—'

'That means we're looking for someone who went missing between eight and … how long did Helen MacNeil say Gordon Smith lived here? Fifty-six years, wasn't it?' The kitchen table thumped into the bed with the sound of cracking wood, as one of the legs gave way. 'So our victim went into the ground sometime between then and eight years ago.'

'If they weren't already here when the Smiths moved in.'

'True. Which makes it *at least* forty-eight years' worth of missing persons to troll through. Assuming anyone missed them enough to report it.' The sideboard was a sod to shift, but it hit the wardrobe with a satisfying crash. 'And, given the storm's currently busy washing the remains out to sea, we'll probably never find out who they were.' Welsh dresser next. Thing weighed a ton. 'Unless Gordon Smith coughs to it, when we catch him, of course.'

And there was sod-all chance of that happening.

The shirt stuck to my back, steam rising from the shoulders of my damp coat. Breathing heavy.

Used to be a lot more fit than this.

Another couple of dining room chairs went flying. 'Mind you, see if I was him? I'd "no comment" everything. No way anyone's going out there, on a crumbling clifftop, to dig up what's left of the bones. Health and Safety would have a prolapse.' The sofa groaned and squealed as I pushed it back, off the rug. 'So Gordon Smith can sit there, smug and quiet, while the North Sea destroys every last bit of evidence, and get away with murder.'

'This is all fascinating, but can we *please* get out of here now?'

I stepped back, one hand rubbing at the dull ache throbbing its way up my spine, puffing and wheezing. *Definitely* used to be fitter than this. Condensation from the window made the walking cane's handle slick against my palm. Cold. Like the dead. 'You want to know what reason number two is?'

'Only if it means we can leave before this horrible old house falls into the sea.'

'Reason number two.' I slid the head of my walking stick under the edge of the living room rug and flipped it up. The wodge of dusty fabric hinged back, flopping over the corpse of a three-bar electric fire. 'Abracadabra!'

Alice crept forwards. Frowned down at the floorboards as she swept her phone's torch across them. 'I bet Penn and Teller are bricking themselves.'

'Sod...' That wasn't right. 'Maybe I cleared the wrong bit?'

'You could get a six-month residency at a swanky Vegas hotel with an act like that.'

The electric fire joined the new pile, as did another bedside cabinet, another mahogany wardrobe, and a bookcase. This time, when I flipped the carpet back, it revealed a trapdoor, with a flush brass handle.

'Oooh...' Alice shuffled forward, Henry trotting along at her side. Then her expression soured. '*Tell me* you're not thinking what I think you're thinking.'

'One way to find out.' I grabbed the handle and pulled.

34

4

The wooden steps creaked and groaned as I inched my way down into the blackness. It was dark enough on the ground floor, but here in the basement? My phone's torch barely made a dent in it. The ancient musty smell of dust and mould thickened the air, along with something rancid and sweaty.

Brick walls on either side of the narrow stairs, the mortar furred and whitened as salt leached out.

Alice's voice worried down from the living room. *'Ash, you really,* genuinely *shouldn't be doing that. What if something happens? You can't—'*

'This would go much faster if you helped, you know?'

At the bottom of the stairs, the basement opened out. Hard to tell how big the space was, given the anaemic beam from my phone, but the sound of my voice echoed back to me. So not exactly tiny.

Mounds of dirt and dust littered the small circle of concrete floor currently visible in the torch app's glow.

I scuffed through them, following the pale light till it pulled another brick wall out of the dark. Inched my way along.

'Ash? I'm serious, Ash, it's too dangerous!'

Since when had that ever stopped us?

More salt-furred bricks. Then a screw poked out of the wall at chest height, the head all rusted and swollen. Someone had wrapped string around the thing, tying it off in a lumpy knot, the rest stretching away into the gloom, like a washing line.

'Ash? Don't make me get DI Malcolmson to arrest you…'

Five or six feet along was another screw, the string looped around it, another length on the other side.

'Ash?'

Hmm…

An ancient Polaroid photo was clipped to the string, with one of those tiny clothes pegs people displayed their Christmas cards with in the seventies. It captured a young woman, seventeen or eighteen, all blonde hair and cheesy grin, standing on one leg in a park somewhere, a bandstand in the background. The colours tainted with orange and brown. Another one hung next to it: a different young woman, her short brown hair spiky, dressed in T-shirt and shorts, the curving line of a beach visible behind her. Next: a young man, early twenties, maybe, doing a terrible job of trying to grow a moustache as he posed with a pint of lager in what looked like a beer garden. Then a girl – couldn't have been much over seventeen – all hunched in as an older man wrapped his arm around her shoulders, the pair of them posed and uncomfortable, in ugly retro sportswear, on a putting course somewhere, with water and hills in the background.

Not exactly your usual basement decorations.

'Ash? I'm not kidding!'

Next Polaroid along showed a laughing man, head thrown back, beard thick and red, eyes shining, arms thrown wide, in front of the Scott Monument in Edinburgh. Then another young woman, wearing jeans and a T-shirt with Tony Blair's face on it, grinning as she sat astride a bicycle on a hedgerow-lined lane somewhere…

There were more, making a strange collection of holiday snaps that never had the same person in them twice. The only common thread was they'd all been taken with a Polaroid camera – that familiar square picture in a white rectangular frame. Tainted with mildew.

'Ash?'

My phone buzzed against a fingertip as I used the sensor on the back to unlock it. Called up the camera, and set it to video.

Which instantly killed the torch app, plunging the basement back into blackness.

Damn.

'ASH, ARE YOU OK? IT'S ALL GONE DARK DOWN THERE…'

'GET YOUR BACKSIDE DOWN HERE – I NEED HELP.'

'IT'S NOT SAFE AND—'

'ALICE!'

'All right, all right…'

I fiddled with my phone till the torch flickered into barely-there life again. Couldn't be much battery left by now.

A bright circle of light bloomed at the bottom of the stairs, followed by the *thunk, thunk, thunk, thunk, thunk* of Converse trainers on wooden steps as Alice finally grumped her way down, Henry's claws *clickity-clacking* behind her. 'I want it on the record that I said this is a terrible idea. If we all die, it's *your* fault. And what is that horrible smell?'

'Thank you. Now shine your torch over here.'

She did, making the wall glow, casting rectangular Polaroid-shaped shadows on the bricks. 'Ash, why does Gordon Smith have other people's holiday photographs hanging up in his basement?'

'Go along the line so I can video it.' The camera killed my torch again, but at least *this* time I could film as Alice shuffled her way from one Polaroid to the next, illuminating each in turn. 'Good, now the other side.'

She turned, sweeping the light across another brick wall to … ah.

Henry let loose a whine.

'Ash?'

There were shackles fixed to the bricks opposite, the chains furry with rust. A mattress on the floor, filthy with brown stains. Heavy-duty stainless-steel hooks, screwed into the beams of the floor above. More brown stains on the concrete floor beneath them.

Another line of Polaroids hung on either side of the shackles. Only in these ones, the people weren't smiling. In these ones the colours were mostly reds and blacks.

Alice crept forwards, pulling a reluctant Henry with her. 'What the hell *is* this place?'

I cleared my throat.

Wasn't easy.

All those small square photographs in their rectangular white 'frames', the greying plastic stained with the dark swirls of bloody fingerprints.

Just like the ones that used to turn up on those birthday cards for Rebecca...

'Ash?'

I swallowed something bitter. 'It's a kill room.'

She inched forwards and stared at one of the photos. 'Oh God. Ash, they're—'

A long, low rumble sounded from somewhere *far* too close. Henry scrabbled round, barking at the end wall, hackles up. Dust drifted down from the joists and floorboards above our heads.

Alice and I turned and stared.

No way that was a good sign.

Then my phone launched into its bland generic ringtone. Vibrating hard against my fingertips. Nearly dropped the damn thing instead of answering it. 'Hello?'

Mother's voice, barely audible over the howling wind: *'GET OUT OF THERE NOW! THE HEADLAND'S GOING!'*

Oh crap.

I took a handful of Alice's coat and shoved her towards the stairs. 'Quick! Outside!'

'No, no, no, no, no...' She stumbled, nearly tripped, righted herself, then ran. Taking Henry and the light with her, leaving me in the pitch-dark.

God's sake...

I limped after them, fumbling with my phone, trying to get the bloody torch app to work as darkness overtook the basement again and Mother's voice crackled out of the tiny speaker:

'ASH, DID YOU HEAR ME? GET OUT OF THERE!'

Finally, a pale glow shone out of the thing and...

Wait a minute: *photographs*. I dropped my walking stick and grabbed at the nearest loop of string, the twine cold and damp as I yanked at it, snapping it free of the rusty screws, Polaroids streaming out from my fist like gory bunting as I hobbled across the concrete floor. Another deep rumble thrummed through the basement, trying to pull my feet from under me. Staggering. Half lurching, half falling up the wooden steps. Bursting out into the living room, just in time for one of those horrible tombstone wardrobes on the pile to keel over, sending me scrabbling backwards out of its way as it crashed down, sealing the trapdoor to the basement.

Jesus.

If I'd been two seconds slower, I would've been stuck down there. Entombed.

Hands snatched at my jacket, hauling me up, into the corridor, and out through the front door. Alice on one side, Mother on the other, Henry running barking circles around us while they bustled me towards the line of temporary fencing. Rain crackled against my shoulders, slashing at any exposed skin as I stuffed the string of Polaroids in my jacket pocket, where they'd be relatively safe. Wind scrabbling at my back, pushing and shoving, screaming out its rage as we barged through the gap in the fence.

Then a fist thumped into my chest, Mother glaring at me with wide eyes and a hard, pinched mouth. 'ARE YOU BLOODY INSANE?'

Alice lunged into a bearhug, pinning my arms to my sides, head buried against my shoulder. 'I thought we'd lost you!'

Gordon Smith's house no longer sat a dozen feet back from the edge of the cliff. The storm had seen to that. The garage had gone, taking about another six foot of headland with it. Now the basement jutted out into the void. That concrete floor was probably the only thing keeping it, and the house above, in one precarious piece.

Yeah. No way in hell we were *ever* going back in there.

Mother turned, face sour as she stared at the house and its eighteen-foot-shorter garden. 'Well, that's our human remains gone, then. So much for that.'

Helen MacNeil's bolt cutters still lay where we'd abandoned them after snipping through the chain that'd held two sections of fencing panel together, and soon as Alice let go of me, I picked the things up, using them as a makeshift walking stick as I limped away from the devouring sea. 'Don't worry, DI Malcolmson, Gordon Smith's got a *lot* more bodies out there.'

Tears of condensation rolled down the small kitchen's windows as we huddled around the table – the air muggy with the heady scent of mince and the steam rising off one soggy police officer and two soggy civilians. All three of us dripping our own personal lakes onto the cracked linoleum floor. The house's owner away seeing to her wee boy and his nightmares.

Warmth seeped into my bones from the mug of hot milky tea clutched in both hands.

Alice had hers pressed against her chest, jacket draped over the back of her chair, frizzy curls plastered to her head.

Mother grimacing as she swallowed another mouthful, phone clamped to her ear. 'No, I understand that, sir, but we need— … Yes, sir, I know, but— … Uh-huh…' She rolled her eyes at me. 'Uh-huh…'

A shiver ran its way through Alice, setting her teeth chattering again.

'Are you OK?'

She shook her head. 'We could've *died* in there.'

'Yes, but we didn't. Now drink your tea.'

A knock on the kitchen door and DC Watt stuck his misshapen head in from the hall. 'Guv?'

Mother looked up. 'Can you give me a minute, sir? Something's come up.' She pinned the phone against her plus-sized bosom. 'What is it, John?'

'I asked DC Elliot to run a PNC check on Gordon Smith: no convictions, but he *was* picked up in 1968 and prosecuted for assaulting a sex worker in Glasgow. Found "not proven". She's got them digging up the paperwork.' Watt scratched at that bald scarred patch on the back of his head. 'Well, Elliot is, not the sex worker.'

'What about his wife?'

'Nothing we can find. *Yet*. Oh, and I've got an address for the brother's croft on the Black Isle. Only he won't be in, because he's doing a sixteen stretch in HMP Edinburgh. Stabbed a GP to death. I've sent the details to N Division; they'll pop up and see if Gordon's there.'

A smile. 'Good boy.' Mother dug her spare hand into her pocket, pulled out a small paper bag, and tossed it over to him. 'Help yourself.' Then back to the phone. 'Sorry about that, sir, getting an update from my team. Now, about that arrest warrant...?'

Alice shuddered, coiling in, shoulders hunched and forward. 'What are we going to do now?'

I stood. 'Don't know about you, but I'm heading back to the flat and changing into something that doesn't squelch when I move. You coming?'

'Can we stop by an off-licence?'

'Don't see why not.' The bolt cutters weren't an *ideal* walking-stick substitute, but they'd do for now.

Watt blocked the doorway, frowning down at the contents of his tiny paper bag, poking a finger in. 'All glued together...' He plucked out a small, pale-yellow lozenge that made sticky screlching noises as it left its mates. Popped it in his mouth. Gave me the kind of smile that begged for a fist to be smashed right into the middle of it. 'Where do you think you're off to?' Sooked his fingertips, then held out his hand, saliva still glistening on the pink skin. 'You've got something of ours.'

'If it's a punch in the gob, you can have it here, or we can take it outside.'

The smile slipped away. 'Mother says you filmed evidence in Smith's basement, so I'm commandeering your phone. You can—'

'Not if you want to keep your teeth, you're not.'

A tug at my sleeve. Alice. 'Ash, maybe we should—'

'You are aware that threatening a police officer is an offence, *Mr* Henderson?'

Alice wriggled past, putting herself between me and the greasy prick with a death wish, same as she'd done with Mother and Helen MacNeil. 'DC Watt, I know this is all very exciting, but it's been a long day and we nearly died in that basement, so maybe we should all take a deep breath and de-escalate this situation before it turns into something contrary to the smooth running of the investigation?'

He pulled his pube-bearded chin in. 'What?'

'After all, we're all on the same side, aren't we, and without Ash's help you'd never have known about the kill room underneath Gordon Smith's house, so why don't we do our best to facilitate an interpersonal rapprochement and we can email you all the footage from the basement and that way everyone's happy, OK? OK. Have you got a business card with your email address on it?'

'Not happening.' Watt folded his arms. 'I want that phone. And you're going nowhere till I get it.'

Right, it was punch-in-the-face time. 'Alice, step aside.'

Mother's voice cut through the muggy air: 'Will the pair of you grow up? This is a murder inquiry, not a willy-measuring competition.'

'He's refusing to hand over vital evidence that—'

'Alice: step – *aside*.'

'One last chance, Henderson: give me that phone!'

'Oh for goodness' sake.' Mother appeared at my shoulder. 'Mr Henderson, do you swear on your mother's life-slash-grave that you'll email the footage to John and me?'

Alice nodded. 'Of course he does.'

'No offence, Dr McDonald, but I'd feel happier hearing it from the man himself.' She poked me in the back. 'Well?'

'I'll email *you* the footage, not this greasy wanked-up slice of pish.'

'I *beg* your pardon?' Watt clenched his jaw.

'You heard.'

A disappointed grunt from Mother. 'Oh let him go, John. We've got enough on our plates without a visit to Accident and Emergency.'

There was some grumbling, too low to make out the actual words, then Watt stepped aside. Made a sarcastic 'after you' gesture.

Prick.

It was difficult, resisting the urge to give him a hard shoulder-barge on the way past, but with Alice bustling down the corridor right behind me, it wasn't really doable. He'd have to take an IOU.

My jacket had cooled down while we were in the kitchen, but it hadn't dried out any, so it clung to my shoulders and back like the cold wet hands of the drowned as I pulled it on and hauled open the front door.

Stopped dead.

Helen MacNeil stood under the tiny porch, wrapped up in a thick waterproof, dripping as the wind clawed at her. Staring at me with puffy, bloodshot eyes. 'You said you'd help find my granddaughter.'

Of course I did. Because I'm far too soft for my own good.

I held out the bolt cutters. 'Thanks for the loan.'

She tucked them under one arm, then dug into her waterproof and came out with a picture frame, about the size of a paperback book. Pressed it into my hands. Voice cracking over the words. 'She wouldn't run away, I know she wouldn't, not after Sophie... Something's happened to her.'

Don't look at Gordon Smith's house. Keep your eyes on Helen MacNeil. Try for a reassuring smile. 'She's ... probably staying with friends. There's no need to—'

'I *spoke* to all her friends, they haven't heard from Leah in weeks.'

Alice tapped me on the shoulder. 'Ash?'

'Not now.' Back to Helen, softening my tone as she wiped a hand across her glistening cheeks. 'You say Leah wouldn't run away, why not?'

'Because her mother left us.' Helen turned her face away. 'She left us.'

'That doesn't mean she—'

'SHE TOOK HER OWN LIFE! OK? SHE KILLED HERSELF!' And there was the Helen MacNeil everyone had always been so afraid of – those bloodshot eyes blazing, mouth a hard vicious line. The woman who could batter a rival firm's drug dealer to death with a pickaxe handle. 'And you *promised* you'd help!'

Yeah, I kinda did.

5

Alice frowned at the rear-view mirror as the little Suzuki lurched its way out of Clachmara. 'He killed her, didn't he? Gordon Smith took Leah MacNeil down to his horrible basement and … did things to her.'

'We don't know that.' The car lumped through another pothole. 'Will you keep your eyes on the road! I'm losing fillings here.'

The windscreen wipers' *squeal-thunk* added a rhythm section to the blowers' roar – enough condensation coming off all three of us to mist-up the windscreen and windows, the air heady with the grubby-animal scent of soggy Scottie dog.

'Why didn't you tell Helen—'

'Because until we know for sure, there's no point making things worse for her. "Oh, yeah, your granddaughter's probably been tortured to death…"' A lump twisted inside my throat. Wouldn't go away when I swallowed. So I cleared it. 'Right now she thinks Leah might come home. At least she's got hope.'

Alice nodded. 'I'm sorry.'

Everyone always was, even after all this time. 'Let's just … change the subject.'

'OK. Yes. Changing the subject it is.' Alice shifted her hands on the steering wheel. 'The photographs we saw in Gordon Smith's basement are indicative of a collective personality. Putting them on display like that allows him to relive the hunt

44

and the kill. Burying the bodies in the garden is about keeping them close. He needs to have them with him.'

'Why would he—'

'Gordon Smith's house is right on the coast – well, even more so now the headland's disintegrating – if you want to dump a body there's plenty of places you could chuck it in the sea and off it goes. He's burying them in the garden because he's a collector, it's the same deal with the photographs.' Alice hunched forwards and rubbed her hand across the fogging windscreen, clearing a porthole. 'He won't have begun there, though. He'd want to keep them closer than that. In the house. I bet that basement wasn't concreted when he moved in, he's done that bit by bit over the years. Probably only started burying them in the garden because he'd run out of room.'

'Thought that was Rose and Fred West?'

The car thumped through yet another bloody pothole.

'The question is, why did he leave his beloved photographs behind? Why not take his collection with him? He can't take their *bodies*, but the photos would be easy enough…'

'Your suspension's going to be ruined, by the way.' As we thunked into three potholes in a row.

'He must have copies, I'd take copies if I was him, I mean think of the nostalgia value when you're reliving past glories and flicking through the souvenirs of all the people you tortured to death, but he's left his kill room behind, hasn't he, so maybe that's because he's been told his house is going to fall into the sea any minute now and in a way that's kind of sexy, isn't it, knowing all this incriminating evidence is sitting *right* there, but no one can ever lay their hands on it, because A: they don't know it exists, and B: everything's going to be washed away in the next big storm.' Alice nodded, agreeing with herself. 'It's all about risk, thrill, and control.'

'You think that's sexy?' I shook my head. 'You forensic psychologists are *weird*.'

'And did Gordon Smith kill them on his own? I mean, it'd be really hard to hide that from your wife, wouldn't it? You can't turn your basement into a torture chamber and graveyard without your other half noticing, can you? How would you explain all the screaming?'

I pulled out my phone. Five percent battery left. A quick scroll through my contacts brought up the one marked 'SHIFTY' and set it ringing. 'Not our problem any more. It's DI Malcolmson's case, remember?'

'I wonder if there was a drop in the murders after his wife died? Couples who kill tend to get caught before one of them drops dead of natural causes.'

A hard Oldcastle accent barked out of the earpiece. *'Detective Inspector David Morrow's phone?'*

'Rhona? It's Ash. Is Shifty there?'

The voice softened. *'Hey, Ash. The big man's interviewing a nonce – you remember Willie McNaughton? Used to flog—'*

'Hardcore German porn to school kids, I remember. Listen—'

'And now they can get it all, online, for free. That's progress for you.'

'Rhona, I need a favour. Leah MacNeil – her gran reported her missing a month ago. Has anything been done about it? And if not, can you get Shifty to kick someone's arse for them till they do? I've got a recent photo, if they need one.' After all, you never knew. Maybe she really *had* run away? Fingers crossed anyway.

'Hold on.' The broken-teeth rattle of Rhona battering the living hell out of her keyboard joined our symphony for windscreen wipers and blowers.

At long last, the potholed horror of Clachmara faded behind us as Alice took a left onto a good old-fashioned crappy B road, heading back towards Oldcastle.

'And while you're at it, have a dig into what happened to her mum.'

'You're not shy, are you?'

'Nope. And make sure...' Silence on the other end. 'Rhona? Hello?'

The screen was black, and poking the fingerprint reader on the back did nothing to change that. Phone was dead.

Alice glanced across the car at me. 'Problem?'

'Don't have a phone charger in here, do you?'

'Back at the flat. Anyway, as I was saying, normally when you've got a couple who kills, one's dominant and one's subservient: Rose to Fred West, Myra to Ian Brady. The dominant partner wants to kill, the subservient partner goes along with it to keep the love of their life happy. So what happens when one of them dies?'

'The world becomes a much better place.'

Wasn't even the third week in November yet, and the big Winslow's in Logansferry already had chocolate Santas, mince pies, and Christmas pudding for sale. An entire shelf dedicated to reduced Halloween tat. And a confusing array of mobile phone charging cables.

Alice draped herself over the trolley's handles, one red-shod foot flat on the floor, the other twisting back and forth on its toes, while she fiddled about on her phone. Face all pinched with concentration.

Why did every bloody mobile manufacturer have to use a different cable?

I picked one that *should* fit, then dumped it in with the Tunnock's Teacakes, Quality Street tin, and multipack of pickled onion Monster Munch.

She straightened up, eyes still glued to her phone, bumping the trolley forward with her hips. It wobbled away a couple of feet, then took an unprompted hard left into the memory cards.

At least it gave me something to lean on while we hobbled around to the drinks aisle.

'You still haven't answered the question.' Scuffing along beside me, like a teenager, using radar to avoid hitting anything while she concentrated on that little screen.

'There's Pizzageddon on Clay Road, and that new place by the station's meant to be pretty good.'

She had the teenager's sigh down pat too. 'No, not dinner – tomorrow.'

This again.

'Alice, can we *please* not—'

'Apart from anything else, it's our crime-fighting anniversary, isn't it? Nine years to the day since we first teamed up to catch bad guys. We should do something to celebrate, that's all.'

'Ah…' Forgotten about that. 'Suppose it is.'

She plucked a box of orange Matchmakers from the shelf as we passed, apparently without even looking at it. 'See?'

'Thought you were the one banging on about not eating properly?'

'Don't change the subject.' A packet of jelly babies joined the rest of her five-a-day. 'And then there's Rebecca.'

Sodding hell. 'I told you I didn't want to—'

'You've never even visited her grave.'

'That's not—'

'It's been *nine years*, Ash.' A shrug. 'And I know the first two weren't your fault, because of … well, what happened with Mrs Kerrigan being a vindictive cow, but it's not healthy to continually avoid the subject.'

I steered the trolley into the drinks aisle, beer and cider forming two walls of a boozy canyon on either side. 'I'm not avoiding—'

'Because sooner or later it's going to come back and bite you, right on the—' The phone in her hand launched into something jaunty and she gave out a small startled squeal, before poking at the screen and putting it to her ear. 'Hello, Bear, how are you getting— … Yes, I know Lewis Talbot's post mortem is happening now, but— … No, it isn't, but— … Yes, but you don't *really* need us, do you, Bear, I mean we can't add anything to— … Yes, Bear.' Her shoulders slumping more with every passing second. 'No, I *am* happy being part of LIRU, honest—'

I poked her in the arm and held out my hand. 'Give.'

She did what she was told.

Detective Superintendent Jacobson's voice rattled in my ear, wanging on about teambuilding. '…*vitally important every member of the team is*—'

'What do you want?'

A pause.

'*Ash? Why aren't you answering your phone?*'

'Stupid thing's run out of battery. And before you ask: no, we won't be attending the post mortem. We almost died an hour ago, thanks to you, so you'll understand if we're not in the mood to watch someone fillet a wee boy who's been dead for a month.'

The visuals would be bad enough, but the smell? On top of everything else we'd been through, tonight? No thanks.

Alice pointed at the shelves, pulled a constipated-frog face, then loped away towards the hard spirits.

'Almost died? Helen MacNeil got violent, did she? Well, you're supposed to be good at handling things like that, it's —'

'We found a kill room in her next-door neighbour's basement. Whole place nearly got washed out to sea with us in it.'

'A kill room? Now, that is interesting… Multiple victims?' Difficult to describe the tone that'd come into Jacobson's voice, but it was a cross between cunning and avarice. *'I take it they'll need our help interpreting the scene? After all, the Lateral Investigative and Review Unit is uniquely positioned to—'*

'There's no one going anywhere near the scene. I wasn't kidding about the place washing out to sea – the headland's crumbling away underneath the property. Doubt it'll last the night.'

'That's a shame. We'll probably wrap up this child-killer case soon, and it'd be nice to have something high-profile to move on to. Still, can't be helped.'

Alice reappeared with a litre of supermarket vodka and a bottle of red wine clutched in her left hand, a twelve-pack of tonic and a bargain-basement brandy cradled in her right arm like a rectangular yellow baby and its alcoholic cuddly toy.

'Now, about this post mortem—'

'No.' I turned the trolley when Alice had finished loading the booze, and pushed for the checkouts. 'In addition to *almost dying* – I did mention that, didn't I? In addition to that, we're both soaked to the skin. And if you think we're going to spend the next four to six hours standing in a freezing cold mortuary, catching our deaths, you can shove LIRU where, as Bernard would say, "the light from our nearest star is permanently occluded".'

'Ash, that's not exactly—'

'AKA: sideways up your hole!'

Silence.

The two old ladies in front of us tremored their way through emptying their trolley onto the checkout conveyor belt: supermarket whisky, white bread, cheese, bacon, cucumber, baby oil, and a jumbo-sized thing of toilet paper. Must've been planning one hell of a party.

'Ash, please remind me: why exactly *do I put up with you on my team?'*

I stuck the 'Next Customer Please' plastic Toblerone down, at the end of the oldies' shopping. 'You want the official reason, or the real one?'

'Ah… Perhaps we should—'

'Officially: it's because my twenty years policing the serial-killer capital of Europe looks good on your stupid brochures. Unofficially: it's because you know sometimes corners have to be cut, rules broken, and heads smashed in, but you don't want to get your hands dirty. You want plausible deniability so none of it blows back on you. And, more importantly, Alice won't work without me.'

She grimaced, then unloaded the vodka, tonic, wine, and brandy onto the conveyor belt, bottles and cans clinking and rattling.

'Have we finished having our sulky tantrum? Because if we have, we might hear me say, "Take the rest of the evening off, Ash. You and Alice have deserved a rest, Ash. Come in fresh tomorrow, Ash."'

Should bloody well think so too.

The last of the shopping went on the belt, to be bleeped through the till by a short man who'd never see seventy again, with a satsuma-orange fake tan and startled-Weetabix hair. The liver spots on his tiny hands trembling as he tried to get the Monster Munch to scan.

'Had to promise Helen MacNeil I'd look into her granddaughter going missing.'

'Unfortunate, but I suppose it won't take up too much of your time.'

Alice reached for her cards, but I waved her away.

'I'll get this lot. Call it an anniversary present.'

'You're getting me a present?'

'Was talking to Alice.' I pinned the phone between my shoulder and ear and went rummaging for my wallet. 'And how long it takes depends on whether or not Leah MacNeil's one of the bodies getting washed out to sea right now. If it is: not so straightforward.'

'Well, do your best, and if you see an in for consultancy services…?'

'You're like a scratched CD, you know that, don't you?' Ah, found it. But pulling the thing out of my jacket pocket brought a cascade of grubby plastic rectangles with it — all pinned to a mouldy length of string. The Polaroids from the basement wall. The ones where the people being photographed weren't on holiday any more. They skittered across the stainless-steel surface, caught in the supermarket's bright lights.

And the wee orange man on the till *stared*. Mouth hanging wider and wider.

All those ripped open bodies. All the screams and pain. All the wasted lives.

Damn things should've been easy to get back into my pocket – they were strung together, for God's sake – but they wriggled and slipped through my fingers like dying fish as I scrambled to gather them up.

The wee orange man mashed his palm down on the panic button. Rising out of his seat, eyes like pickled eggs against his pumpkin skin. 'SECURITY! SECURITY! I NEED SECURITY HERE, NOW!'

Great.

A pair of huge women in black fleeces and combat boots thundered towards us, leaving the front door unthugged. Teeth bared. Fists curled.

'Ash, what's happening? I can hear yelling.'

'I'll call you back.'

Brace yourself…

6

Thug Number One gave me a lopsided scowl from the other side of the dull grey desk. It wasn't a black eye, yet, but it was working on it. Sitting there with her thick arms crossed, muscles bulging through the black T-shirt with 'CASTLE HILL SECURITY LTD.' embroidered on its left breast.

Alice shifted in her seat, setting the plastic groaning as she leaned forward. 'I'm really sorry, Maggie, I'm sure it was an accident, I mean in the middle of everything, heat of the moment, and there's arms and legs and no one really knows what's going on and it's all very—'

'He hit me!' She pointed a thick, stubby finger across the desk at me.

I gave her a nice innocent shrug. 'Oops.'

What can I say, I'm a feminist: if you put Alice in a headlock, man or woman, that's what you get. Lucky I let her off with a black eye, to be honest. Maybe that was sexist of me? Maybe I should've broken her arm too?

'Agnes had to go to A-and-E!'

'The floor was slippery; wasn't my fault she hit her head on the shopping trolley.' Twice. Though hopefully I'd blocked the CCTV camera's view, so no one would be the wiser.

Like I said: feminist.

A knock on the door and Maggie transferred her wonky scowl from me to it. 'COME!'

It clunked open and a thin man in a suit and side parting gave everyone an ingratiating smile. 'I'm sorry to have kept you waiting, but that's the police arrived now and they say Mr Henderson,' a nod in my direction, 'hello,' back to Maggie, 'he definitely *is* working for Police Scotland, so he's not a serial killer or anything, and is perfectly entitled to be in possession of the … disturbing images Mr Turnberry encountered on till number seventeen.'

Pink worked its way up Maggie's wide neck. 'Yes, well…'

The man's smile got a bit more obsequious. 'I'm sorry we had to detain you both, Mr Henderson, Dr McDonald, but given the circumstances, I'm sure you understand. We at Winslow's take our community responsibilities *very* seriously.' He held out a couple of bulging jute bags with snowmen on them. 'Your shopping. On the house. And I've thrown in a fifteen-pound gift voucher as well.'

'Very kind of you.' I stood. Picked my still-damp jacket off the back of my chair. 'Come on, Alice.'

Shifty was waiting for us, bald head gleaming in the strip light of the bare breeze-block corridor, that black eyepatch giving his fat frame a slightly rakish, piratical air. His pale grey suit looked as if a herd of wildebeest had slept in it. Left eye narrowed in disapproval as he shook hands with the man who'd come to get us. 'Thanks, I'll take it from here.' Then turned and marched off, without so much as a word.

I hobbled after him, taking my time, because anything faster than that sent burning daggers lancing through my aching foot. 'What kept you?'

He shoved through the plain door and back onto the shop floor, between the fish counter and the dairy aisle. 'I was interviewing a nonce!'

'At *this* hour? That your way of getting out of Lewis Talbot's post mortem?'

He opened his mouth, then closed it again. 'Shut up.'

Alice bustled alongside, carrying our new jute bags. 'Did your sex offender say anything?'

Shifty gave her the benefit of his evil eye. 'You're *supposed* to keep Ash on a short leash.'

53

'Only, if there's a ring involved, a paedophile ring, I mean, and the killer's a member of it, he might have said something incriminating, he might even want to boast about his crimes, or at least his knowledge of the victims, so did he say anything about anyone saying anything like that?'

'The only thing Willie Bloody McNaughton said was "no comment". And his buggering solicitor just sat there, preening. Like we were questioning his greasy little client about a *parking* violation, not three dead kids.'

Kind of inappropriate, but couldn't help smiling at that one. 'Thought you said McNaughton's solicitor was, and I quote, "completely shaggable".'

'Completely shaggable people don't help paedophiles wriggle their way out of custody!'

We passed the line of tills, the carrot-coloured Mr Turnberry doing his best to avoid eye contact as I limped by number seventeen. 'You let McNaughton go?'

'Didn't have any choice, did I?' Shifty rubbed a hand across his face, pulling the chubby cheeks out of shape. 'A solid day of interviewing child molesters. Going to take a *massive* heap of booze to get that taste out of my mouth.'

Alice nudged him, setting the bottles clinking again. 'Might be able to help you there.'

The automatic doors slid open, and we stepped out beneath the awning, ranks of trolleys sitting chained together on either side.

'OK.' I made it as far as the line of large plastic crates filled with bagged firewood, kindling, and four-litre containers of antifreeze – apparently available at 'BARGAINTASTIC PRICES FOR ALL THE FAMILY!', because whose kids didn't love antifreeze? I settled my backside against the logs and stretched out my right leg, foot throbbing like a malfunctioning microwave. 'Get the car and I'll wait for you here.'

Alice peered out at the rain, hauled her hood up, then turned to Shifty. 'David, do you want to join us for dinner? We're going for a sitty-downy pizza with *loads* of salad!'

'Time is it?' He checked his watch and deflated a couple of

inches. 'Yeah, why not? Supposed to have clocked off hours ago anyway.'

'God, I needed that.' Shifty wiped the froth from his pint off his top lip, smiled and let loose a happy belch.

They'd given us a pretty decent table – for quarter to ten on a Friday night – by the window, looking out across the road to the big Victorian glass slug that was Oldcastle Railway Station. All lit up and glistening in the rain. A row of taxis sitting outside it, their drivers huddled in a bus shelter, smoking fags. Working on cancer and hypothermia all in one go.

'A toast.' Alice raised her large Shiraz. 'To not dying in a serial killer's basement!'

I clinked my Irn-Bru against her glass, then Shifty did the same with his pint and we all drank.

'Speaking of which.' Shifty held his hand out, palm up in front of me.

'What?'

'You know fine, "what". The photos you traumatised Satsuma Joe with, back at the supermarket. They're evidence.'

'I forgot I had them, OK? We nearly got crushed to death and washed out to sea. And since when do you care about evidentiary procedures?'

'Since Professional Standards decided to make me their special little project. Now hand them over.'

I turned in my chair, picked my phone off the windowsill – attached to its new charging cable, stealing the restaurant's electricity. Battery now at a whole ten percent.

'Ash, you can't *keep* stuff like that.'

My phone went back on the windowsill. 'You can have them when I've taken a copy.'

'It's not—'

'What, you're going to bail before your starter arrives and hotfoot it back to the station with them?'

He frowned for a moment, then shrugged those wide shoulders of his. 'No point letting good food go to waste.'

Didn't think so.

Alice helped herself to a breadstick, the words coming out in a wave of crunching and crumbs: 'Do you think Bear would let me do some behavioural evidence analysis for DI Malcolmson?'

'Our Glorious Leader? Without a cost centre to write it to?' Difficult not to laugh at that. 'Not a chance in hell.'

'What if I did it in my spare time, though?'

'Then you're undermining a potential revenue stream.'

She scrunched herself up and fluttered her eyelashes at me. 'Pleeeeeeeease?'

'You're a grown woman in your thirties, don't do that.'

'Pretty pleeeeeeeeeeeease?' Really hamming it up now, hands clutched sideways under her chin, brown curls cascading either side of her beaming face.

'OK, OK.' Anything to make her stop.

'Good.' She shifted her cutlery and napkin out of the way and made come-hither gestures. 'Let's see the photos, then.'

'Sure you want to do that *right* before you eat?'

'The iron's hot, we might as well strike with it.'

I snapped on a pair of blue nitrile gloves and eased the photos from my pocket. Still connected to that mouldy piece of string by the tiny clothes pegs.

Shifty winced. 'You could at least've put them in an evidence bag!'

'Crushed to death and washed out to sea, remember?' I laid them out in front of Alice, one after the other, putting them closer together, so they'd all fit in two lines. 'And if it wasn't for us, no one would even know they existed. So don't be a dick.'

Eleven Polaroids. Each one showing the last horrific moments of some poor sod's life.

Shifty bared his teeth. 'Jesus...'

A row of creases formed between Alice's eyebrows as she frowned at the pictures. 'Victims are male *and* female, so maybe Gordon Smith's bisexual, because there's always a sexual element with this kind of serial killer, even if it's not expressed at the time with the victim present, because what's the point of killing someone if you can't fantasise about it before and afterwards? Of course maybe it's death that turns him on and he's really only torturing people to heighten his and…?' She looked up at me, eyebrows raised.

'Caroline. Smith's wife was called Caroline.'

'Thank you.' Back to the photos. 'He *might* be doing it to heighten their arousal. I wouldn't be surprised if they had sex on that mattress in the basement, right after they killed someone, or even while their victims were dying. They've gone to all the trouble of abducting and torturing someone, who needs Viagra when you've got a rush like that – the power of life and death, someone screaming in agony while you—'

'OK.' Our waiter appeared behind her, looking about as comfortable as a dedicated hipster can when forced into a red-white-and-green waistcoat, dress shirt, and non-ironic bowtie. 'I've got an insalata caprese, antipasto misto platter, and a garlic bread with mozzarella?'

Alice wheeched her napkin over the Polaroids before the waiter could recognise what they were. Pointed at Shifty. 'Garlic bread, Ash is the antipasto, and I'm the salad.' Taking the plate from him before he could interfere with the horror show currently taking place beneath her napkin. 'Thanks.' Then knocking back three big gulps of wine, finishing the glass and holding it out for the waiter. 'And can I have another large Shiraz, please, actually better make it a bottle, no point messing about, is there? That'll be great, excellent, mmmmm, this all smells delicious!'

The waiter's smile looked very uncomfortable, squashed between his handlebar moustache and big beard, as he backed away from our table like it was a rabid dog. 'Yes, wine, definitely.' And he was gone.

She passed her plate across the table to me. 'Can you look after that? And don't eat my mozzarella. Or my tomatoes. Or basil. Actually … don't eat any of it.' Then peeled her napkin back, exposing the bloody images again. 'These were from *one* side of the shackles, weren't they?'

'The string closest the stairs.' Somehow a platter of mixed meat didn't seem all that attractive, not when the Polaroids were sitting there. 'All I could get.'

'I wonder if there's a "before" and "after" for each of the victims? One wall is them alive, the other is them dead. With sex and torture in the middle.'

Great wafts of garlic oozed out of Shifty's starter as he tore a big bite from his huge slice of cheese on toast, white strings looping from his mouth back to the bread, like the ones in the basement. Mumbling through his mouthful. 'You think he rapes them?'

'Maybe, maybe not. I worked on a case in Boston once – got to go over as part of an exchange programme, it's a really nice city, lovely people, but by God it's cold in winter – anyway there was this guy, Chuck Reich. He would abduct men, tie them up, and stab them, but not because he was trying to kill them, he'd stab them in the stomach or the thigh or the buttock and use the holes he'd made to … you know … *pleasure* himself. It was the screaming he liked the best. Maybe Gordon and Caroline were like that?'

Yeah, I *definitely* didn't want the cold meat any more.

'You never told me about Chuck Reich.'

Alice shrugged at me. 'He swore, if he ever got out, he'd come after me and I didn't want you to worry.' She stared down at the photos again. 'Anyway, it was years ago, I'm sure he's a lot less angry now, and it's not like they're ever going to release him, is it? Not after what he did to his lawyer…' She glanced up at me. 'It's OK, you can start eating, I won't mind.'

Nope. Pushed my plate away.

Eleven murder pictures on one side of the shackles, eleven on the other. Which meant twenty-two victims over fifty-six years, the last of which had to be quite a while ago, going by the mould staining those Polaroids.

'So, why did Gordon Smith stop killing?'

'Oh, Ash,' her smile was small and sad, 'what makes you think he's stopped?'

I left the engine running, heaters and blowers on full, as Alice escorted Shifty to his front door. The pair of them wobbly as newborn foals, keeping each other upright. Honestly, they were about as much—

A muffled rendition of the *Buffy* theme burst into life in my pocket and I dragged out my phone. Took the call. 'Rhona?'

'Not too late is it, Guv? Only I got some info for you on Leah MacNeil.'

Outside, Alice was helping Shifty find the keys to his tiny house: a two-up two-down at the end of a curling cul-de-sac in Blackwall Hill. The kind of place that must've looked quite stylish when it was thrown up thirty years ago, on the wrong side of the railway tracks, and left to rot ever since.

'Let me guess – no one's bothered their arse?'

'Bingo. I've rattled some cages and jammed my boot up some bumholes, so at least they'll start looking. Oh, and I managed to dig a bunch of stuff up on the mother, Sophie MacNeil, too. Suicide, sixteen years ago. Poor cow was only twenty.' A slurping noise came down the phone. *'Granny Helen was in HMP Oldcastle at the time, for battering some drug dealer to death, so two-year-old Leah goes to live with the next-door neighbours. Temporary custody, by the look of it.'*

Interesting…

'And Child Protection were happy with that? The Smiths weren't related to her, why didn't she get put into care?'

'No idea. Can find out, if you like, but you'll have to wait till Social Services get in, Monday morning.' More slurping, the words after it mumbled around whatever Rhona was eating. *'Anyway, I say "poor cow", but Sophie wasn't exactly a choirgirl. We've got three arrests for possession with intent, two warnings for fighting, one six-month stretch for assault. Chip off her good old mum's block, that one.'*

Alice and Shifty finally got the door open, and he stumbled inside, leaving Alice to wobble on the top step all alone.

'And Leah's been a chip off her granny's, too. Mostly assault, some petty theft, possession – didn't have enough blow on her to count as dealing, so the arresting officer let her off with a caution – and one theft from a lock-fast place. Guess your mum throwing herself off Clachmara Cliffs screws you up.'

That was a relief, to be honest. At least now we knew Sophie MacNeil hadn't ended up in Gordon Smith's private graveyard.

'They know why she did it?'

'Oh yeah. She left this reeeeeeealy long, rambling suicide note. There's a copy in the file. You want me to read it out to you?'

'Not particularly.'

Alice did an about-face, nearly crashed into the jagged crown of an un-pruned rose tree, and staggered back towards the car. Moving like she was on the deck of a rolling ship.

'It's all boy trouble, and not wanting to be pregnant again, and not being able to cope, and everything being so hard. Six pages of it.' Slurp. 'Looks like it's been written by a drunken spider too.'

It took Alice three goes to get the door open and collapse into the passenger seat. She pulled her chin in, grinned, then let free with a diaphragm-rattling burp. 'Par... Pardon ... me.'

'Thanks, Rhona.'

'Nah, no trouble. I was twiddling my thumbs here anyway. The joys of nightshift.'

There was some fumbling with the seatbelt.

'Ooh, you hear about the post mortem? Your physical evidence guru, AKA: the Pinstriped Prick, says Lewis Talbot was strangled with some sort of silk rope. Maybe a curtain tie, or something from a soft-porn bondage starter set. Don't know about you, but that sounds like an evolving pattern, to me. He's getting more sophisticated.' Slurp, slurp, slurp.

'What on earth are you eating?'

'Bombay Bad Boy, Pot Noodle, nightshift lunch of champions.' An extra-long slurp for effect.

'You're disgusting.'

A laugh, then she hung up, and I slipped the phone back into my pocket.

Turned to look at the wobbly wreck in the passenger seat, still fighting with the seatbelt.

I took the end off her and clicked it home in the buckle. 'You planning on throwing up at some point?'

Alice stuck two thumbs up.

'Wonderful.'

My life just kept getting better and better and better...

7

Rasping snores perfumed the air with garlic, wine and the sour taint of vomit, as I placed the washing-up bowl on the floor beside Alice's bed and tucked her in. Then ruffled the fur between Henry's ears. 'You look after our stinky drunkard, OK?'

He stared back at me with his shiny button eyes, then lowered his head onto her ankles again, curled up on the floral-print duvet.

I clicked the light off. Took one last look.

OK, so she *probably* wasn't going to throw up again. Because, let's face it, there couldn't be much left *to* throw up. Two bottles of wine, plus the large glass of red she'd had while we were waiting for our starters, plus the three brandies she'd downed instead of dessert, and half of Shifty's rum-and-Coke when he wasn't looking. No wonder she'd spent the last half hour evicting everything she'd eaten since breakfast.

Silly sod.

Could it really be *nine* years? Nine years of trying to keep her safe, while we went after murdering arseholes. Nine years of watching her drink herself to death, and clearing up after her. Nine years of violence and killers and pain and horror...

Great. Well done, Ash. That wasn't depressing at all, was it?

Alice wasn't the only silly sod in the place.

I closed the door to her room. Took my mug of tea back through to the lounge.

Had to hand it to Jacobson, he'd actually got us a nice place to stay, instead of the usual manky B-and-Bs. And on Shand Street – very swanky. High up, too: a fourth-floor, self-catering, two-bedroom flat in a new six-storey development, perched on the blade of granite that pierced the heart of Castle Hill. The panoramic windows looked out over the jagged remains of the Old Castle, its tumbledown walls and stone stumps lit up in shades of yellow and red, and beyond that the land dipped away in a tangled ribbon of streetlights. The wide black expanse of Kings River separated them from the regimented roads and houses of Blackwall Hill on the right and Castleview on the left – with the Wynd rising up behind it.

It was almost pretty.

But then Oldcastle always did look better in the dark.

Especially if you couldn't see Kingsmeath.

Sitting on the floor, by its charger, my phone let out the *ding-buzzzz* that announced an incoming text.

The number wasn't recognised, but the message made it clear enough:

> Mr Henderson you promised John you
> wood email that footageage to me!!! Don't
> make me regret thrusting you.

Autocorrect strikes again.

Might as well get it over with.

Mother's business card had gone limp from its stint in my damp pocket, but I dug it out anyway and sent her everything we'd filmed in Gordon Smith's basement, even the duff bits. Then unplugged my phone and settled into the squeaky leather couch.

Pressed play.

Footage was shaky, but the camera lingered long enough on each Polaroid to capture most of the details. The young blonde woman on one leg, in a park. The brunette on a beach. The young guy in a beer garden. The old man and younger woman, looking awkward on a putting green… Then more. And more. All those people, smiling and alive. Then all those people in life-ending agony.

By my count there were sixteen people in the 'before' pictures, and twenty-two in the 'after' ones. Couldn't be sure, but it looked as if most of the first lot were in the second. Not all of them, though. And there were definitely people getting tortured who didn't have 'before' shots.

I went back to the start and pressed play again.

Park; beach; beer garden; putting green; then a man in his mid-twenties and swimming shorts, reclining on a sunlounger, chest and shoulders a painful shade of scarlet, raising a half-coconut with a wee paper umbrella and straw sticking out the top. Two young women, wrapped around each other – one red-haired, the other blonde – caught in the act of laughing, bent nearly double in front of one of those coin-operated binocular things you got at seaside piers. A happy couple, slightly blurred, waving at the camera as the carousel horses they were sitting on galloped past. A teenaged boy wearing a Manchester United top, grinning out of the photo, hot dog in one hand, can of Coke in the other, bunting in the background. A young woman, sat astride a bay pony, crash helmet on, polo shirt and jodhpurs, knee-high riding boots, beaming like this was the best ever day of her life. Rather than the start of the last one.

Clearly, Gordon Smith liked his victims young. The only person over twenty-five was the old guy on the putting green. But then he probably wasn't the target. The young woman he'd been caught so awkwardly cuddling was.

Next: a smiling young woman in an ugly orange-and-brown one-piece swimming costume, face covered in freckles, mousy-blonde hair tucked behind an ear, rolling sand dunes behind her. Then a young man dressed in a smart suit and academic gown, mortarboard on his head as he posed on the steps outside a pillared portico, what had to be a degree clutched in his...

Hold on a minute.

I rewound the footage, back to the ugly swimming costume, and hit pause.

She looked ... familiar.

Well, familiar-ish.

Broad forehead, wide mouth with lots of teeth, long straight nose sitting on a heart-shaped face. A touch overweight. Not *conventionally* pretty – not someone people would stop to stare at in the street if she walked past – just a normal person, whose luck ran out the moment this photograph was taken.

Maybe she was one of the faces from the other set of Polaroids? The 'after' pictures, with their bruises and slashes and blood and screaming. Maybe that's where I'd seen her?

I called them up and flicked through … yup. There she was.

A hard cold lump turned deep inside my stomach.

How could *anyone* do that to someone? How could *that* get your rocks off?

But there was still something else.

Damn.

My jacket lay draped over one of the dining chairs, parked right in front of the radiator, in an attempt to dry the soggy thing out. The framed photo Helen MacNeil had given me still lurked in the side pocket.

The glass was misted with condensation, but a tea towel took care of that.

Two women in the photo: one was Helen MacNeil, smiling for once in her life, a large muscled arm draped across the shoulders of her teenaged granddaughter. It was clearly taken in a photographer's studio – the mottled backdrop and profesional lighting was evidence of that – but while her gran had put in a bit of effort, Leah MacNeil had opted for ripped jeans, a black denim jacket speckled with patches and badges, and a T-shirt for a band I'd never heard of. Wearing so much makeup it looked as if she'd been decorated.

But she had the same heart-shaped face as her grandmother. The same long sharp nose. The same broad forehead. Her hair was dyed a rich purply-blue, but the mousy-blonde roots were clearly visible.

She wasn't the young woman in the Polaroids, but the family resemblance was obvious.

Damn it. God, sodding, *damn* it.

'You were supposed to have killed yourself…'

Maybe it was a coincidence? Someone who looked like her?

I scrolled through to Rhona's number and pressed the button. Listened to it ring as I placed the photo frame on the coffee table, facing me.

Then, *'Guv? If you called up hoping to hear me eating again, all I've got's a—'*

'Sophie MacNeil. Where's her body?'

'Eh?'

'Her body, Rhona, if she killed herself, where is it?'

'Guv, is something wrong?'

'Yes.' Finding it difficult to keep my voice calm and reasonable. 'Now where's her bloody body?'

'Hold on.' Some rustling. *'Is it something I've done? Because if it's… OK, here we go. Procurator Fiscal's judgement was that Sophie MacNeil's remains were washed out to sea. Never recovered. But the suicide note was enough to—'*

'Buggering *hell.*'

'Guv?'

'Sorry, Rhona, got to go. There's a call I need to make.'

Rain lashed at the patrol car as we left the bright lights of Logansferry behind and headed out the Strathmuir road. Blue-and-whites flickering, turning the downpour into sapphires and diamonds as they rattled against the bonnet and windscreen.

Mother slumped in the passenger seat, face sagging, scrubbing at her eyes. 'Why me? Why does crap like this *always* have to happen to me?'

'Yes, because this is all about you.' I shifted in the back seat, sat behind the driver because I wasn't an idiot. 'How do you think Helen MacNeil's going to feel?'

The driver, a spotty-faced lump of gristle in the full Police Scotland black with matching accessories, sniffed. 'Might be a comfort for her: finding out her wee girl didn't commit suicide.'

My hand tightened around the head of my old walking stick. 'Is *that* what you think?' Knuckles aching as I squeezed the polished wood.

Mother groaned. 'Come on, Mr Henderson, he didn't mean anything by that.'

'You think it's *comforting* to find out your daughter was tortured and murdered by a serial killer?' Getting louder with every word. 'You think that'll be an excuse for a party, maybe? Get out the karaoke machine and HAVE A BASTARDING SINGSONG?'

The moron behind the wheel went pink, lips pinched tight together in silence.

'He doesn't know, Mr Henderson. He's young. And a bit thick. Come on, deep breaths.'

I thumped back in my seat. 'Don't see why you needed me on this anyway.'

'Because you've got some sort of weird rapport with Helen MacNeil. And things are hard enough as it is.' Mother seemed to deflate a couple of sizes as darkened fields flashed by the windows. 'We had to do a risk assessment and now the SEB are refusing to search the basement. They won't even go *into* the house. If this was any normal deposition and crime scene, we'd have big plastic marquees up by now, spotlights, generators; there'd be a specialist team digging the garden up and another one going through that kill room with an electron microscope.' A shudder. 'But it's not a normal crime scene, is it? No, of course it isn't, because if it *was*, some DCI would've waltzed in and wheeched it off me by now. It's an utter crapfest, so no one else will touch it with a six-foot cattle prod!'

She had a point.

'What am I supposed to do, Mr Henderson? If I put people in harm's way and something happens, I'm screwed. If I *don't* put them in harm's way, I'm not doing my job, and screwed. Either way: screwed.' She slapped both hands over her face again and smothered a small scream.

'You finished?'

A small bitter laugh jiggled out of her. 'Probably. Top brass have been trying to get shot of me for six years now, well, this'll be the *perfect* opportunity.' She turned in her seat and scowled at the driver. 'You want some career advice, Constable Sullivan? Never have a heart attack on O Division's dime, because if you do the bastards will treat you like a soiled nappy full of radioactive poop!'

PC Sullivan, quite sensibly, kept his mouth shut.

There was hope for the boy yet.

A small village flashed past, the streets empty, the trees thrashing in the wind, overflowing gutters spilling small lakes across the square.

'You hear anything back from N Division?'

Mother sagged even further. 'They sent three patrol cars to Smith's brother's croft. No one there.' Her mouth turned down, lips puckered, like she was sucking on something bitter. 'Said it looked like no one had been there for years. All abandoned and manky. No Gordon Smith. Wherever he's disappeared to, it isn't there.'

A Mobile Incident Unit sat in the middle of the potholed road, about two houses back from the warning fence, lights blazing out in the darkness. It wasn't one of the swanky new ones, either – little more than a grubby shipping container done up in Police Scotland livery with a mobile generator chuntering away behind it.

Mother undid her seatbelt as PC Sullivan parked alongside. Sat there, staring out through the rain-strafed window at Helen MacNeil's house. 'Maybe we should wait till morning?'

'You know what Oldcastle's like: entire police force leaks information like a colander.'

Sullivan stiffened. 'That's not—'

'Yes it is, and keep your gob shut.' I grabbed my walking stick. 'We hold off till morning, this place will be swarming with soggy journalists, wanting to know what it's like living next door to a serial killer. Won't take much for her to put two and two together.' Turned my collar up, and climbed out into the storm. Let the wind slam the car door shut for me. Then banged my hand down on the roof three or four times, raising my voice over the wind. 'DI MALCOLMSON, ARE YOU COMING OR NOT?'

Her door opened and she joined me on the pavement, face a sour sagging scowl. 'This is what I get for answering my phone after midnight. I never learn...' Hunching herself up, lumbering after me as we shouldered our way through the gusts to Helen

MacNeil's front door and the relative shelter of her grubby caravan. She rang the doorbell, then tucked her hands deep in her pockets. 'And how come I'm "DI Malcolmson" now, you always *used* to call me Mother.'

I frowned at her. 'You've been calling me "Mr Henderson" ever since I turned up.'

'I thought you were upset with me for some reason.' She took a hand out again and patted me on the back with it. 'Ash.'

Ah, why not: 'Mother.'

Still no sign of life from the house, so I leaned on the bell again, keeping my thumb there as it *drinnnnnnnged*. Ringing on and on and on and on and—

'*WHAT?*' The door was yanked open, and there stood Helen MacNeil, wrapped up in a tatty old blue dressing gown, bare legs and feet poking out the bottom. Glaring at us with puffy eyes. Short grey hair flat on one side. Fists ready.

Mother looked at me. Raised her eyebrows.

Coward.

I stepped forwards. 'Helen, can we come in, please? I'm … afraid we have some bad news.'

She sat there, staring at me.

I shifted on the couch. 'Are there any questions you'd like to ask?'

Helen MacNeil looked down at my phone again, clutched in her trembling hands. At the image filling the screen: a smiling young woman in an ugly orange-and-brown one-piece swimming costume, face covered in freckles, mousy-blonde hair tucked behind an ear, rolling sand dunes behind her.

PC Sullivan emerged through the living room door, carrying two mugs in each hand, steam rising off them in the chill air. He put the lot on the rickety coffee table, then held one out to Helen. 'Milk and three sugars.'

She blinked. Shook her head. Voice hollow and distant. 'This has to be a mistake…'

And again, Sullivan had the common sense to keep his gob shut.

Mother helped herself to a mug and did the same.

Typical.

'Do you recognise the photograph, Helen?'

'Gordon wouldn't hurt Sophie. He wouldn't. He's been like *family* to us, ever since I was a wee girl. This is bollocks!'

'It's definitely her, though, in the picture?'

'I... It's...' She placed a fingertip on the screen. Then placed my phone on the coffee table, stood, and marched out of the room.

'Pffff...' Mother looked at me over the rim of her mug. 'You have to feel for her.'

'And are you planning on chipping in at any point, or do I have to do *everything* now?'

A smile, then Mother leaned forward and patted me on the knee. 'But you're doing so *well*.'

'You can stuff your patronising—'

Helen marched back in, holding out a Polaroid. 'Look.'

It was almost identical to the one we'd found hanging up in next door's basement. Taken either just before, or just after it. The main difference being that in this version, the woman in the bathing suit was holding a beaming toddler in a pink sundress, floppy white hat on its head. Pinholes speckled the white plastic edges of the photo and its colours were more faded too. A slight grey patina to the whole thing.

'Gordon and Caroline took them for a bank holiday weekend in Aberdeen, when Leah was eighteen months. I was three years into my sentence...'

I turned the Polaroid over: 'BALMEDIE BEACH' printed on the back in neat black felt pen.

'Had it pinned above my bed, in my cell. And every time I saw it, I'd think about them,' Helen narrowed her eyes at me, 'and what I'd do to *you* when I got out.'

The Polaroid clicked down against the coffee table. 'I'm sorry.'

Her chin came up. 'So what if Gordon had a photo of Sophie in his house? He was like a grandfather to—'

'There's another photo. It's...' What good would it do, telling her what he'd done to her daughter? No parent should have

69

to know that. 'Sophie didn't end her own life. She was murdered.'

'If there's another photograph, I want to see it!'

All that blood and pain and horror, captured in one horrible three-inch by three-inch square.

'No.' I stood. Put my phone back in my pocket. 'Trust me, you really don't.'

— happy deathday to you —

8

'...statement that the Justice Secretary, Mark Stalker, has the First Minister's complete support.'

And we all knew what that meant.

'Thank you, Janet.' On the TV screen, a greasy wee man in a too-tight suit pulled on his serious face for the camera. 'Police Scotland are expected to confirm, later today, that remains of a small boy, found in woods to the south of Oldcastle, are those of missing four-year-old, Lewis Talbot. Our crime correspondent Hugh Brimmond is live at the scene for us now. Hugh?'

Outside, it was still dark, the city's lights twinkling in the inky black, as I scooped up another spoonful of porridge. With salt, not sugar. Washed down with a sip of decaf tea.

Rock and roll.

A broad-shouldered rugby type appeared on screen, standing in the dark with some trees behind him, lit up by the headlights of passing cars, rain thrumming down on a red-and-white golf brolly. 'That's right, Bob. We're here in a large stretch of woodland known locally as "The Murders", a name from the sixteenth century that's been horribly prescient...'

'Urgh...' Alice slumped her way in from the kitchen, clanked a big mug of coffee down on the dining table, and collapsed into a chair. Folded over forwards and rested her forehead against the cool glass surface as I finished off the last of my breakfast.

'*…bringing the tragic death toll to three young boys, all under the age of six.*'

'Morning.'

'I said, "Urrrrrrgh!"' Not looking up.

The greasy guy in the suit was back. '*Sport now, and Inverurie Loco Works are looking to make it a hat-trick today as they go up against favourites, Buckie Thistle…*'

'Well, whose fault is that, then?' Downed the last dregs of tea, picked up my bowl and stood. 'Briefing's at quarter to, so better get your bumhole in gear.'

'URGH!'

'Don't "Urgh" me. You know what Jacobson's like when people are late.' Putting on a fairly decent impersonation of the man, even if I say so myself: '"I'd like to remind everyone that LIRU *also* stands for 'Late Is Really Unprofessional'."' Back to normal. 'Hairy wee tosspot that he is.'

A tad harsh, maybe, but what did you expect at quarter past seven on a Saturday morning?

Alice folded her hands over her head. 'Urgh…'

'Don't care. Go get ready.' The flat's kitchen wasn't bad: enough space to throw together a decent meal, if you actually had the time. The clunk-scuff of my limping echoed back from slate tiles and shiny white flat-panel kitchen units.

'*…opening games of the new season. And now here's Valerie with the weather.*'

I stuck the porridge pot and my bowl in to soak. Rinsed out my mug. Raised my voice so it would carry through into the living room. 'You'll be shocked to hear there's been nothing on the news about Gordon Smith and his basement of horrors.'

'*Thanks, Bob. We've got an unsettled couple of days ahead as Storm Trevor continues to track north…*'

'Alice?' Back through the kitchen door.

She'd barely moved. Slumped there, arms dangling, face screwed shut. Groaning.

Oh, for God's sake.

My old walking stick wasn't exactly pristine – the varnish worn off the handle, the rubber tip blackened and cracked – but

74

it was perfect for poking people, so I did. Right in the shoulder. Putting some weight behind the thing. 'You: wretch. Arse in gear. I want your teeth brushed, face washed, hair combed, and ready to go in five minutes.'

Alice's response was barely audible, 'Urgh...'

We followed the curling cobbled sweep of Shand Street, down the hill, moving from one yellowy patch of streetlight to the next – Henry trotting along at my side, Alice's folding umbrella drumming in the rain that pummelled down from a coal-grey sky. Tiny rivers gurgling in the gutters. Past darkened shops with 'To Let / May Sell' in the windows. Boarded-up newsagents, tea shops, and empty banks. A couple of charity shops and a bookies still held on, the grilles down over their grimy windows, waiting for the day to begin, but the baker's was open.

'Wait here.' I handed her Henry's lead, ducked out from under the brolly and limped inside. Came back out again with a mince bridie, a beetroot-and-stovies pie, and a cheese-and-onion pasty, all three turning the paper bag they shared semi-transparent with grease. Handed them over. 'Get those down you.'

'I don't *want* to.'

'Eat.'

She passed me the umbrella and Henry, then grimaced at the bag's contents. 'Don't feel well.'

'Trust me: nothing better for a hangover than baked stuff in pastry.'

'Why do you have to be so mean to me?' But Alice pulled out the bridie, steaming in the cold morning air, bringing with it the rich savoury scent of hot meat and butter, scrunched her eyes closed, and ripped out a big bite. Getting wee golden flakes all down the front of her parka.

Henry bounded along beside her, nose up, sniffing the pastry-scented air. Making hopeful noises as we headed downhill towards St Jasper's Lane.

'Right, soon as the team briefing's over, I want to go jangle Steven Kirk again.'

'Mmmmngghnnphff, mnngnnn mnnnfff?'

'Don't talk with your mouth full.' A four-by-four rattled up the hill, splashing through the lake formed by an overflowing drain and sending out a spray of grimy water that only missed us by an inch. Tosser. 'Kirk was in Kingsmeath when Andrew Brennan went missing, I'd put money on it. The only reason he'd lie about that is because he knows we're onto him.'

'Still don't see why we couldn't have taken the car. It's cold and it's raining and my *head* hurts.' Whine, moan, whinge. But she polished off the bridie anyway, then started on the pie.

'We should speak to his mother's care home: double-check his alibi.'

St Jasper's Lane thickened with traffic – cars and vans heading off to work. An ambulance crawled past with its blue-and-whites off, the driver and passenger looking about as cheerful as a biopsy. More shops here. A young man in turban and leathers, hauling the shutters up outside a vaping shop. A slouch of people, hunched into themselves as they tromped along the uneven pavement. A young woman huddling outside a news-agent's, puffing away on a cigarette as if it was the only thing keeping her upright. A figure, lying on their side in the doorway of a boarded-up nail salon, bundled in a filthy-grey sleeping bag, their back to the road.

The pedestrian crossing bleeped and we followed a knot of women dressed in identical black suits across the road.

Alice looked up from her pie. 'I've been thinking about that profile of Gordon Smith.'

'Don't know why you're bothering, it's not like we don't know who he is.'

Past the King James Theatre – its gaudy billboards advertising the Christmas panto – a droopy old man in a high-viz jacket hosing vomit off the top step.

'That's the point, though,' pastry flakes going flying, *'no one* did. Well, except his wife. And his victims, of course. Everyone else will tell you what a lovely man he was and he'd never hurt a fly and he was always *such* a considerate neighbour who'd give you the shirt off his back and other assorted clichés and actually you might be right about baked goods and hang-overs.' Munching down the last mouthful of pie. 'Could really go something to drink, though, I'm—'

'Here.' I reached into my pocket and pulled out the chilled tin of Irn-Bru I'd got her in the baker's.

'Ooh!' She clicked the ring-pull and gulped away.

'Doesn't matter, in the end, though, does it? We know it was him; Mother's got a lookout request on the go; someone will spot him somewhere; uniform will swoop in and pick him up; and he'll go down for life, with sod-all chance of parole. In the *meantime*, we've got a child-killer to catch. So can we please forget about Gordon Smith? It's not our—'

A juddering belch burst out of Alice, like a lowbrow foghorn. 'I think we should visit Rebecca this morning.'

A bus rumbled past, the steamy windows filled with unhappy faces, pale as margarine and twice as depressing.

'Ash, did you hear me? I said, I think—'

'Can we get on with the day, please? Enough on my plate as it is, without you—'

'It'll be *good* for you, though.'

We turned right, onto Peel Place. The elegant sandstone buildings were blighted by the manky Victorian redbrick lump of O Division Headquarters, like a big hairy wart on a super-model's cheek. Its narrow windows scowled out at the rainy gloom, through bars and grilles. A handful of outside broadcast vans were parked in front of the building: Sky News, BBC, ITV, Channel 4… Getting ready to hear all about the poor wee dead boy found in the woods yesterday.

The BBC lot were doing a piece to camera, the reporter huddled under his red-and-white brolly, trying to stay dry and keep the 'POLICE SCOTLAND' sign in shot at the same time.

'Eat your pasty.'

'You're impossible, you know that, don't you?' She dipped back into the greasy bag, though. 'And we still need to do something for our anniversary: celebratory meal, or something. Somewhere fancy, though, no sticky floors or plastic tablecloths.'

A figure huddled in the lee of the war memorial on the other side of the street – three soldiers in kilts and full WWI pack, bayonets fixed, charging towards the machineguns. She pushed away from the memorial and marched across the road, on an intercept course. Short grey hair plastered to her head, shoulders hunched, bloodshot eyes narrowed against the rain – the bags under them heavy and bruised. Helen MacNeil.

She looked the pair of us up and down, then ignored Alice completely. 'I spent all night on the internet.'

'Didn't they assign you a Family Liaison Officer? They'll keep you up to date on—'

'And I've been googling you.' Stepping closer. 'Thought you were just some thug copper who liked throwing his weight about, but you *know*, don't you? You know what it's like.'

Oh Christ, not this…

'Mrs MacNeil, it's not—'

'You're telling me that Gordon killed my Sophie. That he's killed other people. That the man I let look after my *child* and my *grandchild* was a bloody serial killer!'

I pulled on my best reassuring-police-officer voice. 'Look, it isn't—'

'YOU THINK I'M STUPID?' Bellowing it, right in my face. 'HE KILLED HER TOO, DIDN'T HE?'

Over by the outside broadcast vans, the hyenas were looking our way. Peering out through their windscreens. Scrambling for cameras.

'DIDN'T HE? HE KILLED MY LEAH!'

Alice put a hand on her arm. 'Please, this isn't—'

'DON'T YOU DARE TOUCH ME!' Helen's right hand flashed out, a backhanded slap that sent Alice spinning, stumbling to the ground.

The two silent seconds that followed were broken by Henry growling, hackles up, four little feet set on the wet pavement.

And that was it.

I grabbed a handful of Helen's collar and slammed her backwards into a scabby Land Rover hard enough to set the car's alarm shrieking. Hazard lights flashing their orange warning as I bared my teeth and forced my face into hers. Rain hissing

78

down around us like the end of days. 'You EVER lay a finger on her again and I will FUCKING KILL YOU!'

The growling turned into barking.

Helen grinned back at me, but there was no warmth or humour in it. It was cold and vicious, like her eyes. 'You *know* what it's like.'

I bounced her off the Land Rover again. Then let go. Squatted down beside Alice. Brushed the hair from her face. Helped her sit up. 'Are you OK?'

Her bottom lip was already swelling up. A thin crack of red bisecting it, glistening. 'I'm fine, I'm fine...' Clothes and jacket stained with water where she'd hit the deck.

Helen loomed over us. 'The Birthday Boy took your daughter, didn't he? Tortured and killed her.' A bitter laugh. 'Oh, I know *alllll* about it. Even downloaded the e-book.'

'Come on, let's get you up.'

The car alarm was still screaming as I helped Alice to her feet.

'You OK? Not feeling dizzy or anything?'

She brushed my hands away. 'I'm fine.'

'Good.' I dropped my walking stick and Henry's lead, turned, snatched a handful of Helen's coat and hauled back a fist to—

'Ash, no!' Alice – hanging off my raised arm, pulling it back down again. 'The TV people.'

They were hurrying across the road, getting their cameras up.

I let go and gave Helen another shove. 'You don't touch her again.'

'You were never that squeaky clean, even when you were a copper. So I've got a deal for you: you help me find Gordon Smith before these wankers do, and I'll make it worth your while.'

Deep breath. 'Go home, Mrs MacNeil.'

'I know where an armoured-car job's hidden. Six million in jewellery, paintings, sculptures, antiques, and the like. You help me, you get a third of it.'

'Ash, we have to go!'

The cameras were up on their shoulders now, reporters trotting alongside, microphones out, umbrellas up. Closing in for the kill.

I grabbed my walking stick, turned on my heel, and hobbled off down Peel Place, Henry trotting along beside me, Alice scrambling to catch up.

Her umbrella was all collapsed in on one side, where it had bounced off the pavement.

An idiot in a grey suit, stopped right in front of me, holding out his microphone. Eyes widening when he finally realised I wasn't stopping. He jumped to one side, and the three of us marched past, Helen MacNeil's voice ringing out behind us: *'YOU KNOW WHAT IT'S LIKE!'*

9

Alice shuffled up beside me. 'She still there?'

'Yup.'

Down on the street below, Helen MacNeil was standing in the rain, talking to the Sky News people, glaring at the camera as if it'd refused to pay protection money.

Not our case.

Not our problem.

Not our—

A sharp rapping noise came from the front of the room, followed by a pointed, 'I'm not *boring* you, am I, Ash?'

When I turned, there was Detective Superintendent Jacobson, tapping the tip of his extendable pointer against one of the small room's four whiteboards. He'd peeled off his trademark brown leather jacket, leaving it draped over the back of a chair to drip onto the scabby carpet tiles, exposing a dark red shirt that was about two sizes too big for a wee hairy bloke in tiny square glasses.

He wasn't the only one staring at us.

Professor Bernard Huntly: in his immaculate pinstriped suit, starched white shirt, and pastel silk tie; battleship-grey short-back-and-sides; Sandringham moustache; and a pair of performance eyebrows – both of which were raised as he smirked in our direction.

Dr Sheila Constantine: buried somewhere within a big

padded jacket with a furry collar, a tartan scarf wrapped around her neck and chin, two apple cheeks and button nose poking out over the top. Woolly hat covering most of her thick blonde hair, even though the radiators in here were pounding out heat.

Henry: tail going like a furry windscreen wiper, mouth hanging open, tongue lolling out, the smell of wet dog rising off him like a fusty chemical weapon.

And PC Thingy. No idea what her real name was, because I hadn't been paying attention when Jacobson introduced her. Some no-hoper O Division had lumbered us with, in order to look as if they were cooperating. A stringy scarecrow with oversized hands and a buzzcut, whose nose and chin entered any crime scene about half a step before the rest of her.

Which only left one member of LIRU: Sabir. He wasn't there in person, but his chubby face looked out from a monitor, placed on a wheelie trolley near the front of the room. Mouth a small twitching horror show as he shovelled in crisps, crumbs and stubble on his jowls, bald as a long-dead egg, skin the colour of slightly mouldy beetroot. Someone had stuck a strip across the top of the monitor with 'DS Akhtar' printed on it. Sabir's voice crackled out of the speaker, sounding about as Liverpool as you could get. *'No offence, like, but can we get this thing wrapped up, or wha'? I'm meant to be hackin' into a crime-syndicate an' planting Trojan viruses on their Dark Web servers in twenny-five minutes, and I'd kina like to go for a crap first.'*

'Quite.' Jacobson clicked his pointer against the board again, underlining a bullet-pointed list. 'So, to recap, now everyone's paying attention: eighteenth of June, victim one is strangled by hand. Twentieth of August, victim two is strangled with his own belt. And fourteenth October, victim three is strangled with a silk cord—'

'Actually, Bear,' Professor Huntly held up a manicured finger, 'speaking as this *delightful* little team's physical evidence guru, I think you'll find the strangling ligature was probably a curtain tie.'

That got him a scowl. 'Speaking as this delightful little team's *boss*, you lost "call me 'Bear'" privileges yesterday, when you pissed off the Procurator Fiscal.'

Huntly sniffed. 'I merely pointed out that decomposition products were—'

'Don't make me tell you again!'

A shrug. 'Sorry, Detective Superintendent.'

'Better.' Jacobson frowned at the whiteboard for a moment. 'Now, where was I? Yes, right: silk ligature. No sign of it at the deposition site, so it was taken to and from the scene by our killer.' The pointer came around to aim at Dr Constantine. 'Sheila?'

She dug her hands into her armpits, smothering them in the padded fabric. 'The transition to ligatures isn't the only change: there's a definite difference in how long he takes to kill his victims. With Andrew Brennan he crushes the hyoid bone and the windpipe, so death would be *reasonably* quick. Oscar Harris has a worse time – going by the bruising, our killer tightened and released the belt around his throat three times, before committing to it. Lewis Talbot…' She puffed out a breath and dug her hands in deeper. 'First off, the state of the body didn't help any: four weeks half-buried in the woods. Don't get me wrong, I've post-mortemed worse, but once the soft tissue starts to go, we lose a lot of structural detail. So while it's impossible to say one hundred percent for sure, I *think* he was strangled and revived and strangled and revived at least eight times. And given the infusion of blood in the tissue around his neck, it could've taken anything up to an hour. Maybe an hour and a half.'

PC Thingy whistled. 'Poor wee sod…'

'Another thing: Andrew Brennan suffered multiple broken ribs. Our killer knelt on top of him while he strangled him. No broken ribs on Oscar Harris, and most of the bruising is around the front of the neck, so I think he was probably standing or kneeling behind Oscar while he strangled him. And Lewis Talbot has broken ribs again.'

Outside, in the corridor, someone laughed as they thumped past with a couple of their mates. It faded away like blood down the mortuary drain.

'Anything else?'

Sheila curled her top lip. 'Only that there's evidence of abuse on all three victims. Physical on Andrew and Lewis, but Oscar Harris was definitely sexually abused at some point. Here's the thing though, it was *before* they were killed. And I don't mean immediately before, I mean weeks, possibly months. No sign of semen or penetration of any kind on the bodies.'

Jacobson cleared his throat. 'Thank you, Sheila. Alice?'

Alice shuffled forward in her soggy red Converse trainers, one arm wrapped around herself, the other hand fiddling with the curls by her ear. 'We're seeing a definite progression in his behaviour. Andrew is a victim of chance – he, I mean, our *killer*...' A frown. 'Look, I'm sorry, but I think we need a name for him. Otherwise, it's all going to get pretty confusing on the pronoun front.'

'I have a suggestion,' Huntly straightened his cuffs, a nonchalant wobble to his head, 'Cronus.' He turned to Sheila. 'He was the first of the Titans, in Greek mythology, father of Zeus. Ate his own children, because—'

Sheila hit him. 'We know who Cronus is, you patronising wankspasm.'

'Did you know he castrated his own dad, Uranus, from *inside* his mother's womb? That would rather put the scuppers on a romantic evening, don't you think? You're getting all hot and bothered, next thing you know—'

Jacobson rapped on the whiteboard again. 'All right, if we can stick to the topic in hand?'

'Well...' Alice tilted her head on one side, still twiddling with her hair. 'I suppose we could go with Cronus, but our killer isn't actually eating these boys and it sounds too much like we want him to seem cool when it's probably better if we pick a name that's not going to be something to live up to, if that makes sense, so why don't we call him ... Gòrach? Which is Gaelic for stupid, so we're not putting him on some sort of pedestal, or making people think he's in any way special, which I think we can all agree is counterproductive, and Bernard got to name the last person we were after, so I think it's only fair

I get a turn.' She printed the name up on the board in squeaky green marker pen.

Sabir clicked some buttons and the camera zoomed in on his eye. *'Go-rat-ch?'*

'No, "Gòrach". That back-tick above the "O" is a grave, so you pronounce it "aw", like in caught, or bought, or thought, and the "CH" at the end is an unvoiced dorsal velar non-sibilant fricative, like in "loch".'

'An unvoiced McWhatnow?'

'Imagine making a guttural hissing sound at the back of your throat, like an espresso machine, and you'll be halfway there. Ooh: or if you've ever watched *Star Trek*, the Klingons do it all the time. "Chhhhhh..."'

'Gow-ra-chhhhhhhhhhhh?'

Jacobson pinched the bridge of his nose between two fingers, face creased up. 'I think we're straying from the point. *Again.*'

'Yes. Sorry.' Alice went back to playing with her hair. 'Anyway, *Gòrach* has fantasised about killing a small boy for a long, long time, and then he sees Andrew and he's not prepared for it or anything, but Andrew's there, and no one's looking and this is his chance to finally do what he's been dreaming about. Only it's nothing like how he imagined it and it's messy and Andrew's struggling and Gòrach's panicking and he just wants to get it over with and what if someone sees him and oh my God it was meant to be *so* much better than this... So he abandons the body and runs.

'Andrew's discovered a couple of hours later and it's on the news and in every paper and Gòrach's panicking for real now – they're going to find him, they're going to catch him and he'll go to prison with the perverts and he can't take that, he can't, he'd rather kill himself than go to prison.' She tilted her head to the other side. 'It's all so horrible and scary but, now that he's done it, he can't stop thinking about the power and he's reassessing the experience; maybe it wasn't so bad after all, maybe it was *exciting*, and he's using it to reinforce the fantasy and he's masturbating with the *same hands* he used to strangle a wee boy, and over the next two months he's convincing himself that it'll be perfect next time, because he knows what he's doing now.'

PC Thingy shifted in her seat, face pulled down around the edges, as if she'd trod in something warm and squishy.

'So now Gòrach's looking for the next child to be perfect with and he sees Oscar Harris and this time he's going to get it right and he abducts him and takes him deep into the woods and strangling Andrew with his hands was too scary to do it again and he doesn't want Oscar looking at him, so he uses the boy's own belt and he does it from behind and maybe he doesn't do it right, and Oscar's still breathing, so he tries again, but Oscar still won't die – *why won't the little bastard die?* – so one last time and this time Oscar's dead and how did he manage to make such a mess of it and he's ashamed, so Gòrach hides the body under a rhododendron bush and slinks away.'

Jacobson nodded. 'So he's experimenting?'

'He's *learning*. This time he goes home and watches the media and there's Oscar Harris's parents on TV crying because their son's missing and maybe Gòrach likes that, likes seeing the pain in their eyes and knowing he's the one who did that, that he's got the power of life and death, not just over the children, but over their families too, maybe even the whole city? And he relives killing Oscar and Andrew, over and over, and he takes the best of both murders and puts them together to make a new and *better* fantasy that builds and grows till it's all he can think of, which is when he goes out and abducts Lewis Talbot.' Alice frowned at the whiteboard with the crime-scene photos on it, in all their horrible technicolour glory. 'It's not perfect, but then nothing ever is, but he's in control this time, he takes the silk rope with him, probably carries it about in his pocket for days beforehand, running his fingers over it and daydreaming about that wonderful moment when he finally gets to use it, and when he finds Lewis he's prepared, he takes him out to the middle of nowhere, deep in the woods, where no one will ever find them and Gòrach strangles and resuscitates him and strangles and resuscitates, because he has the power of death *and* life, and what's one without the other, only now he knows he *likes* the look of fear in his victim's eyes, he wants to see it as he kills and brings back and kills and brings back … that beautiful moment when the light flickers out, only to come back on again, so he can snuff it out one more time.'

Silence.

'Andrew was a victim of chance. Oscar was on purpose.' Alice let go of her hair. 'Lewis was the culmination of the first two murders, a return to all the things he loved about killing those little boys.'

'Yawn.' Huntly stretched out his long legs, crossing them at the ankle, exposing a swathe of bright-purple socks. 'This is all very touchy-feely, but – and I hope I'm not speaking out of turn here – perhaps we could have some sort of revelation that *actually* helps us catch him?'

Tit.

Alice pointed at the map that took up Whiteboard Number Four: where brightly coloured magnetic buttons marked the site of each abduction and dead body. 'Andrew Brennan was playing under the railway lines in Kingsmeath when he was murdered. For him to be a victim of opportunity, Gòrach had to be there too. But he went *hunting* for Oscar in Castleview – picked somewhere new to decrease his chance of getting caught – changing things up, going for a slightly older boy from a more affluent family, using the belt instead of his hands, trying new things. But Lewis Talbot is Gòrach's return to form. His return to Kingsmeath. Gòrach's comfortable there, it's his patch. He either grew up there and moved away, or he's never left. He *knows* this place.'

'Hmmph.' Huntly shrugged. 'It's a start, I suppose.'

'He has access to a vehicle – otherwise he wouldn't have been able to take Lewis to where they found the body. He's confident in himself, otherwise he wouldn't have transported his victim so far away from where he abducted him. See, there's that pronoun thing again. Gòrach's either self-employed, or he works shifts, or maybe some job where he's got a lot of autonomy? Otherwise he wouldn't be able to hunt children during the day, and during the week.'

Jacobson scribbled something down in his notebook, then looked up at her. 'What about previous?'

Alice shook her head, setting the curls bouncing. 'He's not had an outlet for these feelings. They've been brewing inside him for years but he hasn't dared do anything about them. That's why he doesn't sexually assault his victims – it's not about them as sexual beings, it's about him and his fantasies. He'd rather go home and replay the murder and masturbate than actually *do* anything with their bodies. Probably thinks that kind of thing is perverted: beneath him.'

'Because what the world really needs is more child-murdering tosspots with a well-developed sense of moral rectitude.'

Alice's shoulders curled up around her ears, eyebrows pinched. 'One more thing: I think this two-month cycle he's on is going to accelerate now he's found what he likes. He took the time between Oscar and Lewis's murders to *learn*. Lewis died in October, it's November now, he's probably already hunting for victim number four. And he'll be a lot better at it, this time.'

'Groan! Sigh. Wilt…' Huntly pulled himself up to his full height, in the back seat, then slumped again. 'Why are we going so *slowly*?'

I turned up the Suzuki's radio – a boy band warbling their way through an autotuned cover of an old Led Zeppelin song. Awful, but with any luck it would drown him out.

Instead, the annoying pinstriped git got louder. 'And why is this car so small? It's like something that comes with a Barbie playset. And it positively *reeks* of wet dog.'

Henry's glistening blackcurrant nose poked over the back seat, hairy eyebrows raised, mouth hanging open in a gaping grin, as if that'd been a compliment.

I gave Professor Bernard Huntly a scowl in the rear-view mirror. 'No one asked you to come.'

'I know. Sadly, it's my burden to be so *incredibly* useful that none can cope without my genius. So when I see a fair maiden in need, how can I possibly refuse to help?'

Outside, the rush hour proved what an oxy-sodding-moron it was – nose-to-tail cars, vans, and lorries, crawling their way across Calderwell Bridge in the pelting rain, while an occasional taxi stuttered past in the empty bus lane. The thick grey river turned pewter by the thin greasy light.

Huntly wriggled in his seat again, turned nearly sideways. 'Honestly, I swear this thing wasn't designed for full-sized human beings. Oompa Loompas, perhaps, but not human beings.'

Alice shrugged when I transferred the scowl to her instead. 'Well, what was I supposed to do? He annoyed Sheila all day yesterday, and it was Bear the day before that, so now it's our turn. You've seen the roster.'

We finally made it to the other side of the river, swinging around the roundabout and onto Montrose Road, heading east. The sign used to read, 'WELCOME TO KINGSMEATH ~ OLDCASTLE'S FRIENDLIEST NEIGHBOURHOOD', but the letters were barely visible under layers and layers of foul-mouthed graffiti.

'Friendliest neighbourhood' my arse.

At least the traffic was a bit lighter here – most of it going the other way, trying to get *out* of Kingsmeath.

Huntly leaned forwards again. 'So, my dear Dr McDonald, have you a plan for when we visit our first deposition-slash-crime scene?'

Alice fixed a smile in place. 'I'm going to look at things.'

'Ah, a very wise choice. I too have "looking at things" in mind.' Huntly wriggled about some more, setting the tiny jeep rocking on its springs. 'I know it's five months since poor Andrew Brennan met his unfortunate end, and it's unlikely anything will have survived the intervening period and this horrible weather, but we troupers must troupe, must we not?'

'I say we pull over, chuck Huntly in the river, and swear blind we haven't seen him.'

'Ash!' She shook her head. 'We're not throwing anyone in the river.'

'How about we fill his pockets with bricks first?'

The railway bridge lumped its way across Kings River on thick stone pilings, the heavy metalwork boxy and functional, rather than elegant and sculptured. It started climbing as soon as it made landfall at Kettle Docks, arching over the road in front of us – a lumpen granite bridge that hung with stalactites of rusting steel.

'No one's filling anyone's pockets with bricks!'

We passed through the gloomy archway, and Alice took a left onto Denholm Road. Heading uphill.

The street had probably been quite grand in its day – sweeping terraces of sandstone townhouses, lined with trees and wrought-iron railings – before they built Castle View and all the smart money moved out, leaving this part of the city to the mercy of town planners, council housing, and tower blocks. Now, the once-fancy buildings of Denholm Road were carved up into multiple occupancy flats, stuffed full of people whose benefits wouldn't stretch to anything less crappy. The trees reduced to vitrified stumps years ago, the railings long gone. The pristine sandstone striped with brown where its satellite-dish acne had rusted away. Blackened by decades of soot and grit and no one caring enough to clean it.

Huntly tapped me on the shoulder. 'Tell me, my dear ex-Detective Inspector, would you like to place a small wager on my turning something up here that will, as they say in the more excitable crime novels, "blow the case wide open"?'

Kept my eyes front. 'And would you like to wager that you'll do something that earns you a punch on the nose before that happens?'

'Oh, I *do* like a challenge!'

Alice pulled the Suzuki in behind the crumbling remains of an outside catering van – a boxy trailer, no bigger than four portaloos strapped together, slouching on flat tyres, its wooden walls bloated and peeling. The words 'SHAKY DAVE'S TATTIE SHACK' sitting proudly above a serving hatch that gaped like a corpse's mouth. She pointed at the junction with William Terrace. 'There's a way through, over there.'

'You, my dear, Dr McDonald, shall be the banker for our bet, this rainy day. Here...' He dug into his wallet and came out with a slithery plastic fiver. 'This says I come up with some *devastating* insight into Gòrach's actions before Mr Henderson deems it necessary to resort to physical violence due to his hyperactive amygdala and sluggish frontal lobe.'

I turned in my seat. 'Are you asking for a fist in the face before we've even left the car?'

'But of course: I do like to make things spicy.' A wink. 'Now, is there any chance we can exit this two-door motorised sardine can before I lose all feeling in my legs?'

'One punch and you'll lose all feeling in your everything.' But I got out anyway and folded the passenger seat forward so he could clamber into the rain like a pinstriped stick insect.

Huntly pulled a rainbow-coloured golf brolly from the rear footwell and popped it open. Standing there, brushing at the damp shoulders of his jacket.

I went back in for the two new-ish umbrellas I'd liberated from the station's Lost-and-Found. Handed the collapsible one to Alice. 'Here.'

She pressed the button and it sprung out, the canopy opening with a *whooomp*. A big smile spread across her face. 'It's a *ladybird*!' Bright red with black dots, a happy face, and sticky-out antennas that wobbled in the rain. It even had six short dangly legs.

'Thought you'd like it.' Mine was a plain black job.

Huntly finished preening, then snapped his fingers. 'Now, dear colleagues, join me at the crime scene, and witness the glory of my unfettered material-evidence genius!' Marching off with his nose in the air.

It was going to be a *very* long day.

10

'Well, isn't this *fun*?' Huntly hunched under his multicoloured brolly, face all puckered and lined, arms drawn in against his chest as he picked his way through the tussocks of pale-green and yellowy-brown grass and the rain hissed down. 'Remind me: whose idiotic idea was it to come out here?'

Our patch of waste ground made a gloomy strip, with the back of William Terrace and Denholm Road on one side, and the fifty-foot cliff that separated them from McArthur Drive on the other. The railway line soared above our heads, held aloft on substantial steel pillars painted in various shades of rust-flecked black. So thickly coated that the rivets were barely visible on some sections.

A long line of bare branches stuck up above the garden fences – beech and sycamore, with broom spilling out in dark-green profusion. The grey ranks of dead nettles wrapped around with curled bramble barbed wire.

Be a miracle if daylight ever made its way down here.

What a horrible place to die...

Alice wandered on ahead, her ladybird brolly thrumming in the downpour. Looking up and down, left and right, turning on the spot, then heading off again. Henry sulked along after her, tail down, whimpering and complaining on the end of his leash. Getting soggier and soggier.

'First observation,' Huntly pointed at the back of the buildings to our right, 'the only way you'd know a child was playing here is if you saw them from the windows, there. Or *you* were here too.'

I shook my head. 'Alice already said that, back at the briefing.'

'Has someone done door-to-doors?'

'No, because *not one* police officer in Oldcastle has ever worked a murder investigation.' I gave him the most sarcastic smile I could muster. 'You muppet.'

'Very well, I see I shall have to increase my levels of brilliance.' His arm swept north, following the line of the tracks above. 'The only entrances to this horrible strip of yuck are where we came in, and up there at Saint Damon of the Green Wood. And it's not as if you'd use this as a rat run to or from anywhere. So why *would* you be here?"

Should've gone with my first thought and thrown him in the river.

'The answer, my dear ex-DI, is "illicit reasons".' Huntly picked his way across to the base of one of the pillars, running the toe of his polished black brogues through the grass around the base. 'Which means the three "D"s: Drink, Drugs, and-slash-or Depravity.'

A thin metallic pinging rang through the air above, getting louder, like a metal rod drawn down a piano wire. Then rattling. And the shadow of a train growled overhead, adding a small shower of dust and grit to the rain.

I checked my watch: 08:32, so that would be the ten past eight to Aberdeen. Late again.

Huntly pulled his shoulders in, squatting beneath his brolly as if trying to make himself as small a target as possible. Only standing up again once the train had passed. 'Call me old-fashioned, but I'm never keen to be spattered with human sewage. And once the train has left the station...' He scuffed his shoe through the grass again. 'And while we're on the subject, who ever heard of Saint Damon? No such beast exists, and I speak as someone who's studied the Catholic faith fairly intensively.'

'You're a Catholic?'

'Well, not any more, obviously – their views on homosexuality being somewhat Levitican – but I was quite the altar boy when I was younger. Had a singing voice that would put joy in the bleakest of hearts. Even *yours*.' He shrugged. Curled his top lip. 'That's the trouble with Oldcastle, you lot have no respect for proper church procedures. You can't just go about making up your own saints without formal permission. Saint Jasper, Saint Damon, Saint Ailsa of the Immaculate Death, Saint Whatever-That-Church-In-The-Wynd is called.'

'Saint Fraser of Ochenbrook.'

'It's sacrilegious. No wonder Pope Innocent the Twelfth excommunicated the lot of you… Aha!' He stared at the grass where his toecap was, then pinned his brolly between his cheek and shoulder – freeing up both hands to snap on a pair of purple nitrile gloves. Bent and retrieved a used syringe, holding it aloft like a prize salmon. 'Voila.'

'That supposed to prove something?'

A condescending smile. 'That this place is being used for the consumption of drugs, my dear ex-Detective Inspector.'

'Wow!' I slapped a hand to my cheek. 'You – don't – say? A patch of waste ground in Kingsmeath being used by druggies? Shock, and indeed, horror! Who would ever have guessed?'

Huntly's eyes narrowed. 'A chap could go off you, you know that, don't you?'

'Every bloody park, kids' playground, and bus shelter from here to Kings Drive is awash with people shooting up. Be more of a surprise if you found somewhere that wasn't.'

He dropped the syringe, rubbed his squeaky purple fingertips together. 'Fine. Then *you* tell me what Gòrach was doing here.'

'Found it!' Alice's voice wafted back to us, through the rain. 'This is where Andrew died.'

'Maybe Gòrach followed him in. Maybe he snatched Andrew off the street and brought him here. Or maybe he knew kids played here so he turns up, hoping some kid will happen past.'

'Or maybe he's already here, shooting up, and then he sees Andrew Brennan and decides to make his high that bit more dangerous?'

'ARE YOU TWO COMING, OR WHAT?'

I shrugged, followed the sound of her voice, damp grass clutching at my trouser legs. 'If you can afford a car, or vehicle, why the hell would you come here to cook up? Why not go somewhere safe, secluded, warm?'

Huntly lumbered along beside me. 'Well, perhaps the good doctor is right and Gòrach lives locally? Or he comes back here to connect to his past...' A frown. 'To be honest, all this behavioural analysis stuff is somewhat beneath my skill level. I make deductions based on facts and realities, I don't do speculative nonsense. What we know is that Gòrach *was* here and *Andrew Brennan* was here, and they can only have come through the gate we did, or the one by the improperly named church.'

Alice stood in a small trampled circle of grass, frowning at the grubby remnants of a large teddy bear someone had cable-tied to a wooden fencepost. One of its arms was missing, the stuffing poking out of multiple holes in its legs. Its stomach spilling out into its lap. A handful of floral tributes lay scattered around it, as if tossed about in a fit of rage, the grimy cellophane wrappers of long-dead bouquets marking where people had paid their respects and not come back to clean them up afterwards.

Henry let loose a whimper and Alice rubbed the fur between his ears. 'Which house was Andrew Brennan's?'

Huntly consulted his phone. 'That one, there.' Pointing down the hill, to the back of William Terrace. 'Mother, younger brother, Andrew, and a succession of the mother's boyfriends. Three of whom are currently taking their ease at Her Majesty's pleasure for extortion, aggravated assault, and domestic violence, respectively. The local numpties interviewed all of her beaux, but to no avail.'

I tilted my head back, let the rain patter against my cheeks and chin. 'Let's say he knows Andrew. Let's say he's watched him play here in the past, what's different about *this* time?'

'Hmph. I'll let the good doctor take that one.'

Alice cleared her throat. 'Well, I mean, you could look on it as a crime of opportunity, like I said this morning, because he's always fantasised about it and the question then has to be why

95

would no one know about the murder, because all it would take is someone looking out of their back window and they'd see you there, strangling a wee boy, wouldn't it?'

Huntly went back to his phone. 'According to the report, the mother called the police when Andrew didn't come in for his dinner. That was a little after five o'clock.'

Back under my umbrella again, I nodded towards the skeletal trees and spiny bushes. 'I checked the weather reports: eighteenth of June, the city was thick with haar. Down here, in the gloom? You'd be lucky to see your hand in front of your face.'

Alice nodded. 'Do you think I could talk to the mother, Ash? Would that be OK?'

'Don't see why not.'

Huntly leaned on the bell, setting its high-pitched trill ringing on and on and on and on.

The building must have been impressive in its day: a grand mid-terrace home with its garden out front, tiled entrance hall, and mahogany staircase, but carving the thing up into six small flats had turned its sweeping grandeur into a claustrophobic warren. The lighting wasn't on in the communal stairwell, hiding *things* in the darkness.

And still the bell trilled.

Alice's boxy wee Suzuki sat at the kerb outside, Henry's nose pressed against the passenger window as the car slowly steamed up, marinating the interior in the stink of wet Scottie dog.

Finally, a man's voice grumbled through the door to Flat 1L, getting louder. *'God's sake, buncha bastards…'* Then the door burst open, revealing a tousle-haired bloke in his mid-forties with tattoos visible on his arms and neck where they poked out of a pink towelling dressing gown two sizes too small for him. Puffy eyes. Chin blue with stubble. A droopy moustache. Squint teeth on show as he bellowed at us. 'STOP RINGING THAT BELL!' Jabbing a hand back inside the flat. 'YES, I WAS ASLEEP: I'M ON BLOODY NIGHTS!'

Huntly took his thumb off the bell. 'So sorry to wake you.' Not sounding in the least bit genuine. 'Is Mrs Brennan home?'

'Why?' The man tucked his chin in, creating a roll of fat around his neck as he looked the pinstriped tit up and down. Clenched his fists. 'You some sort of *lawyer*?' Making that last word sound as if it was code for intestinal parasite.

Alice got herself between the two of them, and gave him a wave. 'Hello, I'm Dr McDonald, but you can call me Alice, if you like, and we're looking to speak to Mrs Brennan, because we're trying to help the police find out what happened to Andrew and why it happened, and who made it happen, of course – that's the really important thing, isn't it – so if you can help us to help them, that'll really help, OK?'

The rolls of fat got deeper. 'Mary's not here.'

'Oh, right, can we come in and wait, because it's—'

'What part of, "I'm on nights" did you not get?' Closing the door on us. 'She's up the church. Been going there every morning since … you know, Andrew.'

'Yes, right, well we can—'

'Hang on.' I stuck the tip of my walking stick in the gap, stopping the door from shutting. 'What lawyers are these, then? The ones you were expecting.'

He stared at his bare feet. 'I need to get back to bed.'

'Professor Huntly, would you be so kind as to lean on this gentleman's bell again?'

A raised eyebrow. 'I hope that's not a euphemism…' But Huntly did as he was asked and that irritating trill rang out once more.

'All right, all right!' Our sleepy friend scrubbed his hands across his face. Sagged. 'It's Mary's ex, Billy's dad. The wanker who broke her arm and knocked out two of her teeth. He's suddenly decided he wants visitation rights.'

Huntly raised the other eyebrow. 'But he's in *prison*.'

'Yeah, but he wants Billy to visit him there. And Billy's only fourteen months, so Mary would have to go with him. And that means Charlie Mitchell gets to screw with her head again. It's all about control with tossers like that.' The man tightened his too-short pink dressing gown about his middle. 'Now, if you don't mind: bugger off so I can go back to sleep.'

* * *

'What do you reckon to our sleepy friend, then?' Water gushed down the gutters on Denholm Road, rain drumming on the roofs and bonnets of the cars, bouncing off the overflowing municipal wheelie bins, as we slogged our way uphill.

Alice peered out from beneath her ladybird umbrella. 'As a suspect? Possible, I suppose – clearing the nest, getting rid of any offspring sired by Mary Brennan's former partners so he can repopulate it with his own, but it doesn't really fit, I mean, why would he go after Oscar Harris and Lewis Talbot as well?' She frowned. 'Unless *they* were killed by someone else, but then we wouldn't see such a clear progression of MO, would we, so on balance I don't think it's likely and anyway wouldn't local police have interviewed him already?'

'Ah, my dear Doctor,' Huntly gave her one of his more patronising smiles, 'you're forgetting one very salient point: the local police are morons.'

Bit harsh, but not necessarily untrue.

The road curved around to the right, coming to a halt at a roundabout circled by shuttered shops. A lone newsagent's was still operating, the sandwich board outside it proclaiming, 'BOY'S BODY FOUND IN WOODS ~ PHOTO EXCLUSIVE!'

From here, Banks Road climbed away on the left, an arched bridge taking it over the raised railway lines. And down below, in the hollow beneath both, lurked the dark grey lump of Saint Damon of the Green Wood. Its jagged spire barely reached road level, the roof done with semicircular slate tiles, like fish scales. Miserable gargoyles. Stained glass that looked as if it'd never seen sunlight or soapy water. A steep set of stairs curled away down into the gloom.

'Well, that's not depressing in any way, shape, or form, is it?' Huntly peered over the railings that separated the pavement from the near-vertical drop to the graveyard, fifty feet below. 'What a silly place to put a church.'

A pair of stone pillars stood amongst the headstones, holding up the railway line, a vast bowed arc of steel allowing it to span the main body of the church, another set of pillars on the far side of its sharp pitched roof.

Alice wrapped an arm around herself. 'Can you imagine being buried down there?'

Not yet.

'Come on: less melodrama, more work.' I opened the gate and led the way, descending the slippery steps. A drift of rubbish had built up at the base of the steep drop, empty crisp packets and plastic bottles mingling with wilting newspapers and take-away containers, stretching out to touch the nearest gravestones.

She was right about not wanting to be buried down here, though. Felt as if we were already halfway to hell, without being another six feet closer.

Lichen covered most of the memorials, obscuring the names and dates. It stretched up the church walls too, joining the thick bank of rambling ivy that crawled across the façade, making those dirty stained-glass windows even darker.

Alice and Huntly followed me through the heavy wooden doors, the three of us dripping on the flagstones, breaths fogging the air as the *plinky-plonk-squawk* of someone not very good practising on the organ filled the vaulted space. The same musical phrase repeated over and over, getting it wrong every time.

'Dear Lord,' Huntly hunched his arms in and shivered, 'colder in here than it is outside...'

Dark too – the only light came from clusters of candle stubs, flickering away in their wrought-iron holders, nowhere near enough of them to dispel the gloom. The cloying scent of incense not quite managing to cover the grubby taint of mould and damp.

Down the far end, looming out of the murk, a twice-life-sized wooden Jesus cried in agony on his oversized cross, eyes screwed shut, mouth open, the blood of his wounds darkened and chipped by time. Ribs visible through the slash in his side.

Rows and rows of hard wooden pews. A marble altar the colour of liver. A lectern decorated with dark metal skulls and bones.

Saint Damon of the Green Wood: about as cheery and welcoming as a landmine.

A woman's head and shoulders were just visible over the pews, by the front of the church. Kneeling in prayer.

She didn't look up as I slid into the space next to her.

'Mrs Brennan?'

Her hair was dark as coal, pulled back from her face and tied with a black ribbon, giving her sharp features a crow-like edge. Bony hands working their way through a string of rosary beads, the fingernails bitten down to ragged stumps. Eyes closed, pale lips moving in silence.

The photo in the case file showed a young woman who'd hung on to her baby weight, smiling away in Montgomery Park, by the boating lake, a baby on her hip and a wee boy at her feet – throwing chunks of sliced white to the ducks. A small happy family, enjoying a day out in the sun.

But those days were long gone.

The organist made another assault on the same passage they'd screwed up at least two dozen times since we'd arrived. Got it wrong again.

And Mary Brennan kept working her way through the rosary.

'Mrs Brennan, my name's Ash Henderson. I'm part of a team who're trying to help the police find out who hurt Andrew. Can we ask you some questions?'

Her eyes screwed tighter shut. 'I'm *praying*!'

'That's OK.' I settled back in my pew. 'We'll wait.'

'Oh, for God's sake...' She thumped her beads down on the shelf built into the back of the pews in front, the one supporting a row of mildew-blackened Bibles. 'What do you want *now*?'

11

'You think I haven't asked that every single day since Andrew…
Since he…' Mary Brennan dug a thumb into her temple, a
menthol cigarette smouldering away in the other hand.
Sheltering beneath the overhang of a gothic memorial to some
silk merchant who'd passed away in the cholera outbreak of
1832.

She took a drag on her cigarette, setting the tip glowing bright
orange in the gloomy morning. 'I ask for God's guidance, I
really do, and I want to believe that it's all part of His holy plan
and that Andrew's at His side. And I tell people I believe in
love and forgiveness. But what I *really* want is for the man who
killed my baby to be tortured in hell for all eternity.'

Alice shuffled her little scarlet feet, rain pattering on her
ladybird brolly's cheery red-and-black surface. 'You don't have
anything to feel ashamed about, Mary, it's natural to be angry.
You wouldn't be human if you weren't.'

'I want to wrap my hands round *his* throat, and squeeze the
life out of him myself. An eye for an eye…'

Yeah, we all knew how that worked out.

My turn: 'And you didn't see anyone hanging around the
place, before it happened? Anyone always walking their dog,
for instance, or taking a bit too much interest in the waste
ground? Maybe someone trying to get the place done up?'

She glowered at me, through a fug of exhaled smoke. 'Why

do you lot always ask the same bloody questions? Why can't you do it the once, then leave me alone? Why do you have to rake it all up, over and over and over?' Cheeks hollowing as she dragged in an angry lungful of menthol. 'How do you think it *feels*?'

Yeah.

The memorial's black marble was cool against my back as I eased further out of the rain. 'What about the people who go out there to take drugs? Would you recognise any regulars? Any names you could give us?' Thankfully, Huntly had taken the not-so-subtle hint and kept his tactless arse in the church, but that didn't mean his druggie theory wasn't worth a go.

'And you never answer anything, do you? You ask and ask and ask, and I get sod all back.'

Alice wrinkled her nose. 'It always looks so easy on the telly, doesn't it? The detectives rock up, ask a couple of questions, there's an ad break, then next thing you know the killer's in handcuffs and everyone lives happily ever after.' She squatted down in front of Mary Brennan, took hold of her free hand. 'It takes a lot longer in real life, and we're really, really sorry about that, but we *have* to find the man who hurt Andrew before he hurts anyone else. So I know it must be almost unbearable, but please: we need your help.'

A shrug, but she didn't take her hand away. 'Local kids use it to drink the booze they've shoplifted... Now and then you'll see someone smoking weed, cos you can't do it inside or you'll get kicked out of your flat. Maybe a couple of junkies, but only when the weather's good. There are nicer places in Kingsmeath than this.' She sucked on her cigarette again, hissing out a cloud of bitter menthol. A hint of steel in her voice: 'You think they're the ones hurt my Andrew?'

Alice shook her head. 'We're keeping an open mind, but it's not likely. They might have seen who did, though. We can get someone to bring round a few mugshots, maybe you can recognise some of them?'

Mary Brennan curled one shoulder up to her ear. 'Maybe.'

'OK.' I took out my phone, called up the memo app and hit

record. 'Can you take us through what happened that day – Thursday the eighteenth – doesn't matter what it is, anything you can remember could help.'

Mary Brennan looked out across the rows of headstones, back towards the waste ground, with the railway line towering above it on thin metal legs. 'It was...' She licked her lips. 'I wasn't ... good that day. Charlie's lawyer came past the day before with the legal papers, you know? Wanting visiting rights to Billy. I...' She bit her top lip. 'So I woke up, Thursday morning, with a killer hangover. What right's that bastard got to demand access to *my* Billy? Never bothered about him before, did he? Not when he could come home reeking of drink and beat the crap out of me.' A shudder ran its way through her, ending with another furious puff of menthol smoke. 'And now, all of a sudden, I'm supposed to take my Billy up to prison to visit his violent arsehole dad?'

She gave a small bitter laugh. 'Yeah, so: hangover like you wouldn't believe. And Andrew's begging me to take him to feed the ducks again, but I *can't*... You try spending all morning throwing up and changing a toddler's shitty nappy.' Deep breath. 'It was kinda cold and foggy, so I bundled him up in his duffel coat, wellies, and mittens, and stuck him out in the back garden. Was supposed to *stay* there, where it's safe.' Mary's voice got quieter and quieter. 'Only he didn't, did he? And now I'm stuck here, every morning, praying for guidance and wishing I could kill the bastard who took my baby...'

Somewhere, on the street above, a lorry went past, rumbling its way across the bridge as Mary Brennan chewed at her ragged nails. Then a train – rattling the rails above us, sending down a smear of grit and dust to clatter against the church roof. The five carriages taking forever to pass as it made its way south towards the station.

I pulled out the wodge of LIRU business cards from my pocket and slipped one free. 'If you remember anything else, anything at all, give me a call.'

She took the small rectangle of card and nodded. Biting her bottom lip. Blinking. Breath shuddering.

103

'I'm so, so sorry.' Alice put her hand on Mary's arm. 'I know you think nobody cares, but we understand, we really do.'

She shook the hand off. Scrubbed away the tears. 'Don't patronise me.'

'Well, maybe *I* don't understand, I mean, how could I – I can empathise, but no one can understand unless they've been through something as horrific as that, but Ash *has*.' Alice pointed at me. 'He knows what it's like.'

'Alice, *don't*.' Not this. Not now. And certainly not today.

'His daughter was taken by a man who tortured and killed her. It might feel like the police don't care, but I promise you, he really, really does.'

The old fire ignited behind my eyes, reached its burning talons deep into my guts. 'I said, that's enough!'

Mary stared at me with hungry eyes. 'Your daughter?'

My Rebecca...

And I'm standing in the kitchen, in my crappy dilapidated council house in Kingsmeath, opening those homemade birthday cards with her photograph on them. One every year. The blood and the pain and the horror in her eyes.

I curled my hands into fists, the knuckles white and aching. 'This isn't—'

'So, you see, Ash and I want to help you find out who did this. We want to make sure they're punished for what happened to Andrew.'

'Someone killed your daughter?'

'Enough.' I backed away from the memorial, into the rain again. Forcing the words through clenched teeth. Jaw throbbing with the pressure. 'I *don't* want to talk about—'

'Mary?' It was a man's voice, slightly high-pitched. A generic Scottish accent that went up at the end. 'I brought you a cup of tea. Thought you might...' He couldn't have been much over five four, with a beer belly that paunched out over the belt of his brown corduroy trousers. A combover that wouldn't have fooled Stevie Wonder on a dark night. A podgy face having difficulty holding onto the wispy beard he'd inflicted upon it. His eyes went wide behind his glasses as he saw me. 'I...' A mug with, 'PRAISE THE LORD FOR TEA & BICCIES!' on it trembled in his hand, steaming beige liquid slopping out to splash against the leg of his cords – darkening the fabric, as if he'd wet himself.

Why did he look so *familiar*…?

Of course: Steven Kirk.

The same Steven Kirk that swore blind he'd been taking care of his dying mother when all those wee boys were abducted and killed. And he just *happened* to be at the same church as Andrew Brennan's mother?

Aye, right.

'Well, well, well.' I stepped closer, letting all that pain and anger sizzle in the words: 'If it isn't the man we were off to see next. Hello, Steven.'

'This isn't… I wasn't…' More tea slopped down his front.

'I think you've got some explaining to do.'

But Kirk was off, the mug flying away to crash against a headstone as he sprinted across the graveyard. Wouldn't have thought a wee fat man would've been able to go that fast.

I lumbered after him, brolly bobbing and weaving – more trouble than it was worth, so I let it fly free. 'COME BACK HERE, YOU GREASY LITTLE GIT!' Not so easy, running through the thick grass with a buggered foot. Gritting my teeth. Pushing through the stabbing jerk every time my right shoe touched down.

But worth it, because Steven Kirk deserved everything that was about to happen to him.

He scrambled over the rear wall of the graveyard and out into the chunk of waste ground beneath the railway lines. I bent into it, sped up, slapped one hand down on top of the wall and swung my legs up and over. Landing awkwardly on my right foot – a red-hot crowbar slamming through the flesh to lever the bones apart.

Kirk wasn't slowing – if anything he was getting faster, accelerating down the slight slope. Increasing the distance between us.

'COME BACK HERE!' Finding it harder and harder to run now, every other step a screaming ball of agony.

He was going to get away.

And after this, it was pretty damned unlikely he'd head home and wait for us to show, like a good boy. He'd disappear. Properly this time.

MOVE FASTER!

Push.

Bite down on the pain and sodding *run*.

A jagged *huff-huff-huff* noise grew louder behind me, then Alice went past, arms and legs pumping, red feet flashing their white soles as she chased after Steven Kirk. Hood thrown back, curly brown hair streaming out behind her in the rain.

Kirk glanced back over his shoulder – face an unhealthy shade of sweaty puce – then put his head down and his elbows up, really going for it. But Alice was fitter. And faster. Getting closer and closer.

Then she was airborne: a flying tackle that slammed into the middle of Kirk's back, sending them both crashing to the wet grass at the base of one of the railway pilings. Rolling over and over, limbs sticking out, then curling up as they struggled.

Only when they stopped, it was Kirk who came out on top, straddling Alice, rearing up, one fist curled back and ready to smash down into her face.

Which is when *I* finally arrived. 'NO YOU DON'T!'

He barely had time to turn and stare at me before I battered into him, tearing him off her and into the grass again. Cracked the bony ridge of my forearm into his nose. Once. Twice. And three time's the charm. Putting my weight behind it. Bouncing his head off the ground as blood spattered out into the gloom. Doing it for every little boy and girl he'd hurt. For the people's *children* he'd brutalised, and tortured, and *killed*.

He screamed, so I smashed my elbow into his mouth as well. Did that again too.

Because let's face it, you have to take the tiny moments of joy when you can get them.

Should castrate the bastard, right here. Stamp on his balls till they burst. See if he still feels like interfering with children after they had to surgically amputate whatever ragged scraps of flesh I left him with down there.

106

His face got another elbowing, my teeth bared as I broke his. Not even bothering to hold back the laughter. Hard and sharp and loud and—

'God's sake, you'll kill him!' Alice's hands grabbed at my arm and collar, hauling me backwards. Off Steven Kirk. Pushing me away. Her face all pinched, eyes shining, nose red, tears on her cheeks. 'Stop it!' Then she was on her knees beside him, wiping the blood from his cheeks and chin with a handkerchief. Holding him as he sobbed.

I stepped back, a dull throbbing spreading down my right arm, making the fingers tingle, breath heaving in my chest. 'I did it … for... He was … trying … to hurt … you.'

Alice glared up at me. 'We're meant to *help* people!' Then she closed her eyes and turned away. 'I can't even look at you.'

Raised voices carried from the church's front doors, down the nave and over the crossing, but by the time they reached the chancel, Saint Damon's gothic pillars and grimy tapestries had reduced it to nothing more than angry noises, stripped clean of actual words, leaving only trouble behind.

I leaned forward in my pew, arms resting on the row in front, and nodded at Mary Brennan. 'Are you OK?'

She blinked back at me. Then stared across the rows of plain wooden benches to a small door set into the far wall. The one Saint Damon's registered first-aider had taken Steven Kirk through. 'I don't understand...'

'How long have you known him?'

'Steven?' A frown. 'Months and months. He helps clean the church.'

Couldn't help glancing around at that: the mildewed Bibles; the cobwebbed carvings; the paintings of religious icons thick with dust; the fourteen Stations of the Cross, so filthy you could barely make out the suffering in them. Oh yeah, Steven Kirk was doing a *great* job.

'Was that before or after Andrew went missing?'

More blinking. Probably trying to process the implications of that.

'*Steven?* But … he's … his mother's dying.'

The angry voices echoed away into silence, then the noise of marching feet – getting louder. One set of clacking heels, one set of squeaky damp rubber soles.

Sounded like it was time for my shouting at.

Across the apse, that small door opened and out came the large woman in a pastel-purple cardigan who'd taken Kirk away to fix him up. Her flushed-pink scalp clearly visible through the thinning, lank, grey hair. Kirk scuffed along beside her, holding a wodge of blue paper towels over his nose and mouth. Looking everywhere but at me.

The marching came to a halt and when I turned, there they were: Alice – who also wasn't looking at me – and an old bloke dressed all in black, except for the flash of white at his throat. Jowls hanging over the lip of his dog collar. A fringe of grey stubble above his pendulous ears. Wire-framed glasses and narrowed baggy eyes. 'What on *God's* earth were you thinking?' Not a local lad. That flat, back-of-the-throat accent definitely marked him out as Dundonian, no matter how hard he was trying to sound posh. 'How *dare* you come into the house of the Lord and assault one of my parishioners!'

Never punched a priest before, but there was a first time for everything.

When I got to my feet, I had nearly a foot on him. Looking down on that grey-fringed bald pate. 'One: it didn't happen in the church. And two: I'm not the one putting the people coming to this church at risk.' I poked a finger into his chest. 'That's you.'

Spluttering. Jowls wobbling. 'I'm calling the police.'

I grabbed a handful of his cassock and spun him around till he was facing Steven Kirk.

'Unhand me!'

Alice glowered at me. 'Ash!'

Tough.

'What's the matter, didn't you run a background check on the man you've got cleaning this tip?'

It was Kirk's turn to glower – over the top of his blue paper towels as they slowly turned a dark shade of purple. Voice all muffled and squishy. 'Yooo brurk mai teefff!'

The priest wriggled free. 'How dare you behave this way in a—'

'But then your team has a habit of covering up for paedophiles, doesn't it? Move them on to a different parish, quash the rumours, silence the victims.'

Those baggy eyes widened as he stared at me, then turned to Kirk. 'He's... What's he talking about, Steven?'

'It'dss nuuunt mai fowwwt!'

'Steven Kirk, former physical therapist, convicted in 1998 of making and distributing indecent images of children, abusing eleven minors at Blackwall Hospital, and the abduction and rape of a seven-year-old boy. On the Sex Offenders' Register for life, aren't you, Steven?'

And now, everyone was staring at him and his wodge of bloody tissues. Not looking quite so sympathetic any more.

The first-aider stepped away from Kirk, wiping her fingers down the front of her cardigan, as if trying to remove the taint of actually touching him.

'Hhh azzolded mei! Thigggh isssnuunt mai fowwwt!'

'I THOUGHT YOU WERE MY FRIEND!' Mary Brennan snatched up one of those manky Bibles and hurled it at him. Face contorted and flushed, spittle flying from her curled lips. 'YOU DIRTY BASTARD!'

He turned and the book bounced off his shoulder, leaves flapping as it fell, like a dying bird.

'I'M GLAD HE BEAT THE SHIT OUT OF YOU!' She sent another one winging Kirk's way – it battered off the top of his bowed head – then another. 'I HOPE YOU BURN IN HELL!'

He'd have a lot of company.

12

'Well, that was … unedifying.' Huntly settled himself down on the bench next to me. Dipped into his inside pocket and came out with a silver hip flask. Unscrewed the top and took a swig. Wiped the neck and proffered it to me. 'You really are somewhat … *volatile* today, aren't you? I mean, even more so than usual.'

High up above, the thick lid of grey had lifted, revealing a cold blue sky with wisps of white, travelling fast. No more rain. The sun was even shining, though none of it made its way down here. A graveyard permanently shrouded in gloom.

Knew how it felt…

Huntly waggled the hip flask.

'Can't.' I pushed it away. 'Pills.'

'Ah yes, the dreaded medication.' He knocked back another swig, then put the flask away again. 'Alice is talking to your friend, Mr Kirk, but it seems he's determined to press charges.'

Course he was.

'Apparently you've knocked out three of his teeth, broken his nose, and cost him his volunteer position at the church.' A frown. 'Difficult to tell which one hurt him the most, to be honest. Seems Father Lucas isn't so keen on a convicted sex offender hanging around with the choirboys and youth groups.'

At least that was something.

'Will you permit me to proffer a tiny morsel of advice, Ash?' Huntly's hand settled onto my shoulder. 'Make yourself scarce.

Soon as Bear finds out you've battered the living bejesus out of a suspect – no matter how well deserved that battering was – he's going to be less than amused.'

I leaned forward, put my arms on my knees and groaned. 'He was here, Bernard. He knew Andrew's mother.'

'And now we can't drag him in and grill him about it, without his lawyer bringing up the aforementioned battering. Which rather undermines our ability to prove he did anything.'

'Yeah.' Head down, hands covering my face. Squeezing.

Stupid Ash Henderson.

'And, as if by magic, here comes a chopper to chop off your head…' The bench shifted as he got to his feet. 'Dr McDonald, don't be too hard on Mr Henderson, he's—'

'A BLOODY IDIOT!'

I stayed where I was, face still covered. 'He was about to punch you in the mouth. Remember that?'

'YOU COULD'VE KILLED HIM!' Gravel crunched as she marched away, then back again. 'What the hell is wrong with you? Why does everything have to be—'

'No!' I dropped my hands. Stood. 'You *always* do this. Every time there's some poor bastard whose child's been killed, you point at me.' Jabbing a thumb at my own chest. 'Enough!'

Alice set her jaw. 'You can't attack every—'

'Rebecca's death isn't some lever you can pull, like it's a bloody one-armed bandit, to make victims pay out in fucking sympathy tokens! HER DEATH MATTERS!' Deep breath. I uncurled my fists. The ground beneath my feet a trembling sea of filthy gravel. 'It matters to *me*.'

'Wow…' Huntly backed off, both hands up. 'Maybe I should give you two a moment.'

Alice closed her mouth. Bit her bottom lip. Looked away. 'I'm sorry.'

Yeah, well, sometimes 'sorry' didn't cut it.

'Come on, Ash, I'm sorry. I didn't think. I'm really, *really* sorry…' Shuffling along beside me as I limped down Denholm Road. 'Ash, *please* talk to me.'

No.

Dragged out my phone and called Shifty instead.

It rang. And rang. And rang.

The rain might have stopped, but the drains were still over-flowing, the gutters making their own rapids where the water hit logjams of filth and rubbish.

Alice lurched in front of me, walking backwards, trying to make eye contact. 'I didn't mean to upset you, I know Rebecca's death must be painful, I was only trying to—'

'DI Morrow?'

'Shifty? It's Ash. I need a lift.'

'Don't be like that, I'll drive you wherever you need to go, it's not a—'

'Oh, Christ, what have you done now?'

'It's important.'

'Ash, *please*!'

'You do realise I'm a detective inspector, right? A detective inspector who's got a murder investigation *on the go. I can't—'*

'Can you give me a lift, or not?'

A long-suffering sigh. *'All right, all right.'* Some scrunching came down the line, then a muffled, *'Rhona? I've got to go out for a while. Keep an eye on things, and for God's sake, don't let the Chief Super put out any more half-arsed statements.'* Then Shifty was back to full volume again. *'Where are you?'*

Alice tried blocking my path. 'Don't do this. I said I'm sorry and I *meant* it.'

I sidestepped her. 'Heading down Denholm, I'll be on Montrose Road, going back towards town.'

'Ash, *please*!' Her voice ringing out behind me as I kept going. 'Ash?'

'OK, I'll be there soon as I can...'

'Ash! Please, we can talk about this!'

Not this time.

'So, are you going to tell me what this is all about?' Shifty was probably going for casual and nonchalant, but it wasn't working.

I kept my face turned to the passenger window as the manky

pool car headed back across Calderwell Bridge. The traffic had eased up a lot since rush hour, sunlight sparking off Kings River like shards of hot glass. Windy enough out there to whip up white horses as the tide tried to fight against it.

'OK.' He pointed at the windscreen as we made landfall on the other side. 'Can you at least tell me where we're going?'

'Steven Kirk's been hanging round the church that leads onto the waste ground where Andrew Brennan was killed. Has been for months.'

'Oh, for God's sake...' Shifty's hands tightened on the wheel, knuckles standing out like ball bearings. 'Blakey *interviewed* him! No mention of it.'

'I cocked up, Shifty.'

He eyed me across the car. 'Do I want to know? Actually, scrap that – I don't. Especially with Professional Bloody Standards poking torches up my fundament.'

Tchaikovsky's 'Danse des Mirlitons' burst out of my pocket. That would be Alice calling. Again.

'You going to get that?'

'Nope.'

We passed a couple of bookies and a charity shop. Pulled up at the traffic lights outside the boarded-up remains of Oldcastle's newest multiplex cinema – still advertising a superhero block-buster from three years ago, the posters' colours faded away to a yellow-and-black duotone.

'Still need to know where we're going, though.'

Good question.

Tchaikovsky faded off into silence as Alice's call went to voicemail.

Maybe it was time?

Wasn't as if the day could get any worse, was it?

'Take a right.'

Soon as the lights changed, he hit the indicators, setting a slew of angry horns honking behind us.

I clicked on the radio, jabbing the buttons till something suitably unhappy groaned out of the car's speakers. We drifted along Nelson Street to the sound of someone else's misery.

Then Tchaikovsky joined in again.

This time I didn't even let it go to voicemail: hit the 'reject call' icon instead.

Shifty shook his head. 'You're going to have to talk to her eventually.'

Maybe. But not right now.

Grey buildings slid by the car windows, grey people slumping past in front of them. Oldcastle in November. The whole bloody city needed a Valium.

On the radio, the song gloomed its way to a depressing finale, replaced by a gravel-voiced woman sitting far too close to the microphone in an attempt to sound sultry and intimate. *'Four Mechanical Mice there, and "Dear Dinosaur". You're listening to* Midmorning Madness *with me, Barbara Chapman, standing in for Annette Peterson. It's half ten and we've got the news coming up, but first, here's a word from our lovely sponsors...'*

'You going back to the flat tonight, or do you need somewhere to crash as well?'

'Don't know, yet.' The way things were going, once Steven Kirk's lawyer got his hooks into me, I'd probably be sleeping in a cell for the weekend, waiting till they got me up in front of a sheriff on Monday.

'...ahar mateys, cos at Blisterin' Barnacles Chip Shop, you landlubbers and salty seadogs can get two fish suppers and a poke of onion rings for the price of one!...'

Tchaikovsky had another go. Didn't make it past the first bar before I hung up on him.

'Look, Ash, it's—'

'Just ... don't, OK?'

'Cluckity cluck, cluck, cluck! Mummy, can we have Chicken MacSporrans for tea tonight? They're new and improved!'

'Of course you can, Timmy, because I know I can trust ScotiaBrand Tasty Chickens to deliver on nutrition and *taste. They're fan-chicken-tastic!'*

I pointed through the grubby windscreen. 'Right at the roundabout.'

We joined the queue of traffic, Shifty shaking his head. 'Only, every time you pair fall out it's me gets stuck in the middle.'

'...*and feel the magic of pantomime as* Sherlock Holmes and the Curse of Tutankhamun's Tomb *comes to the King James Theatre, this December! Fun for all the family! Tickets on sale now!*'

'Well, what am I supposed to do? It's—'

My phone launched into something else for a change: Radiohead's 'Creep', the words 'DSᴜᴘᴛ. Jᴀᴄᴏʙsᴏɴ' glowing in the middle of the screen. To be honest, that took longer than expected. Thought he'd be on the phone yelling at me ages ago.

Ah well.

Nice while it lasted.

Shifty took us out and round onto Castle Drive, the multi-building lumps of Castle Hill Infirmary looming over the houses on our left, the twin towers of its incinerators sending out clouds of white steam to be ripped apart by the wind.

I turned down the radio and took the call. 'Go on then, get it over with.'

'*Ash, Ash, Ash...*' A disappointed noise. Sounding sad, rather than angry. '*You don't make things easy for me, do you? Or yourself. You silly bugger.*'

'It's—'

'*Alice told me what happened and why. And, while I don't approve of people beating the hairy snot out of suspects, I appreciate it's not been easy for you. Not today, anyway.*'

Great: sympathy. The perfect way to make anyone feel even worse about themselves.

'*But that's still no excuse, you complete and utter, total arsehole! You're supposed to be helping us catch Gòrach, not buggering any chance we have of convicting him!*'

'Yeah.'

'*Now I have to spend the next hour pacifying Steven Kirk's lawyer; do you have any idea how hard it'll be getting a warrant to search his house after this? The Procurator Fiscal is going to do her nut.*'

The road curved around a patch of woods on the right, the sharp blade of granite towering on the left, with the crumbling remains of the Old Castle on top.

'*Well? Have you got anything to say for yourself?*'

'Yes: I resign.' Might as well, before he fired me.

'On no, you're not getting away with it that easily. I need you off the Gòrach investigation till this blows over, but if you think I'm giving you gardening leave, you've got another think coming. I'm not paying you to sit about doing sod all: you can go be a massive pain in someone else's backside for a change. I'm sure DI Malcolmson would be delighted to have you muck up her *caseload for a change.'*

No…

That dragged my shoulders down. 'In that case, I'm *definitely* resigning.'

'Have fun in Mother's Misfit Mob, Ash. Try not to cock anything else up, eh?' And with that, Jacobson was gone.

Wonderful. Just. Sodding. Wonderful.

When I opened my eyes, Shifty was squinting at me.

'You look like someone's slapped a cold jobbie in your Pot Noodle.'

To be honest, that would've been an improvement.

Never liked Tarbeth Park.

Saint Bartholomew's Episcopal Cathedral dominated the semi-manicured grassland, rearing up in all its jagged granite glory, the copper-coated spire scratching at the sky in shades of greeny-brown. All buttresses and lancet windows. Like Saint Damon's on steroids, only out in the sunlight, rather than down in a dank rainswept hollow. God knew what kind of sins Oldcastle had to atone for in the sixteenth century, but going by the size of Saint Bartholomew's, they were many and heinous.

Shifty stuck the pool car in one of the parking spots reserved for emergency vehicles. Cleared his throat. 'Want me to come with you?'

'Not really.'

He nodded, but clambered out after me, anyway. Scuffing along at my side as I limp-hobbled my way past the retractable metal bollards and onto the slick cobbled road that jinked in towards the cathedral's nave end. Gusts of frigid air shoved us along, making our coattails flap out in front of us as we followed the road, heading for the biggest graveyard in the city. Well, if you didn't count the plague pits in Shortstaine.

Shifty stuck his hands deep in his pockets, good eye narrowed as he squinted out into the sunshine. Raised his voice over the howling wind. 'Least it's stopped raining.'

From here, the view stretched down, across the park, to the river's glittering grey ribbon, then across to Cowskillin – with its rows of pre-war terraced houses and the abandoned hulk of City Stadium. Lots of browns and greys, because who wouldn't want to live somewhere completely devoid of charm or life?

Maybe the idea was that the ranks of the dead wouldn't see anything to make them jealous?

Saint Bartholomew's Graveyard sat a good ten-minute limp from the cathedral, as if distancing itself from the wages of all that sin, encircled by a four-foot-high stone wall. Guarded by a large wrought-iron gate, 'Mors In Nobis Ponere Debemus Confidunt In Deum' inscribed in metalwork above the entrance. As if that meant anything to anyone.

Shifty, thankfully, kept his mouth shut and followed me inside.

The part nearest the gate was filled with the oldest head-stones: short, blunt, ugly things where most of the carving had been eaten away by weather and lichen, leaving nothing but the ghost of memorials behind. The wind badgered us through the Victorian part, where being buried became all about outdoing your dead neighbours. Seeing who could have the swankiest granite mausoleums, or fanciest marble statues of weeping angels and cherubs. Celtic crosses big enough to crucify someone on. The Georgians were even worse. But the further back from the main path they got, the humbler the graves became.

And then we reached the far side and the modern burial plots, where shiny black headstones with gold lettering sprouted in ordered rows. Photos of loved ones engraved into their surfaces. Wilting flowers and rotting teddy bears slumped against the cold dead stone. Where the grief was still fresh enough to hurt.

Lines and lines and lines of them, with a chunk of woodland

rising in the background – branches writhing, the last of their leaves torn away to soar free in the gale.

'Erm, not meaning to be funny, or anything,' Shifty did a slow three-sixty, 'but do you know where she is?'

'Yeah.' Never been here in my life, but I knew. 'Thanks, but maybe I'd better do this bit on my own.'

I left him there and headed down a gravel path fringed with weeds, to a section by the back wall. A pair of plain grey stones, each with a fresh bunch of carnations in front of them. That would've been Michelle. Because she'd always been the more responsible parent.

HERE LIES REBECCA HENDERSON
BELOVED DAUGHTER, SISTER, & FRIEND
TORN FROM THIS EARTH FAR TOO SOON

My little girl.

Girls, Ash. Look at the other headstone.

No.

For God's sake, it's been *nine* years.

Deep breath.

But when I tried … it…

HERE LIES KATIE HENDERSON

My eyes slid off the shiny grey marble, like it'd been greased. Hauled down by the weight of guilt. My fault. My fault she was dead.

Wire and dead leaves filled my chest, pushing their way up to knot in the middle of my throat, not letting the breath in.

I stepped back, focused on Rebecca's final resting place again. Because at least I wasn't responsible for that one.

Huffed out a rattling lungful of bitter air.

They were only graves.

Then why was every beat of my shrivelled-up heart like being kicked in the chest?

The carved golden letters swam out of focus and no amount

of blinking would get them to snap back again. Standing there, amongst the dead, as the wind whipped at my back. As it howled and screeched through the headstones. As it *raged*.

I closed my eyes.

Aberdeen beach, when Rebecca was three, the sun hot on my bare back and legs. A picnic in the golden sands, looking out at the supply vessels waiting to come into harbour. Rebecca: testing her courage against the North Sea, chasing the waves as they retreated down the sand, turning around to squeal her way back to us as they doubled back on her.

Only Rebecca's face … is a blur. Her face isn't the only thing that wouldn't come into focus: the bright-red swimming suit, the sturdy little legs and arms, her curly hair.

Why can't I see her? Why can't I—

Rebecca: tied to a chair in a dank basement, her pale skin smeared with scarlet, slashed and burned and bruised. Eyes wide. Screaming behind a duct-tape gag. The number '5' scratched into the corner of the bloodstained Polaroid picture, mounted on a homemade birthday card.

No.

I snapped my eyes open again, but that image was burned forever on the back of my retinas.

All these years. All these years and I still couldn't—

'Ash?' A woman's voice, behind me, sounding pleased and amused. 'Ash Henderson, it *is* you. Well, well, well…'

I closed my eyes.

Apparently today *could* get worse after all.

13

She settled onto the bench next to me, hands in the pockets of her burgundy overcoat, shoulders hunched. Auburn hair escaping from beneath a shapeless woolly hat that was probably meant to look chic, but came off more like a stolen tea-cosy. Jennifer Prentice. She'd lost a chunk of weight, grown hard about the eyes and mouth. Forehead suspiciously smooth and immobile.

Wind whipped at the grass around us, thrashing the bushes, making trees creak like a galleon under full sail. It was billed as an 'area of quiet contemplation and peace', but the reality was four rusty park benches, arranged around a 'fountain of remembrance'. Which turned out to be a sludge-filled concrete roundel with weeds growing out of the rusting pipe where water probably hadn't sprayed for years.

Jennifer looked me up and down, as if assessing the damage. 'So how's it going with you and Whatshername: the Detective Superintendent woman?'

'None of your business.' Besides: that wound was much too raw for prodding.

'Oh, I *am* sorry.' A shrug. 'You never return my calls, Ash. A girl might begin to think you didn't like her.'

A 'girl' would be right.

'What do you want, Jennifer?'

'Aren't you going to ask me how I found you?'

120

And give her the satisfaction of showing off? 'Nope.'

'Used to think that strong-silent act of yours was quite sexy. Now? I'm not so sure.' Nudging me with her shoulder. 'A tiny birdie tells me you're the man to talk to about,' she left a pause, leaning in closer, as if that was going to build up dramatic tension, '*The Coffinmaker*.'

I held up my middle finger. 'One: sod off.' Index finger next, flipping her the 'V's. 'Two: never even heard of "The Coffinmaker".' The third finger went up. 'And three: you really think I'm going to talk to you after what you did?'

A pout. 'All I did was write a book about the Birthday Boy, Ash. I was there too, remember?' Another nudge. 'But I'm really pleased you read it.'

'You turned my daughter's murder into torture porn!'

'Ah...' She wilted a bit under my stare. Shrugged. 'OK, so I had to take some *artistic liberties* with events, but my editor insisted. What's a girl to do?' She was probably going for a contrite expression, but with half her face immobilised, it didn't really work.

How did I ever think it'd be a good idea to cheat on my wife with someone so shallow and greedy and vile? What the hell was wrong with me?

'Go away, Jennifer.'

'And "The Coffinmaker" is what we're calling Gordon Smith. From Clachmara? The man with the "Kill Room" in his basement?' She took her hand from her pocket and slipped it through the crook of my arm. As if we were dating. 'I've been talking to the neighbours. Did you know he's a set designer? Worked for theatres all over the UK – the new Sherlock Holmes thing on at the King James? That's one of his. Anyway,' lowering her voice, as if the graves on all sides were full of eavesdroppers, 'whenever some neighbour-kid's pet died, he'd build a small coffin for it out of plywood, paint it up all fancy, so the kid could have a proper funeral. Course, everyone thought he was being a sweet, thoughtful old guy, but now? Creepy as hell, don't you think?' She leaned back again, flashing a smile that barely moved her frozen face. 'Hence, "The Coffinmaker".'

God save us from tabloid hacks with overactive imaginations.

A magpie landed on the edge of the sludge-filled fountain, cackling at us, as if we were responsible for the horrible weather. Beady black eyes staring. Head tilted to one side as it popped down onto the gravel path.

'Ash?' Jennifer gave my arm a squeeze. 'I've heard rumours you were in Smith's basement. That you've got films and photographs. Of the victims.'

The magpie found the crushed triangular box of a prepacked sandwich, bashing its beak against the crumpled plastic window, trying to get at whatever was left inside.

'And I was thinking, *obviously* we couldn't publish the photos themselves, not with us being a family newspaper and everything, but there's definitely a book in it, right? "*Kill Room: the hunt for the Coffinmaker.*" You and me could do that.' Her words, soft and warm against my ear as she leaned in again. 'We could do *all sorts* of things. Like we used to, remember?'

A final jab and the plastic ruptured, spilling toenails of brown crust out onto the gravel as wind whipped the container away.

Jennifer pulled herself closer, till the warmth of her body leached through into my ribs. 'I could do that thing you like?'

I'd rather swallow a pint of bleach.

'Well? What did the Wicked Witch of the Wank want?' Shifty emerged from the shadow of a mausoleum, his one remaining eye narrowed to a suspicious slit.

'Chucking in the river.' Turning out to be a bit of a theme today.

He followed me back down the path and out through the big iron gates. Into the full force of the howling wind. High overhead, pale grey clouds snaked across the sky, but down here it was strong enough to turn the simple task of heading for the pool car into an undignified lurch.

Didn't make getting the Vauxhall's doors open exactly easy, either.

We tumbled inside, the wind slamming them shut.

Shifty wriggled in his seat. 'How'd she know we were here?'

'No idea. And I don't care.'

He started the engine. 'Can't believe you used to shag that. Lucky your poor wee willy didn't shrivel up and drop off with the cold.' A three-point turn. 'We finished now? Can I go back to my *actual* job?'

'Yeah.'

Half of St Bartholomew's Road had already been converted into the kind of luxury flats that cost more than most police officers would earn in ten years, the billboards outside advertising, 'SPACIOUS EXECUTIVE APARTMENTS WITH RIVER VIEWS!'

'Shifty?' I cleared my throat. Watched the unsold flats go by. 'Thanks. For taking me to see Rebecca.'

'You're a daft bugger, you know that, don't you?' His hand left the gearstick and thumped down on my arm. Gave it a squeeze. 'How long we been best friends for, thirty years? No way I'd let you go on your own.'

Even after everything we'd been through.

Couldn't help smiling. 'You'll have me welling up in a minute.' The flats gave way to unconverted warehouses and rat-infested alleyways. 'Actually, speaking of *best* friends, any chance you can give me a lift out to Clachmara?'

'Oh, for God's sake...'

The pool car rocked on its springs as we crested the hill and looked down on what was left of Clachmara. About another twenty foot of headland had disappeared, swallowed by the North Sea. Waves smashed against what was left, sending up massive spumes of white that were slammed away by the howling wind.

Half of Gordon Smith's house had gone, the roof caved in on most of what was left.

No rain this time, instead we were greeted by blue skies and churning grey sea. Crumbling yellow-green gardens. The houses looking every bit as depressing in daylight as they had last night. The road was a lot busier, though.

That manky Mobile Incident Unit had been shifted back a couple of houses – now a large white van sat in front of it, while little figures in high-viz outfits and hardhats struggled a new line of temporary fencing into place. Dragging segments from the back of a dirty-big flatbed truck. Looked as if Helen MacNeil's place was no longer considered safe. She'd love that. Wonder what poor sod had to break the news?

The caravan that'd sat on the drive had followed the MIU inland. Now it sat in the driveway of a boarded-up house, two doors down. Well, where else was she going to go?

This side of the Mobile Incident Unit, a couple of patrol cars were parked sideways across the road, holding back a knot of four-by-fours and hatchbacks. The familiar cluster of outside broadcast vans had relocated here from Divisional Headquarters, ready to give Clachmara its miserable turn in the spotlight.

'Wow…' Shifty peered out at the crumbling village and shook his head, setting his jowls wobbling. 'What a shitehole.' Weaving the pool car through the minefield of potholes. 'And you were in *that* last night?' Pointing through the windscreen at the remains of Gordon Smith's house. 'You're dafter than you look. And that's saying something.'

He took us past the outside broadcast vans, the four-by-fours, and hatchbacks – where telephoto lenses were jabbed out through hastily opened windows in our direction – and up to the patrol-car barrier. Flashed his warrant card at the PC behind the wheel of the nearest one, and hooked a thumb off to the side.

A nod, and the Constable reversed far enough to let us squeeze through.

'Don't say I'm never good to you.' Shifty pulled up behind the Mobile Incident Unit.

Would've thought all that rain last night might have scrubbed it clean, but the thing was even mankier today – its white walls stained a dirty beige.

'Thanks, Shifty.' I unclipped my seatbelt, grabbed my walking stick.

'Hoy, Ash!' He leaned across the car as I shoved my way out into the wind. 'You'll have to speak to Alice at some point.

124

Might as well put on your big boy pants and do it sooner rather than later.'

'Bye, Shifty.' Let the wind slam the car door for me. Staggered over to the kerb as he turned the fusty Vauxhall round and headed back towards town.

Right, time to get out of this howling-bastard gale. Every single window in the MIU was steamed up, but the door wouldn't budge. Thumping the handle up and down didn't help either. So I hammered on the door with the head of my walking stick. 'OPEN UP, YOU LAZY BUNCH OF SODS!'

'Excuse me, sir?' It was the patrol car's driver – the one who'd reversed out of the way – clasping his peaked cap to his head, leaning into the gusts, high-viz vest snapping and crackling against his stabproof. 'Sorry, sir, but they're not in there.' Pointing across the road with his free hand, towards a cheerless bungalow. 'Said the wind was making it impossible to get anything done.'

Course it was.

Mildew filled the gloomy living room with its ancient eldritch scent, fighting against whatever horrible aftershave DC Watt splashed on all over this morning. Mother's team had kitted the place out with two whiteboards – propped against the peeling wallpaper – and a TV on a stand. They'd even brought in the handful of cheap office chairs that came free with the Mobile Incident Unit, and a solitary Formica desk. Three ancient laptops grumbled away on top: screens glowing, fans whirring. Other than that, the room was empty. Even the carpet was gone, leaving behind an expanse of grubby floorboards that creaked and groaned beneath my feet. The houses on this street must've been built from the same set of plans, because a rectangle of solid wood sat in the middle of the floor: a trapdoor down to the basement.

Wonder if anyone had thought to check it for bodies yet?

Mother fiddled with a remote control, frowning as she jabbed it at the black TV screen. Getting nothing back for her efforts. 'Work, you horrible piece of nonsense...'

I cleared my throat and she turned.

Favoured me with a not-quite-smile. 'Ash. Detective Superintendent Jacobson said you might be joining us for a while. Are you any good with TVs?'

A snort from Watt as he stuck an A3 printout to the wall with a handful of thumbtacks. 'Laying low, is what I heard. And I don't see why we need some *civilian* screwing up our investigation.'

'You know John, of course,' pointing her remote at the weaselly pube-bearded git, 'and this is DS Dorothy Hodgkin.'

A middle-aged woman in a wheelchair gave me a cheery wave. Black leather jacket on over a thick red shirt, blue jeans rolled up and pinned where her legs came to an abrupt halt – not much above the knee. Long brown hair coiling down either side of a round face. Big grin. 'But you can call me "Dotty".'

'Ash.'

Watt stepped back to admire his handiwork. 'There we go.'

It was a photograph – head and shoulders of a man with a wide easy smile, wrinkles around his eyes and mouth that looked as if he'd done a lot of laughing over the last six or seven decades. Grey hair, just about clinging to the fringes of a high forehead, eyebrows that sprouted outwards in curling tufts. A neatly trimmed Santa beard.

Watt produced a pen and printed, 'GORDON SMITH (75)' across the bottom of the picture.

Mother nodded. 'Very good, John.'

'Got it from the theatre – it's in the programme for that Sherlock Holmes panto.' He stuck another printout next to it: an old-fashioned boxy grey Mercedes. Watt had added a mock-up of Smith's number plate underneath the photograph, along with the car's make and model details.

'Well done. Very thorough. Now, I think we should…' Light bloomed in the gloomy room as the bare bulb above our heads stuttered into life.

Call Me Dotty punched the air. '*Yes!*'

A woman peered in through the living room door – tall, with

broad shoulders and a long rectangular face; strawberry blonde hair down past her shoulders, that somehow managed to look expertly styled, even though it was blowing a force nine outside. Striking blue-green eyes, twinkling as she mugged a huge grin. Dark, fitted suit. Soft Invernesian accent. 'Talked the electricity board into plugging us back in again.'

'Lovely.' Dotty spun her wheelchair around. 'Any chance of a cuppa, then? I'm gasping.'

Mother brought the remote to bear again. 'Ash, this is Detective Constable Elliot. Amanda, and everyone else, this is ex-Detective Inspector Ash Henderson from the Lateral Investigative and Review Unit.' Giving Watt a pointed look. 'Mr Henderson has worked on a *lot* of serial killer investigations. He's going to be joining the team for a while, as a consultant.'

DC Elliot held her hand out for shaking. Had a grip on her that could crush a concrete bollard. 'Mr Henderson. Mother told me all about your trip into Gordon Smith's basement. That took some guts!'

Gritted my teeth. 'Any chance I can have my fingers back in one piece...?' It was as if she'd wrapped each of my knuckles in the heating-element-wire from a toaster and set it to eleven.

'Oh, I'm sorry!' Pink rushing up her neck, setting her pale cheeks glowing.

I stuffed the crushed paw under my armpit. 'Arthritis.'

'God, I'm such a *klutz*.'

Mother handed her a mug with 'WORLD'S GREATEST DETECTIVE INSPECTOR' on it. 'Amanda, if you're making, I'd love a coffee, and I'm sure Mr Henderson would like one too.'

'Yes, right. Coffee.' She turned and marched from the room, thumping the door closed behind her.

'You'll have to excuse DC Elliot, Ash, she doesn't know her own strength sometimes.' Mother jabbed the remote at the blank TV again. Slumped. Held it out in my direction. 'Don't suppose you know anything about these things, do you?'

With the curtains shut, the room was plunged into darkness, the only light coming from the TV screen as everyone perched on their plastic chairs, staring as what I'd recorded in Gordon Smith's basement played out in all its shaky horrible glory. Yet again.

Alice's voice crackled out of the TV's speaker: *'What the hell is this place?'*

The picture swam into a gloomy sea of grey-black pixels, then back to the light again as a string of Polaroids came into focus, the colours blown out by the glow from Alice's phone. Taking in one torture scene after another.

'Ash?'

My voice sounded weird. Higher than normal, a little shaky. *'It's a kill room.'*

'Oh God. Ash, they're—'

A muffled rumble and the Polaroids shook, faded out of focus into a grainy scrabble of blacks and greys. Henry's barks stabbed out like gunshots and the screen went dark.

The distorted double-echo of my phone recording its own generic ringtone.

'Hello?'

Mother shifted in her seat, grimacing as a tinny version of her own voice burst into the room. *'GET OUT OF THERE NOW! THE HEADLAND'S GOING!'*

Then it all became a confused smear of barely visible shapes rushing across the screen.

Me: *'Quick! Outside!'*

Alice: *'No, no, no, no, no…'* The screen darkened as she ran away, taking the light with her.

'ASH, DID YOU HEAR ME? GET OUT OF THERE!'

A hissing click, and the picture changed to a solid blue with 'HDMI1' in the top left corner.

Mother poked the remote and turned the TV off, plunging the room into darkness. 'Comments? Questions? Suggestions?'

'Leah MacNeil is dead, isn't she?' DC Elliot got up and hauled back the curtains, sending up a whoomph of dust – it glowed in the sunlight that spilled through the grubby glass.

A sniff from Watt. 'Of *course* she's dead. She disappears, Friday the ninth, Gordon Smith waltzes off into the wild-blue-yonder

128

one week later. Whatever's left of her will have washed out to sea by now.'

'It's all a disaster...' Mother levered herself out of her seat and slumped over to the window. Shoulders hunched as she stared out, across the road at Helen MacNeil's caravan. Then turned to face the new line of fencing, separating the world from what was left of Smith's house. 'There's bodies over there. Evidence. And we can't get anywhere near it.'

'Well, how about this?' Dotty wheeled herself over to join Mother. Craning her neck to look over the sill. 'They won't let us put an SOC team in Gordon Smith's garden, in case the whole thing gets washed away, so what if there was some way to have SOC officers in there, but keep them safe too?'

Another sniff. 'No way anyone would be daft enough to take that risk.' Watt stood, one hand straying to that bald scarred patch at the back of his head. 'Even if you managed to come up with a solution, by the time you'd done a risk assessment, got volunteers organised, set everything up, and put them to work, the garden would be gone.'

'Well, that's hardly the attitude, is it?'

'All I'm saying is: it's not doable. You couldn't follow any evidentiary procedures at all, there wouldn't be time. Best case scenario: they leap over there, dig like crazy and drag back everything they can before disaster strikes. How's that going to stand up in court?'

'What if...' Dotty squeaked her chair from side to side. 'We could get everyone a harness and someone holds onto the other end, ready to pull them back if something happens?'

That got her a laugh. 'And if you're too slow? They die. No one's going to let you do that.'

'OK, well, what if we got, like, a big crane?' She stuck her arm out, palm down, fingers dangling as she mimed it. 'You could lower a bunch of people suspended from a frame, so if the ground goes, they can't fall anywhere.'

'It's blowing a gale out there! Might as well make a wind chime out of their battered bleeding corpses.'

He was a prick, but he had a point.

Mother raised an eyebrow in my direction. 'I notice *you're* keeping very quiet.'

'Yup.'

'Ooh!' Dotty dumped her mimed crane. 'If we can't get anyone to go into the basement, how about we use a drone instead?'

Watt covered his face with a hand, speaking with the slow clear deliberation of someone explaining why you don't stick fireworks up your brother's bum to a particularly thick four-year-old. 'It's – too – windy.'

'Oh.' She stuck her nose in the air. 'At least I'm trying!'

DC Elliot shrugged. 'Sorry, I've got nothing.'

'So, that's it: we're doomed,' Mother sagged back against the windowsill. 'Without the remains, how are we supposed to identify Smith's victims?'

Ah well. Suppose I might as well play nice.

'Actually,' my empty coffee cup clunked down on the desk, 'I *might* know someone who can help you with that...'

14

Sabir made a sound like a deflating beach ball. *'Yer not asking much, are yez?'*

I leaned against the wall and shrugged. 'Well, if you think it's too difficult...?'

The master bedroom had been stripped bare, like the lounge, but this time they'd even taken the curtains. A large brown stain reached out from the far corner, across the ceiling, spreading down the wall, and finishing up in a patch of twisted floorboards – blackened with mould.

'You see, I've been telling everyone what a computer genius you are, but if you think this one's too hard for you, I completely understand.'

'Ash, yer a total—'

'Won't make me think any less of you, if this is *way* beyond your skill level.'

Outside, the TV crews were getting ready for the lunchtime bulletins. Reporters bracing themselves against the battering wind, scarves and hair flying out like an eighties rock video. Cameramen lurching about as they tried to frame their microphone-wielding idiot, Gordon Smith's house, the headland, and the Mobile Incident Unit, all in the one shot. While at the same time cutting every other channel's camera crew from the scene.

'Is this reverse-psychology bullshit supposed to werk on me, like? Cos if it is, I've got some bad news for yez.'

'Come on, Sabir! It'll only take you a couple of minutes. And I can give you a cost code too.'

'*Really?*'

'All I want you to do is run the Polaroids in the footage against every misper database in the UK, going back fifty-six years. Piece of cake.'

A sharp intake of breath. '*Fifty-six years? Are you off your haggis-munching—*'

'No, you're right, Sabir, better make it sixty.'

'*Yez never said nothing about fifty-six years! Half the bloody records probably ain't even been digitised, never mind put online. Yez're off yer head if you think—*'

'Unless, of course, it's beyond even *your* immense talents?'

Silence.

The BBC lot were getting into a stushie with the Channel 4 brigade: the reporters banging their chests together like elephant seals while the camera crew tried to look the other way.

'Well?'

'*All right, all right. I can run the ferst set, but you've got bugger-all chance with the second. No way you'll get an image match with people bein' tortured. Facial recognition's good, but there's limits.*'

'Couldn't you clean them up? Digitally alter them so they look normal?'

'*Oh yeah, and then I'll climb aboard me flying unicorn and go—*'

'Look, if you can't—'

'*This isn't* CSI Oldcastle! *I can only do what's actually bloody possible in the* real *world. And you better gerra cost code for me, Ash, cos if you don't—*'

'Thanks, Sabir, you're a star.' Then hung up, before he could change his mind. According to my phone, there were eight missed calls from 'DR MCFRUITLOOP' and about a dozen text messages. Well tough, Alice could bloody well stew.

Back in the living room, the curtains were shut again, that lonely lightbulb casting hard shadows on the bare walls. DC Elliot was fishing about inside a big lumpy printer, scowling at the mechanisms as she poked. Swearing under her breath while Watt pinned up a blurry still from the video I'd taken in Gordon

Smith's basement. It was the young man in the beer garden, toasting whoever was taking the picture. Smith, presumably. Or his wife.

Maybe they took turns picking victims and killing them?

The photo was one of three – the young woman on one leg, and the other young woman on the beach.

'Where's DI Malcolmson?'

'Hmmm?' Elliot looked up from her rummaging. 'Sorry, yes: she's off shouting at someone, I think.'

Watt stepped back to admire his handiwork. 'Some moron from the *Glasgow Tribune* tried to sneak through the fence. Have you *still* not got that printer working, Amanda?'

'It's not my fault it jams on every other page, is it?' She hauled a crumpled sheet of ink-smeared paper from the machine's innards, and clunked the lid shut again. 'Try it now.'

I left them to it.

Headed down the hall and out the front door.

Mother stood in the garden, curly ginger hair whipping around her head in the wind, throwing her arms about while a young man in an ill-fitting suit withered before her.

He had a face full of acne and teeth, a single solid eyebrow wriggling its way across his brow. A big digital camera slung around his neck. Knees bent, hands raised as if to ward off blows. 'I'm sorry, I'm sorry!'

'YOU COULD'VE DIED, YOU IDIOT! WHAT WOULD YOUR POOR MUM THINK IF YOU GOT CRUSHED TO DEATH AND WASHED OUT TO SEA?'

'I'm *sorry*—'

'BECAUSE I'D BE THE ONE WHO'D HAVE TO TELL HER, HER LITTLE BOY HAD STUPIDED HIMSELF TO DEATH!'

'I'm sorry!'

'GO ON, GET OUT OF MY SIGHT.' She stabbed a finger westward, away from the cliffs. 'AND DON'T YOU *EVER* LET ME CATCH YOU DOING ANYTHING LIKE THAT AGAIN!'

The wee loon scuttled off, jacket snapping about him as the wind tore at his back.

'Were you trying to make him cry?'

Mother turned. 'Ah, Ash. Any luck with your IT guru?'

'Going to take a look for us, but we'll probably have to give him a cost code to write his time against.'

She sagged, turned, and leaned her thick white fists on the garden wall. 'Everyone always wants money, these days. Whatever happened to going out and catching crooks? Now it's all cost centres and codes and balance sheets and budget forecasts.'

'Look on the bright side,' I pointed across the road, 'you'll save a fortune, not having to pay for a search team, or the scene examination lot.'

A deep *dark* rumbling noise juddered its way through the gale as another chunk of Gordon Smith's garden disappeared into the North Sea, taking a four-foot segment of wall and roof with it. The TV crews all swung their cameras around to capture the excitement. No doubt that would get featured on the lunchtime news.

She shook her head. 'Going to be almost impossible to get a sound conviction on this one.' Raised a hand towards the crumbling bungalow with its tumbledown roof. 'No physical evidence, no bodies, no forensics tying Smith to the crimes... Be lucky if we can even prove there've *been* crimes. Any semi-conscious defence solicitor will tear us a fresh bumhole.'

No wonder the top brass had lumbered Mother and her Misfit Mob with the case. Every Superintendent, DCI, and DI in O Division would be running full speed in the opposite direction to this career-killing crapfest.

The camera crews stayed where they were, obviously hoping for a repeat performance.

'Wouldn't be the first time someone got sent down for murder with no body.'

'Jack thinks I should pack it all in. Give up the glamorous life of a police officer and go on cruises instead. Play golf. Do the garden. Spend more time with the grandchildren.'

'Sounds exciting.'

'You haven't met my grandkids.' She frowned for a moment, then sniffed. 'Tell your IT guru he can have eight hours and not a penny more. In the meantime, what are *you* going to do?'

Good question.

'Think I'll go see a man about a croft.'

'When DS Franklin gets back, you can take her with you. She's driving everyone else round the bend, don't see why you should be the exception, just because you're new.'

Oh joy.

'What?'

Sitting in the driver's seat, Detective Sergeant Franklin tightened her jaw, eyes fixed straight ahead as the dual carriageway climbed Friarton Bridge, arching over the River Tay. Hands tight around the wheel, knuckles paling her skin. She'd hung the black suit jacket up in the back, her white shirt fitted and a touch more revealing than was *strictly* necessary. Some would call her handsome, striking, maybe even beautiful – as long as they hadn't had to share a crappy Police Scotland pool car with her.

'Come on, out with it: you've been shooting daggers at me since before Dundee.'

Still nothing.

'Not my fault you got assigned to this job, is it? That was your guvnor.'

She bared perfect white teeth. 'It's because I'm black, isn't it?'

'What is, the sulking?'

Franklin put her foot down, the needle creeping up closer to eighty as she swung the ancient Ford Focus out into the other lane to overtake a Megabus. 'I'm a *detective sergeant*, you're not even a police officer!'

'And that's a problem, because…?'

'I am not a bloody chauffeur! *You* should be driving *me*, not the other way round.'

She snapped the car back into the inside lane, getting an angry flash of headlights and a variety of rude hand gestures from a fat woman in a people carrier.

'Are you always like this?'

'I'm not *like* anything.'

'God, it's no wonder Mother wanted shot of you for the day.' I stretched out my right leg, rotating the ankle, setting it clicking. Easing out the burning. 'And the reason *you're* driving *me*, Detective Sergeant, is one: I used to be a DI, and two: you don't have a bullet hole in your foot. Which makes driving anything a massive pain in the ... foot.' Tried for a smile. 'Much like yourself.'

Not so much as a twinkle.

'So, shall we get on with the obligatory bonding getting-to-know-each-other bollocks, or are you planning on seething all the way to Edinburgh?'

She tightened her jaw again.

'Fair enough.' I reclined my seat and closed my eyes. 'You can wake me up when we get there.'

Something sharp poked me in the shoulder. 'We're nearly there.'

I sat up, blinked. Didn't bother stifling a yawn.

We were on a residential street that could've been anywhere in Scotland: short rows of small terraced houses; the occasional bungalow; two-storey blocks of flats arranged around a central stairwell; grey harling, pink harling, bus lanes and speed cameras. Wouldn't think Saughton was lurking just out of sight.

Franklin pulled up at the junction, sitting there with the indicators clicking, waiting for two taxis and a removals van to pass. 'You snore.'

'And you have all the interpersonal charm of a post mortem. But you don't hear me going on about it, do you?'

She took the corner, up the small hill, and round into the car park.

Suppose one of us should try being a grown-up.

'Look, we're going to have to work together for a couple of days, so maybe we could try and keep the mutual loathing down to a gentle simmer? Or we could even have a bash at starting over?' I held out my hand as she killed the ignition. 'Ash Henderson, former Detective Inspector. Of course, that was

136

back when it was still Oldcastle Police, before Police Scotland ruined everything and we all went to rat shit in a handcart.'

She looked down at my proffered hand, then up at me. Curled her top lip. And climbed out of the car. Grabbed her jacket from the back and marched off towards the ugly Lego-brick lump of a building lurking behind a weird green-roofed visitor centre. They'd stuck the words 'HMP EDINBURGH' on the prison's façade, above a three-storey wall of tinted glass, framed with beige cladding, but it was like putting stockings-and-suspenders on a pig and hoping no one would notice it wasn't a glamour model.

Franklin stopped by the line of bollards, turned, and threw her arms out. 'ARE YOU COMING OR NOT?'

Oh yeah, she was *definitely* a charmer.

'Sorry to keep you waiting...' An ingratiating smile pulled at the man's face. He'd slicked his hair into a greasy side parting that didn't really go with the pink polo shirt – stretched tight across a chest and arms that clearly spent a *lot* of time in the gym. Thick black-rimmed glasses perched on a horsey nose. iPad clutched under one arm. 'If you'd like to follow me?'

We abandoned the small waiting room, Franklin simmering away behind me, glowering at everything and everyone as we followed the bloke down grey concrete corridors that stank of fresh paint.

'We're having a spruce up: going for something a bit more cheery.' A hand came out to wave at the bland walls. 'This'll all be bright primary colours when it's done. I wanted a mural, but there wasn't the budget.' A combination of ID card and pincodes got us through a series of thick doors with safety-glass inserts, opening and closing to a running commentary on what colour what wall was going to end up.

Not sure if he was nervous, or really liked the sound of his own voice.

'And this is us, here.' He ushered us through into a small meeting room.

No windows. Instead, a watercolour painting of Edinburgh

137

Castle – as imagined by a six-year-old with no artistic skill whatsoever – took pride of place on the far wall. A lone pot plant sagged in the corner, its plastic leaves drooping. One manky coffee table, and four uncomfortable-looking chairs upholstered in vile patterned fabric.

Two occupants: a prison officer, every bit as over-muscled as our guide, leaning with her back against the wall, off-blonde hair pulled into a saggy ponytail; and a man in his late sixties, early seventies. He looked up from a plastic cup of something brown, ran his deep-set eyes across me, then did the same with Franklin.

Leered.

'Hello, *darling*. You're a vision to warm a man's heart, aren't you?' He had a sharp face, not helped by the pointy goatee dangling off the end of his chin. He'd swept his grey hair forward, probably thought it covered that bald shiny crown, but it gave him a look of Nero's pervier uncle. Prison sweatshirt and jogging bottoms. A pair of white trainers that had never seen the outside world. And never would. 'Tell you, this place is full of poofs and wankers, so it does a body good to see a *real* woman for a change. Instead of these muscly dykes.' He turned his smile on the prison officer. 'No offence, Shona.'

Shona narrowed her eyes, but didn't say anything. Not while there were witnesses present, anyway.

There was a pause as Franklin's cheeks darkened. Winding herself up to a proper explosion.

OK. Time to be the grown-up again.

'Mr Smith.' I settled into one of the other chairs. 'You know why we're here?'

'Oh aye: saw it on the lunchtime news. My wee brother's been a naughty boy, has he?'

'Runs in the family.' A smile. 'Detective Sergeant, would you care to refresh everyone's memory?'

Franklin pulled a printout from her suit pocket. 'Peter Smith, currently serving sixteen years in Saughton—'

'Actually,' our guide raised a hand, 'the official name is HMP Edinburgh, so if you don't mind…?'

Her back stiffened. '*Fine.*' That one word making it clear it really wasn't. 'Serving sixteen years in "HMP Edinburgh" for murdering a GP. According to the file, you stabbed her thirty-two times.'

Smith shrugged. 'Tempers became heated.'

'Then there's the three years you did in Oldcastle for aggravated assault, the stint for attempted abduction, and a four-year stay at Peterhead Prison for sexually assaulting a pregnant schoolteacher.'

A wistful look slid its way across his face. 'I've led quite the colourful life, haven't I?'

'Not to mention the four allegations of rape.'

Another shrug.

I hooked my walking stick over the back of the chair next to mine. 'Tell us about your brother, Peter. What's Gordon like?'

'Now you're asking.' He sat back, knees spread far apart, crotch pointing in Franklin's direction. 'You heard about the coffins, yes? Making them for the kids if their pets died? Aye, that's not new, Gordy's been doing that all his life. Turned out a lovely one to bury the neighbour's Dachshund in, painted it like a racing car and everything.' Smith shook his head. 'Course the dog wasn't dead. At least, not when it went *into* the coffin. Could hear it whining as Gordy shovelled the soil in on top. Ashes to ashes, and all that.'

No one said anything.

'Always thought it was a bit of a cliché, myself, but that was Gordy for you. And he learned to hide it well, had to give him that. By his eighth birthday, you'd never have known how screwed up he was inside. Always smiling, singing happy tunes to himself. Course I knew about the humane traps he used on the mice in the basement.' Smith winked at Franklin. 'Oh yes, the *traps* were humane, but what he did to those wee mice when everyone went to sleep? That wasn't humane at all...'

Our guide cleared his throat. The prison officer, Shona, shifted against the wall, fidgeting with her keys. The central heating pinged and gurgled.

'Poor wee Gordy never was ... robust like me. He let it get

to him. So Dad used to batter the living hell out of us, so what? Even the sexual stuff, you don't have to let that define you, do you? Bet there's millions of people out there been interfered with and never killed anyone.'

I sat forward. '*You* killed someone.'

'That's not the same thing at all: Dr Griffiths had it coming. If she'd been any sort of real doctor, she would've caught Caroline's cancer before it was too late to do anything about it, wouldn't she?' He poked his cheek out with his tongue, head wobbling in faux-modesty. 'When you think about it, I did the NHS a favour, taking that useless cow out of the gene pool.'

Now that was interesting...

I threw Franklin a glance to see if she'd spotted it, but she was still busy with her scowling.

'Anyway,' Smith waved away the notion, 'that stuff with the animals: Gordy's way of coping, wasn't it? I'm sure he had nothing to do with all those alleged dead bodies you *say* you found, but can't produce. Because "the nasty storm's eaten them all".' Smith wasn't making a very good job of hiding his smile. 'Allegedly. If they ever existed in the first place.'

Sometimes, all you needed to do was leave a long enough gap in an interview, and the suspect would scramble to fill it with something incriminating. But when I gave it a go, Peter Smith settled back in his seat, hands behind his head, legs out, ankles crossed.

OK.

'Tell me about your croft...?' I raised my eyebrows at Franklin.

She checked her notes. 'Wester Brae of Kinbeachie.'

'Not much to tell. Ninety-three acres, most of it bog and reeds. Loads of gorse. And it's a *farm*, not a croft.' He sniffed, pursed his lips. 'Inherited it off an uncle. He was "hands on" with wee boys too. Suppose it must've run in the family...' Smith frowned down at his hands. The fingers seemed to have worked themselves into a knot. He unlaced them, one by one. 'To be honest, it's amazing Gordon and me turned out as well as we did.'

Talk about setting a low bar.

'And who's looking after this "farm" while you're in here?'

'Nah,' he waved that away, 'nothing worth looking after. Animals all died years ago. Nothing left but weeds and mud and a farmhouse you wouldn't keep dogs in. Whole place needs burning to the ground.' A smile. 'No point salting the earth, though, sod all grows there anyway.'

Franklin pulled her chin up. 'And where do you think your brother is now?'

That leer returned. 'He'd like you.'

'He's not at your so called farm, we checked. So where is he?'

'See, we share a taste in women, Gordon and me.' Peter sat forward. 'Young and tight. Bet you know how to treat a man, don't you? With your low-cut top and pert firm breasts.'

That imminent-explosion look was back on Franklin's face again.

OK, time to get this back on track. I cut in before she could open her mouth. 'Let me get this straight, Mr Smith: you murdered a woman because she didn't diagnose your sister-in-law's bowel cancer early enough? Does that sound *reasonable* to you?'

The smile slipped from his face. 'Think you lot have had enough of my time.' He stood, gave Franklin another once-over. 'Don't fancy coming back to my cell with me, do you, sweet-cheeks? Sure I can show you some moves that'll get your knickers dripping. No?'

Franklin bared her teeth, fists curled. 'No.'

'Ah well, just have to use my imagination, won't I?' He gave the front of his joggy bots a squeeze. 'Be thinking about you, later.'

She didn't stop swearing till we were back in the car.

15

I opened my mouth, but Franklin got there first:

'Don't, OK? Don't say a *bloody* word. That misogynistic, sexist, slimy old… Gah!' She stuck her foot down as the lights changed, wheeching out onto the roundabout. Following the road markings for A71 WEST ~ THE NORTH. Slamming on the brakes again as the next set of lights turned red before we could cross them. Bashing the flat of her palm against the steering wheel. 'Damn it!'

'Come on, he can't be the first creepy weirdo who perved on you to mess with your head.'

'He did *not* mess with my—'

'Difficult to focus on what someone's saying if you're standing there dreaming about battering his face off the floor six or seven times.'

She scowled across the car at me. 'I was focused!'

'Green.'

'What?'

Pointing through the windscreen. 'The light's gone green.'

'Bloody hell…' She nearly stalled it, but got the pool car kangarooing around to the exit.

'OK, well if you were so focused and non-distracted, what did you make of the sister-in-law thing?'

Down the slip road. 'What sister-in-law thing?'

'See?' God save us from detective sergeants with a chip on

their shoulder. 'Peter Smith says he murdered Dr Griffiths because she cocked up Caroline Smith's cancer diagnosis. He killed for his sister-in-law. Not his sister, not his wife, his *sister-in-law*.'

'So what? Maybe they're a close family.'

'Yeah, that's what I'm worried about. It's—'

My phone launched into its bland generic ringtone, and when I pulled it out, there was 'DI Malcolmson' in the middle of the screen. Ah well, might as well. It was that or talk to smiler, here. I hit the button. 'Hello?'

'Ash, it's Mother. How are you and Rosalind getting on?'

'Like a house on fire.' People running, screaming, dying...

'That's nice. Listen, you don't fancy doing a teensy favour for me, do you? We put an appeal out on the lunchtime news, did you hear it? Anyway, people have been calling with sightings.'

'And let me guess: some timewasting loony thinks they've seen Gordon Smith in Edinburgh.'

'And Portree, Kingussie, Clydebank, Hawick, Aberystwyth, Torquay, Billingborough, Methil... So if you can swing past and check, while you're in the area, that'd be a great help.'

Hard not to groan at that.

'I know, I know, but it's worth a try, isn't it?'

Not really. That was the trouble with police work, though. Ninety-six percent of it was a complete waste of time and the other four percent got you in trouble with Professional Standards.

'Have the labs got back with anything from those Polaroids? The ones I gave DI Morrow?'

'DI Morr...? Oh, you mean Shifty? No, not yet. John's chasing them.'

'Get them to compare any DNA, blood, or fingerprints with Peter Smith – Gordon's brother. Doing a sixteen stretch in Saughton.'

Silence from the other end of the phone.

I leaned towards Franklin. 'Better get in the right-hand lane, we're going back to Edinburgh.'

'Oh, for God's sake. Make up your mind...' But she yanked on the steering wheel anyway, sending the Ford Focus careening across the white rumble strip and inches from the rear end of an articulated lorry. A blare of horn from the white Transit we'd just cut in front of. Then out into the overtaking lane, accelerating past the lorry and up the hill, as if we hadn't been seconds away from 'Five Dead In Motorway Pileup Horror'.

I forced down the fizzy feeling that'd clamped onto my bowels. Went back to the phone. 'You still there?'

'Is there something you're not telling me, Ash? Why all this interest in Gordon Smith's brother?'

'Call it ex-DI's intuition. Now, where are we meant to be heading?'

'You'll like this: be a treat for you.'

Why did that sound highly unlikely?

'Well how was I supposed to know there wasn't any parking?' Franklin stomped past the National Gallery, moping her way between the waist-high sections of temporary fencing and into a world of glittering lights. The thick meaty scent of charcoal and sausages mingled with piped Christmas carols and the whirrrrrr of someone making Irn-Bru-flavoured candyfloss.

'Can we get on with this, please?'

The sky had gone from bright blue to a dark indigo as we'd tramped all the way from the multistorey round the back of the Traverse Theatre, down Lothian Road, and along Princes Street. Fighting our way through the seething swamp of bloody tourists and bloody-minded locals. Now a sliver of burning red lined the top of the surrounding buildings, doing nothing to compete with the twee gaudy horror of Edinburgh's Christmas Market.

Lines of small wooden stalls were arranged in three 'streets', bedecked with multicoloured lights, bells, stars, oversized candy canes, and bits of pine tree, as if Santa had vomited all over it. Stall after stall after stall, selling tat, tat, and more tat.

Towering over everything, a slow-motion Ferris wheel glittered its way around, overshadowing the gloomy blackened spires of the Scott Monument. And everywhere you looked: fairy lights. Fairy lights and more bloody tourists.

144

This early in the season, it shouldn't have been busy, but it *was*. People jammed in everywhere, circulating at a snail's pace. Taking selfies, blocking the way, drinking bargain-basement Glühwein from a stall manned by a bloke who wouldn't have looked out of place on the Sex Offenders' Register.

Franklin stared at the seething masses, teeth bared. 'This is a *monumental* waste of time.'

'Of course it is. Even if Gordon Smith *was* here, he'll be long gone by now.' I gave her the side-eye. 'Especially after your parking.'

'That wasn't my fault!'

A stall down the end – past one selling socks and gloves, one selling 'HANDMADE ARTISANAL CHEESES!', one selling tea-lights in the shape of Edinburgh tenements, and one entirely dedicated to vile flavours of fudge – had a big circular metal grille suspended over a smouldering bowl of red-hot charcoal. An array of golden sausages drifted around in a lazy circle as the woman in charge poked at them with a set of tongs. The smell alone was enough to set my stomach growling. Been a long time since that bowl of salted porridge and cup of decaf tea.

Franklin sniffed, did a three-sixty. 'So where do we begin this utter waste of time?'

I held up two fingers to the lady with the tongs. 'One brat-wurst, one currywurst. All the trimmings.'

'Reet you are, pet.'

Franklin stared up at the string of lights that looped from pole to pole, running the length of the fake street. 'Think the market's got CCTV? They have to have CCTV, right?'

I took delivery of the sausages, smothered in sauerkraut and crispy onions. Handed over a tenner. Got very little of it back. 'Here.'

'What?' Franklin looked at the proffered currywurst as if it'd recently come out the back end of an Alsatian.

'You'd rather have the bratwurst?'

'We pull the CCTV from when Gordon Smith was spotted and we have a look. We see anything, we alert local plod and get them to launch a proper manhunt.'

Gave the sausage a waggle. 'You wanting this, or not?'

She rolled her eyes, then accepted the thing as if she was doing me a favour. Slathered it in tomato sauce and yellow mustard from the squeezy plastic bottles by the till. First thing she'd done all day that wasn't annoying.

I followed her lead. 'According to Mother, Gordon was spotted at two fifteen, near the helter-skelter.'

'That's how you know this is bollocks.' Franklin took a bite off the end of her sausage, getting a mustard moustache for her troubles as we wandered down the aisle between two rows of stalls. Talking with her mouth full. 'He's on the run from the police, no way he's stopping off here to play on the slides.'

True.

The bratwurst snapped between my teeth, setting free an explosion of meaty smoky goodness, sweet and sharp at the same time. 'Might as well go see if anyone down there recognises him. We're here anyway.'

So we dawdled through the 'Nutella and crepes' section, the tower cakes, the scented candles, munching our way through a very late lunch.

The Scott Monument loomed above us, in all its grim gothic glory.

I stopped. Frowned up at it.

Moved over to the left.

Then forward a couple of paces.

Far as I could tell, this was exactly where Gordon Smith must've been standing when he took that Polaroid – the one with the bearded man in it, arms wide, head thrown back, laughing. You didn't pose like that for a stranger, did you? No, whoever took the photo, they had to be someone you knew. Someone you felt comfortable with.

Franklin seemed to realise I wasn't with her any more, because she turned and stomped back towards me. 'Thought we were supposed to be *working*, not sightseeing.'

'You do realise, now I've bought you a sausage, you have to be less of a grumpy tosser, don't you?'

Franklin wiped the splodges of red and yellow from her cheeks and chin. 'I am *not* a grumpy tosser.'

'You've had a massive retractable bollard up your backside since I met you, and I'm renowned for my charming wit.' Sort of. On a good day. 'So come on, then: why the grump?'

She tossed her napkin into the nearest bin. 'Do you have *any* idea how hard it is to be a woman in the police force? Try being black on top of that. So far this week I've been propositioned four times, groped once, called a "coloured monkey bitch", a "fascist darkie", and told to go back where I came from. Which, for the record, is about a twenty-five-minute bus ride that way.' Pointing in the vague direction of Waverley Station. 'And let's not forget the eighty-two-year-old woman who used the N-word so much she must've got a discount for bulk, and spat on me for daring to suggest she couldn't put rat poison down for her neighbour's dog, even if it *does* crap on her lawn. So you'll excuse me if I'm a bit less than sodding cheerful about it!'

Jesus…

'I'm sorry.' It'd be nice to think Scotland was better than that. That we were more enlightened and accepting and welcoming. That we were just a *wee* bit brighter. Always depressing to be reminded we had our fair share of thick-as-pig-shit racist wankers, same as everywhere else. 'Did you arrest her? The old lady?'

Franklin gave a snort. 'She's eighty-two, what are the courts going to do?'

True.

'Give me her address, then: I'll go round and crap on her lawn myself.'

That almost got me a smile.

We took the steep, leaf-slippery slope down at the end of the fake street.

The sky was dark as ink, our breaths glowing in the light of the yellow-and-red helter-skelter – tall as a four-storey building, ringed around with flickering bulbs. A carousel sat next to it, slowly rotating to the sound of 'Scotland the Brave', played on an oom-cha organ, wooden horses rising and falling, taking squealing children round and round in the flash of two dozen parents' phones.

Franklin's face softened. 'I used to love those when I was little…'

'Don't see why not. Once we've checked with the helter-skelter people.'

She raised a perfectly plucked eyebrow at me. And I swear to God, that was almost a smile playing at the corner of her lips. 'I'm a grown woman.'

'Never too old to play on a wooden horsey, though, are you.'

There was a queue outside the helter-skelter: people in padded jackets snaking their way up a set of wooden steps to where a fat man in a black bomber jacket and Santa hat was checking tickets, before letting them inside to climb to the top.

Franklin pulled out her warrant card and flashed it at the tourists. 'Police, we need to get past. Excuse me. Thank you. Police.' Working her way up the stairs with me limping along behind. 'Sorry, police business. Thank you. Sir? I need you to step out of the way for a moment. Thanks.' Until we were face to face with our bouncer in a jolly hat.

He gave her a scowl. 'No swicking the queue.'

'Police.' She stuck her warrant card under his podgy nose. Then dug into her pocket and pulled out a folded A4 sheet. Stuck that under his nose instead. 'Have you seen this man?'

A frown. Mouth pursed and pulled to one side as he examined the printout.

An impatient tut from the woman next to me. Checking her watch.

But the man in the bomber jacket wasn't to be rushed.

Eventually he shook his head, setting the white furry bobble on the end of his Santa hat wobbling. 'Sorry.'

I peered over Franklin's shoulder. 'You been on shift all afternoon?'

A nod, setting the bobble going again. 'Since one.'

She gave the sheet another go. 'And you're *certain*?'

'Oh aye, I'm good with faces, me. That bloke's no' been on my ride the day.'

Ah well, it'd been worth a try.

We thumped our way down the stairs again and out onto the path.

She put her printout away. 'So what now?'

'You want a go on the carousel before or after we check for CCTV?'

A wistful look slid across Franklin's face as she turned to gaze at the merry-go-round, its flashing lights playing across her skin, sparkling in her eyes. 'I'm a grown woman, and we're supposed to be working, so—'

'Both it is, then.'

A white picket fence separated the thing from the walkway, with a perky middle-aged woman, dressed as an elf, in charge of the gate. 'Hello.' Beaming like hers was the best job in the world. 'Are you here to ride the carousel?'

'Come on, Mr Henderson, we don't have time to—'

'One adult, please.'

'This is ridiculous, I'm not going to—'

'Listen up, Detective Sergeant: life is fleeting, short, and horrible. Take whatever joy you can, *where* you can.'

The elf put a hand on her heart. 'Oh, that's so true...' Then did her perky thing again. 'Now, have you got a token? Because, if you don't, there's a machine up by the—'

'Tenner. No questions asked. And failing that,' pulled out my old warrant card – the one I should've handed back years ago, 'police business.'

'Done.' She opened the gate and waved Franklin through. Throwing in an elaborate bow for good measure as she swept a hand towards the shiny wooden horses. 'This way, my lady, your noble steed awaits!'

First time around the circuit, Franklin looked vaguely embarrassed, sitting there on her filigreed golden horse with red and blue swirls. The second revolution brought a smile with it. And by the third time around she was grinning away as 'Flower of Scotland' omm-cha'd out of the carousel's organ.

And you know what? There were worse ways to have spent a tenner.

Maybe now she'd be less of a pain in my—

Tchaikovsky's 'Danse des Mirlitons' blared out in my pocket, clashing with the merry-go-round soundtrack.

Alice.

Reject, or take the call?

My shoulders drooped.

Shifty was right, I'd have to speak to her sooner or later.

I moved away from the picket fence, shouldering my way through the crowds to a quieter spot. Hit the green button. 'Alice.'

'Ash?' Sounding breathless, as if she was walking fast. *'I can't talk for long. Listen, I'm really, really,* really *sorry.'*

A Japanese family lumbered past, almost swallowed in their huge padded coats, hoods up like gnomes. Then a couple of Eastern-European men in Manchester United replica shirts, their bare arms semi-blue with cold and pebbled with goose bumps.

'Ash? Did you hear, I really am sorry.'

'So you should be.'

'Oh, Ash…'

'It hurts every time you do it, but *today*?'

A couple of the local plod smiled and nodded their way through the crowds, conspicuous in their high-viz waistcoats, stabproof vests and peaked caps.

'I know, I'm an idiot… David tells me you went to see her. Rebecca.'

Or what was left of her.

'Yeah.'

The Christmas Market was a sea of faces. Happy people, bored people, families, couples, none of whose lives had been torn apart one bloodied Polaroid at a time.

'We don't have to talk about it right now, but you know I'm here for you. If you want me to be?'

A sigh dragged my shoulders down. 'Yeah.'

'I wanted you to know that I've … had a word with Steven Kirk. He's…' She cleared her throat. *'I told the investigating officer that he … attacked me on the waste ground. That he had … a knife. That you were only trying to protect me.'*

'You didn't have to lie, it's—'

'It's my fault you did what you did, Ash. If I hadn't … used Rebecca's death like that—'

'Yeah. Well.' Deep breath. 'Thanks for trying to fix it.'

A gaggle of Aberdonians posed for selfies with the helter-skelter in the background, pouting like constipated ducks. Three Brummies laughed their way past, sharing a plastic tray of something cheesy. Those two police officers stopped for photos with a group of Americans.

'And I really am so, so sorry … Henry misses you.'

I puffed out a breath. 'Look, as it's nine years since we started catching bad guys, maybe we *should* go somewhere fancy for dinner. I could…'

Hold on a minute.

'Ash?'

There – in the swarm of faces, gazing along the row of fairground attractions and off towards the line of stalls. A young woman: heart-shaped face, broad forehead, long sharp nose. Wisps of bright-violet hair sticking out from the edge of her hoodie.

Nah. It couldn't be.

'Ash, I've got to go, Bear's got a press—'

I hung up, slipped the phone back in my pocket.

Maybe it was?

Shouldered my way through a group of German tourists, waiting to get on the waltzers. Dodged a gaggle of septuagenarians dressed up as schoolgirls and rattling a collection bucket.

The young woman looked away, but those wisps of hair fluoresced in the harsh festive lighting.

Past a young family trying to get their toddler to stop screeching his head off, a cloud of candyfloss grounded on the tarmac at his feet.

Closing the gap.

It *couldn't* be her. But if it was…

I slipped around a couple arguing over the head of a miserable-looking young girl in a wheelchair.

Reached out. And grabbed the young woman's arm.

She spun to face me.

'Leah? Leah MacNeil?'

And at that her eyes went wide. 'Shit...'

It *was* her.

'Your gran's been worried sick, she needs—'

'GET AWAY FROM ME, YOU PERVERT!' Leah wrenched her arm free, and she was off.

16

'Leah!'

She barged through a knot of tourists, sending plastic cups of Glühwein and paper cartons of bratwurst flying. 'HE'S TRYING TO TOUCH ME! HELP!'

God's sake…

I lumbered after her, but the crowd was turning. Staring at me.

'KEEP AWAY FROM ME YOU RAPIST BASTARD!'

I shoved through the same group but someone shoulder-checked me on the way. Got my walking stick slammed in his guts in return.

He doubled over, staggered out of the way, but Leah was widening the gap.

'HELP! HELP, POLICE!'

Over by the candyfloss stall, that pair of uniformed officers meerkated above the crowds, and both of them were *definitely* looking in my direction.

'LEAH! I NEED TO TALK TO YOU!' Shoving past the idiots blocking my way.

Only good thing about this was: she had to wade through the sea of people too. If it wasn't for the crowd she'd be long gone by now.

'HE TOUCHED MY BREASTS! POLICE!'

A bellowing Edinburgh accent burst across from the uniforms. 'HOY, YOU! COME BACK HERE!'

She'd made it as far as the ramp leading up to where the market's edge ran along the side of the Royal Scottish Academy, its sandstone façade stained in shades of red, yellow, and green in the flashing festive lights.

'LEAH! YOUR MOTHER DIDN'T KILL HERSELF! SHE—'

'HE'S A PERVERT! STOP HIM! HELP ME!'

People had their phones out now, filming as I struggled after her.

A woman's voice, cutting through the press of duffel coats and parkas: 'You should be ashamed of yourself! Leave that poor girl alone!'

'STOP, POLICE!'

No chance.

An overweight bloke in an ill-fitting Santa suit stepped out in front of me, shoulders back, chest out, chin up. 'You going *nowhere*, mate! You're—' My right knee smacked him right in the balls and he collapsed, both hands clutching himself as he retched.

Another stepped up – American, going by the stars-and-stripes puffa jacket and buzzcut. 'We don't take kindly to perverts.'

'I'm not a pervert, you moron.' I shoved him out of the way, hurrying after her. 'LEAH!'

A hand grabbed the collar of my coat. So I threw an elbow back, felt it connect with something solid as a grunt burst out behind me and the hand let go.

'LEAH!'

Through to a gap in the crowds, limping as fast as humanly possible up the ramp, every other step jarring steak knives through my stupid foot.

She was frozen, outside the stall with that 'HANDMADE ARTISANAL CHEESES!' sign over it. Staring at me. Must've heard what I'd said about her mother. It wasn't—

Something solid slammed into the small of my back and that was it – my walking stick went flying as I, and whoever tackled me, crashed to the soggy grey carpeting. Another grunt.

Bloody Americans never could take a telling, could they?

I snapped another elbow back, aiming high this time. The

jarring thud resonated through my arm as it landed. With any luck, breaking the bugger's nose.

The weight reared off me, then someone else piled on. Hands scrabbling for my left wrist. That same Edinburgh accent: 'LIE STILL! YOU'RE UNDER ARREST!'

'Get off me you idiot!'

And Leah just stood there, staring.

'I SAID LIE STILL!'

They twisted my left hand back, putting on the pressure, dragging the arm with it as barbed wire screamed through the wrist joint. Going for the classic hammer lock-and-bar.

'I'm working for the police!' The words shoved out through gritted teeth as they upped the pressure on my arm. It wasn't too late, though: I dug my right hand into my jacket pocket and hauled out that wodge of LIRU business cards.

'JIMMY, GET HIS OTHER HAND!'

'I thing he broge by node...'

I hurled the whole block at Leah. They made it a good ten or twelve feet before breaking apart into their individual pieces, spinning and whirling like heavy cubist snowflakes. About half a dozen fluttered to the ground at her feet.

'STOP STRUGGLING!'

Another pair of hands grabbed my outstretched arm.

'I'M TRYING TO HELP, LEAH! YOU NEED TO TALK TO ME!'

She blinked at me a couple of times. Then bent down and plucked one of the cards from the ground. Clutched it to her chest.

Then turned and ran.

The cold metal bar of a handcuff clicked around my left wrist, someone forcing their weight down on top of my head, shoving my face into the damp carpet.

'YOU'RE NICKED!'

Singing wafted through from somewhere down the corridor – a wobbly baritone, serenading the rest of the cellblock with an X-rated version of 'A Froggy Would a Wooing Go'.

The blue plastic-coated mattress creaked beneath me as I rolled over onto my back and stared up at the words in stencilled blue lettering on the ceiling. 'CRIMESTOPPERS: Anonymous Information About Crime Could Earn A Cash Reward' and an 0800 number. Nothing like taking advantage of a captive audience...

Everything in here smelled of disinfectant. Which was comforting in some ways – at least it meant they'd cleaned it recently – and disturbing in others – what the hell had someone done in here to require drenching *everything* in Dettol?

To be honest, given how crappy a day I was having, it was actually nice to lie down in the peace and quiet. If you didn't count the filthy song. No one demanding anything. Nothing to achieve. No one to disappoint.

And it hadn't *all* been a waste of time, had it? At least now we knew Leah was still alive. She hadn't been tortured to death and buried in Gordon Smith's garden. At least she'd been spared that.

Helen MacNeil, too. Her granddaughter wasn't dead.

Of course, it didn't change what had happened to her daughter, Sophie.

What Gordon Smith had done to her.

All laid out in grisly detail in that bloody Polaroid. A small white rectangle bordering a horrible square picture, the image smeared with dried gore...

Like the ones that used to arrive on Rebecca's birthday. Getting worse and worse every year. Until I couldn't even picture my little girl's face without seeing them.

She would've been twenty-six today. Could've been married with kids by now. A happy family of her own, rather than the fractured mess left behind when the Birthday Boy took her.

Polaroids.

Wonder how many sick bastards out there used them to record their handiwork? How many of them spent every night wanking themselves raw to the image of someone's son or daughter being torn apart?

Helen MacNeil was right: I knew how it felt. And it didn't matter that she hadn't been a doting mother, or even a medi-ocre one – whether or not she spent most of Sophie's life in prison and the rest of it enforcing for the mob. Sophie was her child and Gordon Smith took her, same as the Birthday Boy took Rebecca.

So now, only *one* thing was certain: I was going to find Gordon Smith, and I was going to make him pay. For Sophie. For Rebecca. And for every other child out there who'd suffered at—

The cell door banged open, the sound reverberating off the bare concrete walls.

'Henderson! On your feet.' A Police Custody And Security Officer filled the doorway: an unassuming middle-aged man with thinning hair, grey moustache and soul patch. Glasses. Like a disappointed uncle, in his black polo shirt and black jeans. Only you could tell from the way he held himself he was ex-job. Done his time in the force and couldn't adapt to life on the outside, so came back to work as civilian support. Strange how much ex-cops were like ex-cons. Same problem, different sides of the cell door.

I swung my legs around, placed my stocking soles on the cold terrazzo floor. 'Any chance I can get my walking stick back, if I promise not to go the full Rambo?'

'Arse in gear; the Super wants to see you.'

Take that as a no, then.

A tall thin woman looked me up and down as I shuffled into the small room, in my socks. She was dressed in formal Police Scotland black, wiry arms poking out from the sleeves of her T-shirt, a silver crown on both lapels. Probably best not to stare at the big hairy mole poking out beneath the line of her sharp jaw.

I nodded. 'Superintendent.'

She wasn't the only one in here. Franklin leaned back against a row of grey filing cabinets, and a uniformed PC scowled out from a pair of bloodshot eyes, the skin beneath them darkening in purple arcs. Crusty flakes of dark scarlet clinging to both nostrils.

'Mr Henderson.' The Super folded her arms. 'Would you like

to explain why I shouldn't charge you with a public order offence, resisting arrest, and assaulting a police officer?'

'Because you know who I am, or DS Franklin wouldn't be here.' I tipped my head toward her – Franklin rolled her eyes and pulled a face. 'I was in pursuit of a witness in a murder investigation, when your … let's be nice and call them "halfwit minions" carried out an unprovoked assault and illegal detention.'

The PC with the black eyes soured his mouth. 'Now wait a buggering minute! We were doing our—'

'All right, Constable Marshall. I'm sure Mr Henderson meant "halfwit minions" in a nice way. Didn't you, Mr Henderson?'

Franklin shot me a glare: play nice.

Yeah, she was probably right.

'Of course I did. It was banter, that's all. No offence, etc.'

'Good. Now, I believe you have something to say to Constable Marshall?'

Another glare from Franklin.

'I'm sorry about your nose. I thought you were that idiot American, back for another go.'

The Superintendent raised an eyebrow at the PC. 'And Constable Marshall, I believe you have something to say to Mr Henderson?'

He looked as if he was trying to force a pineapple up his arsehole, the wrong way around, but eventually he managed to shove it in: 'I'm sorry we mistook you for a sex offender, but given the circumstances…'

I puffed out a breath. Nodded. 'She kinda screwed with the lot of us.'

A smile from the Superintendent. 'Well, I'm glad we got that all sorted out.' She turned, plucked a large, bulky, brown paper bag from the room's tiny desk and tossed it in my direction. Followed it up with my walking stick. 'You're free to go.'

The bag was heavy – that would be my shoes, belt, jacket, and everything else they'd confiscated when they banged me up in here. 'One thing, before we go.'

Her shoulders dipped. 'What?'

'I need someone to go through the CCTV from the Christmas Market, from noon till three. We're after an IC-one male, mid-seventies.' I pointed at Franklin. 'She's got a photo. Suspect is responsible for at least a dozen deaths: Gordon Smith.'

The Superintendent grimaced. 'You're not asking for much, are you? That'll take ages.'

'And a lookout request for Leah MacNeil wouldn't hurt either.'

'Think they're going to find anything?' Franklin took the rusty Ford Focus through the traffic-cone chicane, crawling past road-works that stretched for miles and miles and miles... Little orange lights winking in the darkness.

'Leah MacNeil, or Gordon Smith?'

'Smith.'

We passed beneath the motorway matrix sign – its metallic gantry partially covered in scaffolding – 'WARNING: HIGH WINDS ~ NO HIGH-SIDED VEHICLES'.

'Nah. He's got away with it for decades, that takes care and planning. He's not stupid enough to stick around now he knows we're after him. He'll have taken one look at the news and done a runner. Changed his appearance. What he's *not* doing is hanging about the Edinburgh Christmas Market, buying "arti-sanal cheeses" and horrible fudge.'

'Hmph...'

The Forth Bridge loomed into view on the right, like three skeletal Apatosaurus wading their way across the water, brown-red silhouettes in the reflected glow of the city's lights, caught against an angry, burnt-umber sky. And between us and it, the lonely stick figure of the Forth Road Bridge. Hanging there like a pale ghost. Empty, while we drudged our way through a slow-motion contraflow.

Franklin chewed on her lip, wrinkles bunching up between her neatly plucked brows in the beams of advancing headlights. 'Maybe we should get onto Interpol? See if he's gone abroad somewhere?'

'Maybe. It's worth a—'

My phone buzzed in my pocket. Text message.

SABIR4TEHPOOL:

> Still running those Polaroids against the
> misper DBs. No results yet. But I got
> locations for most of them if UR
> interested?
> Solid pain in my Arsenal BTW
> & where's my cost code?!?!?!?!?!
>
> ＼ʕ❍益❍ʔ／

Franklin looked at me. 'Something important?'
'Not really.'
I thumbed out a reply.

> Finger out, Sabir. I've told everyone you're
> an IT whizz kid with superhuman powers.
> Making me look bad here!

SEND.
He'd like that. Be a bit of motivation for him.

The first of the bridge's towers crawled past, its cables stretched out like the sail of a ship.

'You know what worries me?' I stuck my phone on the dusty dashboard. 'Leah MacNeil just *happens* to be in Edinburgh when we are. *Where* we are. That not strike you as a massive coincidence?'

'Not really. When I worked for E Division, mispers were always turning up there. You've run away from home, where are you going to go: Dundee? Aberdeen? Fraserburgh? Oldcastle? No, you head to the capital city, where the streets are paved with opportunities and tourists.'

My phone buzzed again.
SABIR4TEHPOOL:

> Cheeky jock haggis-munching
> wankmonkey!
> U should be made up I'm helping U at all!
> At least it gives U idiots somewhere 2
> look!!!!!

160

Ah, got to love the wit and wisdom of lazy IT people.

> Again: making me look bad here, Sabir. I
> need names for those faces. Poor sods
> deserve that much, don't they?
> We owe it to them and their families.

Might be laying it on a *smidgeon* too thick there, but what the hell.

SEND.

'Besides, the Christmas Market's bound to be a draw, isn't it? All those flashing lights. Half the smackheads, stoners, and junkies in the city will be like moths round a porch light.'

'True.'

And on the traffic crawled.

Just after six, time for the news.

I reached for the radio, clicked it on. 'What did Mother say when you told her Leah MacNeil was alive?'

A woman's voice crackled out of the speaker. '*...four Federal buildings, claiming it was "America's punishment for supporting the rights of gays and coloureds." The White House issued a statement...*'

'Ah, about that.'

'You did tell her, didn't you?'

'*...retribution would be both swift and disproportionate. ~ Reality TV star and tabloid journalist Marian Shires has been found guilty of murdering Kelly Strickland in a drunken brawl outside notorious Glasgow nightclub...*'

Franklin kept her eyes front, mouth closed.

'Why didn't you tell her?'

'Well, I ... didn't see Leah, did I? Not personally.'

'*...sentencing later this month. ~ The hunt continues for the man thought to be responsible for the death of at least twenty people in Oldcastle today, after human remains were spotted as Storm Trevor made landfall to the east of the city...*'

'You think I'm making it *up*?'

'Well, maybe not "making it up", but I didn't—'

'I bought you a sausage, and a go on the carousel!'

'*...police are keen to trace the whereabouts of Gordon Smith, last* *seen in Clachmara four weeks ago. ~ BBC Scotland has announced a major new crime drama to be shot in the picturesque northeast town of Portsoy. Based on the novels of J.C. Williams,* PC Munro and the Poisoner's Cat *will…'*

'I thought you'd like to tell her yourself, without me taking credit?'

Aye, right.

'I was *not* making it up.' Pulled out my phone and picked 'DI MALCOLMSON' from the list. Listened to it ringing. 'Thought you and I had actually managed to—'

'Ash?'

'…Justice Secretary, Mark Stalker, continues to deny any wrongdoing after…'

I clicked the radio off. 'Leah MacNeil's alive. I saw her at the Christmas Market, but a pair of Edinburgh's finest tackled me before I could get to her.'

'Oh, that is *good news! I was certain she'd be one of Gordon Smith's victims. Her gran's going to be delighted.'*

'You need to get a warrant sorted for whoever Leah's mobile phone provider is: get her location tracked.'

We finally reached the other side of the bridge and Franklin wove us through another traffic-cone chicane. The space between vehicles opened up as people accelerated.

Still nothing from Mother.

'Hello, you there?'

Maybe reception wasn't good in Fife?

'Ash, if Leah's alive – and I'm very glad she is – then it's exactly what officers thought in the first place: she's not been murdered or abducted, she's left home. And she's an adult, so she's perfectly within her rights to do that. We don't have any grounds for a warrant.'

'Her mum's been killed by the serial killer living next door, don't you think she deserves to know?'

A long pause was followed by what might have been a groan. *'I do, but she has* rights. *No judge is going to give us a warrant for that. Let's be happy she didn't end up in Gordon Smith's torture base-ment.'* A strangled straining noise came down the line. *'Not that there's much of it left; lost another dozen feet of headland today. And*

162

these idiot journalists are still *sneaking through the safety fence, trying to get photos! It's pitch-black out there, what are they going to see?'*

She was probably right about the warrant, but that didn't make it any less crap.

'You'll tell Helen MacNeil her granddaughter's OK?'

More silence.

We overtook an articulated lorry – 'MRS LOVETT'S FABULOUS FAMILY PIES ~ PACKED FULL OF DELICIOUSNESS!' – following the signs for Perth and Dundee.

'Hello? Are you still—'

'Actually, Ash, given that you've got such a good rapport with her—'

'Oh, for God's sake!'

'I think it might be better coming from you.'

Because we'd got on so *well* this morning, outside Divisional Headquarters.

Looked as if someone up there hated me almost as much as I hated them...

17

Oh for...

Just when things couldn't *possibly* get any worse.

Helen MacNeil was framed, dead centre, in the pool car's headlights, standing in the middle of the road, right in front of the Mobile Incident Unit, hands wrapped around the throat of some idiot in a Barbour jacket, while a soundman tried to prise her off and a cameraman filmed it.

I undid my seatbelt. 'Out, now!'

Franklin and I both scrambled from the car – the howling wind slamming against my chest, ripping the car door from my fingers. She ducked into the back seat for a moment and came out with an extendable baton, clacking it out to full length as we closed the gap.

The MIU's wall boomed as Helen shoved her victim against it. His hands scrabbled at her forearms, eyes bulging, teeth bared in a red-faced rictus that went all the way up to his retreating hairline. Glasses all squint.

Franklin was faster than me. 'THAT'S ENOUGH! LET HIM GO!' Closing in on Helen, baton raised.

No way that was going to end well. Being filmed battering a woman who'd just found out her daughter had been *murdered*? Broadcast to the nation on the evening news?

Please don't let this be going out live...

I limped after Franklin, fast as possible. 'DON'T!'

A thin shaky warble came from the red-faced man. 'Please … help … meeeee.' Head rattling back and forward, glasses shaking loose as Helen throttled him.

Franklin planted her feet. 'LET HIM GO, NOW!' Readying herself, baton up, poised to slash down.

God's sake, did no one do the Officer Safety Training courses any more?

I lurched over there, dropped my walking stick, made a claw of my right hand and dug it into the hard flesh a couple of inches in from Helen's hipbone. Hobbled past, speeding up, dragging her off balance, twisting her away from the victim.

'Aaaargh!' She let go of his throat and slammed into the MIU, head bouncing off the grubby wall.

The man in the Barbour jacket collapsed to his knees, one hand clutching his neck as he coughed and wheezed and spluttered.

Helen aimed a kick at his head, but I grabbed a handful of her collar and pulled. The foot went wide and she tumbled to the potholed tarmac.

'CUT IT OUT!' Getting between the two of them: arms out, blocking the way.

She wiped a hand across her twisted mouth, glaring at the man. 'You want to know how it feels? THAT'S how it feels!'

His back hunched as he dragged in breath after wheezing breath.

'*That's* how it feels to know your wee girls were killed by a man you thought was one of the family.' Helen slumped back against the MIU. 'It feels like that…'

The kitchen of Mother's commandeered house was bare, except for its abandoned cabinets and one crappy plastic chair from the Mobile Incident Unit. An earwax-coloured kettle rumbled to a boil, filling the room with pale damp steam, thickening the condensation that covered the window.

Helen MacNeil sagged in the solitary chair, head down, chin against her chest. 'Got a letter from the council this morning.' She dug into a pocket and pulled out a crumpled envelope.

Hurled it down on the table. 'Gave me *two hours* to get out of my house, oh and by the way, we want sixteen grand to tear it down and ship away whatever's left for "environmentally responsible disposal". Which means chuck it in landfill.' Shook her head. 'No wonder Gordon up and left.'

Soon as his name was out of her mouth, her face soured. 'Then that bunch of fannies come round, with their camera...'

Ah you had to love the media. All the compassion of a starving hyena.

'"How does it feel?"' She pulled her shoulders in, shrinking in her seat. Voice so quiet it was barely audible. 'Why do they have to *ask* things like that?'

'Because they're wankers.'

The mugs weren't exactly dishwasher clean, but they'd do. I made two cups, heavy on the sugar with one. Handed it over.

'Drink this.'

She took a sip, grimaced, looked up at me, then away again. 'Don't take sugar.'

'Tough. Drink it.'

Shockingly enough, Helen MacNeil actually did what she was told. Nursing the mug against her flat stomach. '"How does it feel to know your daughter and granddaughter were tortured to death by a man you trusted?" How the fuck do they think it feels?'

To be honest, the strangling thing was a pretty good analogy.

I smiled at her. 'Well, I've got good news for you on that one: Gordon Smith didn't kill Leah. She's alive. I saw her today in Edinburgh.'

Helen *stared* at me. Mouth hanging open. 'Leah...?'

'Tried speaking to her, but a pair of local plod decided they'd get in the way. But she's alive.'

'Oh, thank God.' Helen's face slackened, a deep breath whoomping out of her. 'She's *alive*.'

'Don't know if she'll get in touch, or not, but...' A shrug. 'Maybe.'

'She's alive...' Helen's shoulders trembled, she put a hand over her eyes. And sat there, weeping in almost total silence.

Rocking in her cheap plastic seat, in an abandoned kitchen, at the end of the world.

A deep, dark rumble sounded, setting the bare lightbulb swinging on the end of its cobweb-tinselled cord.

I stood there and drank my tea.

Strange to think I could've happily strangled *her* this morning. Or caved her head in. Now? Hard not to feel sorry for Helen. Her granddaughter might have escaped Gordon Smith, but her daughter hadn't. And you had to admit—

A barrage erupted at the front of the house – someone pounding on the front door. Followed by a clatter of feet on bare floorboards.

I stuck my head out of the kitchen and there was Franklin, with Mother right behind her – blocking most of the corridor.

Cold air whipped in through the open front door, a man trembling on the threshold, eyes wide, shock scrawled across his features. 'You… You've got to… There's been an accident! The cliff gave way…'

Grabbed my coat from the kitchen worktop, my walking stick from where I'd hooked it on a cupboard handle, and limped out after them.

It wasn't raining, exactly, instead a thin drizzle slapped into us, driven by storm-force winds. Stealing all heat from my exposed hands and face.

Mother grabbed the man by the lapels. 'Where?'

A trembling hand came up to point through the temporary fencing. Into the darkness.

'Damn it.' She let him go. 'Torches! I need torches!'

Franklin sprinted for the pool car, plipping the locks and rummaging through the boot as DC Watt emerged from the house, hauling on a waxed jacket, a teeny LED torch clutched between his teeth.

She returned from the boot with a pair of big Maglites, each one a good foot long. Held one out to me as she hurried past.

I clicked it on and followed her.

The fence ran straight across the road, each one of the junctions chained and padlocked, until we got between Helen

MacNeil's house and her nearest surviving neighbour's place. Someone had snipped the chain clean through, leaving it dangling against the metal upright.

'Idiot…' Franklin yanked it free. 'OVER HERE!' Then slipped through the unchained gap, following her torch beam through a drooping swathe of green-and-yellow grass. Slowing to a walk now.

'You do realise this is a *very* stupid thing to be doing?' I hobbled along beside her, running my light along the edge of the garden. A waist-high brick wall separated Helen's house from Gordon Smith's. Now that the council had taken the old temporary fencing away, that small wall was the only thing between us and the storm.

We stopped when we got to it, wind tearing at our clothes, pushing and shoving like a schoolroom bully.

'WHAT DO YOU THINK?' Having to raise her voice now, over the angry boom of waves crashing against the headland.

I slid my torch across Gordon Smith's back garden, to the point where the autumn-bleached grass ended in a ragged black line. 'I THINK WE SHOULD TURN ROUND, RIGHT NOW, AND GET THE HELL OUT OF HERE.' Took a deep breath, then clambered over the wall.

'YEAH, THAT'S WHAT I THINK TOO.'

'ANYONE STUPID ENOUGH TO COME OUT IN *THIS* DESERVES ALL THEY GET.' I inched my way closer to the edge, bending my knees, hunkering down, turning sideways-on to make less of a target for the wind.

There wasn't much of Gordon Smith's house left: eighteen, maybe nineteen feet? Which meant the kill room had already gone, taking any forensic evidence with it. The living room, with its avalanche of ancient furniture, had gone too. And nearly all of the roof – what was left, clinging to the joists still fixed to its gable end. But nothing would…

Hold on, what was that?

'ASH?'

'SHUT UP A MINUTE!' Head on one side. 'CAN YOU HEAR THAT?'

It was hard to make anything out, over the crashing waves and bellowing wind, but there was definitely *something* there.

I inched closer. Then closer still.

Franklin grabbed my hand and stepped behind me. Acting as an anchor. 'JUST IN CASE!'

Another torch snaked across the ravaged grass – till its tiny white spotlight found us. Then Mother's voice: 'WHAT THE HELL ARE YOU IDIOTS PLAYING AT? GET BACK HERE THIS INSTANT!'

OK, only a couple of yards till the garden came to a sudden and deadly stop.

Closer...

Closer...

'I'M NOT KIDDING: YOU GET BACK HERE RIGHT NOW!'

One yard. What was that, three feet?

Three feet to the roaring maw of the North Sea.

Oh God...

I dropped to my knees. 'GRAB MY FOOT!'

Franklin let go of my hand and wrapped her fingers around my left ankle. 'THIS IS STUPID!'

'I KNOW!' Edging closer to the edge.

Two feet.

One foot.

And then there was nothing between me and Norway but a cold violent death.

'ANYTHING?'

'HOLD ON!' I poked my torch over the edge, running along the tattered cliff edge beneath me. Dark soil, crumbling, making little avalanches that were torn away by the wind. A couple of pipes, poking out into nothingness. Some wires...

Oh. *Shit*.

The harsh white circle of light slid up the body of a young man, hanging there, still as the dead, a high-pitched moan rattling out of his throat. A young man in a soil-smeared, ill-fitting suit, with a face full of acne and a monobrow. Mouth open and twitching, showing off all those uneven teeth. A big digital camera hanging around his neck. The idiot Mother had shouted at. The one she'd told not to go anywhere near the headland again.

Well, that had worked, hadn't it?

He had both arms up above his head, hands clenched tight around a loop of flat fabric. Dark. Like, maybe the handle of a duffel bag, or a rucksack strap? It disappeared into the cliff. Something buried in Gordon Smith's back garden.

I ran the torch downwards. Nothing beneath him to stand on, or break his fall, it was straight down to the angry sea. Grooves in the crumbling muddy cliff face where his feet had scrabbled at it.

Dark waves smashed themselves against the headland, thirty or forty feet below, sending up massive gouts of spray. Each blow like a sledgehammer, *BOOOOOM*ing out, and hissing in. Like the ragged breath of some huge malevolent beast.

OK, so as long as whatever it was he'd caught hold of stayed where it was, and he didn't let go, we could do this. 'WE'RE GOING TO GET YOU OUT OF THERE!'

He stared back at me and the moan got louder.

Back, over my shoulder: 'WE NEED A ROPE!'

Franklin tightened her grip on my ankle, turned. 'WE NEED A ROPE!'

Mother's voice cut through the screaming wind. 'DON'T STAND THERE LIKE A LEMON, JOHN, GET SOME ROPE!'

I wriggled over a couple of feet to the right, until I was directly above the hanging man. 'YOU'RE A BLOODY IDIOT, YOU KNOW THAT, DON'T YOU?'

Tears sparked in the torchlight. His mouth moved, but whatever he'd said it wasn't loud enough to make out over the storm.

'WHAT?'

'I DON'T... I DON'T WANT ... TO DIE! PLEASE DON'T LET ME DIE!'

What the bloody hell did he think I was trying to do, here?

'IT'S OK, WE...'

Another rumble, and off to the left a piece of cliff tumbled into the crashing waves. Like an enormous hand had scooped a chunk of it away, leaving an overhang behind. Moments later the rumbling got louder as the overhang crumbled, tearing a slab of Gordon Smith's back garden with it.

The young man *screamed*.

And the falling earth filled the air with that mouldy-brown-bread scent of broken soil.

I twisted my head around to Franklin. 'WHERE'S THAT BLOODY ROPE?'

'I DON'T KNOW!' Over her shoulder again. 'MOTHER! WE NEED THAT ROPE, NOW!'

'GET OUT OF THERE!'

I reached down with my right hand. Fingers straining. About a foot and a half too short. 'CAN YOU PULL YOURSELF UP?'

He stared at me, then bit his bottom lip, tears streaking the mud on his face. Shoulders bunching as he hauled on the strap, feet scrambling at the dirt. Still not close enough to grab. 'I *CAN'T!*' Then sagged back again, sobbing.

My torch beam ripped across the grass till Franklin was caught in the light. 'FOR GOD'S SAKE: WHAT'S KEEPING THEM?'

A large shape loomed out of the darkness behind her: Mother. She crouched down by Franklin's feet and tossed something forwards.

It landed with a clanking slither, level with my chest. A length of chain – the one that was meant to be holding those two fencing panels together, with the padlock still firmly shut on the last two links.

Better than nothing.

The padlock fitted into my palm, chain hanging down between my fingers as I clenched it in my fist, then flipped the end over the cliff edge. 'GRAB HOLD!'

It dangled about three inches above his hands.

He stared back at me, arms trembling. 'I CAN'T!'

A wave smashed into the cliff beneath him, tearing loose a chunk of dirt and rocks.

'GRAB THE BLOODY THING, YOU MORON!'

His left hand twitched, then let go of the strap, fingers stretching up for the chain's end.

'COME ON, YOU CAN DO IT!'

Feet digging into the mud, trembling with the effort, straining, reaching…

Another wave battered in, sending up a wall of spray, hiding his flailing legs for a moment.

Then the ground beneath my chest slumped, dropping a good six inches. 'Shit!'

'ASH!' Franklin's hands tightened around my ankle as a semicircle the size of a couch cracked all around me.

His eyes went even wider. Screaming. The thing he was holding onto slid towards him, pulling away from the crumbling cliff face, slipping free.

It was a big holdall, the red fabric stained almost black by its time in the earth.

I dropped the chain and lunged, fingers curling around the buckle where the strap fixed to the bag. Muscles straining across my shoulders. Joints yanked taut by the sudden weight. Knuckles full of burning rubble. Teeth gritted. But holding on…

'ASH, GET OUT OF THERE!'

'PULL ME BACK! PULL ME BACK, NOW!' Staring down at him. 'DON'T YOU BLOODY DARE LET GO! WE'RE GOING TO—'

The ground to either side gave way, clattering down, battering into his face and chest, muffling his screams as the weight on the other end of the strap disappeared. Arms pinwheeling as he fell.

'NO!'

I careened forwards – nothing supporting my chest any more, the torch tumbling end-over-end until the next wave smashed into the cliff and swallowed it.

'AAAAAAAAAAAAAAAAAAAAAAAARGH!'

18

A second set of hands wrapped around my other ankle, stopping me from falling any further forward, then a third pair snatched at my trouser leg. All of them hauling me backwards, onto semi-solid ground again.

Wet grass against my grateful cheeks and forehead.

Oh *Christ*, that had been close.

The hands let go and I rolled over. Let the cool drizzle slam down on me. Breath rattling in my chest. *Alive.*

Then the hands returned, pulling me to my feet.

DC Watt thrust my walking stick into my hand. 'NOW CAN WE GET OUT OF HERE?'

'GOD, YES!' I hobbled after him, Franklin, and Mother, wind jostling at my back. Clambered over the low wall, and into Helen MacNeil's garden again.

Soon as we'd put twenty feet between ourselves and the wall, Mother swung her arm back and battered me one across the chest. 'WHAT THE BUGGERING HELL WERE YOU THINKING? YOU COULD'VE DIED! YOU NEARLY GOT US *ALL* KILLED!' She hit me again. 'YOU IDIOT!'

'I COULDN'T SAVE HIM! I TRIED, BUT I COULDN'T...'

'AND WHERE DID YOU GET THAT?' Jabbing a finger at the filthy red holdall, still clutched in my right hand.

It was heavier than it looked; there was definitely something inside. And given where the thing had been buried, didn't exactly take a genius to guess what that was…

'Are you OK?' Franklin leaned back against the stainless-steel work surface next to me, arms wrapped around herself, keeping her voice low. 'Because you look like death.' The words came out in a small plume of white fog.

The throat-catching smell of bleach and punctured bowels filled the ancient mortuary, like thick brown soup. At one point, the wall tiles had probably been white, but they'd turned a grubby ivory, the colour of a smoker's teeth. Black tiles on the floor – chipped and cracked, their grout stained grey even after generations-worth of disinfectant. A wall of refrigerated drawers, the names of their occupants printed in dry-erase marker on white plastic rectangles. Three cutting tables with drainage channels, their metal surfaces scarred and scratched. The middle one bearing an ugly bundle wrapped in black-plastic bin bags secured with duct tape.

No one else in here but us.

No one *living*, anyway.

I cleared my throat. 'Thank you. You know, for not letting me fall.'

'Meh…' She shrugged. 'You bought me a sausage and a go on the carousel, remember?' Then shivered. 'Absolutely soaked to the bone, here. These idiots going to be much longer?'

According to the mortuary clock, it was nine o'clock already.

So much for a conciliatory crime-fighting-anniversary dinner with Alice.

'Teabag doesn't like working overtime. Mother will have to drag him down here like a sulky child.'

Above us, the sounds of Castle Hill Infirmary oozed through the ceiling. The hum and buzz of heating and electricity, the bang and clank of trolleys and floor polishers. Life.

Down here, the only sounds were us and the faint whirring hiss coming from that bank of refrigerated drawers.

Franklin cleared her throat. 'You didn't answer the question. *Are* you OK? I mean, I feel bad enough and I didn't even see him, never mind watch him fall.'

'I'm fine.'

'I only heard the screaming, but to actually *be* there, holding the other end of—'

'All right! All right, I get it.' Maybe sounding a bit more defensive there than I'd hoped, going by Franklin's raised eyebrows. 'Look, he was an arsehole, OK? What kind of moron ignores a direct telling, all the warning notices, cuts through the chain, and sods about on the crumbling headland in the middle of a storm? Yes, he died – tragedy, thoughts and prayers etc. – but he nearly got you, me, Mother, and Watt killed too. And while Watt's death wouldn't exactly be a great loss to humanity, the rest of us deserve better.'

She pulled her head back, making a tiny double chin. 'You really have it in for John, don't you? What did he do?'

'He's a dick.'

A shrug. 'True. But if you need to talk to someone about what happened, don't be a macho idiot about it. It doesn't impress anyone.' Franklin had another shiver. 'Why do mortuaries have to be so *cold*?'

'You can knock off, if you like? Doesn't need both of us here for chain of evidence.'

She rolled her eyes. 'You're not a police officer any more, remember?'

'True.' I straightened up. 'In that case, *you* stay here, and I'll see if I can break into Teabag's office and get a brew on.'

Franklin munched her way through a third Jammie Dodger, getting crumbs down the front of her overcoat. 'So I punched him.'

'Good. Sounds like the prick deserved it.' The tea was almost gone, only a couple of biscuits left in the packet.

'Only it turns out breaking a superintendent's nose *isn't* a good career move.' She shrugged. 'It's not *that* bad, being in the Misfit Mob. OK, so we don't get the best of cases, and I do miss Edinburgh...' She chewed on the inside of her cheek. 'Don't get me wrong, Oldcastle's all right—'

'Oldcastle's a shithole.' I drained the last of my tea. Stood there, head turned... 'Stick those biscuits in your pocket!'

'What?' Looking at me as if I'd proposed getting naked and romping on one of the dissecting tables.

I snatched up the Jammie Dodgers and stuffed the packet in her overcoat pocket. Took the mug from her hand and limped across the cutting room.

'Hey, I was drinking that!'

Teabag's office was a gloryhole of paperwork and things in specimen jars. Barely enough room for the roll-top desk and green-leather swivel chair squeezed in amongst the shelves and filing cabinets. Both mugs went back in his in-tray. And I was out again, just in time to shut the door behind me, before the double ones at the far end of the mortuary banged open and in marched Mother and Teabag.

It looked as if he was on his way to some sort of Jeremy Clarkson convention, in blue jeans, an untucked white shirt, and a tweed jacket. His floppy fringe was a touch greyer than it used to be, the jaw not quite as square – a line of fat softening it and deepening the dimple in his chin. Thin wire-rimmed glasses glinting in the mortuary's strip lights as he puffed out a long breath. 'Before we begin, I want everyone to understand that this is *not* a post mortem. This is an initial, and very *brief*, impression of the forensic evidence. Assuming there is any.'

He stopped in the middle of the room and frowned down at the bin-bag package. 'I assume this is it?'

Mother pulled on a pained smile, then nodded. 'Yes, Professor Twining.'

'Very well. ALFRED!'

A pause.

'AAAAAAAAAALFRRRRRRRRRRRRRED!' Teabag marched across the room to his office, took his keys out, then made puzzled expressions when the door swung open without him unlocking it. 'That's odd, could've *sworn*… Never mind.' Looked back over his shoulder. 'Wheels up, ten minutes. Assuming Alfred actually shows.' Then disappeared inside.

Mother slouched over to join us at the work surface. 'That man is – and I hope you'll excuse my language, Rosalind – a complete and utter turdjacket.' She hoicked up the sleeves of her Police Scotland fleece, exposing those tattooed forearms. Pulled a face. 'Apparently, our beloved Chief Superintendent isn't too impressed that we let a journalist die on our watch.'

What?

I stared at her.

'I know, I know: I was there, remember? But if you see him coming, take my advice and run. Turns out the media are less interested in your heroics trying to *save* Nick James, than they are in our not adequately ensuring that he couldn't cut through a padlocked chain on a clearly marked safety fence, in the pitch-sodding-dark, and sneak through to get himself killed.' She let her head fall back and grimaced at the greying ceiling tiles. 'Some days, I *hate* my job.'

Franklin reached into a pocket and came out with a Jammie Dodger. 'Fancy a biscuit? We definitely didn't steal them from Professor Twining's office.'

That got her a smile.

The biscuit disappeared in two bites, to be followed by a crumb-spilling sigh. 'Don't suppose your IT guru has come up with anything, has he, Ash?'

'Says he's got locations for most of the photographs, but no IDs yet.'

The smile faded away. 'The universe hates me, doesn't it?'

A voice, from over by the main doors: 'Evenin' all.' A middle-aged man scuffed into the mortuary, headphones around his neck, hair scraped back in a thinning ponytail that exposed about sixty percent of his shiny head, a greying beard trimmed to within an inch of its death. All done up in pale-blue hospital scrubs, backpack slung over one shoulder. 'DI Henderson! As I live and breathe.'

'Alf.'

He nodded his head towards the closed office door. 'The Prof here yet, or do I have time to nip out for a fag?'

And right on cue: Teabag emerged, having changed into a rustling white Tyvek oversuit, white wellies, and a thick brown rubber apron. 'Alfred, get scrubbed up: we're doing a quick surface examination, then I've got a dinner party to get back to.'

'Right you are, Prof.'

'The rest of you better put on protective gear. Let's not have a repeat of the Robert Bradbury fiasco.'

We all struggled into disposable SOC suits, finishing off with safety goggles, face masks, blue plastic booties, and purple nitrile gloves. Then joined Alf and Teabag at the central table. All gathered around that bin-bag package like ghosts at the feast.

Alf switched on a big digital camera and took a couple of test shots. 'All working.'

'Then I'll begin.' Teabag's scalpel sizzled through the black plastic, opening it up like dark flower petals, exposing the red holdall within as Alf snapped away. 'Has this been tested for fingerprints, fibres, or DNA?'

Mother shook her head. 'You always moan when you don't get first go with remains.'

'I do *not* moan. I apply constructive criticism when people don't prioritise the correct chain of forensic hierarchies.' He took hold of the zip and pulled. Nothing. Tugged. Still nothing. So he sliced along the stitching next to it instead. Pulled the sides apart.

A dark, leathery smell joined the mortuary's foul bouquet, tainted with a compost earthiness.

Whatever was in there, it'd been dead a long, long time.

'Hmm...' Teabag peered into the slit. 'Better move this to the end of the table. We're going to need some room.'

Soon as it was relocated, he reached in and came out with a dirty length of what looked like grey-brown tubing, about an inch and a half wide, maybe fourteen inches long, both ends ragged and chipped. He laid it down on the stainless-steel surface with an audible click, then went back in for another piece of piping with ragged ends – this one thinner and curved – and laid it out near the end of the table, on the opposite side to the first bit.

The next two things were definitely ribs. They got clicked down in the proper anatomical place. Then a pelvis. A shoulder blade. Then what looked like the head of a femur.

'You can see here, that the remains have been dismembered.'

Turning the smooth head of bone over to expose the ragged end. 'Probably an axe, going by the fractures and splintering. A saw would leave much cleaner cuts in the bone.'

A radius and ulna were next, both parts of the arm bone cut short and splintered.

'Your victim was most likely dead at the time, because, let's face it, dismembering someone with an axe would be *fairly* difficult if they were still alive. And even if you tried, they wouldn't be for long.' Teabag dipped into the bag again and again, humming away to himself as he reassembled a human skeleton on the cutting table in front of us. 'I know it's not to everyone's taste, but I rather enjoy this part. I completely get why people like a good jigsaw puzzle.'

Finally he stepped back, hands on his hips. 'Well, I can safely say your victim is dead.'

Alf was the only one who laughed at that. But it didn't sound convincing.

'As you can see, we're missing a number of phalanges, mostly distal and middle,' pointing a purple finger at the body's hands and feet. 'Given the body was most likely dismembered to make it fit in the holdall, you wouldn't need to take the fingers off, would you? So, and this is nothing more than an educated guess, but I think they could've been removed before death. Which suggests to me that your victim was murdered.'

If Teabag thought he was getting a round of applause for that, he was in for a disappointment. Not when we had the 'after' set of Polaroids.

'These additional kerf marks on both sets of forearms, thighs, and shins – you see how they're nowhere near the dismemberment points? And the ones on the skull?' Pointing at a trio of dark lines carved into the bone above the right eye socket. 'That makes me suspect they *might* be ante-mortem too. And then there's the broken-slash-missing teeth…'

He pinged off his gloves, into an open bin marked 'Medical Waste Only'. Removed his face mask. 'Don't quote me on this, but I think there's a good chance your victim was tortured quite extensively before they died. Male, five-nine, I can't speculate

179

on ethnicity before we've done DNA testing. And for that, and everything else, you'll have to wait till tomorrow.' He took off his thick rubber apron and draped it over one of the empty cutting tables. 'We start at nine o'clock sharp – you should arrange for a forensic anthropologist to be in attendance. In the meantime, thank you for not asking any stupid questions, and I'm going back to my boeuf bourguignon and friends.'

With that, Teabag marched off into his office, thunking the door shut behind him.

Mother pulled a face. 'I don't know about anyone else, but I am now officially *gagging* for a glass of wine. Rosalind, Ash?'

I pushed away from the dissecting table and its collection of bones. 'Can't: pills. Besides, I've got a prior appointment...'

I unlocked the front door and hobbled into the flat. Eyes full of grit. My back aching like it'd been holding the world up for two years too long. All that weight pressing down on my shoulders – still aching from trying to haul Nick James up from the abyss...

Come on, Ash, dead was dead. At least you *tried*.

And failed.

The pair of heavy carrier bags swung in my other hand as I limped down the hall, letting loose the spicy-cumin scent of curry.

'Hello? You still up?'

No reply.

Was only quarter to ten. Maybe she'd gone out?

'Alice?'

She was in the living room, slumped at the dining table, with a pile of paperwork, her laptop, and two half-bottles of something the wee off-licence on Shand Street passed off as 'SINGLE MALT SCOTCH WHISKEY'. One of them was empty, the other heading that way.

I picked it up and screwed the top back on. 'You have to stop drinking this gut-rot. They can't even spell "whisky" properly – stuff's probably fifty-fifty antifreeze and horse piss.'

She raised her head from the table. A big oval red patch

180

where the skin had been pressing into the glass surface. A string of drool still connecting her to it. She blinked puffy bloodshot eyes. Wiped the drool away with the back of her hand. 'Whhtmsit?'

'Have you eaten anything, or just drunk yourself into a stupor?' Thunking the carryout down on the table. 'Punjabi Castle. Got you a chicken dhansak, coconut rice, saag paneer, onion bhajee, and a heap of poppadoms.' Voice getting harder and sharper. 'You want to eat it first, or should I flush the whole lot down the toilet now and save you the effort of vomiting it up?'

'I... Drnn't shhhowwtme.'

'I'm not shouting at you. You were the one who said we should do something to mark nine years, remember? This morning? Back when you were *sober*.'

Alice placed the palms of her hands against the glass top, arms stiff – keeping her upright. Blinking and shaking her head, as if she was trying to get it to work again. 'Had to ... profile.'

'YOU CAN'T KEEP DOING THIS!' Picking up the lighter of the two bags and hurling it down in front of her. The muffled crash of a dozen poppadoms shattering. 'You're drinking your-self – to – death.'

Tears sparkled at the corners of her eyes, nose going dark pink. 'Henry always said—'

'Henry was an idiot! The only reason he didn't die of liver failure is he killed himself first. Is *that* what you want?'

'Ash, why are you being like—'

'I NEARLY DIED TONIGHT!'

A muffled *BOOM, BOOM, BOOM*, sounded through the floor beneath us as the tosser downstairs got in on the act.

I raised my left foot and battered it down three times, good and hard. 'MIND YOUR OWN BLOODY BUSINESS, OR I'LL COME DOWN THERE AND MIND IT FOR YOU!' Breathing hard. Heat rushing through my cheeks and brain. Pulsing at the back of my eyes. 'I nearly died.' Turning away. 'I won't always be here to take care of you.'

Her reflection in the floor-to-ceiling windows wiped away

its tears and wobbled to its feet. Picked its way around the table, leaning on the glass for support. Then she was behind me. Wrapping her arms around me, her face buried between my shoulders. Voice catching, popping with snot and pain. 'He ... he took ... another one, Ash. Gòrach ... abducted ... another little boy. Because ... because I ... because I can't *catch* him!'

And I let a journalist die.

Yeah, today had turned out to be some day.

I turned around and hugged her back.

Because, sometimes, what else could you do?

— things can always get worse —

19

'...increased tensions in the Middle East, after the downing of that British Airways flight...'

Porridge, with salt, and a cup of decaf tea. Living. The. Sodding. High. Life.

Alice's half bottle of gut-rot still sat at the end of the table, its badly spelled label reflecting in the glass. The sound of retching echoing out through the closed bathroom door as she got rid of the rest of it.

Darkness pressed against the flat's windows, the city's lights twinkling in the early morning gloom.

A teeny whinge, and there was Henry, looking up at me with his shiny black eyes. Tail wagging. Thick pink tongue hanging out the corner of his mouth.

Oh to be a wee Scottie dog with nothing to worry about but who was going to feed him, and take him out to pee on things. No dead journalists on his conscience. No murdered children.

'...tributes paid to the crew of the Ocean-Gold Harvester, lost in Storm Trevor on Friday when it was buried in a landslip...'

He closed his eyes and widened his grin as I ruffled the hair between his ears.

'Give us a minute to finish this, and we'll go for a wee walk. It's—'

A harsh trilling came from the corridor. Was that the *bell*?

'Right, you wee horror, no stealing Daddy's porridge. Sit. Staaaaayyyyy…'

He looked at my finger as if it was the most exciting thing in the world and wagged his tail even harder.

Thick as custard.

Down the corridor. I peered through the spyhole set into the front door, because in Oldcastle you never knew.

Franklin's face stared back at me, all distorted and bulbous in the fisheye lens. I let her in.

She frowned me up and down. 'Are you not ready yet?' She'd bundled up in a thick puffa jacket, with a scarlet scarf wrapped around her throat. Tartan bunnet on her head.

'Ready for what?' Limping back to the living room and my rapidly cooling porridge.

'Morning Prayers. Mother wants everyone there, and you can't drive, remember? Pain in the foot?' A what-can-you-do shrug, playing it nonchalant. 'So … you OK today? You know, after last night and—'

'I'm fine.' Well, other than having a go at Alice when I got home, and the horrible dream, and the ache digging its teeth into my shoulders. Other than that? Just peachy.

'God save us from macho…' She froze as she caught sight of Henry. Then squatted down in front of the wee lad and ruffled his ears. 'You're a sweetie, aren't you? Yes you are.' Pulling on a pout. 'Yes you are!'

Henry lapped it up.

'…five-year-old, missing since yesterday evening. Colin Broadbent is in Oldcastle for us. Colin, what are the police saying?'

'Thanks, Siobhan. Toby Macmillan disappeared from his home in the city's Kingsmeath area at seven—'

I killed the TV and polished off my porridge. Dumped my bowl in the sink. 'Give us two minutes and we can head.'

'Always wanted a dog, but Mark's allergic.' Cupping our lad's hairy wee face in her hands. 'Oooh, you're lovely…' Then up to me: 'What's his name?'

'Henry. And he's had breakfast, so don't believe a word if he says he's wasting away.'

The bathroom door thunked open and Alice slouched out, dressed in mismatched tartan jammies, the top buttoned up all wrong, showing off a slice of stomach the colour of old yoghurt. Yawning and scratching, head looking like something horrible had happened to one of the hairier Muppets.

Franklin stared at her, cheeks darkening as she abandoned Henry and stood. Brushed her hands down the front of her jacket. 'Sorry, I didn't know you had … company.'

'Franklin, this is Dr McDonald: Lateral Investigative and Review Unit. Alice, this is DS Franklin: Misfit Mob.'

'Urgh…' Alice scuffed past and disappeared into the kitchen.

Franklin pointed down the hall. 'I can wait in the car?'

'I'll only be a minute. Have a seat.'

When I got back from brushing my teeth, Franklin was still standing where I'd left her. Shifting from foot to foot as Alice slouched over a large steaming mug of hot chocolate – going by the smell.

Neither of them seemed to realise I was there.

The bags under Alice's eyes had darkened, a puffiness to both them and her cheeks, the beginnings of creases forming on either side of her chin. Looking more mid-forties than early-thirties. She rubbed a hand across her shiny forehead. 'Sorry, I don't mean to be rude, I might be a *teensy* bit hungover.'

Franklin nodded. Looking even more stiff and uncomfortable. 'Not a problem.'

'When I started out, I had a mentor who claimed alcohol was the key to "forging non-linear connections in behavioural evidence analysis by dampening down areas of modal control in the brain, allowing the forensic psychologist to experience a heightened state of detached-consciousness processing" the only problem being that you end up drunk thirty percent of the day, operating normally for twenty percent, and hungover the rest of the time.' All this, whoomped out in a non-stop rattle. 'Sorry, I'm babbling, I babble when I'm nervous, and how long does it have to take for paracetamol and ibuprofen to kick in?' Almost sobbing at the end there.

'Well … maybe your mentor…?'

Alice folded forwards, forehead on the table. 'Henry.'

'Henry?' Franklin pulled her chin in and stared at the hairy black face gazing up at her with his tail wagging. '*He's* your mentor?' Backing off a pace from the clearly crazy lady.

'Dr Henry Forrester, he's dead now. We named our dog after him.'

'OK. So, basically, your mentor, Henry, who isn't the dog, told you to get drunk a lot and that'll help you think like serial killers?'

Alice raised a hand, and gave her a thumbs-up.

'No offence, but he sounds like an idiot.'

I cleared my throat and Franklin turned. Blushed again.

'Mr Henderson. Are you ready?'

'When you are.' Pulling on my coat. 'Alice, you looking after Henry today, or are you too hungover?'

'I'm *dying*…'

'Fair enough. I'm taking some of your business cards, OK? Chucked the last of mine at Leah MacNeil yesterday.' I dug a dozen or so out of her satchel, stuck them in my pocket, then grabbed the wee man's lead from the shelving unit. 'Franklin, you don't mind if he joins us today?'

And her face lit up, like it had on the carousel. Then she hauled on a blanket of studied nonchalance. 'Suppose so. Why not?'

'Good.' Alice got a kiss on the top of her head. 'Shower. You smell like a dead person.' Henry came running soon as I jangled his lead. 'Come on, teeny monster, we're off to catch some bad guys.'

Hopefully.

The darkened countryside streaked past the pool car's windows, twinkling lights of distant farmhouses drifting by in slower motion.

Hands wrapped around the wheel, Franklin glanced across the car at me. Probably thought she was being subtle.

'What?'

'Nothing.'

Henry poked his head through from the back seat, panting away, looking up at me then at Franklin, as if trying to figure out if either of us had any sausages.

Franklin did it again. 'Only, you and Dr McDonald ... they're OK with you two working together? I mean, I know LIRU isn't *strictly* speaking Police Scotland, and you're both civilians, but still.'

'Why wouldn't they be OK with us working together?'

'You know, if you're,' she pulled her mouth out and down, jerking her chin up a couple of times, 'at it?'

Eh?

'At what?'

'It. You know, sex. In a relationship. Shagging.'

I stared back across the car. 'Are you *insane*?'

'You're not—'

'She's young enough to be my daughter!'

'Yes, but you middle-aged men like—'

'I am *not* sleeping with Alice! We're ... I don't know, family?'

Franklin stuck her eyes on the road again. 'None of my business anyway.'

'Christ knows what would happen if I wasn't there to look after— Oh, for God's sake.' My phone blared out 'I Am the Walrus'. Which could only mean one person. I pulled it free and pressed the button. 'Sabir? Not like you to surface before noon.'

'Not gone to bed yet, been too busy shagging yer ma.'

'She's still dead, Sabir.'

'I'm not that fussy, these days. You seen yer email yet? Sent yez a list of them locations in the photos. And youse should be wershipping the ground I walk on for that. You got any idea how hard it is to write an algorithm that does a reverse image lookup, with wildcarding, for backgrounds *across all of Google Maps and every image posted to Facebook in the last six years? See if I wasn't a total IT god, you wouldn't have a—'*

'Are you planning on getting to the point at all, here?'

'How come no bugger appreciates a proper banging genius in their lifetime? Anyway, I got youse all them locations and...?'

'If you're waiting for a thank you, you're going to be there a while.'

'God, you've gorra right cob on, this morning, haven't ya? The "and", at the end there, refers to the fact that I know who one of yer victims is.'

My phone dinged and buzzed in my hand. Incoming text message.

Sᴀʙɪʀ4TᴇʜPᴏᴏʟ:

> Keith Whatley AKA: Simpson Kinkaid (stage
> name)
> Was in B&TB panto in Edinburgh
> Went missing 32 years ago

The message came with a professional headshot – it was the laughing man from Princes Street Gardens, the one in front of the Scott Monument. Same beard, but doing a smoulder for the camera this time.

Another ding-buzz. This time it was a bunch of web links, including one for Simpson Kinkaid's Wikipedia page.

'Ye got all that?'

'What's B-and-TB, when it's at home?'

'Beauty and the Beast, *you cultureless div. Don't youse never go to the theatre?'*

'And let me guess, Gordon Smith did the set for them?'

'No idea, crap like that's way *below me paygrade. Get yer bizzie mates to find out. Till then, I'm gonna roll back on top of yer ma and see if I can't hump her back to life. Laters.'* He hung up.

One down.

I called up the footage I'd shot in Smith's basement, pausing it at the Polaroid in question. Spooled it forward till it got to the matching one from the other side of the room. The one after Gordon Smith and his wife had been at him. The one with all the blood and frozen screaming.

Franklin was looking at me again. 'Something important?'

'Got an ID on the bearded guy.' Slid my finger across the progress bar, restoring him to life again. Went a bit too far. Ended up with the young woman on the beach, T-shirt and shorts. Then the young man trying to grow a moustache. Then the young woman and older man, in ugly sportswear, on a putting course. And back to Keith Whatley, AKA: Simpson Kinkaid, again.

It was … weird. Risky. Abducting and murdering someone you'd worked with: that would leave a trail. Why would Gordon Smith take that chance? Or did he feel invincible thirty-two years ago? He'd got away with it so many times before, why would anyone make the connection?

Still, it was worth a look.

I thumbed out a reply to Sabir's last text:

> See if you can get a cast list for all the productions Gordon Smith did sets for and run them against the misper database. Might find this wasn't the only actor he took a fancy to.

SEND.

Took barely a minute for the reply to come winging back. SABIR4TEHPOOL:

> Do one.
> UR 8 hours is up.
> No pay – no play.
> ⌐∩⌐ (ಠ__ಠ) ⌐∩⌐

Ah well, it'd been worth a try.

Ooh, on the other hand, this would be the *perfect* thing to lumber Detective Constable John Watt with.

'Erm… Mr Henderson? What's with the evil smile?'

Watt indeed?

A thin line of pale blue ran along the horizon as we climbed out of the manky old Ford Focus. No wind. No rain. No thundering waves pounding at the headland. Instead it was actually kind of pleasant. And surprisingly warm for mid-November.

The small handful of working streetlights cast their cheery

yellow glow into the pre-dawn gloom, someone's cockerel crowing out its morning greeting. And, blessing of blessings, no sign of any outside broadcast vans or journalists. Not yet, anyway.

Franklin frowned at me. 'You're doing that smile again.'

'Am I?'

'Yes, and it's creepy, so please stop.'

I clunked my door shut and she locked the car.

Henry danced a couple of circles on the end of his lead, letting loose a ripple of small happy barks. Before sniffing one of the front tyres and widdling on it. Scraping his back paws on the pitted tarmac.

The curtains twitched on Helen MacNeil's caravan.

Great.

Thirty seconds later she was out, hurrying across the road and following the three of us up the path to Mother's commandeered basecamp. 'Are they searching for my Leah?'

'Mrs MacNeil.' I stopped. Turned. 'E Division have a lookout request on the go for her, but she's—'

'You have to find her!' Hard strong hands grabbing at my lapels. 'You have to bring her back.'

Down by my ankles, Henry growled.

'It's...' I went for that reassuring-police-officer voice again: 'I've asked for a warrant to track her phone.' Which was true. Helen didn't need to know that Mother had turned me down flat.

'Your weird girl was right: I should've put a tracking app on Leah's mobile when I had the chance. But it's too late for that. I need you to *find* her!'

'We're doing everything we can.' Trying to sound sincere and convincing. 'But you know what police budgets are like. Maybe you could try getting a private detective? Johnston and Gench, in Shortstaine are good. Or there's McLean and McNee, in Logansferry?'

She let go and stepped back. 'You're not going to help me, are you?'

I raised my eyebrows at Franklin, but she just stood there.

Then seemed to twig, because she made a great show of looking at her watch. 'I'm sorry, Mrs MacNeil, but Mr Henderson and I are late for our morning briefing. We've got a killer to catch.'

'I'll chase up the lookout request and make sure Edinburgh are still on it. I promise.'

Franklin took hold of my sleeve. 'We really do have to go.'

Helen glowered at me. 'Leah's all I've got left.'

'I know. But in the meantime, I'm going to try catching the bastard who murdered your daughter.'

20

'Any questions?' Mother folded her thick arms and leaned back against the windowsill. Behind her, that line of pale blue had reached up the sky, a smear of red replacing it on the horizon. The outside broadcast vans had arrived at last, bringing with them a flotilla of hatchbacks and four-by-fours. All ready for the media circus to kick off once more.

Especially now one of their own had died.

The team was gathered in their cheap and nasty plastic chairs, Henry curled up at my feet – making tiny whimpery noises as his paws twitched. Chasing something in his dreams.

DC Elliot put her hand up. 'Simpson Kinkaid: are we going public with that? And if we are, has anyone delivered the death message to his next of kin? Or are we holding off telling them?'

'Official line from on high is: we're holding off for now.' She pointed. 'You look like you've got one, John.'

He arched an eyebrow and tilted his head towards the window. 'Who's handling the press?'

Mother stretched out her jaw, as if she was having difficulty swallowing something. 'Our beloved leader will be addressing the nation this morning. And, in the absence of any real bones to throw them, and after what happened last night, I expect we'll get a bit of a kicking.'

'Speaking of bones,' Elliot again, 'what about the post mortem?'

'Nine sharp. Anyone want to volunteer and join me? Anyone? Hello?'

No one made eye contact.

'Of course you don't, because you all want to sod off on a jolly, don't you?' She chewed on her lip for a moment. 'Bunch of ingrates.' Pointed at me. 'Ash?'

I produced the printout of Sabir's locations. 'The only place we can't ID is the bicycle-and-hedgerow picture. Other twelve range from Tiree to Malaga.'

Mother folded her arms. 'And before anyone asks: no. You can't go to Malaga.'

'Awww…' Dotty slouched in her wheelchair.

'Pick up your assignments from Rosalind on the way out. And don't—'

The living room door creaked open and in strode a large man in the full Police Scotland black, peaked cap tucked under one bulky arm. Face like a slab of granite that'd been carved by a sadist. Inspector's pips. 'As you were.'

Henry scrabbled to his feet, claws clicking on the bare wooden floorboards as he turned to face the newcomer.

Mother tried for a smile, but it wasn't very convincing. 'Inspector Samson, to what do we owe this—'

'The Chief Superintendent would like a word.' Making it sound like a death sentence.

'I see.' She dusted herself down. 'Right, well, let me tidy up here and—'

'With *all* of you.'

Right on cue, in stalked Chief Superintendent McEwan. Ducking slightly to get through the doorway without banging his head. Military moustache drawn in a hard sharp line above a hard sharp mouth. He removed his pcakcd cap – revealing a shiny pate surrounded by close-cropped grey hair – and handed it to Samson.

The pair of them were bookends, more like bouncers than police officers.

McEwan took his time to glare at everyone in the ensuing silence. Then turned to Mother, voice a deep rumbling baritone, calm and flat, as if nothing at all was wrong in the world. 'Detective Inspector Malcolmson, would you be so kind as to explain to me why I've got half the world's press CRAWLING UP MY ARSEHOLE WITH HOBNAIL BOOTS ON?'

Henry scrabbled around behind me, peering out past my legs. Tail down.

Give Mother her due, she didn't even flinch. 'Perhaps this isn't the—'

'I know we don't expect much of your team. But Divisional Investigative *Support* is supposed to do precisely what its name suggests: support investigations, NOT GET JOURNALISTS KILLED!' Going redder and redder.

'Now that's not fair, we—'

'Have you *any* idea how difficult you've made my job? You.' Jabbing his finger at her. 'All of you! YOU'RE A BLOODY DISGRACE!'

Mother pulled her chin in, shoulders back. 'My team has done *nothing* wrong. You can criticise me all you like, but—'

'Nothing *wrong*? Your team does nothing *but* wrong! If they were capable of anything else, they wouldn't *be* in your team!' He was actually trembling now, flecks of spittle glowing in the light of that one bare bulb. 'You're an unprofessional—'

I thumped my walking stick down on the desk, making the collection of paperwork dance. 'Shut up, you bloviating, half-arsed, jumped-up, overbearing PRICK!' Because he wasn't the only one who could do the shouting thing.

A pause, then Henry found his courage again, popping out from behind me to growl at McEwan.

The head of Oldcastle police stared at me. Eyes growing wider. Mouth curdling. 'How *dare* you talk to me like—'

'Oh, fuck off. You were an arsehole when I was in the Job and you're an even bigger arsehole now.' Closing the gap between us to poking distance. Jabbing a finger in his pompous chest. 'DC Watt, DS Franklin, and DI Malcolmson *risked their lives* last night, trying to save a moron journalist who wouldn't take a telling and stay away from the cliffs!'

'The media have been very clear that—'

'So what if the press are crawling up your backside? So what if they're screaming for scapegoats?'

'This isn't—'

'Your job isn't to help *them*, your job is to stand behind your bloody officers! No, you know what: it's to stand *in front* of your officers and take the flack so they can keep on DOING THEIR BLOODY JOBS!' Another poke, hard enough to send him flinching back a step. 'SO GROW A PAIR OF BALLS, GO OUT THERE, AND DO YOURS!'

His eyes bulged, white teeth bared, moustache twitching.

Then Inspector Samson cleared his throat. 'Sorry, sir, but we're live on the BBC in two minutes.'

Some more twitching and glowering.

Henry barked at him.

'Sir?'

McEwan's nostrils flared as he stuck his nose in the air, then he turned and marched from the room, snatching his hat out of Samson's hands as he went.

The inspector shook his head. Hissed out a long slow breath. 'Between you and me? That probably wasn't a great idea.'

I gave him the benefit of a cold shark smile. 'You can tell your boss: he briefs against the Misfit Mob, I'll go straight to the press and tell them *all* about Deborah Stalker.'

That got a frown from Samson. 'Who's—'

'You'll find out tomorrow, when it's all over the front pages.'

'Right. Well. Yes.' He backed from the room. 'I'd better...' Samson turned and hurried away down the corridor. *'Sir? Chief Superintendent? Sir, I need to talk to you!'*

The front door clunked shut and silence settled into the gloomy mildewed house.

Dotty blew out a long, hard breath. 'Bloody hell. Ash Henderson, you absolute *monster*!' Clapping her hands and mugging at me. It built into a slightly embarrassed round of applause from the team that ended with a wee hug from Mother.

Nice to be appreciated for a change.

Henry did his round-and-round dance again, as if he'd been wholly responsible for chasing McEwan away.

Watt grabbed the remote and turned the TV on, flicking through to BBC One, where the same reporter they'd had in town all week was doing his piece to camera.

'…*tragic death of Nick James from the* Glasgow Tribune, *prompting fierce criticism of the police presence here in Clachmara.'* He moved a pace to the side, the camera following him. *'I'm joined now by the head of O Division, Chief Superintendent McEwan.'*

And there was McEwan, turned slightly away from the camera, with Samson whispering something in his ear. He looked up, face a *lot* paler than it had been during his rant.

'Chief Superintendent, how do you respond to accusations that your officers were negligent in ensuring the safety of media teams in the area?'

Watt folded his arms. 'Negligent my arse.'

'I'm…' McEwan cleared his throat. Glanced back towards Samson. Then faced the camera again. *'My team did everything it possibly could to prevent this tragic death.'* Getting into the stride of it, popping his chin up. *'Let's not forget that three of my officers put their own lives at great risk trying to rescue Mr James, after he ignored repeated warnings to stay away from the cliff…'*

'Well, well, well.' Watt smiled. 'Looks like Shouty McShoutface isn't so shouty after all.'

'…utmost confidence in my officers to track down Gordon Smith and bring him to justice. And we'd once again ask anyone who has any information on Smith's whereabouts to get in touch with Police Scotland on…'

'All right, John,' Mother waved at the screen, 'I don't think we need to see any more.'

He killed the TV.

'Now, where were we? Ah yes, assignments. Rosalind?'

Franklin opened a folder and pulled out a wodge of paper. 'John: in light of Simpson Kinkaid appearing in one of Gordon Smith's pantos, we need you to get together a cast list of every show Smith worked on and see if anyone else has been reported missing.'

'Noooo…' Watt wrapped his arms around his head and curled up in his seat. 'Why can't *Amanda* do it?'

'Because Amanda and Dotty will be visiting Aberdeen, Fochabers, and Inverness.' Franklin passed across two printouts: blow-ups of the 'before' Polaroids: the guy at a graduation ceremony, the young woman on a pony, and the bloke in the beer garden. 'No point going to Balmedie, we know the victim there was Sophie MacNeil.'

A big smile from Dotty. 'Girls' road trip!'

I hobbled over to the printouts that DC Elliot and Watt had pinned up, opposite Gordon Smith's headshot. The same thirteen blown-up Polaroids that Franklin was handing out – the ones from the 'before' set – made a wide-spaced grid on the fusty wallpaper. If there was a corresponding 'after' picture, it was stuck underneath the living one, which left four smiling people with no corresponding torture shot.

The remaining eleven unmatched 'after' pics formed a second grid. Where they would probably stay, unknown and unnamed. But *hopefully* not unrevenged.

Someone had added Sophie's name to the bottom of her picture in blue sharpie. They'd done the same with Simpson Kinkaid. Leaving eleven unknowns on the 'before' grid. Well, fourteen, if you counted people, rather than pictures. The happy couple on a carousel: photographed in Glasgow, according to Sabir. The two young women hugging on the seafront: Brighton. And the older man and younger woman posing awkwardly on a putting course: Rothesay.

'Mr Henderson and I will take—'

'Does this look *familiar* to you?'

Franklin pursed her lips and lowered the chunk of paperwork in her hand. 'I'm in the middle of—'

'No, come look. Here.'

She rolled her eyes, groaned, then sloped over. 'What now?' Glanced at the photographs. 'Yes, it's a carousel. Wish I'd never let you—'

'Not the carousel, *this* pair. On the putting course. He not remind you of someone?'

Creases appeared between her perfect eyebrows and she leaned in to stare. '…Maybe?'

199

'Cos he reminds me of Gordon Smith's brother: Slimy Pete.'
Only in the picture he had to be about thirty, maybe forty years
younger? Instead of that swept-forwards Nero hairstyle, he had
a full head of frothy brown curls, a Peter Sutcliffe beard, and a
turquoise-and-red shell suit.

'Now you've said it? Yeah… Kind of.' She poked the picture.
'Same piggy eyes.'

'Think we should go pay Bute a visit?'

Franklin held up her paperwork again. 'Way ahead of you.
We're down for Cupar, Glasgow, and Rothesay.'

'In *one* day, are you off your head? Do you have any idea
how long that'll take?'

She poked at her phone, then held the screen out in front
of me. A map of Scotland with a wiggly blue line stretching
nearly all the way across it with a narrow loop on the right-
hand side. 'Seven hours, fifty-five minutes. Should be back here
by … twenty to four?'

'Assuming we don't actually stop the car, or do any police
work when we get where we're going, or pause for two minutes
every now and then so Henry can have a wee!'

The little man perked his ears up at the mention of his name.

Mother appeared, unfurling the crinkly white top to a bag
of sweets. 'What are we arguing about now?'

'Detective Sergeant Franklin seems to think Police Scotland
are going to lend us one of those old blue public call boxes,
and that it'll actually travel in space and time.'

'That's nice.' Mother took hold of my arm and led me over to
the window, where the outside broadcast units were still lined up,
their various journalists doing pieces to camera as the sky lightened
above them. 'Listen, about this post mortem, you heard Professor
Twining, we're supposed to get a forensic anthropologist to attend.'

'So go find one.'

'I *can't*. The woman I always use from Dundee has sodded
off to Lancaster University, and everyone else is away working
in godforsaken parts of the globe. Like Guildford.'

No idea why *her* lack of staff was *my* problem… But that
wasn't exactly being a team player, was it? Play nice.

'Could always try the next-door neighbour – the pregnant one.' Pointing through the wall and off to the right. 'OK, she's not qualified, but better than nothing. Maybe.'

'Oh, God.' Mother covered her face with her hands. 'And it had all been going so well...'

The sun finally made it over the horizon, painting the world in shades of gold and amber as Franklin worked the pool car through Logansferry. Even the harbour looked attractive in this light. As we drove up the dual carriageway, the view between the buildings opened up, giving a clear line of sight across the river and up into the bleak horror of Kingsmeath. Not even the sunrise could make that place look like anything other than what it was: dark, depressing, and dangerous. A twisted nest of cheap council housing and brutalist tower blocks.

Should've bulldozed the place years ago.

The Luftwaffe had spent all their energy bombing the Logansferry docks, could they not have flattened Kingsmeath while they were at it? Was that so much to ask?

And yes, *technically* most of the place had only been built after the war, but that was no excuse.

I stretched out my right leg, setting the tortured ankle clicking as the bombs fell, wiping the whole area off the map.

'You're doing that weird evil smiling thing again.'

'What can I say, I'm a cheery individual.' Sometimes.

Henry nudged his nose through from the back seat, rubbing his muzzle against my arm till he got a scratch.

I gave Franklin the side-eye. 'I'm assuming that's why you decided to partner up with me again, today: my winning charm.'

'Best of a bad lot, to be honest. Dotty's lovely, but she'll drive you insane after thirty minutes, John's a dick, and Amanda is...' Franklin screwed her face into a thoughtful pout.

'Bit too earnest? Eager to please? OTT?'

'Could say that, yes. On top of other things.'

'Go on then: what did she do wrong to end up in Mother's Misfit Mob?'

'You'd have to ask *her* that.' Franklin joined the queue for the roundabout, stuck behind a bread van and an eighteen-wheeler full of vegan sausage rolls – going by the branding. 'What really matters is that I get to hang about with Henry all day. You're just collateral damage, so—'

Radiohead's 'Creep' started up in my pocket: Detective Superintendent Jacobson.

She nodded. 'You want to answer that?'

'Not really.' But I pulled out my phone anyway. Swiped the button. 'What now? I'm on secondment, remember?'

'Ash? Sabir says you've still not sent him that cost code for his eight hours. And while I've got you: Steven Kirk.'

'I'm sure I emailed it across.' Which was a lie.

'Kirk's solicitor is threatening us with all manner of horrible things, Ash. I do not want LIRU getting sued because you roughed up a nonce. Understand?'

'Tell Sabir to check his spam folder, maybe it ended up in there?'

'Alice says she's had a word with Kirk, but I need this done belt-and-braces style.'

'I can try resending it, if you like?'

'Yes, excellent attempt at evasion, but you're not wriggling out of this one. You're meeting with Kirk's solicitor ASAP, and that's final.'

Franklin took us around the big roundabout and onto Camburn Drive. The traffic lightening up as we hit the ring road through the woods.

'Can't today, we're on our way to Fife, Glasgow, and Bute.'

'Don't care, as long as you stop off past HMP Oldcastle on the way. Because if you don't *– and let me make myself really clear here – if you* don't*, I'm going to make it my mission in life to cut you loose, point out the "accountability for own actions" clause in your contract, and make sure Steven Kirk's legal team nail you to the courtroom floor. By your testicles!'*

The rotten bastard would as well.

'That's not exactly—'

'And send Sabir that cost code! I'm not running a charity here.'

Then silence. He'd hung up.

Lovely.

I slipped my phone back into my pocket. Gave Franklin an apologetic smile.

She pulled her chin in. Clearly suspicious. 'What?'

'Slight change of plan.'

A groan. 'Of course there is...'

21

Strange how much one prison looked like any other these days. Well, assuming it wasn't built in the late eighteen hundreds. The new ones, though, were more community centre than penal institution. From the outside, anyway.

Inside, it didn't matter where you were, it always smelled of too much air freshener trying to cover up the animal funk of too many people crammed into one place for too long and never allowed to go anywhere.

Out in the real world, Franklin wandered past, her shape distorted by the wall of tinted glass that fronted the main entrance, Henry trotting along at her side on the end of his leash – nose down and sniffing. Searching for interesting things to widdle on.

The officer on reception frowned at my ID for a while, porn-star moustache twitching as if he was trying not to read the words out loud. Then it twitched up at me instead. 'And you want to see...?'

'Kenneth Dewar.'

'Right. Mr Dewar.' He swivelled his chair around and called across to a beefy woman in matching white short-sleeved shirt, epaulettes, black tie and trousers. No moustache, though. 'HOY, JESS, YOU SEEN MILKY-MILKY ANYWHERE?'

The voice that bellowed back was remarkably posh. 'HAVING A WEEP, ROUND THE BACK OF THE BINS!'

'CHEERS!' A finger swung around to point at a door this side of the security scanners, X-ray machines, and conveyor belt, marked 'AUTHORISED PERSONNEL ONLY'. 'Mr Dewar will be on your left. I'll buzz you through.'

Kenneth Dewar didn't look the type to be having a cry behind the prison's collection of massive wheelie bins, but there he was: broad shoulders; thinning hair, swept back from a tanned scalp; jet-black leather jacket; sitting on the kerb with his knees up against his chest, one arm wrapped around them, the other hand covering his face as he rocked back and forth. Breath coming out in sharp little jags. An untouched vending-machine cup of something frothy and brown resting on the tarmac at his booted feet.

The kind of person Alice would've been all over. Trying to help him through his pain, instead of leaving the poor bugger to blub in peace. Which I would've done, if there weren't a million more important things to be getting on with.

'Mr Dewar?' I flashed my ID, even though he couldn't see it. 'My name's Ash Henderson, Lateral Investigative and Review Unit. I believe we need to talk?'

He blinked at me between his fingers. Hauled in a deep wobbly breath. Then scrubbed at his face. Sniffed. 'Yes. Right. Of course. Sorry.' Stood, wiping his hand down the leg of his blue jeans. Then held it out for shaking. 'Kenny.'

All covered in tears and snot? Don't think so.

I limped over to the opposite wall instead, where a tiny sliver of sunlight had made it through the chain-link and barbed wire. 'So, Kenny, I hear you represent Steven Kirk.'

He stooped and picked up his cup of brown. Gave himself a shake. His eyes might've been bloodshot, but they were still bright sapphire with a dark border. Wolf's eyes. A strong jaw and muscular neck. Large hands at the end of brawny forearms. Exactly Shifty's type. But then Shifty always had terrible taste in men.

Dewar pulled his head up and nodded. Bit his lip. Then looked away again. 'Have you any idea what it's like having to represent people like Steven Kirk, day in, day out? Because no one else will even be in the same room as them?'

I shrugged. 'You don't have to do it.'

A short, bitter laugh. 'Doesn't matter what they've done: *everyone* has the right to legal representation. Even Steven Kirk. Because if we don't, what's next? Maybe we should do away with the judicial process altogether? Instead of judges and juries we should give police officers guns and you can execute anyone you think's broken the law?' Dewar shook his head. 'There's enough fascist regimes in the world without us joining them.' The breath that rattled out of him was long and sad. 'So this is how I spend my days.' One hand sweeping up to indicate the prison. 'Wading through the child abusers, rapists, and everyone else you wouldn't touch with a cattle prod.'

Oh, I would – especially if it was fully charged.

I settled back against the wall. 'What does Kirk want?'

'You know what the rest of my morning looks like? Helping a man who murdered his wife and two daughters rehearse for a "diminished-responsibility" plea, on the grounds that he thought one of the girls wasn't his, so they all had to die. Then prepare some sort of argument so a *complete* animal can get visiting rights to his toddler, even though he beat the living crap out of its mother. Short break for lunch. Followed by a woman who filmed herself abusing and killing a wee boy. She wants to sue the prison for not letting her publish the slash-fic novel she's written about Jimmy Bloody Savile granting wishes at Hogwarts…' Dewar's shoulders slumped, head thrown back to stare up at the cold blue sky. 'Should've listened to my mother and gone into the priesthood.'

A seagull screeched by, overhead.

'Nah.' I gave him a small smile. 'If you did that, you'd *still* have to deal with paedos, rapists, and freaks, only you'd have to absolve them of their sins, then send them off on their merry way, safe in the knowledge they were going to do it all over again. Imagine having that on your conscience.'

He let his head fall forward, staring at his cup of vending-machine brown as he nodded. 'True.' Took a sip. 'Steven wanted to press charges for assault, even though Dr ... McDonald is it?'

I nodded.

'Even though Dr McDonald claims *he* assaulted *her* and you were only trying to save her.' Another bitter laugh. 'Which you and I know is utter bollocks. You gave Steven Kirk a good kicking, because he deserved one.' Dewar took a deep breath. 'So here's what I'm going to propose: you make a full and *sincere* apology. Police Scotland – or your LIRU lot, don't care which – make a modest financial settlement to acknowledge his pain and distress. Somewhere in the ballpark of eight to ten grand should do it. And I talk Steven into dropping the charges. Mary Brennan's screaming for his head on a spike now she knows he was cosying up to her in church. That should give us some leverage.'

Eight to ten grand. Not sure if Detective Superintendent Jacobson would go for that, but you never knew...

'Thank you.'

'Yeah.' Dewar took another sip. 'And in return, I need you do me a favour, OK?'

The silence stretched.

That gull soared past once more, bringing a couple of squawking friends with it.

Outside the high fences, a car horn brayed.

'You're supposed to ask what the favour is.'

'OK... What is it?'

Kenneth Dewar downed the last of his drink and flipped the empty wax-paper cup into the nearest bin. 'Steven Kirk didn't kill Andrew Brennan, or any of those other wee boys – he's got an alibi that I can't tell you about. A proper one. Nothing to do with looking after his dying mother.'

'Something that violates his SRO?' AKA: something that could get him wheeched right back to prison for being a sketchy child-molesting bastard.

'That would be one *possible* interpretation, but I can't confirm or deny it, because even a perverted monster like Steven Kirk is covered by client confidentiality.' Deep breath. 'But I want something in return.'

'What, in addition to your cut of the eight grand?' I took out one of Alice's business cards, scored out her mobile number and printed my own in its place. Held it out. 'In case you change your mind about that client confidentiality. Off the record, of course. Anonymously, if you like?'

'I want you to promise me you'll find the man who killed those wee boys.' Dewar bit his bottom lip and nodded. 'You find him, and you make him *pay*.'

'How *much?*' Jacobson sounded as if I'd just stabbed him.

'Eight. Well, eight to ten.' I shifted the phone to the other ear as the pool car *thrummmm-thump-thrummmm-thump-thrummmm-thumped* its way across the Tay Road Bridge. The river sparkled in the sunlight, a massive slab of slate grey, scarred by the passage of an RNLI lifeboat. A handful of Jackup rigs reaching their latticework ladders into a dull-blue sky.

'*Thousand pounds?*'

'No, jelly babies.'

A smile played at the edge of Franklin's mouth, but she kept her face front, following a wee sandwich van with 'BINGO BRENDA'S BAPS, BUTTERIES, & BRIDIES!' on it, at a stately fifty miles per hour.

'*I don't think you're in any position to be sarcastic, do you?*'

'Kenny Dewar is adamant Steven Kirk isn't our boy. He was doing something else at the time. Something that breaches his Sexual Risk Order.'

'*Ten thousand pounds! Do you have* any *idea what that'll do to my budget?*'

'Kirk's not going to make something like that up, is he? Well, maybe to get away with abduction and murder...'

'*How can you not take this seriously?*'

Thrummmm-thump-thrummmm-thump-thrummmm-thump.

'Look, it happened, and I'm sorry, but it happened.' I sagged back in my seat. 'Kirk weaselled his way into Saint Damon's, got himself a nice little volunteer job where he could slither up to Mary Brennan. It all kind of ... happened.'

'*Thought you said you went for him because he attacked Alice?*'

'That happened after.' Almost. From my slouched position, the road behind us was dead centre in the rear-view mirror. A wee open-topped sports car, driven by a wrinkly old lady with wild grey hair. A dumpy Mini the colour of dung. A dull-yellow Volkswagen Golf clarted in rust. And behind them the grey swathe of Dundee as it faded into the distance behind us.

Say what you like about the place, at least it was trying – with its V&A museum and redevelopment and infrastructure plan. More than Oldcastle was doing.

'Ash?'

Oh, right. Jacobson.

'Look, we've got personal liability insurance, haven't we? Use that.'

Silence from the other end of the phone.

Thrummmm-thump-thrummmm-thump-thrummmm-thump.

Then, *'How do you manage to be the biggest ache in my rectum, Ash? You're in a team with Professor Bernard Huntly, for God's sake, you shouldn't even come close!'*

'And see if you can chase up Sabir, eh? He's had his eight hours – about time he produced the goods and got us some IDs.'

'The ice is thin, Ash, and you're skating very, very heavily.'

'Yeah.' I hung up and put my phone away. 'I know.'

Franklin held up her printout of the young woman standing on one leg, then shuffled around until the real-life bandstand lined up with the one in the photograph. In the picture, a blob of pink flowers and a wavy line of red and yellow ones punctuated the grass, but here, in the middle of November, Haugh Park was all faded yellows and browns. No leaves on the trees.

She nodded. 'Definitely the same place.'

Sabir was good for something, then.

We wandered back up the path, Henry having a good sniff at everything, past some sort of memorial statue, and stopped at the roundabout.

'What now?' Franklin pointed left, where the road curved

past a big sandstone lump of a building. 'Police station's that way. Go have a dig through their missing persons' database?'

'Would be sensible.' I limped across to the other side of the roundabout, Henry trotting along at my side, tail up and waving. Making for Cupar town centre. 'So, you nip off and do that.'

She hurried after me, rolled her eyes. 'Come on then, out with it.'

'Nothing at all. It's the sensible thing to do. Like I said.'

'And what will *you* be doing, while I'm digging through fifty-six years' worth of misper records?'

'The cops aren't the only ones who keep tabs on missing people.'

'Ash Henderson, I thought you were dead!' Vera Abbot held her arms wide for a hug. A spattering of stains marred the front of her flouncy paisley-patterned blouse, dog hairs on the legs of her baggy red trousers, a pair of knee-high boots that probably hadn't seen a lick of shoe polish since she'd bought them some time in the eighties. The long brown hair was gone, instead it was a short-back-and-sides in shades of grey and white, making her ears stick out even more than normal, dangly gold earrings hanging from the lobes. Dark eyes and a slightly ratty smile, emphasised by the collection of creases and laughter lines.

Up close she exuded the mismatched scents of sharp Olbas Oil and stale cigarettes, as she planted a *'mmmwah'* on both my cheeks.

Then stepped back to give me a proper once-over. 'You're far too thin. How's Michelle? Or are you still seeing that stripper, Susie?'

'Susanne, and no.'

'Oh, too bad. I know how middle-aged men like you put great store in boinking a twenty-four-year-old.'

Vera's office was a sea of paperwork: shelves on the walls, groaning with stacks and stacks of it, file boxes lining the room – three deep and four high in places. A drift of printouts and newspaper cuttings buried her desk. More on the windowsills, blocking off the bottom half of a view out over the Crossgate to the Chinese restaurant opposite.

She bent double, patting her hands on her knees, and beamed at Henry. 'And who's this handsome wee lad?'

'My sidekick. Police Scotland just can't get the staff any more.'

'True.' Vera thumped back into her office chair, setting it rocking on groaning springs. 'Tea?' Dipping into a desk drawer and coming out with a bottle of Glenfiddich. 'Or something stronger, perhaps?'

I cleared a stack of newspapers off the room's only other chair and eased myself into it. 'Can't: pills. And it's not even ten o'clock, yet.'

'True, shouldn't be a cliché, should we?' She popped the whisky back in her desk. Then took a deep breath. 'SANDY! TWO TEAS! AND NIP DOWN THE BAKER'S FOR A COUPLE OF SAUSAGE BUTTIES!' Vera winked at Henry. 'AND AN EXTRA SAUSAGE!'

A loud teenager groan rattled out from somewhere down the hall, followed by a grudging, *'All right, all right...'* and a door thunking shut.

'The joy of interns.' Vera creaked her seat from side to side, smiling at me like a deranged squirrel. 'Now, I'm guessing you didn't come here to chat about the good old days, and it's too early for a booty call, so what can the *Fife Daily Examiner* do for you? Is this about those murdered little boys? Saw another one went missing yester—'

'You still keep that big file full of missing persons?'

Her eyes widened at me, eyebrows going up. 'You have piqued my interest, Mr Henderson. And would there be an exclusive in it for me?'

'Depends.'

'You know what the other really lovely thing about interns is? You can get them to do *all* sorts and call it work experience.' Vera gave a wee nonchalant shrug. 'Like digitising the entire archive. Fancy a wee squint?'

Damn right I did.

22

I polished off the last mouthful of sausage butty and washed it down with milky tea as a young man in a tartan shirt and polka-dot tie poked at the keyboard on a shiny new laptop. It looked as if he'd modelled his haircut on Vera's, only with a vaguely obscene quiff. Peering through small round glasses at the array of black-and-white images on his screen. An accent so Fife you could've designed rollercoasters with it – up and down and up and down and up again. 'See, the real trick is getting the metadata right when you're putting the stuff into the database in the first place.'

Vera leaned back against an overflowing filing cabinet in what passed for the *Fife Daily Examiner*'s newsroom – barely big enough to fit in yet more towers of file boxes, an old dining table, and four wooden chairs. 'You still haven't said why we're looking for this woman, Ash.'

'Haven't I?'

The young man poked at the keyboard some more. 'Right, so if we eliminate anyone from the last fifteen years, male, blonde, or over thirty…' The images refreshed on his screen, narrowing down the field. 'Then we cut off anything more than sixty years ago…' They changed again. 'And that gives us fifty-six possibles.' He looked up at me with a wee swaggery wobble to his head. 'You want me to flick through them?'

No, I was standing here for the good of my health.

'Please.'

'Right.' A woman's face filled the screen – too old to be standing on one leg and with completely the wrong shape of nose. 'Well?'

'Keep going, I'll tell you when to stop.'

Face after face clicked past, each one staying there for no more than a couple of seconds, their names flashing up underneath the pictures. A list of info down the side: names, dates, all that kind of stuff. Some were professional photo-studio jobs, others were more informal, some blurry and grainy, some done down the local nick with a height chart in the background, some wedding pics, and some were those cheesy end-of-year ones they used to do in secondary schools.

'Stop!' I leaned in. 'Go back a couple.'

He did.

And there she was: Julia Kennedy. Fifteen years old – definitely younger than she looked – grinning out at us in front of a mottled background. Blue blazer with the school crest on the breast pocket, white shirt, blue tie with yellow-and-red diagonal stripes, straight skirt. A butterfly hairgrip, holding her side parting in place. Missing for the last thirty-five years.

Took some doing, but I kept my face as still as possible. As if it didn't really matter one way or another that we'd found her.

The printer in the corner creaked and whirred into life, chugging out three or four sheets of A4.

Vera wheeched them out of the tray. Pursed her lips as she frowned at them. 'I remember this one: her mother was in absolute bits for years. DI Dickie fancied the stepdad for it, kept waiting for Julia's remains to turn up, but they never did.' A grey eyebrow waggled at me. 'Until now? Is that why you're here, you've found her body?'

'Nope. We found her *photo* and wanted to know who she was.' I held my hand out and, eventually, Vera handed the printouts over. 'You know what investigations are like these days: every stupid little thing has to be followed up.'

'Because if you've found her body and you're not telling me, I'd—'

'We *haven't* found her body.' Which was true. 'And I promise if anything comes up, I'll let you know.' The folded sheets went in my pocket. 'In the meantime, do me a favour and stay away from the family. No point getting their hopes up for nothing.'

Vera narrowed her eyes and squinted at me for a while in silence. Then nodded. 'Deal. But you better not stiff me, Ash Henderson.'

'Would I?'

'Yes, you bloody well would!'

'Don't know why you're glowering at me. I IDed our victim, didn't I?' I pushed my seat back, reclining it and stretching out my right leg. Trying to work the crackling knots out of the tortured ankle as Franklin scowled her way along the M8.

Her suit might have started the day a smart shade of black, but it'd developed an off-grey patina, spotted with the occasional clump of fluff. 'I was digging through those bloody boxes for ages, while you were swanning about having sausage butties and cups of tea!'

'Well, one of us had to take the official route, didn't they? Besides, we got a result – that's all that matters.' Trying to rub some life back into my calf.

That was the trouble with a walking stick. It was good for belting people with, but after a while the whole 'hobbling about' thing set every other muscle in my body squint and aching.

'Hmmph!'

'Look, if I buy you a sausage butty when we get to Glasgow, will that cheer you up?' Reclining my seat even further, till I could see the motorway behind us in the rear-view mirror. 'Getting to be a bit of a habit.'

'Oh ha-ha.'

Yup – it was definitely still there. 'Can you see what I see?'

'I'm *not* playing I Spy with you.'

'No, you twit. Three cars back: Rusty VW Golf.'

'Yellow?'

'Been following us since we left Cupar.'

Franklin shrugged. 'So what? Lots of people drive to Glasgow. Even Fifers.'

'It followed us across the Tay Road Bridge, too.'

She pulled herself closer to the mirror, squinting at it. 'Can't see the number plate… Journalists?'

'Maybe.' Or maybe not.

'Want me to lose them?' Tightening her grip on the steering wheel. No doubt looking forward to another go at 'FIVE DEAD IN MOTORWAY PILEUP HORROR'.

'Nah. Let's see if we can't front them up when we get to Glasgow.'

Franklin's shoulders dipped an inch and she loosened her grip. 'Suppose…'

Yeah, I was no fun.

We stood in the shadow of the Nelson Monument – a stubby dirty Cleopatra's needle that didn't provide nearly enough shelter from the wind whipping in up the Clyde. Bringing with it the peppery-ozone scent of impending snow.

Detective Chief Inspector McManus nodded her head towards the squat glazed bulk of the People's Palace – a silvered jellyfish, washed up in the middle distance – then held up the printout in a gloved hand. She had a large, powerful frame; hair scraped back from a high forehead; small piercing eyes. Voice trying hard to lose the tenement twang and almost succeeding. 'That's it there, just visible between the carousel horses.'

Sabir and his magic algorithms strike again.

'Any idea who they are?'

Something chugged by on the river behind us, accompanied by the faint *bmmtssshhh-bmmtssshhh-bmmtssshhh* of dance music played too loud on cheap speakers.

I turned, but McManus was staring off in the opposite direction. Watching as Franklin and Henry wandered through a double avenue of trees, the wee lad's nose down and tail up. 'She's very pretty.'

'She's a *he*. Scottie dog.'

That got me a withering look. 'Not the terrier, the Detective Sergeant.'

'Oh, you soon get over that if you have to spend any time with her.' I poked the printout in McManus's hand. 'Who are they?'

'Hmm?' McManus dragged herself back to the photo: a man and a woman, waving at the camera as their carousel horses galloped by. He had sideburns and a leather waistcoat, one of those flouncy ceilidh shirts unlaced far enough to expose a 'V' of pelt-covered chest, shoulder-length brown hair bouncing out behind him. Maybe mid-twenties. The woman was a good five or six years younger, mousy-blonde hair in a bulbous bob, wide white smile stretching her happy round face. Long, floaty, floral-print dress, ridden up at the side showing a flash of pale thigh. 'No idea.'

McManus lowered the printout. 'One of our history buffs managed to date the picture, though. Going by the fairground, the positioning of the stalls, and the terrible fashion sense, this was taken forty-two years ago, sometime between the fifteenth and twenty-first of April. Circus was in town. I've got people going through the archives for all missing person reports within a three-month window.'

'Let me guess,' I leaned back against the monument, 'stacks and stacks of dusty boxes?'

'It's like that scene at the end of *Raiders of the Lost Ark*. And every time I even suggest getting everything digitised?'

'Budget cutbacks?'

'Can barely afford to police the streets as it is.'

'You should get yourself some interns.'

Franklin and Henry made one more pass around the trees and headed back towards us.

McManus stared at them, a slightly droopy wistful look on her face. 'Course, there's no guarantee they were even reported missing here. People come on holiday to Glasgow all the time. Could've been from anywhere.'

True.

I dug my hands deeper into my pockets. 'You want some unsolicited advice?'

'Not really.' Curling her lip.

'The last senior officer who perved on DS Franklin ended up with a broken nose. Ask E Division.'

'I do like a challenge…' McManus returned the printout. 'Where you off to next?'

'Bute. Smith photographed his brother and a young woman on a putting course.'

'Oh, shame.' Clearing her throat as Franklin and Henry got closer. 'I could've come with you. You know … to help facilitate access and inter-divisional cooperation with local resources, but that's K Division's patch.'

Aye, and there were no prizes for guessing whose inter-divisional cooperation Detective Chief Inspector McManus was trying to access. Standing up straighter and smiling as Franklin finally arrived with the wee hairy boy.

No prizes at all.

The pool car passed under a raised walkway, and the landscape opened out to the right – the wide River Clyde a choppy blue smear with hills and mountains disappearing into the lowering sky on the other side – while we roared along the dual carriageway.

'*Tell you, it's an absolute nightmare.*' Rhona gave a disgusted grunt. '*Soon as Toby Macmillan was reported missing:* total *media feeding frenzy.* "*Is missing five-year-old the latest Oldcastle Child-Strangler victim?*" *Second editions are all* "*picture exclusive, pages four to nine*", *and opinion pieces from every mouth-breathing halfwit who ever wanked into a sock. Shifty looks like his head's going to pop like an over-ripe pluke any second now. Doesn't help that your wee friend's hungover as hell. Been sick three times already this morning.*'

'Do me a favour and keep an eye on Alice, OK?'

Rhona groaned. Then, '*OK, OK. But if she pukes all over me, you're for it.*'

Franklin overtook a big green articulated lorry with the ScotiaBrand Tasty Chickens logo down the side, and, 'ONLY A CLUCKING IDIOT WOULDN'T LOVE SCOTIABRAND CHICKEN MACSPORRANS!' Someone had finger-painted, 'VEGAN REVOLUTIONARY ARMY!!!' and 'MEAT IS MURDER!!!' underneath, in the grime.

'And while you're there, chase up Edinburgh plod for me, will you? Supposed to have a lookout request on the go for Leah MacNeil. Make sure they're not sat on their arses twiddling their thumbs.'

'Yeah. You'll have to wait till I'm done here, though. Got a media briefing in five. Hopefully I won't be spending most of it holding Her Ladyship's hair back as she barfs all over the front row.' The smile in Rhona's voice was loud and clear. *'Not that most of them wouldn't deserve it, mind. Then it's back to interviewing nonces for the rest of the day. Which is about as—'*

'Thanks, Rhona.' I hung up. Tapped the phone against my palm. Might be worth tuning in to listen. Then again, if Alice really was in that bad a state, maybe better not.

We passed a minibus full of grumpy-faced pensioners. A taxi with a sobbing man in the back. A Transit with two blokes singing along to something in the front. An ancient Ford towing a trailer full of logs.

Then a wide stretch of nothing but us and the river and the hills.

Franklin risked a glance back over her shoulder, even though there was a perfectly good rear-view mirror, right there. 'They still following us?'

'Will you keep your eyes on the road?'

'I can't see them, maybe they've... No. Rusty yellow Volkswagen Golf at twelve o'clock.'

I tried not to grimace, I really did. 'Of course they're at twelve o'clock, they're *following* us.' Poked at the screen on my phone, bringing up the web browser and scrolling down the Calmac timetable. 'OK, we've missed the twelve fifteen, and the next ferry's not till one.'

She glanced at the dashboard clock. 'Plenty of time.'

'Ah... According to this, we need to be there twenty minutes before it sails.'

'Going to be tight, then.' The car's engine changed pitch as she put her foot down and the needle crept up to eighty. 'Can't believe we didn't make the Golf, back in Glasgow.'

I slithered down in my seat. Three cars back, the Volkswagen accelerated to match our speed, pulling out to overtake the red van in front of it.

Gotcha.

Sat up straight again, turned in my seat and pointed my phone's camera at the rear windscreen.

And immediately, Henry popped up like a gopher, big happy head filling the picture. 'Get down, you daft lump.'

He stayed where he was, but his expression got even more glaikit.

Took hold of his collar and pulled him into the footwell. 'Stay!' Then took the shot. Turned and faced the front again.

'You get them?'

'Find out soon enough.' Calling up the photo showed it wasn't great, but there was *just* enough grainy detail when I zoomed in to make out the number plate. Right. Rhona was already doing me a favour, so I texted the pic to Shifty instead.

> Run this through the PNC for me.
> I need an ID, address, and anything else
> you can get on the driver.
> They've been following us.

Send.

The response was surprisingly prompt, given he was meant to be giving a media briefing.

Shifty:

> I am not your bloody skivvy! I'm running a
> bloody murder inquiry here! I've got three
> dead kids and one missing!!!!!!!

Which was actually a fair point. He really *did* have more important things to do.

I smiled across the car at Franklin. 'You haven't got DC Watt's mobile number, have you?'

219

23

Franklin stood at the front rail, peering down into the ferry's loading bay. The huge metal prow was raised, like the open beak of a vast blue-and-white metal parrot, banging and clanging coming from below as the last of the vehicles was driven on board. 'Any sign of it?'

Wind grabbed at her hair, making it stream out to the side, water breaking in spumes of white against the dock's pilings. Henry scuttered up and down on the end of his leash, ears flapping.

'Over there.' I raised a finger and pointed, past the apron with its twelve lines reserved for vehicles waiting to board – two of which were already full, ready for the next sailing – to the parking area away to the right, down by the pebbly shore. Where that rusty yellow Golf now lurked. 'Must've missed the loading cut-off, so they either abandon the car, or abandon the chase.'

'Hmmm…' She narrowed her eyes at it. 'So they're definitely on board.'

'Came a hell of a long way to give up now.'

Franklin turned, resting her back against the rail instead, looking up at the wheelhouse as it towered over us. Picking the hair out of her mouth and setting it free to writhe in the wind again. 'Still nothing from John?'

'Useless as he is ugly.' I tried to flex out the knots in my right leg. 'You want to run the PNC check instead?'

'I'm not your—'

'Do it myself, but they tend to frown on members of the public hacking into the Police National Computer.'

She made a pained expression, then slumped. 'Fine, but you owe me a sausage butty, remember?'

'Deal.' I handed her Henry's lead and sodded off inside.

'Thanks.' I pocketed my change, picked up the cardboard coffee-holder thing and the wee paper bag with the not-sausage-butties in it.

The ferry was busier than you'd think, for the one o'clock sailing on a blustery Sunday in November. The outside seating area at the stern was virtually empty, though. Instead people were clustered inside, on the rows of vinyl seats or around the puggy machines – feeding in their money and pressing buttons to a soundtrack of dings, tweedles, and flashing lights.

A couple of fake-tan tourists in neon hiking gear were going pale and sweaty as the ferry forged its way against the wind. Deck rising and falling, wallowing from side to side. Making limping anywhere with two decaf lattes and a pair of pre-packaged cake slices even more difficult than usual.

Should've been paying more attention to where I was going, but I was more concerned with not falling on my backside, and thumped sideways into a fat bearded bloke in a stripy top. 'Sorry.'

'Sorry.' An apologetic shrug, even though I was the one who'd barged into him.

Still, at least…

'Are you all right?' He put a hand on my arm. 'Only, you look like you've seen a—'

'Hold this.' I thrust the coffees and cakes at him, then pushed past, heading for the narrow passageway through to the other seating area.

Rows of angled seats, a couple of small tables, lots of bored-looking people, and a handful of screaming children running in circles. Piles of luggage against the bulkheads – wheelie cases and cardboard boxes of things.

Where the hell was…

There: by the window, staring out at the darkening sky.

I limped straight over, thumped a hand down on her shoulder. 'What's the matter, couldn't get your car on the boat?'

Helen MacNeil froze for a moment, then turned and scowled at me. 'It's a free country.'

'I *told* you I'd chase up that lookout request, and I did. They're looking for her.'

Franklin burst into the passenger area, dragging Henry with her, making a beeline for me. 'Ash: you'll never guess who owns that yellow…' She stopped and stared at Helen.

'You're too late. I already know.' Pointing.

'What's *she* doing here?' Franklin stepped closer. 'What are you doing here, Mrs MacNeil?'

Wait.

I looked at Franklin. 'It's her car.'

'No, it belongs to Nick James, the journalist who got washed away yesterday.'

Great. Of course it did.

'You *stole* a dead reporter's car?'

Helen opened her mouth, but a voice behind me got there first, 'Technically, *we borrowed it.*' No need to turn around to know who that was: Jennifer Bloody Prentice.

I turned on my heel, and limped off. Pausing only to retrieve my coffees and cakes from the confused-looking bearded bloke.

Jennifer's voice brayed out behind me. *'Oh come on, Ash, don't be like that!'*

'…all drivers return to their vehicles…' The nasal announcement echoed through the metal stairwell as I hobbled down to the car deck, the air thick with the scent of diesel. Walking stick clanging on the steps.

Franklin was waiting for me, leaning on the roof of our manky Ford Focus, eyes narrowed, mouth pursed. Voice hard and clipped. 'Like to tell me what that was all about?'

'No.'

She climbed inside. Pulled on her seatbelt as I settled into the passenger seat. Radiated Arctic cold at me. 'So, according to Ms Prentice, she had an arrangement with Nick James, where she could use his car if she needed to go incognito.'

'And you believed her? That woman could lie for Scotland. If they ever make it an Olympic sport, she'd beat Donald Trump.'

Henry scrabbled his way between the front seats, covering the handbrake and grinning up at me with his tongue hanging out. That was the trouble with Vera giving the greedy wee sod a sausage.

Muscles rippled along Franklin's jaw. 'Prentice says you're helping her write a book about Gordon Smith: "The Coffinmaker ~ hunting the world's most dangerous serial killer".'

'Hmmph.' She'd changed the title then.

The car thrummed as the ferry's engines changed tone – a loud growl you could feel in your chest.

Franklin's voice rose over it, spitting out the words as she bashed a hand off the steering wheel. 'What the hell were you thinking? We're in the middle of an investigation and you're passing info to a *journalist*?'

'Of course I'm not.'

A grating siren blared out, orange lights flashing as we bumped to a halt.

Franklin started the engine. Glared at me. 'You've got a bloody cheek, writing about a case we're still working on! You two-faced—'

'I'm not writing anything! I want sod all to do with Jennifer … *Pain-In-The-Arse* Prentice, and I told her that. But she won't take no for a bloody answer.'

'Then why did she tell me—'

'Because she's a liar!' My hands ached into tight fists. 'I told you that already. You really think I'm going to slip her information? After what she did?'

Franklin's mouth opened. Then closed again. 'What did she do?'

'None of your *sodding* business.'

The sirens got louder as a flap in the stern hinged down, a

223

fat bloke in high-viz and a hardhat directing the cars and lorries out through it into the cold grey light of the afternoon.

Two minutes later we were rattling off the ferry and up onto dry land again, in a fug of angry silence.

Rothesay curved around the water, a marina full of yachts sitting between the ferry terminal and a line of old brown brick buildings. A three-sided town square straight ahead. And more bland buildings to the right. Someone had painted the last lot in faded shades of pastel yellow, pink and blue, presumably in an effort to distract tourists from their unin-spired façades.

But in front of them sat the flat green carpet of a putting course. Three couples slowly whacking their way around it in jumpers and woolly hats.

Franklin jerked her chin at them, forcing a hint of jolly into her voice, as if that would make everything all right. 'Looks like we found our photo location.' Turned right, onto the main road. 'God's sake, is there *nowhere* to park?'

A weird end-of-the-pier-style building sat alongside the putting green – a big domed middle, fronted by a pair of red-roofed pagodas. Then another putting course on the other side. Another group of idiots out braving the wind.

I pointed. 'Pull in there.'

'It's a bus stop.'

'You're a police officer. We're hunting a serial killer!'

'It's still a bus stop.'

'I've got a blue badge. Stop the damn car.'

'Right!' She slammed on the brakes, getting an angry fusillade of horn blasts from the Transit van behind us. 'Out. You get out here and *I'll* go find somewhere to park.'

And just like that, we were back at war again.

'Fine.' I clipped on Henry's lead as the Transit launched into another barrage. 'Come on, wee man.'

He followed me out onto the road, and as soon as I'd closed the door, Franklin roared off.

God save us from unreasonable detective bloody sergeants.

Henry and I crossed over to the other side, stomping along

the pavement that skirted the putting course. Then took the tarmac path into it and did a lap of an ornamental fountain – its sprays of water jerking and twisting away in the wind. Definitely a lot colder than it'd been back home.

We followed a line of blue railings, up a long ramp, and out onto the promenade.

Had to admit, the view wasn't half bad. Green-and-grey hills, buffeted by fast-moving clouds, light and shadow moving across the concrete-coloured sea. Probably was quite something in summer.

In November, it was freezing, though.

Henry sniffed at pretty much everything we passed, widdling on half of it as we hunched our way along the waterfront. Seals bobbing in the troubled water. Herring gulls scrawking as they scudded past, sideways.

Might not be a bad place to retire, this.

'There you are.' Franklin, hands on her hips, padded jacket zipped up to her neck. She cleared her throat. 'I'm sorry. I didn't know you and this Prentice woman had a history. I didn't mean to upset you.'

Like I was a sulky toddler.

A sigh rattled out to be whipped away by the wind.

Maybe I was? Barging about, whingeing and moaning…

Yeah.

I nodded. 'Don't worry about it.'

'Good. Thank you.' Franklin stomped her feet on the tarmac. 'Now we're all friends again, can we get this over with, please? Losing all feeling in my toes here.'

Might as well.

I pulled out the photo of Peter Smith and the unidentified young woman, the paper crumpling in my hand as the wind tried to whip it from my grasp. 'Over there?'

We went back down the ramp, out onto the putting course.

According to the flag, this was hole number seventeen, looking back towards the sea and the hills beyond, a palm tree off to one side.

'Waste of time, of course.'

'What is?' Franklin dug her hands into her padded pockets, shoulders curled up around her ears.

'All … this. Pointless. We should be out there hunting Gordon Smith, not faffing about here.'

'You really are a ray of sunshine today, aren't you?' But she was smiling. 'What about the victims' families? Don't they deserve to know what happened to their loved ones?'

'Of course they do, but that's not as important as catching the scumbag who *killed* them.'

Franklin gave me a half nod, half shrug. 'Tell you what, how about I get us a couple of putters and we can play a round? Might cheer you up a bit. You can pretend it's like a go on the "wooden horsies".'

'No thanks.' I turned and hobbled across the grass, making for the road again.

'Oh come on, Ash, I'm trying to apologise here!' Hurrying after us. 'What's wrong with putting?'

'Once upon a time, there was a man called Adam Robinson. He found out his wife was having an affair with someone at her golf club, so do you know what he did?'

'Talk to her about it, like a rational grown-up?'

We'd reached the pavement. Stood there, waiting for a break in the traffic.

'He started saving up his urine.'

'OK, not so rational, then.'

A taxi drifted by and I hurpled across the road behind it, making the other side as an open-topped bus rumbled past. Kept going down a narrow street between one of the few branches Royal Bank of Scotland *hadn't* shut and a carpet shop.

'Adam collected it in two-litre bottles, you know, like Diet Coke, that kind of thing. Then once a week, he'd take the most mature samples and go up the golf course in the dead of night. Filled each and every hole, from the first to the eighteenth with his rancid piss.'

'Why on earth would he—'

'So that every time someone sunk a putt, they'd have to stick their hand in the hole to fish out their ball.'

226

Franklin's mouth opened wide, tongue sticking out, eyes creased almost shut. 'Oh… Yuck!'

We crossed another road, and entered another tiny street, passed yet another carpet shop.

'He kept that up for six months, then decided the only thing left to do was march into the clubhouse with a shotgun and blow holes in every male over the age of fifteen.'

We emerged from the tiny street into a big open space, with a moat and a partially collapsed castle in the middle of it. A saltire flag snapping and crackling in the wind above.

'Killed three people, crippled six, injured about a dozen.' I shook my head. 'Genuinely a *terrible* shot.'

'What happened?'

A gull worried away at a discarded polystyrene container, chips spilling out into the gutter.

Henry rushed at it, firing out sharp-edged barks till the lead brought him up short.

Unimpressed, the gull stared back and kept on pecking.

'Well, by the time an Armed Response Unit got there, Adam had barricaded himself in the golf pro's office, with his wife and a bottle of Glenfarclas he'd liberated from the club bar.'

'This doesn't have a happy ending, does it?'

'Hell no.' We followed the road, around the castle. 'Took the crime-scene cleaners *four days* to dig all the tiny bits of skull out of the wooden panelling. So, no: I'm not keen on a game of putting.'

A wet popping wheezing noise gurgled out of Franklin and she rubbed at her stomach. 'You still owe me that sausage butty.'

I leaned on the windowsill, rolling my right ankle in small clicking circles. That's what I got for walking all the way to Rothesay Police Station from the putting course.

Our meeting room was pretty much identical to the ones you'd find in any Police Scotland building. Someone had tried to glam it up with a series of ugly watercolours and a wilting pot plant, but it hadn't really worked.

Pulling back the vertical blinds had revealed a view out across a twenty-foot strip of flat roof and over the road to a weird boxy building in pink granite with a sign fixed to its black front door: 'CARPET SHOP BEHIND CHURCH ↗'.

What the hell was it with Rothesay and carpet shops? How much carpet did one small town need?

Henry had found himself a spot by the radiator, curled up and dead to the world, making wheezy snoring noises as we waited. And waited. And waited.

I checked my watch: twenty past two. 'I'm giving it five more minutes, then sod the lot of them.'

'Absolutely starving...' She slumped back in her chair at the empty meeting table. Stared at the ceiling. 'How long's it been?'

'Over half an hour.'

'And not so much as a biscuit.'

'Ah, now you mention it.' I dug into my jacket pocket and came out with the two pre-packaged slices of cake I'd bought on the ferry. Each about the size of a small remote control. Held them out. 'You want a cranberry-and-pistachio slice, or rocky road?'

'Yes!' She took both. Ripped open the plastic and tore a big bite out of the knobbly chocolate slice. The words all mushy as she chewed. 'So are you going to tell me what it was Jennifer Prentice did?'

'No.'

More chewing. 'She showed me a text from Nick James saying she could borrow the car whenever she liked.'

'Probably nicked his phone and sent it to herself.'

Franklin chomped on another mouthful. 'You really don't like her, do you?'

'That woman's a complete—'

The meeting room door creaked open and in marched a stiff-backed bald bloke in the full Police Scotland black. Three pips on his epaulettes and a full-bore Highlands and Islands accent that lilted higher than expected. 'I understand you're...' His face pulled in around his scrunched lips. 'Is that a *dog*? We don't allow dogs in the station.'

228

Henry stayed where he was, but Franklin stood to attention. Hiding the rocky road slice behind her back. 'Sir.'

Another uniform hurpled in after him, this one a good head shorter than his boss, his official-issue T-shirt stretched over a decent-sized beer belly. A thick brown beard covering his cheeks and chin. Saggy eyes. 'Sorry to keep you waiting...' All smiles and handshakes.

His fingers lingered over Franklin's.

She slid her hand free and wiped it on her trouser leg, soon as he wasn't looking.

The Chief Inspector stuck his nose in the air. 'Detective Sergeant Rosalind Franklin, I understand you want to search through all of our historical missing person reports?'

'Yes, sir.'

A cold fish eye swivelled in my direction. 'And *this* is?'

'Mr Henderson. He's with the Lateral Investigative and Review Unit. We're—'

'While I'm quite happy to allow *police* officers access to our records, I draw the line at civilians. And dogs.' He snapped his fingers. 'Sergeant Campbell will assist you. Sergeant Campbell, please make sure you escort Mr Henderson from the premises first.' He turned on his heel, as if it was a parade ground manoeuvre, and marched from the room, head up, shoulders back.

Prick.

Sergeant Campbell grimaced. 'Sorry about that. The Chief can be a tad ... brusque?' He placed a hand on Franklin's shoulder. 'But I'm sure *we'll* get on like the best of friends.' Rounding it off with a greasy smile.

Yeah, he was going to end up with a broken nose, like her old boss in Edinburgh.

24

'Here we go, son. You want any sauces or mustard wi' that?' The woman in the black shirt and red waistcoat – both of which were too small for her – clinked the plate down on the table in front of me. Then brushed the grey hair from her eyes and leaned in, dropping her voice to a whisper. 'And I've got the chef to do a cheeky sausage for yer dug, too.' Wink.

'Thanks. This'll be great.'

She squatted down to pet Henry. 'Who's a lovely wee boy, then? Oh, you're just pure *gorgeous*, so you are.'

Our table was next to the window, with a view out over the castle's remains, moat glinting in the golden light as the sun sank lower in the sky. More seagulls strutting about on the pavement, looking for an unsuspecting tourist to mug.

One more ruffle, then the waitress straightened up, beaming down at the lad. 'Oh, he's smashing.'

I dipped into my pocket and came out with the printout – Peter Smith and the unknown woman, standing together on the putting course. Passed it across. 'Don't suppose you recognise either of them, do you?'

'Hold on...' She produced a pair of reading glasses and perched them on the end of her nose, peering at the photograph. 'Shell suits? Before my time, son, I've only been here thirty years. I can ask the chef, though? *She's* been here since the dawn of time.'

'That would be great.'

She plucked Henry's sausage from the plate and tossed it to him. Smiling like a proud granny as the wee lad snatched it out of the air. 'Clever boy!'

Then she was off, taking the printout with her, while I dipped a chip in my tiny dish of mayonnaise and Henry scarfed his cheeky sausage.

Sitting on the tabletop, my phone dinged and buzzed.

RHONA:

> Chased up E Division – they've done posters.
> Beat cops & cars keeping an eye out.
> Maybe they'll get lucky & find Leah?
> Doubt it though.

So did I.

Bit awkward: poking out a reply one-handed, but it left the other one free to scoop up my burger with chargrilled halloumi and mushrooms. Chewing while I texted.

> Thanks Rhona. How's Shifty holding up?

SEND.

Good burger. Have to make sure and tell Franklin all about it. She'd *like* that...

> Having a late lunch with Henry: very nice food.
> Have you punched Sergeant Campbell in the face yet? Twat that he is.

SEND.

I'd barely managed another bite before the phone ding-buzzed again.

DS FRANKLIN:

> WHAT AN UTTER WASTE OF TIME!

231

They've brought every missing person file
out from storage going back to Noah's Ark.
It'll take DAYS to go through this lot!

Buzz-ding.
DS FRANKLIN:

And I'm starving. They haven't even
offered me a cup of tea, and we've been
here for ages!
Turned my back for 2 minutes and
Campbell had my other cake slice!

Yeah, he'd looked the type. Still, I'm sure I could make her feel better:

If it's any consolation, Henry's eaten that
sausage I was going to buy you. He says
it was delicious.

SEND.

Sometimes, it was the simple things in life that gave you pleasure.

I was halfway through my burger before the next text came in.

RHONA:

Chief Super's in giving Shifty a pep talk
now.
Can hear it through the wall.
Lots of shouting & swearing.
Apparently we're an incompetent bunch of
arseholes.
Kid's mother was all over the lunchtime
news saying the same thing.
Which is great when we're the ones
slogging our guts out trying to find her kid
before some sicko strangles him.

Chief Superintendent Angus McEwan, the gift that kept on giving.

As if the team didn't know how important it was to find Toby Macmillan. As if they didn't know the first twenty-four hours were the most important. As if they didn't know Toby was probably already dead. Because, let's face it, Gòrach wasn't really about the delayed gratification, was he? Well, except when it came to strangling his victims. *That* he liked to take his time over.

Crunched my way through a couple of chips.

Unless that was part of his evolving MO, of course. Andrew Brennan is a victim of opportunity: no planning involved, dumped where he was killed. Oscar Harris: abducted, killed and the body hidden. Lewis Talbot: abducted, taken deep into the woods, killed over a *long* time, then hidden so well we didn't find his body for nearly two months.

Maybe Gòrach had got himself a hideaway: somewhere he could keep a small boy for a few days? God knew there were enough abandoned buildings and shacks in the thick swathe of forest that ran from Camburn Woods to the Murders. Moncuir Wood alone was big enough to lose a small town in.

Might be worth chasing up.

> Shifty,
> Got an idea for you: get a thermal-imaging
> camera and a helicopter. Do a sweep of
> the woods. See if you can pick up Toby
> Macmillan's heat signature.

SEND.

Another bite of burger. Chewing as I stared out the window at the castle.

Wonder what Alice was up to…

Look at me: sitting here; shoving fried food into my face, one-handed; crouched over my phone like a braindead teenager. Supposed to be a grown man.

> Rhona tells me you've been puking your
> ring all day. Perhaps it's time to lay off the

booze for a while, before we have to have
an intervention?
Henry says "Hi."

Send.

You know, an intervention might not be such a bad idea. Maybe it'd help Alice live to see her thirty-third birthday.

'So *this* is where you've been hiding.'

Wonderful.

And Mother thought the universe hated *her*.

I looked up and there was Jennifer Prentice, hauling out the chair opposite and sinking into it.

Big glass of red wine in one hand. A tight smile that barely dented her frozen face. 'Wasn't hard to find you, in case you're wondering. Your pretty little detective sergeant girl said you'd both skipped lunch, so I looked for the nearest restaurant to the police station, open on a Sunday afternoon, that lets dogs in. And there you were, sitting in the window.'

I went back to my burger. 'Sod off, Jennifer.'

'She's *quite* something, isn't she? DS Franklin? Bet she'd be great in a threesome. That lovely dark skin of hers, all naked and glistening. It'd look *very* sexy next to mine, wouldn't it? Our limbs intertwined, lips and tongues exploring each other. You'd *like* that.'

And with that delightful image, the burger curdled in my mouth.

I dumped the rest of it back on the plate. 'Whatever you want, might as well bugger off right now, because you're not getting it.'

Ding-buzz.

Unknown Number:

I'm sorry

Odd...

Maybe Alice had borrowed a phone from one of Shifty's team and that's why the number wasn't recognised? That's what happened when you got too drunk to put your mobile on to charge overnight.

'Now, Ash, is that any way to talk to an old friend? One who has a proposition for you?' Jennifer's wink wasn't anywhere near as appealing as the waitress's. 'And not a sexual one this time.' She looked over her shoulder.

I followed her gaze.

Helen MacNeil was outside, standing with her arms folded, back against the railings, coat buffeted by the wind. Face like she was trying to stare down the world.

'Thank God, right? I mean, can you imagine *that* in the nude?' Jennifer faked a shudder. Then leaned forwards. Glanced left and right as if someone might be eavesdropping. 'Six *million* pounds. I checked it out: Steve Jericho's place got knocked over fifteen years ago. Hallelujah Bingo, cash-in-transit job. Official report was they made off with twenty grand, but *unofficially* Steve Jericho had got his hands on Nigel Cavendish's stash – all the stuff he'd robbed from private collections and museums, going back to the seventies.'

'Cavendish?' Why did that name sound—

'Hacked to pieces in his living room with a machete. Anyway, Helen says Billy "the Axe" Macgregor was the one who nicked Steve Jericho's stuff. No one ever found the armoured car, or its driver.' Jennifer's eyes widened. 'She says it's still in Oldcastle, and she knows *where*.'

'Did you follow me all the way here for that?' I scrubbed my hands clean on the napkin. 'Not interested.'

'Four million for her and two million for *us*.' A glistening pink tongue flickered around Jennifer's lips. 'That's *one million pounds* each, all we have to do is find Gordon Smith. And you're doing that anyway! It's a win-win.' She sat back and toasted me with her glass, before downing a mouthful.

Ding-buzz.

Unknown Number:

> I didn't want 2 let them arrest U but I had
> 2 run
> grandad doesn't like it when I talk 2
> people

Wait a minute.

Wait a bloody sodding minute.

Ding-buzz.

Unknown Number:

> We go 2 the Xmas market every year as a
> treat but U was shouting at me & the
> police was there & if they cot us he would
> B V angry
> I don't want 2 make him angry

I scraped my chair back, grabbed the phone and stuffed it into my pocket. 'I'm not going to do *anything* with you, Jennifer. Not now. Not ever.' Gave her a smile as I hauled on my jacket. 'And Helen offered me two million, so why the hell would I need you?' Picked up my walking stick and Henry's lead. Nodded at the half-eaten burger and chips. 'You can finish that if you like.'

Dumped fifteen quid on the bar on the way past, and limped into the windy sunshine.

Fiddled my phone out again and hit the call icon at the top of the two unknown text messages. It rang twice, then disconnected.

Ding-buzz.

Unknown Number:

> U can't call me!!!!!!!! Grandad doesn't no I
> have this phone! He can't find out!!!!! If
> he finds out it'll upset him & he'll be angry
> with me!!!!!!!

Holy shit. It *was* her.

> Leah, tell me where you are and we'll
> come get you. You don't have to be
> scared, we can fix this if you tell me
> where you are.

Send.

Ding-buzz.

UNKNOWN NUMBER:

> I don't no where we R! I'm frightened!!!
> He's bin there all my live & I love him but
> he scares me so much
> He's coming back I have 2 go!!!

Right, there was only one thing for it.

> Leah, I need you to keep your phone
> switched on for me, so we can trace your
> location. Turn the volume and the vibrate
> setting off, and leave the phone switched
> on.
> We'll find you, I promise!

SEND.

Soon as it went, I called Mother.

'DI Malcolmson?'

'It's Ash. Remember...'

Helen MacNeil was staring at me.

By rights, I should go over there and tell her.

Tell her what? That her granddaughter isn't safe and laying low in Edinburgh after all? That she's been grabbed by Gordon Smith, and can't get away because she's terrified of him? That we had no idea where she was now? How *exactly* was that going to help?

Yeah. Maybe not.

I gave Helen a small wave instead and limped off down the High Street, towards the ferry terminal.

'Ash? Remember what?'

Keeping my voice low, in case Helen decided to follow. 'You *really* need to get that warrant out for Leah MacNeil's mobile phone. She's been in touch: Leah's with Gordon Smith.' I ducked around the corner – sheltering in the lee of an off-licence – out of the wind and Helen's line of sight. 'You still there?'

'*Ash, I hate to be a cynical Charlotte, but some might think this was a bit convenient, given your—*'

'Fine: I'll forward you the texts. Hold on.' I did, sending my

237

replies on too. 'She's with him and she's scared. If you get a warrant, we get *her*. And if we get her...?'

'*We get him.*' The sound went all scrunched, as if Mother had put a hand over her phone's microphone. '*John, whatever you're doing, stop it and get a warrant for Leah MacNeil's mobile phone location!*'

DC Watt's reply was too muffled to make out. Probably whingeing, knowing him.

And Mother was back. '*Any luck IDing the Bute victim?*'

'Had to leave that to Franklin and a sergeant. The local Chief Inspector doesn't think civilians should have access to missing person archives. Doesn't allow dogs in his station, either.'

'*He sounds lovely.*'

'Nothing's been digitised. It's going to take them a *long* time to wade through everything. And the last ferry back to the mainland's at seven.'

'*Hold on...*'

'Anything from Dotty and Elliot?'

Silence.

A couple of Russian tourists trundled their wheelie suitcases past, arguing about something.

A taxi stopped to let an old man, bent like a question mark, hobble into the off-licence behind me. Techno music vibrating out through the car windows.

'I'm sorry if I'm boring you, but—'

'*There's another ferry. If you go up to ... Rhubodach? Am I saying that right? Last one from there sails at nine. Think Rosalind could be finished by then?*'

'No idea. Maybe?'

'*Let me know if not and we'll get a B-and-B sorted. And keep all your receipts!*' With that, she hung up.

Henry thumped down at my feet, staring up at me as if I was the divine provider of sausages.

'Better hope she gets us somewhere that takes greedy hairy monsters, or you're sleeping in the car tonight.'

That didn't seem to dent his enthusiasm any, instead his tail wagged even harder.

'Scuse me?' It was the waitress from the restaurant, arms wrapped around herself, grey hair flailing in the wind.

'I put the money on the counter.'

'Oh, I know, thanks. No, you left *this* behind.' Holding out the printout of Peter Smith and the young woman. 'I asked Elsie, but she doesn't recognise either of them, so I showed it round all the staff and customers.' Her mouth made a creased zigzag. 'Sorry. Maybe someone else knows who they are though?' She pointed across the square, at a narrow street between a jewellery shop and a red-painted bar with a couple of Tennent's 'T's hanging outside. 'You could try the Black Bull? The library's got a book group, meets there on Sunday evenings: seven for half seven. Mostly gossipy auld wifies and nosy auld mannies, but that's maybe what you're after, son?'

Worth a go.

Till then, probably better make myself useful.

25

Thick, muggy air followed me out into the cold and wind. Lingering for a second as the pub door shut behind me, before the wind snatched it away.

Streetlights gleamed against the raven darkness, illuminating the curling seafront, headlights sweeping their way along the road as the occasional figure hurried somewhere warmer.

Henry cocked his leg against a downpipe, then we headed off along the pavement, following the map on my phone to the next location. Past shuttered cafés and antique shops.

The scent of hot fat and sharp vinegar drifted after us – the siren call of an empty chippy – as my phone launched into its default ringtone, the words, 'DS FRANKLIN' replacing the map.

'Hello?'

'This is an absolute nightmare. There's a huge stack of boxes left, and we've only got as far as 1970!'

'You're having fun then?'

She sounded muffled and distant, as if she had the phone on the table and her head in her hands. *'Only upside is Sergeant Campbell clocked off at five, on the dot, so I don't have to put up with his sleazy gitbaggery any more.'*

'Mother wants to know if you'll be done in time for us to catch the nine o'clock ferry from Rhubodach.'

'Nine tonight? Not a chance in hell.'

Bed-and-breakfast in sunny Rothesay for us, then.

'I'm going to be stuck here for hours.' A groan rumbled down the phone. 'And while I'm slogging my way through three tons of missing person reports, what are you—'

'Pub crawl. Well, technically it's a "pub limp", but you get the picture.'

Franklin's voice got a *lot* louder. 'Oh for God's—'

'Teetotal, remember? Pills. I'm showing that photo of Peter Smith and the girl to anyone old enough to remember shell suits being a thing. Every bar and hotel I can find. And failing that, there's a book club meets in one of the bars at half seven. Meant to be full of oldies.'

'Worth a try, I suppose.'

Henry and I kept going.

'You were right in the first place: when we were on the putting course. This is a complete waste of time.'

'Yup.' I paused outside a little place advertising Karaoke and Tennent's Lager. The muffled sound of someone slaughtering a country-and-western tune oozed out through the pub windows, rising to a horrible blare as the door banged open and a couple of middle-aged women scurried out in a fit of the shrieking giggles. They huddled in the lee of a parked Transit van and lit a couple of cigarettes, eyeing me as they smoked – like I was a piece of meat, found at the back of the fridge, with a dodgy sell-by date.

'You know what we should've done? We should've gone back to HMP Edinburgh and shoved that photo in Peter Smith's face. Demanded to know who she was.'

'Yeah. But he'd just sit there and deny everything, wouldn't he? All we'd achieve is giving him something else to wank about after lights out.'

'Thanks for that image.'

'Give me a shout when you're ready to pack it in for the night.' I put the phone away and pushed through into yet another noisy crowded bar.

It would've been classified as a 'light drizzle', if it hadn't been jabbed in like needles on a howling wind, as Henry and I

241

struggled our way back along Argyle Street. The warmth of tea and a Jaffa Cake at the Robertson Hotel a swiftly fading memory.

Which meant we'd tried every hotel on the seafront, every bed-and-breakfast, and every bar. Except one.

The gale slammed itself against my chest, stabbing its needles deeper into my face, making the streetlights sway in the darkness. Misty shadows dancing around them. Henry more out for a drag than a walk, whimpering on the end of his leash like a petulant wee hairy anchor.

Past old stone buildings with bay windows, their lights on, showing off warm domestic scenes as the sensible people stayed inside, out of the horrible night. Jammy bastards.

On the other side of the road, waves smashed themselves against the seawall, white spray curling over the metal railings to spatter down against the pavement.

Should've made Franklin hand over the keys to the pool car, sore foot or not. Couldn't hurt more than it did right now, anyway. It was as if someone was taking a cordless drill to the bloody thing, screeching hole after ragged hole into the bones every time my right foot hit the paving slabs. If I'd been driving, it'd still hurt, but at least I'd be dry.

I dug the hand with Henry's lead deeper into my pocket, the one clutching my walking stick aching and numb all at the same time.

So much for retiring to sunny Rothesay. They could—

Oh, for God's sake.

My phone, doing its basic ringtone again.

I limped across the road, into a car park outside what looked like a cross between an art deco swimming pool and a car showroom, all concrete and glass, lights blazing in its windows, kept going till I was under the overhanging portico and out of the wind and rain. Hauled out my mobile and stabbed the button. 'What?'

The sound of a band rehearsing boomed out from the floor above.

'Not the friendliest of welcomes I've had, Ash.' Mother. *'I was*

calling to say I've got you and Rosalind rooms at the Hotel Sokoloff, but maybe you'd rather sleep in the car instead?'

'It's blowing a gale, I'm cold, I'm soaked through, and my foot's killing me because I've been hobbling all over Rothesay for the last four and a half hours, trying to ID your murder victim!' Adding an extra scoop of sarcasm to my voice. 'So *excuse me* if I'm not in the most sociable of bloody moods.'

The band launched into a grating cover of an old Foo Fighters song, even though the drummer *really* wasn't up to it.

They'd staggered their way to the chorus before Mother came back on the line. *'And has your sore foot discovered anything?'*

'Yes. That it hates sodding about in the buggering wind and rain.' I leaned back against the steel pillar holding up the concrete portico. Huffed out a breath. 'No one knows who she is. Got one place left to try.'

'Dotty and Amanda have IDed our graduating student. According to Aberdeen University, he's Alex Yates. Got a two-one in Law, 1978. Parents reported him missing three days after the ceremony.'

'Anyone told them yet?'

'The Chief Super still doesn't want any of this getting out till we've got Gordon Smith in custody. And before you say anything: no, I don't think it's fair either.' Mother's voice sagged. *'Dotty couldn't get an ID for the girl on the horse in Fochabers, or the young man in the Inverness beer garden. And we're* still *no nearer to laying our hands on Smith.'*

Thirty / forty years was a long time. People moved away. They died.

'Then we've got no choice: hit the media with Gordon Smith's "before" Polaroids. Someone has to know who they are.'

Upstairs, the half-arsed rendition of 'All My Life' sputtered to a halt. Then started again from the beginning. And the drummer was still terrible.

'Chief Superintendent McEwan won't like that.'

'Tough. You're thinking of retiring anyway: cruises, golf, gardening, and grandchildren, remember?'

'Don't you start. Get enough of that from my Jack.'

Henry whined on the end of his leash, wee sides shivering, tail between his legs, fur all slicked down and dripping.

'And I thought your IT guru was supposed to get us IDs: what happened to those eight hours I paid him for?'

Good question.

The Black Bull's monochrome frontage was sandwiched between an angling shop and a café, its olde-worlde mock-Dickensian windows looking out over the marina to the ferry terminal. As Henry and I limped over the threshold, a wall of warm air wrapped its welcoming arms around us, bringing with it the sound of laughter.

Busy in here.

Henry and I worked our way through the crowd to the small bar, where a young woman with far too many piercings and a lopsided haircut was pulling pints of Belhaven. 'What can I get you, love?' As if she was a Glasgow granny.

'Looking for the book club.'

She pointed off to her left, through a narrow passageway. 'Down there, take a right. Drink?'

'Pot of tea. Decaf, if you've got it?' Talk about painting the town beige…

'Aye, I'll get someone to take it through to you.'

I handed over the cash and then Henry and I squeezed through the gap at the end of the bar; past another, longer bar; and turned right, into a large-ish nook, with a tartan-carpeted floor, red bench seating, and a bunch of old folks – most of them women – sitting around seven wooden tables. The eighth was empty, so we commandeered it: me collapsing into the padded seating, Henry collapsing under the table. The pair of us looking as if we'd swum here.

Everyone else had a paperback in front of them: black cover, moody shot of a crumbly warehouse, author's name in big yellow lettering. That would be a crime novel, then.

I stretched my right leg out, teeth gritted as the ankle moaned and clicked and complained at the top of its voice.

A large woman, going bald on top, leaned over from the next table. 'You're new, aren't you?'

'Actually, I'm not—'

'Here you go.' A wee tray with a small metal pot of tea, mug, bowl of sugar sachets, and a thing of milk clicked down in front of me. Packet of shortbread on the side. Then the spotty youth who'd delivered it turned and hurried from the room before anyone could order anything from him.

She leaned in again. 'Where were we? Yes, so, you're new and—'

'All right, everyone, we all here?' A smiling woman in a floaty grey top, body warmer, and council lanyard stood at the head of the room, holding the book in her hand. Blonde hair with a half-inch of grey roots on show. 'Welcome, everyone, to the Rothesay Library Criminally Good Book Club! Who'd like to start?'

A flurry of hands.

'Maureen?'

The woman next to me lowered her hand. 'I don't understand why it had to be so *gory*! I mean, a man who collects dead animals in a steading, it's horrible.'

Someone else nodded. 'It was offensive, if you ask me. Sickeningly, cynically, offensive.'

I unwrapped the two tiny shortbread biscuits and fed one to Henry under the table.

'What about the characters? Anyone?'

'Yes.' Another woman, this one done up in a trouser suit with lacquered hair. 'That *lesbian* police officer. She was so revolting! Always talking and swearing and scratching and digging at her underwear. I didn't like her at all: she *ruined* the whole book.'

Someone else nodded. 'Not that there's anything wrong with female lesbians in crime fiction.'

'Well, of course not, but there *is* when it's nothing but an excuse for blasphemy and crude so-called "humour".'

I poured my tea.

'Can we please have a proper crime novel, next time? Like one of those nice Ann Cleeves ones.'

'Oh, yes, I *do* like her books. She was lovely when she came to the crime-writing festival, too.'

And on, and on, and on they went, as I drank my decaf tea and finished the remaining biscuit.

Soon as I was done, I dug out the printout and levered myself to my foot – keeping the right one off the tartan carpet, so it wouldn't sting so much. 'Speaking of murder investigations,' I flashed my expired warrant card at them, 'do any of you recognise the people in this picture?'

The woman with the lacquered hair pursed her lips and glared at me, clearly not happy at being interrupted mid-rant about how terrible it was that anyone could enjoy a book where children got murdered.

Tough.

Welcome to the real world.

I passed the picture to Maureen. 'Take your time, this would have been in the 1980s.' Gave the rest of the room a bit of serious eye contact. 'Anyone remember a young woman going missing back then?'

The librarian fiddled with her lanyard. 'My cousin ran off with an American tourist. And there was Sheila Fraser – everyone thought her dad did her in and got rid of the body. Or Effie Parsons?'

One of the auld mannies shook his head, setting his combover bouncing. 'Naw, that was in the seventies – having an affair with that Glaswegian artist bloke who used to come here and paint nudie women all the time.'

'Sorry, never seen her before.' Maureen handed the printout to the next table.

They all huddled over it, muttering away to each other.

'All right, not Effie Parsons then.' The librarian creased up her forehead. 'What about Georgina Kerr? The police searched every house, bothy, shed, and outbuilding on the island, looking for her.'

The picture had nearly made it all the way around the book club.

Still, it'd been worth a try.

My phone ding-buzzed, deep in my damp pocket. When I pulled it out the screen was misted up. Had to wipe the condensation off with my shirt.

UNKNOWN NUMBER:

> I have 2 hide my phone! If he finds it I
> don't no what he'll do
> Please save me!!! I want 2 go home!!!

Damn.

I nodded at the book club. 'Excuse me a minute.'

Slipped from the tartan nook, then out the back door. Into that narrow street that the waitress from lunch had pointed to. Into the drizzle too.

Quick hobble across the road, to shelter in a shop doorway. Somewhere nice and secluded to poke out a reply.

> Leave your phone on, Leah – we need to
> latch onto the mobile signal so we can find
> out where you are and come get you.
> Be brave!

SEND.

Ding-buzz.

UNKNOWN NUMBER:

> I'll try!!! But don't no how much charge
> I've got left

Time to give Mother a kick up the backside.

She answered on the third ring. *'Ash? Have you—'*

'What's happening with that warrant?'

'Were you always this rude, because—'

'Leah's been in touch again: she's going to leave her phone on so we can trace it. Now where's that warrant?'

'John's trying to serve it now.' Mother sounded as if she was deflating. *'Of course, at this time on a Sunday evening, chances are her mobile provider won't be—'*

'You've got till Leah's phone runs out of battery to *find* her. Gordon Smith's not going to let her recharge the damn thing – we've got one chance and that's it!'

'I know, I know... We're pushing as hard as we can, Ash, we really are.'

'Then push *harder*.' I hung up. Stuffed the phone back in my pocket. Slumped against the shop's doors, staring up at the black wooden ceiling.

Smith hadn't hurt Leah yet, but that couldn't last. It wasn't as if he'd had any qualms butchering her mum, and he'd been like a grandfather to *her* too.

'*Erm, excuse me?*' Woman's voice.

When I looked down, there was one of the Rothesay Library crime book club's members. One who'd sat quietly through most of it, nursing a large glass of white wine.

'Sorry. Erm, hi, I'm Aileen. Aileen McCaskill?' She tried on a pained smile. Her wrinkled waterproof and creased forehead made it look as if she'd shrunk into herself over the years, thin jowly neck protruding from the cowl of a thick orange jumper like a turtle. Watery blue eyes blinking up at me in the gloom of the shop doorway. 'Told everyone I was off for a cigarette.' She pulled out a pack, fingers covering the graphic warning image as she opened the top and offered me one.

'Thanks, but I don't.'

'Quite right too. Filthy habit.' But she lit one anyway, sucking on it with her eyes closed, setting the tip glowing a hot orange. Then letting out a lungful of smoke in a juddery breath. Another couple of puffs. 'I…' She cleared her throat. Looked away, down the street, towards the square. 'That woman in the picture. With the man? I think it might be my sister.'

She huffed out a breath, smoke-free this time. 'Linda was … could be difficult. Oh God, could she ever.' Aileen bit her lips together. Shook her head. Stubbed her cigarette out, even though she'd barely touched it. 'Drinking, boys, staying out late, failing all her O levels. Broke…' Deep breath. 'Broke my mum's heart when Linda left: up and walked out one morning, didn't even say goodbye. At least, that's what we *thought*.' Aileen dug into her waterproof and produced a tatty leather wallet. Clutching it in trembling fingers. 'Was my dad's.' She flipped the thing open and held it up to the greasy streetlight, revealing a faded photograph of two teenaged girls: one in pastel-green trousers; the other, pastel yellow; matching baggy grey-and-blue

248

jumpers with the popped collars of their shirts sticking out the neckholes. Big hair.

When I looked up from the photo, Aileen was staring at me, her eyes a lot waterier than before, a lot more needy, the tip of her nose pinkening.

She pointed at the girl in green trousers. 'That's Linda. You see?' She reached out and took hold of my sleeve. 'It's *her*, isn't it? The girl in your photo, with the ugly man in the shell suit? It's my sister...'

Had to admit, it looked a *lot* like the woman in the photo with a young Peter Smith.

'When did she go missing?'

'June twelfth, 1985. It was my seventeenth birthday...' A small, sour laugh. 'Always thought she'd picked the date just to spite me. It's not my fault I was a year older, is it? That I got new stuff and she had to make do with my hand-me-downs. God, how she *hated* that.' Aileen let go of my arm and wiped the tears from her cheeks. 'But she ... she didn't, did she?' The words coming quicker and quicker. 'She didn't run away. If she'd run away, you wouldn't be here, showing her photo round. It was him, wasn't it? The man in the picture *did* something to her.'

Something horrible.

If it was her.

The date was about right, going by the clothes and the haircuts. And the resemblance to the young woman in the photo was undeniable. But without a body or any forensic evidence to compare? With nothing but two stills taken from mobile phone footage in a darkened basement? Impossible to know for sure.

Aileen stared up at me, her father's wallet clutched to her chest, bottom lip wobbling as her eyes filled up again.

What was better: false hope, or certainty and closure?

That whole year when I'd thought Rebecca had run away from home, when in reality she was already long dead. Hoping she'd walk in the door one day as if nothing had ever happened. Then that first homemade birthday card landed on the doormat and I found out what had really happened to my little girl.

But Aileen deserved the truth, didn't she? No matter how much it hurt.

I nodded. 'I'm sorry.'

Her mouth opened wide, the bottom lip curled in over her teeth as dark pink flushed her cheeks, eyes screwed tightly shut. The silent scream made her knees bend and her hands curl into claws. Then a painful breath howled into her lungs and roared out in a jagged wail.

So I opened my arms, wrapped Aileen in a hug and held her as she sobbed.

Because Helen MacNeil was right: I knew how it felt.

26

I closed the taxi door and Aileen blinked up at me from the back seat, face all puffy and streaked with mascara. Then turned to face front as the old Ford puttered away down the narrow lane, took a right at the junction, and disappeared.

Jesus.

I sagged back against the empty shop doorway, pulled out my phone, and called Franklin.

'For God's sake, what now? *I'm going as fast as I can, but there's three tonnes of—'*

'Our girl's Linda McCaskill: sixteen, went missing twelfth of June, 1985.'

Silence from the other end.

Then, *'How did you—'*

'Old-fashioned legwork. See if there's a misper report.'

More silence.

'McCaskill, McCaskill, McCaskill... Here we go. Linda McCaskill.' Some rustling, then a groan. *'If it isn't her, it looks a* hell *of a lot like her. But without a body?'*

'Yup.' I checked my watch. 'Five past eight. We got time to finish up and make the last ferry at nine?'

'You are *kidding, aren't you? Have you forgotten how much paper-work it takes to turn a missing person into a murder victim? Be lucky if I'm out of here before midnight!'*

True.

'Then wrap it up; you can finish in the morning.'

'*But*—'

'We'll have to spend the night in Rothesay anyway, so there's no point busting your hump. Might as well grab dinner.'

But you know whose hump *was* worth busting?

Sabir's.

Soon as I'd hung up, I gave the useless wee sod a call.

The sound of explosions and machineguns rattled in the background. '*This better be important, like, I'm savin' the werld from Nazi zombies, here.*'

'Where are my IDs?'

'*Hello, Sabir. How are you, Sabir. You're my favourite, you are, Sabir.*'

'Oh, sorry, let me try that again. Hello, Sabir, where – are – my – sodding – IDs – you – lazy – tosser?'

'*A guy could go off you.*' The sounds of war came to an abrupt halt. '*I've got web crawlers going through every Friends Reunited and LinkedIn profile on the net. Every missing persons' database too, including a few I'm not meant to have access to an' all. Cough, cough, GCHQ, cough, cough.*' A slurping noise. '*See, your trouble is you know bugger all about information technology. You watch one episode of* Dr Who *and think you're an expert, but I can't search for stuff that's never seen a computer in its puff!*'

'I thought you were meant to be—'

'*You wanna better result? Try looking for people who didn't fall off the globe thirty years ago, you utter divvy! I'm doing me best here.*'

Yeah...

'Fair enough.' I limped across the road again to the Black Bull's back door. 'Do me a favour, though?'

'*What, another one?*'

'DS Watt's got a warrant for locating Leah MacNeil's mobile phone. He's an idiot.'

'*And you think calling us a "lazy tosser" is going to make me want to help youse?*'

I leaned my walking stick against the pub wall, closed my eyes, pinched the bridge of my nose with my free hand, and did my best not to swear. 'I'm sorry, Sabir. You're a tech guru, and DS Watt's an idiot, and I want to find Leah MacNeil before Gordon Smith tortures her to death.'

'Bleedin' heck: you and the melodrama.' A wet raspberry noise. *'Hold on.'* The phone scrunched and squealed for a minute. Then Sabir was back. *'Right, let's see what's on the system…'* Keys rattled. *'OK. … Jesus, your lad Watt's spellin's appalling.'* More keys. *'He's got it set up all wrong too. Give us a minute…'*

I ducked back into the warmth, retrieved Henry and the printout, gave the lacquer-haired harridan a big smile, then headed outside again. 'Any idea where she is?'

'Can you shut yer gob for two minutes and let us werk?'

Fair enough.

We limped out of the lane and into the square, wind shoving against my spine, drizzle stabbing the nape of my neck. Past a tiny, closed, windowless newsagent's with a big advert for Tunnock's on one side of the door and a sandwich board screwed to the wall on the other: 'HAS OLDCASTLE CHILD-STRANGLER STRUCK AGAIN?'

Knowing our luck? Definitely.

Across the square and down a cobbled road lined with wee shops, two banks, a huge Ladbrokes, cafés, and chemists. The only thing open was a small pub, the sound of a singalong in full-throated roar as we went by, bringing with it the funky scent of spilled beer and crowded bodies.

And nothing from Sabir's end yet, but the clatter of oversized fingers on a noisy keyboard.

We'd made it as far as the Co-op on Bridge Street, cutting across the car park to the relative safety of the overhang above the main doors, before he was back.

'You still there?'

'Where else am I going to be?'

Henry got tied up outside, and I hobbled in, grabbing a basket on the way past.

'One, you're entirely correct: DC Watt is an idiot, and I am a tech guru. Two: I've fixed it so it werks now – muppet didn't understand a mobile's IMEI number and its phone number aren't interchangeable. Three: I've been through the data they've got.'

'And?' Limping along the aisles to the one with face creams, shampoos, medicines, and various toiletries.

'*Got her phone being handed off between cell towers heading north up the M9 between Linlithgow and Junction Nine. Then it goes dark about three and a half miles south of Stirling. Either she's switched it off, or it's outta battery, like.*'

Two cheap toothbrushes went in the basket along with a couple of bottom-of-the-range toothpastes. 'Address?'

'*It's the Stirling Services: they've gorra food court, tourist info centre, petrol station, and a Travelodge. So unless your Leah's stopped for a touch of the early-evening budget-hotel delight, followed by a romantic Berger King, I don't think so.*'

'Sod it.' Down the aisles again, looking for the pet food.

'*Till she terns it on again, the system can't find her. You want us to set up an alert, if she does? Straight to yer phone, like.*'

'Thanks, Sabir.'

'*Now, if ye'll excuse us, I've got a werld to save.*' And he was gone.

Franklin wriggled out of her soaking jacket and collapsed into the chair opposite mine, mouth pulled into a grimace. 'Bloody hell...' Plucked a napkin from the table and scrubbed the water from her face. 'Absolutely *starving*.'

'Hold on a minute...' I finished adding Leah's mobile to my contacts, picking a different text-alert sound and ringtone so it'd be obvious when she tried to get in touch. Then pushed the bottle I'd ordered across the table to Franklin, flecks of condensation beading on the glass. 'Got you a Cobra.'

The Chinese restaurant was tucked down a side street, within view of the putting course and seafront beyond. Warm in here, even as rain drummed against the steamed-up window, the air rich with five spice and sesame oil.

Franklin leaned over to one side and peered under the table. 'Where's Henry?'

'Back at the hotel, tucking into a tin of own-brand meaty chunks in gravy and filling the room with wet-dog stench.' I called up the map on my phone and placed it on the table between us. 'According to Leah's mobile provider, Gordon Smith is heading north.'

Franklin frowned at it. 'Going back to his brother's farm on the Black Isle?'

'That's Mother's guess.'

She picked up the menu and frowned at that instead. 'He'd be an idiot, though. Surely he knows we'd be waiting for him?'

'And you don't get away with killing people for fifty-six years by being an idiot.'

'Szechuan ribs, crispy seaweed, Kung Pao chicken, egg fried rice.' Franklin turned and waved at the waitress. 'You want to split a thing of noodles?'

'I'm getting some anyway; we can share, if you like.' I wheeched a couple of fingers across the phone's screen, scrolling up the A9, past Perth and on to Inverness. 'He knows we're after him, but he *doesn't* know we can track Leah's phone… Assuming she switches it on again.'

The waitress wandered over and Franklin ordered, then thrust the menu at me.

'Can I have the spring rolls, salt-and-pepper king prawns, and … mushroom chow mein?'

'Oh, and a thing of prawn crackers!'

Soon as the waitress was gone, I zoomed out the map. 'There's a lot of Scotland you can get to from Stirling.'

'Yes, but most of it's easier from the M90. If you're heading north from Edinburgh, why not go straight up to Perth? Why the detour?'

Good question.

One thing sprung to mind: 'Think he's got property there?'

'Not according to the Land Registry. The place in Clachmara was it.'

'What about his brother, or his wife?'

Franklin raised an eyebrow. 'Now *that's* worth chasing up.' She looked up as the waitress returned with a heaped bowl of prawn crackers. Had to be enough there for at least six people. 'Perfect, thanks.' Franklin scooped up three or four of the curled white discs and stuffed them into her mouth, one after the other. Eyes closed. Making happy humming noises as she crunched.

I bit the edge off one – still hot from the deep fat. 'Unless Smith's going the long way round on purpose? Tootling along in his ugly old Mercedes, staying off the main road so we don't catch him on the ANPR cameras. Thinks he can sneak up to the Black Isle without anyone noticing.'

She stuffed in another prawn cracker. 'He'd still have to be an idiot.'

The map on my phone shifted under a grease-free finger till the Black Isle filled the screen. That knobbly peninsula, just across the water from Inverness. Not really big enough to lose yourself in, if you didn't want to be found. Assuming anyone was looking, of course.

'Highlands and Islands *have* got the farm staked out, don't they?'

Franklin paused, cracker half-in half-out of her mouth. 'Yeah. Bound to.' But she didn't sound convinced.

Still… Wouldn't hurt to check tomorrow: make sure someone *was* actually watching the place. But at least that was N Division's problem, not mine.

'OK,' I pocketed my phone again, 'so we hit Stirling tomorrow. How long do you need to finish up here?'

'Could probably palm most of it off on sleazy Sergeant Campbell. I've got all the important bits done anyway. Even *he* couldn't cock up the rest.'

'Good. If we get the nine o'clock ferry, we can be in Stirling by eleven-ish?'

'Doable.' She rubbed her hands together as the starters arrived, diving straight into the ribs. And that was it as far as sensible conversation was concerned.

Too busy eating.

'So, is your room nice?' Alice, doing her best to sound upbeat and cheery, and not getting anywhere close.

'You'd love it. Great view out over the sea and all the mountains in the background.' Or at least there probably was, if you had a room at the front of the Hotel Sokoloff. I cleared a port-hole in the steamed-up window, looking out over a car park and a building site. A nearly-full skip overflowing in the rain.

'*How's Henry?*'

The wee lad was curled up at the foot of the bed, making snuffling snores, paws twitching as he dreamed. His dirty-grey wet-dog stench filled every corner of the room, like a coat of horrible paint.

'You asked me that already, remember?'

'*Yes. Right.*' A heavy breath.

'Is everything OK?' I pulled the curtains shut and sat down on the bed. 'You sound all … squirrely.'

'*You didn't see the Sunday papers? The tabloids found out that Gòrach garrottes his victims, so now they're calling him the "Oldcastle Child-Strangler" and it's all over the front pages and everyone on the team's looking at me as if it's my fault we can't catch him and—*'

'It's not your fault!'

'*Bear says we have to interview all the sex offenders again, but that won't help, I mean, the profile clearly shows that Gòrach hasn't been in trouble with the law before, or if he has it's been for petty things like shoplifting or setting fire to the bins outside a takeaway or something minor like that, but he's not going to be on the Sex Offenders' Register, because this, what he's doing, it's been a journey for him trying to work out what his sexuality really is and how it works, and Bear's going in the wrong direction and Toby Macmillan is going to turn up dead and strangled and it'll all be my fault for not catching Gòrach and everyone will hate me and I'm horrible and useless at my job and why aren't you here to help?*'

Never ceased to amaze that she could do all of that in what sounded like one breath.

'I can't always be there, Alice. I wish I could be, but I can't.'

Just like I wasn't there for Rebecca. Or Katie…

The duvet *whoomphed* beneath me as I slumped onto it, lying flat on my back, one hand covering my face. 'And it's not all on you, OK? Jacobson's the one in charge, if everything goes tits-up it's *his* fault, not yours. Do what you can.'

'*Urgh…*'

'So the question is: what *are* you going to do?'

She made a noise like a deflating beach ball. *'I don't know. I want to rework the profile, but I genuinely can't face anything stronger than Lucozade and Irn-Bru. Everything else bounces.'*

'So try doing it sober for a change. To hell with what Henry Forrester said, you're not his minion any more, you're a highly respected forensic psychologist who's caught dozens of sick bastards and saved countless lives.'

'Then why do I still feel like a total—'

'Beating yourself up isn't helping, OK?'

Silence.

Henry stirred at the foot of the bed, let out a huge pink yawn, then curled up and went back to snoring again.

'Alice?'

'You were right: what you said to Bear. I really won't *work without you. Going by the way I'm stumbling about, achieving sod all, I'm starting to think I* can't. *Come back to Oldcastle. Please!'*

'You don't need me to function, Alice, and you don't need Henry Bloody Forrester. It's time to drag your arse out from his shadow, stand on your own two little red trainers, and do it *your* way.'

She let out a long rusty whine. Then, *'You're right, you're right.'*

'Of course I am.'

Twice in one day.

First time for everything.

— should auld acquaintance be forgot —

27

'…*unprecedented scenes in Holyrood as naked protestors stormed the Debating Chamber on Sunday*…'

I hauled on my left sock, then worked the right one over the puckered circle of scar tissue that marked the middle of my right foot. Smiling as the room's TV screen filled with bare-arsed people – all of whom had anti-government slogans scrawled across their chests and backs, while someone at the BBC blurred out all their naughty bits.

'…*amongst growing calls for the Justice Secretary, Mark Stalker, to resign in light of allegations he*…'

Shoes next. Then shirt. Tucking it into my trousers as the photo of a small boy appeared on the screen: blond curly hair, blue eyes, chubby cheeks, cheeky smile as he mugged for the camera, clutching a guinea pig.

'*Fears are growing for missing five-year-old, Toby Macmillan, as police teams search woodland in Oldcastle. We go live, now, to Hugh Brimmond at the scene. Hugh?*'

Toby and his guinea pig disappeared, replaced by a shot of a parking area in what was probably Moncuir Wood. Headlights pierced the darkness: a couple of patrol cars blocked the road, with two police Transit vans and a trio of minibuses sitting behind a cordon of blue-and-white tape. SOC-suited figures milling about, like pale grey ghosts in the middle distance, waiting for the sun to rise so they could get started.

The camera panned around until the standard BBC roving reporter was onscreen, hunched up in a padded jacket, breath clouding in the camera lights. *'Thank you, Siobhan. Tragedy shrouds the deep dark woods here in Oldcastle...'*

My phone buzzed on the bedside table, turning on the varnished wood, then the opening guitar chugs of 'Eye of the Tiger' burst out of the speaker. That would be Shifty, then.

I grabbed the remote and muted the TV as Hugh from the BBC launched into some bollocks about symbolism and fairy tales and children going missing in the woods.

'Shifty?'

'I swear to God, I'm going kill someone before this morning's out.'

'Going well, then.'

'Is it buggery. I put in a request for a helicopter and thermal-imaging camera, you know what they said? They said, "Sod off, Oldcastle, we've only got one helicopter and Strathclyde needs it." How the hell am I supposed to find Toby Macmillan if they don't give me the right kit?'

I settled on the edge of the bed and ruffled Henry's furry head. 'If it's any consolation, you're on telly right now.' After all, one of those small figures in the white suits was probably him.

'You hear that?' There was a moment's silence, then what sounded like the far-off pounding *whirrrrrrrrr* of someone trying to beat partially-set concrete with an electric whisk. *'Sky News have got a bloody helicopter. The BBC have got a bloody helicopter. Everyone's got a bloody helicopter except the poor sod who actually needs one: me!'*

'Well ... what about drones, then? Surely someone at the university's got a few they can lend you. Part of a research project or something?'

'If this was America, I could shove my badge in the pilot's face and say, "I'm commandeering this helicopter!" And if he said no, I could shoot the bastard.'

'No luck with your sex offenders, then?'

'Why does everything have – to – be – so – bloody – hard? Why can't I get an easy case for a change?'

I stood and pulled on my jacket. 'If it makes you feel any better, I'm heading down for a massive hotel-breakfast fry-up.'

'No, it doesn't. And we've been through every nonce, stott, and greasy bastard in Oldcastle already. Twice.'

'Then stop being a dick and go talk to Alice. She thinks this guy's not on the Sex Offenders' Register, because he's never done anything like this before. He's learning as he goes.'

'Aaaaargh... How's that supposed to help me? Instead of a finite pool of known kiddie fiddlers, I've got to interview every tosser in the whole place? This isn't... God's sake, what now?'

It went quiet for a bit, some muffled conversation barely audible in the background.

On the screen, Hugh the roving reporter marched across the car park, to the cordon. Where Chief Superintendent McEwan and his sidekick, Inspector Samson, were standing, in full dress uniform, with clipboards out and chins up. Soon as the other news crews got there, McEwan nodded and launched into a speech. No idea what he was saying, but it'd be the usual platitudes and look-at-me-being-all-in-charge bollocks he always came out with at these things. Not worth unmuting him for, anyway.

Then, Shifty was back: 'Look, I've got to go. Apparently no one can find their arse with both hands unless I'm there to show them the bloody way!' And with that, he hung up.

Say what you like about being kicked off the force, at least it meant I didn't have to run around after tosspots like Chief Superintendent McEwan.

'Right,' I pointed at Henry, 'if you stay here, and you're a good boy, I'll bring you back something greasy from the breakfast buffet.'

He grinned back at me.

Little sod was going to be the size of a beach ball by the time we got home.

The sun had barely cleared the horizon as Henry and I wandered along the promenade. Four big fat seals rolled in the gilded water, gulls wheeling overhead. Bit of a nip in the air, but at least it'd stopped raining. Should be a nice day, for a change.

Monday morning rush hour was in full swing. Which in Rothesay wasn't saying much. A half dozen cars, the odd taxi. That open-topped bus again. Ten past eight – not even the carpet shops would be open yet.

I nipped across the road to a café, bought a decaf latte, then went back to the promenade to drink it. Chucking a tatty old tennis ball for Henry to fetch. The wee man scurrying about on clockwork legs, tail thumping back and forth like this was the best day of his life.

Ah, to be a daft, slightly stinky, Scottie dog.

My phone launched into a weird unfamiliar ringtone and I dragged it out, leaning against the blue railings, watching a couple of tiny fishing boats puttering out into the morning light. The words, 'LEAH MACNEIL' sat in the middle of the screen.

I jabbed the button. 'Leah? It's Ash Henderson, are you OK?'

Nothing from the other end.

'Hello?'

A scrunching, popping noise, then a voice so muffled it was barely audible: *'I'm frightened... He's... I love him, but ... he did something last night, something ... something terrible. He's ... he's scaring me so much...'*

'Leah?'

She didn't sound like an eighteen-year-old, she sounded like a terrified child.

'He's in paying for the petrol and I don't know what to do.'

'Get out of there, Leah. Get out of there and run!'

'I can't.'

'Is there another car at the petrol station? Someone you could go to?'

'He's locked the car and I can't get out. ... Please help me!'

Come on, Ash, *think*.

'OK, where are you?'

'I don't know, he... We're ... it looks like a supermarket, maybe?'

'What kind? Can you see any road signs? Landmarks? Anything that'd help us find you?'

'Oh God, he's coming back!' Her voice getting even harder to

make out. As if she'd stuck her phone in a pocket, or something.

Then a clunk, a thump, and the sound of something crackling.

A man's voice, talking at full volume. *'Sorry, Caroline, they didn't have any of the jelly beans you like, so I got jelly babies instead. Hope that's OK?'*

A click.

The man again: *'What? No, I don't think so. It's too dangerous.'*

Whoever he was talking to, not a single hint of what they said made it down to my end. Not even mumbling.

'Yes, that's what I was thinking too. What about you, Leah?'

'Erm...' A pause. *'If you think it's a good idea?'*

'Got to trust Caroline, she knows about this kind of thing.'

'OK...'

My phone ding-buzzed.

ROBOSABIR:

>>Target Phone Activation Detected
>>Requesting Location Data

About time too.

Ding-buzz.

ROBOSABIR:

>>Triangulating Source
>>Pending

Come on, come on...

'Now, what shall we listen to today? How about ... Götterdämmerung?' A small laugh. *'Remember we played it all night when we had that young woman from Dundee to stay? You remember that, Caroline? Oh, wow, did she have a great set of lungs on her. Screamed and screamed and screamed.'*

Then silence. Leah had ended the call.

Ding-buzz.

ROBOSABIR:

>>Target Phone Disconnected

Damn it.

She must've switched the thing off as well.

I pulled up my contacts and called the real Sabir.

Took him nearly a dozen rings to answer. *'What the bloody hell do youse want now?'* Followed by a full-mouthed yawn.

'Did you get a location or not?'

'Mornin', Sabir. You're sounding dead sexy today, Sabir. Hope yer not too shagged out from humping my ma all night, Sabir.'

'I got a text on my phone saying Leah had activated her phone.'

'Youse are welcome.'

'I need a location!'

'How the hell am I supposed to know where they are? I've been asleep! You woke us up!'

'It's nearly twenty past eight.'

'And I've been up most the night, trying to track down a bunch of internet kiddie fiddlers, so excuse *me if I'm not at your beck and bloody call twenny-four hours a day!'*

Off in the distance, sunlight flared off something white on the water, followed by the long mournful cry of a ship's horn.

'OK, OK. Sorry.'

'It takes time for the system to triangulate data from mobile phone towers. If your Leah doesn't leave her phone on long enough, there's sod all I can do about it.'

'Can we at least … guesstimate where she is?'

A moany grumbling noise rattled out of the phone. *'I'll have a go. But I'm promisin' nothing.'* He hung up.

So close.

The shining dot in the distance grew, making a beeline for Rothesay. That'd be the ferry from Wemyss Bay. The one we'd be taking back to the mainland.

Of course, the big question was: who on earth had Gordon Smith been talking to in the car? 'Caroline', his wife, died four years ago of bowel cancer… Or that's what Helen MacNeil had told us. So was he talking to himself, someone else, or maybe even Leah? Did he think his neighbour's eighteen-year-old grand-daughter was the woman he'd married nearly half a century ago?

Might explain why he'd kept her alive.

And if Leah had half a brain about her, it was a delusion she'd be playing along with.

Mind you, he'd also spoken to Leah by name. But that could be part of it, couldn't it? If he had dementia, or something so he couldn't tell who was who?

This was all really Alice's field, rather than mine.

What was it she'd said? Something about not knowing what happens when one half of a couple-that-kill dies? Maybe the dominant one mourns for a couple of days, then goes out and finds himself another accomplice? Whether she wants to be, or not.

Especially when Leah said he'd done something terrible last night. Maybe it...

Ah.

Speak of the Devil's neighbour.

Helen MacNeil stood in the middle of the promenade, scowling back at me, hands curled into fists at her sides.

I nodded. 'Helen.' Bent down and grabbed Henry as he returned the tatty ball. Clipped his lead on again. Just in case.

She didn't move. 'You *know* what it's like.'

'Yeah.' Welcome to the world's most horrible club. I peered past her, towards the strange pavilion thing that bisected the putting course. 'What happened to your "friend"?' Adding a stab of bitterness to that last word.

'All she wants is dirt for her book, she doesn't give a damn about Sophie or me.'

What could I do but shrug? 'You want my advice? Avoid Jennifer Prentice like a weeping sore. She's poisonous.'

'I want Gordon Smith.' Helen's chin came up. 'He *deserves* to suffer for what he did to my Sophie. For what he did to all those people!' Her left arm trembled, as if she was having difficulty keeping it under control. 'But they won't do that, will they. They'll arrest him, if they catch him at all, and they'll try him, and they'll stick him in some cushy psychiatric hospital with all the other whackjobs, feed him and water him and dose him up with all the best drugs.' The arm shook harder. 'While my Sophie GOT TORTURED TO DEATH!'

Helen's face flushed.

I took a breath. Tried to sound reasonable. 'You don't know Sophie was—'

'SHE TOLD ME!' Jabbing a finger back towards the town centre. 'Jennifer. She showed me the Polaroids – the other ones. The ones he took *after* what he did to them.'

Oh, for God's sake.

I let my head fall back and stared up at the sapphire sky.

Oldcastle Police strikes again. Couldn't keep a secret if you stitched it inside the useless bastards.

Helen's voice dropped. 'Jennifer had a copy on her phone – of Sophie, in the basement...' Voice wobbling as much as her fist now. 'She showed me... She *sent* them to me.'

And I knew how *that* felt as well.

Every year on Rebecca's birthday: another homemade card from the bastard who killed her, with a photo of my baby girl being tortured on it.

Took some doing, but I cleared the knot out of my throat. 'She shouldn't have done that.'

Helen stepped closer. 'That six million: I'll split it with you, straight down the middle. Three *million* pounds, if you help me find Gordon Smith before the police do.'

It was like a weight pushing down on my shoulders. 'I can't, it's—'

'*Four* million! OK?' Throwing her arms out, eyes shining as the tears welled up. 'Five? You can take the bloody lot if you want: all six million!' Her arms fell back to her sides and she sagged. Shrinking into herself. 'I don't care. I want him to know how my Sophie felt when he killed her. I want my hands round his throat, staring into his eyes as he gurgles and thrashes and pleads, his blood smeared up to my elbows, bits of him lying on the concrete floor.'

I leaned back against the railing. 'It won't bring Sophie back, Helen.'

'No.' She ground the heel of one hand into her eye, wiping away the tears. 'But it'll make me feel a hell of a lot better.'

Yeah, it probably would.

'We're heading back to the mainland on the next ferry. You could do worse than nick Jennifer Prentice's car and abandon her here.'

With any luck she'd try to swim home.

And drown.

Twenty minutes out of Rothesay, I stepped out of the ferry toilets and there she was. Looked as if Helen hadn't managed to lose her after all.

'Ash.' A semi-frozen smile. 'I hope you washed your hands.'

I limped straight past her. 'Whatever you want, Jennifer, you can bugger off.'

'Oh, don't be so sulky.' She eased up beside me, keeping pace. 'I know things finished on a slightly sour note with us, but that doesn't mean we can't be friends.'

'Go away, Jennifer.'

'One *million* pounds each. Think what you could do with the money: retire, have a decent holiday for a change. You could finally marry off that daughter substitute you've been hauling around since Katie died.'

I had to squeeze the words out through clenched teeth: 'You remembering I'm a feminist?'

'You're not going to hit me, Ash. Not unless I hit you first – you're sweetly old-fashioned that way. I *know* you, remember?'

Through the doors and into the outside seating area at the back of the boat, looking out over the shining blue water and the purpled hills.

'We had some lovely times, didn't we, Ash? When things weren't going well with you and your wife, I didn't put any pressure on you, did I? Didn't make scenes or demands. It was simple, uncomplicated, sweaty … *fun*.' She scooted around in front of me, backing towards the handrail. The twin red-and-black exhausts towering overhead, keeping the diesel fumes away from the passengers. 'We could have that again. No judgement, no pressure, no commitments.'

The metal handrail was cold against my forearms. Leaning on it, taking the weight off my foot. 'You don't give up, do you?'

'Like the Energiser Bunny,' Jennifer licked her lips and winked, 'remember?'

Yeah.

She linked her arm through mine. 'It wasn't *all* bad, was it?'

I puffed out a breath. 'No. Suppose not.'

'There you go.' Bumping her shoulder into mine. 'Not such a grumpy Gus, after all.'

We stood there in silence, or at least what passed for it with the ferry's massive diesel engine making the deck vibrate beneath us.

'This book you're writing…'

'"Garden of Bones", brackets, "hunting Scotland's most notorious serial killer: The Coffinmaker".' A frown tried to force its way onto her frozen forehead. 'Or is the subtitle too long? Putting his name on the end there seems to undermine the drama, doesn't it? But readers need to know who it's about when they see it in the supermarket.'

'It'd be … tasteful's the wrong word, but you know what I mean?'

She squeezed my arm harder. 'No lurid prose. No lingering on the grisly details.' A my-hands-are-tied shrug. 'The publishers will probably insist on photographs, you know what they're like, but it'll be a *proper* piece of investigative journalism. Not sensationalist in any way. Respectful to the victims and their families.'

I nodded. 'OK.'

Jennifer pressed her lips against my cheek, breathing deep. 'I have missed you, you know. Even if you were horrid to me.'

'Come on then.' I turned my back to the railing and pulled out my phone. Called up the camera app and set it to selfie mode. 'Squeeze in.'

An actual, real smile broke across her lower face. It might not have moved the rest of it, but it sparkled in her eyes as she huddled in and pouted for the camera.

I pressed the button.

Frowned at the screen. 'Think my camera's buggered…'

'Here,' she pulled out her phone instead – something fancy in a jewelled case – held it out and up, pouted again. 'Say cheese.'

Click.

'Can I see?'

'Course you can.' Jennifer passed me her phone, and there we were, the pair of us together again. Side by side at the ferry's railing. Her nestled in under my arm, pulled in tight, as if we were still lying sticky with sweat in that Travelodge on Greenwood Street, the duvet rumpled around our ankles. She looked really, really happy.

I turned and hurled her phone – not straight back, where it might crash down onto the car deck, but at the perfect angle to send it sailing over the side, twirling end-over-end. Didn't see it hit the water, but it was enough to know it did.

'MY PHONE!' Jennifer stared at me. Then gripped the railing and looked out at the point where her phone and its fancy jewelled case had disappeared. 'ARE YOU OFF YOUR BLOODY HEAD?'

I leaned in close. Kept my voice nice and friendly. 'You shouldn't have shown Helen MacNeil the photo of what Gordon Smith did to her daughter. You – repulsive – *fucking* – vulture.'

Then turned on my heel and limped away.

Jennifer's voice boomed out behind me, getting higher and sharper with every word. 'THIS ISN'T OVER, ASH HENDERSON! IT'S NOT OVER BY A LONG WAY! I'LL MAKE YOU WISH YOU WERE NEVER BORN!'

She could join the queue.

28

The pool car roared past the Cumbernauld junction, Franklin keeping the needle hovering around seventy-five. Snarling as she overtook cars and lorries as if their merely being on the road this morning was a personal affront to her.

I reclined my seat far enough to check the rear-view mirror.

Yup, Nick James's fusty yellow Golf was still there. Only now Jennifer wasn't trying to hide the fact. And she wasn't alone in the car, so it looked as if Helen hadn't told her what she could do with her self-serving exploitative bollocks after all.

Disappointing.

Still, if I couldn't break the pair of them up, at least I'd had the pleasure of chucking Jennifer's phone in the sea.

Mind you, it probably hadn't been the best of ideas, antagonising her like that. She wasn't exactly renowned for her forgiving nature. And, while chucking her phone in the sea would get rid of the pictures she'd got from whichever O Division scumbag had leaked Smith's Polaroids, there was no way she hadn't backed them up. So a temporary fix at best. One that would come with a side order of Botox-faced vengeance.

Lucky me…

Too late to worry about it now, though. Have to—

My phone launched into its generic ringtone. 'Unknown Number' filling the screen.

I jabbed the button. 'Leah?'

'Oh, sorry.' A man's voice, the words twisted by a heavy Orcadian accent. *'Is Detective Inspector Ash Henderson there?'*

Damn it.

Franklin looked at me, across the car, eyebrows raised.

Shook my head at her. 'Speaking.'

'Thomas Sinclair, from the Land Registry Office? You wanted to know if there was any property in Stirling belonging to a Peter or Caroline Smith?'

A row of ugly warehouses drifted by on the other side of the motorway.

Nothing more from Thomas Sinclair.

'And?'

'Oh, sorry, I was waiting on you. Anyway, we had a look and the answer is yes. Well, it is and it isn't, if that makes sense?'

Not even vaguely.

'Obviously "Smith" is a very popular surname, so there's quite a few properties in Stirling owned by various Smiths, but once we eliminated everyone with the wrong first name we ended up with six properties. Two Carolines, and four Peters.'

You wee beauty.

'Can you email me over the details?'

Two minutes later I was scrolling through the addresses and Cumbernauld's warehouses were a thin grey smear in the rear-view mirror.

Time to go to work.

The first Peter Smith on the list peered out at us through thick round glasses, no hair on his head, a threadbare cardigan on his back. 'No, I've not got no brothers, and my wife's called June. Do you need to talk to her? Hold on.' He turned, raising his voice at the hallway. 'JUNE! PEOPLE FROM THE SOMETHING-OR-OTHER WANT TO SPEAK TO YOU!'

Caroline Smith curled her top lip, cigarette dangling from the corner of her mouth, a Yorkshire terrier on her hip like a small child. Mid-thirties, and definitely not dead from bowel cancer.

'Naw, never heard of them, like. Is this about them council bins that got set on fire? Cos I *totally* know who did that.'

Peter Smith Number Two wasn't in, but his husband was. A short man in tartan trousers and a biker jacket. Blond Andy Warhol bob, Gary Larson glasses, and a great big wine glass, half-full of red. He sniffed at the photo. 'Naw, it's not my Pete, my Pete's in banking. But, you know, not in an evil money-grabbing bastard kind of way. Well, maybe a teensy bit.' A smile. 'I *adore* your hair, by the way. Wish I had hair like that.'

Franklin's cheeks darkened a fraction. 'Yes, well, thank you for your time.'

The second Caroline Smith owned a small boxy mid-terrace two-up two-down, opposite a playing field. She slouched against her doorframe, in a purple velour tracksuit, the top open to expose a T-shirt with 'IN YOUR DREAMS, LOSER!' on it. Her shock of cherry-red curls going grey at the roots. She squinted at the picture of Gordon Smith in Franklin's hand, then shook her head. 'Sorry, love, I'd really like to help, but I've never seen the man. And my husband's called Bob: he's in the RAF.'

I leaned back against the car, phone clamped to my ear as Shifty moaned and whined.

'Utter bunch of useless bollocks. Tramped about five miles through these bloody woods already today and what have we found so far?'

Franklin was off talking to a short ugly man with taxi-door ears and the kind of face you could use to frighten small children. Standing on his doorstep with her arms folded. Body language about as defensive as it got.

'Go on then.'

'We've found three shopping trollies, a bunch of dead dogs, and a massive pile of fly-tipped medical waste. I'll be washing the smell out for bloody weeks. And is McEwan appreciative of all our efforts? Is he buggery!'

'No sign of Toby Macmillan, then?'

'Oh, didn't I mention that? We found him half an hour in, he's back with his mum and dad right now, eating ice cream and dancing

the bastarding fandango!' A small pause. *'Of course we didn't find him. There's miles and miles of these bloody woods, how am I supposed to find one little boy in all this?'*

'So delegate. Go speak to Alice and see if you can't actually achieve something today.'

'And, of course, it's all my fault we haven't found anything. I didn't even want to come out here, it was that idiot DCI Poncy Powel's idea to search the woods, but shite never sticks to…' A groan. *'Sodding hell. Sorry, got to go. We're getting another "motivational" speech from McEwan. If I get any more motivated I'm going to swing for someone!'*

Shifty hung up and I settled back to enjoy the sun on my face. You wouldn't think it'd been thumping down with rain all week.

'OK, thanks anyway.' Franklin sagged when the ugly man's front door shut, turned, and slumped her way up the garden path and out onto the street again. 'Feel like I've just *stepped* in something.'

Henry beamed up at her, tail going like a windscreen wiper on full.

'How'd you get on?'

'Nothing doing.' She dropped down into a squat and Henry flopped over on his back, exposing his black hairy tummy for her to rub. Tart that he was. 'Tell you, *that* Peter Smith had "welcome to the Sex Offenders' Register" written all over him in magic marker. Stared at my breasts the whole time I was talking to him. Barely even looked at the photo.'

'Yup, perverts will do that.'

She stood, wiping her tummy-rubbing hand on her trouser leg. 'One more Peter Smith to go.' A long hissing breath. 'This is another complete waste of time, isn't it?'

'Come on then, we'll get him done, then it's lunchtime.'

'Naw, sorry.' Our last Peter Smith of the day shook his head, setting long straight dark hair swinging like a curtain across his white-painted face. Piercings glinting in his ears and nose. Lots of leather. Couldn't be a day over twenty-two.

Franklin took a step back and peered up at the big gothic

275

townhouse on the outskirts of Stirling. Large, gated garden. Lots of trees and lawn. A small black cat washing its bum on the rim of an ornamental fountain, completely ignoring Henry. 'Do you really own all this?'

He nodded. 'Six numbers and the bonus ball.'

'OK. Thanks anyway.'

We headed down the gravel drive, through the wrought-iron gates, and over to our manky pool car. I opened the back door and let Henry hop inside. 'So much for that.'

Franklin stared back across the road. 'I'd *love* a house like that.'

'Lunch?'

'How come *I* never win the lottery?' She climbed in behind the wheel.

'Do you actually *play* the lottery?' I got into the passenger side.

'That's not the point. So, where are we lunching?'

'You know, I think Pasty Peter The Goth fancied you, so if you want to go back and chat him up, he'd probably let you have it in the divorce settlement.'

'Don't tempt me.' She started the car and headed back towards the main road. 'I feel like a nice big salad. Think there's a good salad place in Stirling?'

Sitting in their rancid-yellow Golf, Helen MacNeil and Jennifer Prentice watched us go by, then pulled out after us. Couldn't have been the most exciting of days for them, following us around. But at least they'd—

'Ash! Salad places: Stirling.'

'No idea. Has to be somewhere, though. Failing that … curry?'

'For *lunch*? That Prentice woman was right, you really are off your head. It's—'

My phone belted out 'I Am the Walrus', so I answered it. 'Sabir. Have you got some good news for me, for a change?'

'*Oh, I got some good news for youse indeed. That Sabir is the King of Tech. High priest of Databases. Emperor of the Digital World!*'

'You missed out Lord of the Pies.'

Franklin took a right, making for the centre of town.

'*Was that you cracking a* joke*? Dear God, there's a ferst. You had a head injury, or summat?*'

'What do you want, Sabir?'

'You was after a guesstimate, remember? Where Leah MacNeil was when she called you this morning, but didn't stay on long enough to trace? Well, I've done it. Call came from somewhere in the vicinity of the Sainsbury's on, and I kid you not, "Back O' Hill Road". Website says it's on "Drip Road" which is equally as bad, but you can't even get into it from there, it's all fenced—'

'How big an area are we talking about?'

'Within four to five hundred metres. So draw yourself a circle a kilometre wide around the supermarket and she was calling from somewhere inside that.'

'And let me guess, the Sainsbury's has a petrol station?'

'El Bingo, signor.'

'So why do you sound so bloody smug? That's next to sod-all use to me.'

'Because Sabir is Emperor of the Digital werld. And his imperial majesty went and did some searching, and guess what he terned up within that kilometre circle? Pauses for applause…'

'All right, stop milking it.'

'There's an industrial estate round the back of the supermarket, on Glendevon Drive. And one of the warehouses there is owned by this production company that puts on loads of pantomimes all over the UK. They use it to store props and scenery. You know, in case yer wanting to put on Cinderella and can't be arsed making your own pumpkin coach, like. And I was thinking, who do we know that might have access to a pantomime scenery store?'

'I take it all back, Sabir. You're a certified genius!'

'First sensible thing I've heard from your tartan-munchin' mouth all year.' And with that he hung up.

Franklin frowned at me. 'You're doing that creepy smile thing again.'

Oh yes.

Ridiculous though it sounded, Back O' Hill Industrial Estate was pretty aptly named. Being as it was around the back of the dirty-big hill that Stirling Castle sat on top of. Although the castle wasn't visible from down here. What *was* visible was a small collection of Portakabins, lockups, and old-fashioned warehouses – the single-storey kind with brick walls and corrugated metal cladding.

Franklin drove us into the compact warren of streets and buildings, hunched over the steering wheel and gazing up at the signage as we drifted deeper and deeper inside. 'What's it called?'

I checked Sabir's text. '"Williamson and Norris Theatrical Logistics Limited". Bit of a mouthful.'

We turned another corner, and there it was, lurking at the end of the road. A long double-width warehouse with twin rust-red roofs and grey harled walls – bearing a very understated sign with the company name on it. Bars in all the windows. Shuttered loading bay that looked big enough to take an articulated lorry.

Had to admit, it didn't exactly reek of pantomime magic.

Franklin parked in the empty row of spaces in front of the small office. 'No lights on. Think anyone's in?'

'One way to find out.'

The air was sharp, but seasoned with the deep-mahogany scent of onions fried in burger fat, coming from a bright red food van with 'Fiona's Fantastic Fried-Food Emporium!' in gold lettering down the side, parked outside a shuttered unit. A line of blokes in oily overalls queueing in front of the open hatch.

Nick James's fusty Volkswagen Golf pulled up on the far side of it, Helen and Jennifer sitting there, watching as we locked the pool car and tried the warehouse's main door.

The handle rattled when Franklin jiggled it up and down, but that was it. She cupped her hands against one of the office windows and peered inside. 'Can't see anyone.'

'OK.' Back to Sabir's email. In addition to the company name, address, and for some unknown reason its VAT registration, he'd included a phone number with an Edinburgh dialling code. 'We give them a call…' I raised an eyebrow. 'Unless you want to boot in the door? I would, but,' pointing at my foot with the walking stick, 'bullet hole.'

'Without a warrant?' She pulled her chin in. 'Might be how they did things back when you were in the job, but we don't pull that crap any more. Can you imagine Gordon Smith getting away with everything because we screwed up on a technicality?'

Think the body we dragged out of his garden in a holdall *might* carry the day on that front, but what the hell. 'Fine. You call the company, then we go grab lunch.'

'So much for a nice big salad.' Franklin ripped another bite out of her bacon-and-cheese haggis burger, chewing as she rested her bum against the pool car's bonnet. Face upturned to the sun.

'It's got salad *in* it, doesn't it?' I scooped a sporkful of glistening grey-and-brown stovies from my squeaky polystyrene tray. Not bad. Needed pepper, though. And pickled beetroot.

'Two slices of tomato and some iceberg don't count.'

'Surely *chips* count.'

'Only in Glasgow.' But that didn't stop Franklin munching her way through them all, then polishing off her burger while Henry sat at her feet, gazing up at her as if he was in love. Especially when she dropped him the occasional scrap of burger, bun, or bacon.

She wiped her mouth and hands clean on a napkin, then popped her wrist out from its starched white cuff and peered at her watch. 'One forty-two. Shouldn't be long now.'

Helen and Jennifer still hadn't moved. Still sitting there, in a dead journalist's car. Still scowling through the windscreen. Watching us.

To be honest, given Helen's reputation, it was amazing she had this much patience. Jennifer, on the other hand, would probably be using the time to plot her revenge.

Well, tough. She deserved all she'd got.

I scooped up the last mouthful of mystery meat and potatoes. 'Wonder why Smith took Leah here, to the warehouse.' Sooked the memory of stovies off my plastic spork. 'Collecting something? Dropping something off? Or checking something was still where he'd left it?'

'You know what *I've* been wondering?' Franklin pulled a small container of hand sanitiser from her jacket and pumped a couple of squirts onto a palm. Had a good scrub with it. 'Why did Gordon Smith leave his Polaroid photos behind? Why not take them with him?'

'Hmph. Alice asked the same thing.'

'Well, they're not hard to transport, are they? You could pop the lot in your pocket and no one would even know they're there.'

As was evidenced at the Winslow's supermarket checkout on Friday night.

She folded her arms. 'I've read the profile your Dr McDonald wrote: Gordon Smith's meant to be a "collector". So why leave his collection behind?' A frown. 'Or maybe it was only the *old* Polaroids he left behind? Maybe he took the newer ones with him?'

'What age are you?'

Franklin stared at me. 'Why?'

'Because back in the bad old day, before your time, if you wanted to take photographs you had three choices: build your own darkroom, develop and print them yourself; take the film down to Boots and get them to do it for you; or buy a Polaroid camera. Gordon Smith wants a photo to remember his victims by: option one's a pain in the backside, number two will get him arrested, but number three's nice and easy.'

'Come on then, Methuselah, out with it.'

'Fast forward ten, maybe fifteen years and domestic video cameras are affordable. You don't need static images any more.'

'You can film everything you're doing and watch it back to your dirty little heart's content.' She nodded. 'Makes sense. Then, before you know it, you've got a smartphone and every-one's a documentary filmmaker. You can carry your entire collection of homemade torture porn in your pocket.'

'He left the Polaroids behind, because he's got copies on his phone.' Only *he* didn't have to do it, in a rush, in the pitch-dark, while the bloody house crumbled into the North Sea.

'Maybe we can...' She stared over my shoulder.

A grey two-seater sports car had turned into our dead-end street, top thrown back, a grinning man in a flat cap behind the wheel. It growled into the parking space two down from our manky Ford Focus, as if it was worried about catching something.

He gave us a wave with his tan-leather driving gloves and buzzed the roof up again, before getting out and marching around. Not the tallest – barely scraping five feet, if that – the slightly bandy legs probably didn't help. His yellowy-tartan hoodie was unzipped, showing off a T-shirt with 'He's Behind You!' on it, and when he whipped off his bunnet a shock of bright-orange hair stuck up at the front of a bald head so shiny it looked as if it'd been polished. He performed an elaborate bow for Franklin, snatching up her hand to kiss it. 'My dear Officer Franklin, you're even more delightful in person than you sounded on the phone.'

And before she could say anything, or punch him, he skipped away and grabbed my hand for shaking instead.

'Louis Williamson, Panto McHaggis Productions! Delighted, etc.' Pumping my arm up and down. 'I understand you'd like a wee tour of our prop-and-set store?' He pulled a knot of keys from his pocket and jangled them all the way to the door. Unlocked it. Then turned, arms out, blocking the way. 'Lemme see your warrant, coppers!'

Franklin blinked at him, then at me, then back at him again.

OK, I'll bite: 'Do we *need* a warrant, Mr Williamson?'

'Not really, I just love it when they say that on the telly. Ooh, and: "you'll never take me alive, you doity rats!"' He turned and skip-hopped over the threshold. 'Shall we?'

Strip lights pinged and flickered into life as I stepped inside – revealing rows and rows and rows of metal shelving towering over us. Each unit packed with labelled boxes and crates.

Signs dangled from the rafters, dividing the place up like the aisles of a supermarket, each one marked with the name of a show: 'Cinderella', 'Aladdin', 'Mother Goose'…

Henry's claws clicked on the concrete floor, Franklin bringing up the rear, closing the door behind her.

'I've always wanted to do a panto version of *The Maltese*

Falcon, but apparently you can't get the rights for love nor money.' He cast a furtive glance up and down the aisle, then hauled on a stage whisper. 'Strictly *entre nous*, we're in talks with Ian Rankin's people. Early days yet, but fingers crossed!' A wink, then Louis Williamson swept his arms up and out. 'Anyway, welcome to my emporium of theatrical delights!'

'We'd like to talk to you about Gordon Smith.'

'Ah…' His arms fell back to his sides. 'Yes, I heard about that unfortunate business with his house and that poor reporter who *died*. Tragic, simply tragic.'

'And all the murders, of course.'

'Quite.' He wrinkled his nose, as if he'd caught scent of something rancid. 'Well, Gordon has worked with us since mine dear papa ran the operation. He's a dab hand at stage sets, every single panto we put on is designed by Gordon Smith.' Pointing down the aisles. 'Would you like to see them? It's no trouble, really.' And with that Louis did an about-face hop and led the way down 'DICK WHITTINGTON' and along 'SWEENEY TODD' to the breeze-block wall that marked the join between the two ware-houses. 'Here we go.' Performing another low bow for Franklin as he ushered her through the open double doors.

She kept her hands clutched up by her chest, where he couldn't grab and kiss them again.

'Sorry, the lights don't work, I'm afraid. I've called and called and called the maintenance company, but will they send anyone out?' He flicked the switch up and down a few times, to demon-strate. 'Of course they won't.'

It wasn't *completely* dark in here – a thin greasy light oozed in through grubby skylights in the corrugated roof, barely bright enough to make small gloomy islands beneath them. Back in the prop store, it'd been difficult to get a sense of how big the place was – all carved up into segments by the rows of shelving, like that – but this one was *huge*.

The same set of signage hung from the rafters, but ninety percent of it was illegible in the dismal light. No shelving, instead clumps of metal cages and racks holding sections of scenery and rolls of backdrops, lurked in the shadows – their flat-pack villages and laundries and caves and castles and forests fading into murky silhouettes.

'This might help.' Louis picked a handlamp from a shelf by the doors, banging it a couple of times against his palm until a hard white beam lanced out into the dusty air. 'Please, do feel free to look around. I shall hover nearby ready to assist, should I be needed. Rub the lamp three times and, as if by magic, Louis shall appear!'

'Thanks.' You utter freak.

Franklin accepted the proffered handlamp and we wandered away into the racks of scenery, Henry scampering off ahead, then rushing back to run circles around us and off he went again. Happy gunshot barks in the darkness.

She kept her voice down to a whisper, swinging the torch beam across what looked like the disassembled walls of a teeny Post Office. 'What are we looking for?'

'Something out of place. Something weird. I don't know.'

'*Everything* in here looks weird.' Her torch drifted past a huge dragon's head.

'Gordon Smith didn't pop past for old times' sake. He came here for a reason. And Leah said he did something terrible last night. Maybe this is where he did it.'

We made our way past Cinderella's kitchen, Aladdin's cave, and what looked like a steam train, if steam trains came in kit form.

'Could've been lying low? He knows we're looking for him, so he steers clear of the hotels and B-and-Bs. Doesn't want to get recognised.'

'Possible… What's that over there?'

In my day, pantomime had been *Dick Whittington*, *Aladdin*, *Cinderella*, and *Jack and the Beanstalk*, or if you were really unlucky: *Mother Goose*. But Panto McHaggis Productions had branched out into previously uncharted territory.

A partially constructed set sat in the back corner, furthest away from the door we'd come in through. Details sprang into life as Franklin played her torch over it, then faded away into darkness again. It was big and gothic, with chipboard flying buttresses and painted-on gargoyles. A big slab-like table in the middle, flanked by the kind of Van de Graaff generators that featured in many an old-fashioned horror film. Bulky lumps of fake machinery with oversized cogs and levers. And right at the back, a workbench covered in vials and retorts and distillation equipment. It looked as if they'd been full once, but now the glass bore coloured tidemarks where the liquid inside had evaporated. Cobwebs everywhere.

Shelves lined the fake granite wall above the glasswork, each one home to rows and rows of glass jars that glittered in the torchlight.

'Holy mother of God...' Franklin's torch froze.

The small jars had rubber spiders and things floating in yellowy liquid, but the bigger ones contained something a lot more horrible and a lot more real.

She licked her lips. 'Can you see what I'm seeing?'

Row upon row of severed human heads.

29

'Jesus...' There had to be two, maybe three dozen of them up there, squashed into large screw-top jars.

Franklin dragged her eyes away from the collection and yanked out her phone, fumbling with the screen. 'I'll call it in.'

'Hello.' Louis stepped out from behind an oversized coffin. 'Magnificent, isn't it?'

I turned, holding a hand up at chest height. 'I'm going to have to ask you to step back, sir. This is now an active crime scene.'

'It is? How *exciting*!' He pursed his lips as he looked around the set. 'Why?'

Seriously?

'Who else has keys to the warehouse? Does Gordon Smith have keys?'

'Well, of course he does. He's working on this, right now. Well, he was, anyway. Before all the ... unpleasantness.' A big smile as Louis gazed at the set. 'You have to admit, though, he's one *hell* of an artist!'

Franklin turned her back on us, one finger in her ear. 'Mother? It's me, we need an SOC team down here, ASAP. And a pathologist, Procurator Fiscal, the whole shooting match.'

'This is slated for His Majesty's Theatre in Aberdeen, next Christmas: *Frankenstein and the Christmas Monster Mash*. It's a working title.' He stepped onto the set. 'We've got a heap of original songs being written and you should *see* the special effects.'

'I don't know, at least … thirty, maybe more. Severed heads.' Franklin's back stiffened. 'No, I haven't been drinking! … Why would I make something like that up?'

'Ah.' Louis raised a finger. 'I think there might be a misunderstanding.' As he scuttled over to the workbench.

'Step away from the evidence!'

He smiled at me. 'It's not what you think.'

'Of course I'm serious! For God's sake, Mother: there's about thirty severed heads down here in—'

'No! No, they're not real! They're not: look!' Louis scrambled up onto the bench, and grabbed one of the jars off its shelf before *I* could grab *him*. 'It's me, see? It's my face. They're part of the set dressing.' Holding it out.

Oh.

Up close it definitely was him, nose pressed against the glass, bright-orange shock of hair on top of… The head didn't actually have a top, it had a thin circular rim instead.

Louis pulled another from the shelf. 'They're really easy to make. All you do is you squish your nose against a window and take three pictures – two profiles, one full-face – and you stick them together in Photoshop, then you print them out on waterproof stock, and you slip them into a head-sized jar full of water and some food colouring. Look: there's nothing else in there.' He tilted the jar in his hands, showing off the bottom. Nothing inside but the printout.

Franklin paced back and forth in front of the Van de Graaff generators. 'I don't know. Far as we can tell Gordon Smith must've been keeping them down here for years. It's an extension of—'

I cleared my throat. 'Franklin?'

'—horrific collection. The Polaroids weren't enough any more, so he's—'

'FRANKLIN!'

She turned and glared at me. 'Do you mind? I'm trying to—'

'It's all make-believe.' I unscrewed the jar with Louis's head

286

in it and pulled the printout free. Held it there, dripping on the warehouse floor. 'They're fakes.'

Her face creased shut, jaw clenched as she curled up at the knees for a moment. Then stood. Eyes closed, free hand clasping her forehead. 'No, I'm still here, Mother. I...' Deep breath. 'There's been a misunderstanding.'

'Now this one, right here is the holy grail, as far as I'm concerned.' Louis held up another head-in-a-jar. Fiddled about with the lid. Then beamed with pride as the head inside blinked then started to sing. The words coming out all muffled and tinny:

'Frankenstein's a friend of mine,
Although he fed me strychnine,
And pickled my poor head in brine
We're still chums and it's all fine...'

'Got a prototype manufactured by this wonderful boutique electronics firm in South Korea – semi-flexible curved screen that takes pre-filmed footage on USB and displays it. Bluetooth to the theatre sound system. Cost an absolute *fortune* to develop, but can you imagine a dozen of them singing along while the monster dances for the kiddies?' He clicked the thing off and tucked it under his arm. 'What a show!'

I stared up at the shelf with its collection of heads. Then raised an eyebrow at Franklin. 'Just to be on the safe side?'

She rolled her eyes, huffed out a breath, but clambered up onto the bench anyway and clinked her way through the jars. Taking each one off its shelf, turning it upside down, then putting it back again. 'All fakes.'

Louis shrugged. 'Not sure if I should say "sorry" or not. I mean, I'm sorry it got everyone so worked up, but on the other hand, it's nice they're *not* real, isn't it?'

She climbed down again, brushing dust and fake cobwebs off the knees of her suit trousers. 'So why was Gordon Smith here last night?'

'I honestly and truly have no idea.'

*   *   *

Franklin's feet left scuff marks in the dust as we followed her torch in a slow-motion tour of the warehouse, stopping to examine each cluster of scenery. 'Of course, Mother now thinks I'm an idiot.'

'No one thinks you're an idiot.' I raised my voice. 'HENNNNNRY?' His name echoed back at me from the corrugated metal roof. 'Where are you, you horrible stinker? HENNNNNNNRY?'

She glanced over her shoulder, in the vague direction of where we'd left Louis Williamson, by the Frankenstein set. 'So we're right back where we started from.'

'Smith was here for a *reason*.'

'How am I supposed to be taken seriously when I'm calling my DI and banging on about severed heads in jars? Mother thought I was making it all up!' Franklin's shoulders drooped as she swung the torch around another pile of scenery. This one looked like it might fit together into a barber's shop, complete with an oversized leather chair that had more than a whiff of the dentist about it and a big set of hinges at the back. 'Taken me three years to prove I'm rehabilitated enough to transfer out to another team, and now I look like a cast-iron grade A...' She stopped.

I limped past a couple of feet, then turned. 'No one thinks you're an idiot, OK? Now, can we get on with—'

'This "something strange" we're looking for.' She wobbled the torch beam around in a small circle. 'Would it be something like that?'

It was the bedroom scene from *Goldilocks and the Three Bears*, partially erected against the wall, in a gap between two racks of flat-pack trees, mountains, and a gingerbread house. And someone had clearly been sleeping in all three of the beds – the covers rumpled and pulled back, indentations in the pillows where their heads had been.

'OK, so what do we do now?' Franklin stayed where she was as I hobbled closer.

Three beds. Gordon Smith, Leah MacNeil, and the unknown woman from the car? Assuming she was even real, of course.

Or maybe, if Leah was Smith's twisted idea of a substitute wife, he'd found a fresh victim for them to torture and kill together?

She did say he'd done something terrible last night…

'We need to get an SOC team down here after all – test the beds, see if we can get a DNA match.'

Franklin groaned. 'Bit of a comedown, isn't it? Severed heads to a couple of unmade beds?'

Henry's bark rattled back from the roof and walls, before fading away into silence.

'Could be worse: at least we found something.'

'And can you imagine what Mother's going to say when I call her?' Franklin pulled out her phone and grimaced at it. '"Are you sure you're not making it up this time as well, Rosalind? Only you got rather overexcited about the heads-in-jars thing, remember?"'

Another bark from Henry. Then the skitter of his little clawed feet on the concrete as he scampered in out of the gloom to wheech around me twice then drop a manky tennis ball at my feet. The thing was almost bald, what was left of its bright-yellow fur stained a grimy brown. Glistening with slavers.

Well if he thought I was picking *that* up and throwing it for him, he was in for a disappointment.

Another bark, then Henry snatched it up in his mouth and disappeared off in the direction he'd just come from.

Thick as mince.

I gave Franklin a shrug. 'Three beds: Gordon Smith, Leah MacNeil, and, potentially, a new victim. Do we have a choice?'

'God's sake.' She poked at her phone, then held the thing to her ear. Sighed. 'Mother? It's Rosalind. I need an SOC team. … Yes, very funny, but— … No. No, this isn't the same thing as last time…'

I limped after Henry, pulling out his lead.

Probably best not to have him charging about the place compromising any evidence. Assuming it really *had* been Gordon Smith and Leah MacNeil in Daddy and Mummy Bears' beds, and not some lazy night watchman.

'Henry? Come on, you wee sod, time for you to go back in the car.'

Another bark, up ahead in the gloom.

Took out my phone and started the torch app, its small circle of cold white light dissipating after only a couple of feet. Limping past bits of a library – all the books painted on – and what might have been the bow of a pirate ship.

'Henry! Get your hairy arse back here.'

Two small spheres glowed in the darkness, a couple of feet above the ground: Henry's eyes.

'You're a massive pain in my backside, you know that, don't you?'

A bark.

He was turning tight circles in front of yet another lump of disassembled scenery, only this one was covered in a huge blue plastic tarpaulin. And the thing he was circling was that manky tennis ball. Still, at least it kept him where he'd be easy to grab.

My phone ding-buzzed in my hand.

ROBOSABIR:

>>Target Phone Activation Detected
>>Requesting Location Data

Leah had turned her mobile on again.

Ding-buzz.

ROBOSABIR:

>>Triangulating Source
>>Pending

Maybe this time we'd get lucky?

Henry hunkered down, forelegs extended towards me, bum in the air, tail whooshing from side to side. Then he snatched up the vile tennis ball in his gob, turned, and off he went, scurrying away into the depths of the warehouse again. Little idiot.

'HENRY! STOP BUGGERING ABOUT! HEEL!'

Bark.

Knew we should've got a cat.

Pretty certain he'd found something unwholesome to roll in as well, given the horrible sour sausagey odour he'd left behind. Well, it was either that, or my fault for letting him eat all that crap over the last two days. God knew Henry could fart with the best of them.

I hobbled after him, into the darkness.

Well from now on he was getting nothing but dog food till his digestion settled down. No more treats.

Ding-buzz.

RoboSabir:

> >>Target Phone Located
> >>56.678808, -2.876107
> >>56.678892, -2.875771
> >>56.678982, -2.875412

What was that meant to be, some sort of error message?

And then it dawned – latitude and longitude. They were map coordinates.

When I copied and pasted the first one into my phone's map, it jumped straight to the A90, north of Forfar. The second one took it slightly further along the road. As did the third.

Which meant Gordon Smith was either heading for Oldcastle or Aberdeen.

I killed the torch app, plunging the surrounding stage sets into gloom again, and called Mother.

'If you're calling about your unmade beds, it's—'

'Leah's on the move. Sabir's got her mobile signal heading north on the A90.'

'It is? Why didn't we...' The sound went all muffled again. *'John, what's happening with Leah MacNeil's mobile phone? ... Well find out! Ash says she's being tracked right now! ... Go! Quick, quick!'*

My phone ding-buzzed again. Another text from RoboSabir with three lots of coordinates in it, and this time when I pasted the first set into my map, it came up with the slip road onto the A9402. So *definitely* heading for Oldcastle. 'You need to get an Armed Response Unit ready.'

'Thank you, Ash "I Was A DI Before You Were" Henderson, but

this isn't my first psychotic maniac.' A scrunching noise as she put her hand over the mouthpiece. *'Amanda! I need a dog unit and a firearms team, ASAP! Oh, and an OSU as well, might as well go in mob-handed. Then get the car: we're going hunting!'*

'Good. Franklin and I can be with you in—'

'You've got an SOC team on the way, remember? You need to be there for chain of evidence. Or have you completely forgotten what being a police officer involves?'

Damn it.

A muffled voice in the background – and whiny with it, so probably DC Watt. *'I've got them sending me live updates on Leah's phone's location. See?'*

'Right, I have to go.'

'Let me know how it...' But the line was silent. She'd hung up.

Thank you, Ash. You've done a great job, Ash. We couldn't have caught him without you, Ash.

Hmm... This was probably how Sabir felt.

My phone ding-buzzed again with three more coordinates, marking Leah's course towards Oldcastle.

Had to admit, it hurt to be left out at the grand finale. Would've been nice to be there while Gordon Smith resisted arrest. And maybe pile in to help subdue him. In a proportional-and-appropriate-level-of-force kind of way, of course. With a few sneaky kicks in the balls for luck.

Henry was doing his circular dance again when I caught up with him, next to Cinderella's kitchen – going by the laminated sign – but this time, as he tried to scurry off, I grabbed the smelly sod by the collar and snapped on his lead.

Ding-buzz.

Didn't seem to faze him any, though, he just grinned at me, tongue lolling out the side of his mouth.

'You're a stinky idiot, you know that, don't you?'

Weird: up close he didn't smell *nearly* as bad.

Must've been a bout of post-haggis-burger flatulence, then.

I let him pick up his vile tennis ball and we made our way back through the mounds of disassembled scenery.

Ding-buzz.

That nasty sausage-like smell was still there as we passed the tarpaulin-covered rack.

'How does one wee dog manage to produce a lingering...'

But what if it wasn't Henry?

None of the other sections of scenery were covered with tarpaulin, they were all open to the dusty warehouse air.

Yeah...

Ding-buzz.

I hooked his lead around the metal upright of the nearest rack and left him there.

Took hold of the tarpaulin's bottom corner.

Hauled it up and to the side. Flinging it back.

The breath turned to concrete in my throat as I stared at what'd been hidden underneath.

Now I knew what Gordon Smith had been doing here last night.

30

'But…' Franklin stood there, mouth hanging open. 'There's… I mean, are we sure this isn't another, you know, prop?' Sounding hopeful.

Couldn't blame her.

It was a cobbled-together version of the far wall in Gordon Smith's kill room. Shackles, for the wrists and ankles, fixed to chains that were bolted to a makeshift frame. Only this time the poor bastard he'd tortured was still hanging there.

Or at least, what was left of them.

Which explained that sour *meaty* smell.

She whistled out a breath. 'That's a lot of blood.'

The body's feet were twisted over onto their sides, in a wide plastic tub, submerged nearly up to their ankles in dark shiny viscous liquid.

This time, instead of *ding-buzz*, my phone went *pop-ding*. The text-alert noise I'd set for Leah.

> I don't no what to do!!! He's always been
> grandad 2 me but he's so so scary now
> I wanted 2 stop him but I couldn't I just
> want 2 cry all the time
> Please help me!!

Scary?

Scary didn't even *begin* to describe what Gordon Smith had done to the poor sod in front of me.

'What have you found this time?' Louis Williamson came bounding up, performing an OTT skip-and-a-hop, elbows out, as he came to a halt. As if he was on stage. 'Is this...' Then his eyes went wide and he lurched back a couple of steps. Grabbed hold of the nearest rack of scenery with one hand, the other clasped over his mouth. 'Oh Jesus...'

I turned, arms out, doing my best to block his view. 'Mr Williamson, I'm going to have to ask you to back away from the—'

'It's *him*, isn't it: that drama student who went missing? It was on the local radio this morning, his mum was frantic...'

'Drama student?'

'David something or other, didn't come home last night. He's... He *was* missing. Oh...' Louis swallowed. Shook his head. 'I think I'm going to be—' Both hands covered his mouth now, as he hurried away into the gloom.

I turned to Franklin.

She grimaced. Pulled out her phone. 'I know, I know. I'll call it in.'

Didn't take long for C Division to send out its best and brightest. Now the warehouse rang to the echoes of bodies in SOC suits rustling around, shouting at and to each other. Camera flashes flickering back from the surrounding scenery, lighting up the gloom like a mini thunderstorm. The clack and whine merging into the background noise.

Ding-buzz.

RoboSabir again. Only this time there was only the one coordinate. And according to my map it was halfway down Kittiwake Avenue in Logansferry. Looked as if Leah and Gordon Smith had finally got where they were going. I forwarded the text to Mother. Along with:

> They've stopped moving – Watt should
> have an address by now.
> Have you got your teams ready to go in?

295

SEND.

Not long to go before all this was over. Bit of an anti-climax, to be honest.

I called up Leah's contact and sent her one as well:

> You have to be strong, Leah. We know
> where you are and we're on our way. It'll
> all be over very, very soon!

My finger hovered over the 'SEND' icon.

What if she wasn't the only one reading her texts? What if *Smith* had got access to her phone? He'd probably slit her throat and run for it, before Mother and her team could get there. We'd never get another chance like this. Was it really worth the risk?

I deleted everything but the first sentence and tried again:

> You have to be strong, Leah.
> We WILL find you and Gordon Smith won't
> be able to hurt you, or anyone else, ever
> again.

SEND.

One more for good luck:

> But I need you to tell me what happened
> last night. We found a young man's body
> today. His mum and dad have a right to
> know what happened to him.

SEND.

Well, it was worth a try, anyway.

'Milk, no sugar.' Franklin wandered over and handed me a polystyrene cup full of something beige. 'They didn't have decaf.'

'Scuse me, coming through, beep beep.' A pair of techs trundled a portable generator past on squeaky wheels, closely followed by another pair carrying big work lights on bigger stands.

'Thanks.' It tasted every bit as nasty as it looked.

She took a sip of whatever it was she'd got herself. 'I miss anything?'

'Not yet, but that might change.' Pointing in the direction the techs had disappeared, as a figure in the full Smurf outfit *zwip-zwopped* their way towards us.

Stopped and pulled her facemask down. Her accent was semi-posh southern English, with a slight hint of Essex about it. 'Which one of you's the senior officer?' The words spat out hard and fast. Like a typewriter.

Franklin stood up straighter. 'I am.' Stuck her hand out for shaking. 'Detective Sergeant Rosalind Franklin. This is Ash Henderson, he's a consultant.'

'Ex-DI.' In case anyone cared.

The newcomer snapped off her nitrile gloves and gave Franklin's hand a brief up-and-down. 'DCI Jane Jopson.' Pulled back her hood, revealing a long ash-blonde bob. Flashed the kind of smile that showed off a good chunk of gum above her top teeth. 'Well, we'll need the family to ID his body, assuming the mortuary can make it presentable…' She glanced back, over her shoulder. 'Which doesn't seem likely, given the state of it. But I think it's safe to say our victim's David Quinn. Sixteen. His parents reported him missing last night when he didn't come home from a friend's house.' Jopson tapped the side of her neck. 'Port stain birthmark.'

The *chuff-chuff-chuff* of a generator starting came from behind her, rattling up to a diesel growl. Then those big work lights flickered into life, bouncing off the roof, spreading enough illumination to see by, even all the way over here.

'Any idea where our victim was abducted?'

Jopson looked at me, as if I'd slithered out from under a rock. 'Before we go any further, let's get one thing clear, ex-DI Haroldson—'

'Henderson.'

'Whatever. This, right here?' Describing a circle with one finger. 'Is *my* investigation. I'm the one running it. And even if you *were* still in the job, I'd outrank you. So for now, *I'll* be the one asking the questions.' Another smile, but this one cold and sharp. 'Let's start with: what makes you think this was your "Coffinmaker"?'

'The MO, ma'am.' Franklin was actually standing to attention now. 'It's virtually identical, all except for leaving the body behind. Normally he buries them in his garden.'

'I see. What's his usual abduction methodology?'

'Unknown, ma'am. The most recent victim we know about is from sixteen years ago.'

'Well, that's not *entirely* true, is it?' I leaned back against the nearest chunk of scenery. 'We know he befriends them first. Otherwise he couldn't get them to pose for their photographs the way he does.' Because ex-DI Haroldson wasn't an idiot.

Franklin's cheeks darkened. 'Well, yes. There is that. He takes photos of his victims before he abducts them, ma'am. And photos of them after he's … finished with their bodies.'

'I see.' Jopson nodded. 'And this "Coffinmaker", Gordon Smith, he worked here, did he?'

'All over the country. Designing sets for theatrical productions.' Franklin pointed. 'He did all these.'

'Right, well thank you for your help, DS Franklin. Ex-DI Haroldson. I'll be in touch if we need anything else. In the meantime, you can give Sergeant Marland your statements. And shoes.' And with that, she turned her back and *zwip-zwopped* away again.

I turned to Franklin. 'You total, and utter, crawler.'

Those cheeks darkened again. 'I am *not* a crawler.'

'"Yes, ma'am. No, ma'am. Look at me, all standing to attention and being efficient, ma'am."'

'There's nothing wrong with being efficient!'

Couldn't keep the smile hidden any longer. 'Crawler.'

'Hmph.' She folded her arms, then looked left and right. 'Any idea where this Sergeant Marland's—'

My phone burst into song. 'DI Malcolmson', according to the screen. 'Mother?'

'All right, I said I'd keep you in the loop, so consider yourself looped.' The sound was a bit tinny, with an underlying growl to it, as if she was in a car.

Franklin leaned closer. 'Have they got him?'

'Not yet.' Back to the phone. 'You got all your teams?'

'Shockingly enough, yes. Dogs, Guns, and Thugs. Did think about holding off and doing it in the wee small hours, but what if Smith moves on? Or goes out?'

'Or kills Leah MacNeil.'

'That's the scenario I'm trying not to think about, thank you very much.' The engine got louder. 'Here we go…'

A wee man in a double-breasted three-piece pinstriped suit that gave him the air of a 1920's gangster, lumbered out from behind a lump of scenery. His arms were a lot longer than they had any right being as well. As if an orangutan had escaped from the zoo by dressing like a bank manager. Hair slicked into a severe side parting. And when he smiled no two of his teeth pointed in the same direction. 'DS Franklin?'

I pointed at her.

Scrunching noises came down the line, followed by the *whoomph, whoomph, whoomph*, of Mother's breath as she ran.

The splintering *boom* of a door being whacked off its hinges by a big red door key.

Muffled voices in the background: *'GO, GO, GO!'*

'POLICE! NOBODY MOVE!'

Whoomph, whoomph, whoomph…

'DS Franklin, I'm DS Marland, but you can call me Colin, if you like? Good. Yes.'

'LIVING ROOM: CLEAR!'

'Now, the chief tells me you're the ones who discovered the body, is that right?' Pulling out a black police-issue notebook. 'I'd like you to take me through the series of events, starting from how you found yourself at the warehouse, here.'

I stuck a finger in my other ear and limped away a dozen paces.

'KITCHEN: CLEAR!'

More banging and crashing.

Whoomph, whoomph, whoomph…

Thumba-thumba-thumba-thumba…

Was that feet, thundering up a set of wooden stairs?

My phone announced an incoming text with that strange *pop-ding* again.

LEAH MACNEIL:

> Am I going 2 have 2 go 2 prison? He
> made me watch I didn't want 2 but he
> made me & it was horrible & I can't stop
> shaking

Another splintering *boom* – the noise tinny, because I didn't have the phone to my ear.

'YOU ON THE GROUND! ON THE GROUND NOW!'

A woman's voice, high-pitched and trembling. *'I'm on the toilet!'* Was that Leah? It sounded too old to be her, though. And the accent wasn't right, either.

'BEDROOM ONE: CLEAR!'

Whoomph, whoomph, whoomph…

Crashing. Something heavy hitting the floor.

'YOU: DON'T MOVE! MOVE AND I WILL SHOOT YOU!'

A man's voice. *'I don't understand, why are you—'*

'HANDS ON YOUR HEAD! KNEEL! KNEEL ON THE BLOODY FLOOR, NOW!'

They'd got him.

Then Mother's voice, loud and clear. *'Let me through, come on, Dougie, move your bottom, there's a good boy.'*

'Please, I don't know why you're—'

'SHUT UP! I SAID HANDS ON YOUR HEAD, BEFORE I BLOW IT OFF!'

'All right, Keith, you can stop…' The silence seemed to stretch for a week. Then, *'Keith?'*

'Yes, Mother?'

'Who the hell is this?'

Oh, for the love of Christ. I slapped my free hand over my eyes. They'd raided the wrong house.

Chaos on the other end of the phone. Lots of banging and crashing and swearing. Most of which seemed to be coming from Mother.

I left Franklin telling DS Marland how we'd entered the warehouse, and wandered away through the door to the prop store.

Along 'JACK AND THE BEANSTALK', past the office where Louis Williamson was scrunched up in a swivel chair, elbows on his knees, bald head in his hands, that tuft of bright-orange hair poking out between his clenched fingers.

The expensive prototype head-in-a-jar was on the desk behind him, still singing away to itself:

'Frankenstein he is a mate,
And though you'd think that we'd all hate,
The man who did decapitate,
Us all, but we still think he's great!'

I stepped into the darkening afternoon. Only half three, but already the sun was nearly at the horizon, painting the clouds that hunkered there in shades of violent pink and eggshell blue. Our manky pool car had been joined by half a dozen others, and a trio of patrol cars too – their reflective livery glowing in the fading light. And a surprisingly clean Transit van, with SOC techs humping blue plastic crates from the back doors and into the warehouse.

No sign of the national press yet, but that would change soon enough.

Pop-ding.

Another text cut through the tinny shouting coming out of my phone's speaker.

LEAH MACNEIL:

> I didn't want the boy 2 die I didn't want
> grandad 2 kill him
> But I didn't no how 2 stop him I wish I
> did I really really wish I did

Henry was on his hind legs in the back of our dirty Ford Focus, nose making pale snotty smears across the glass. Happy barking as I got closer.

Mother's voice came down the line. *'Well this is an unmitigated cocking shambles, isn't it?'*

Then someone else – might have been DC Watt, it was certainly whiny enough. *'It's not my fault! This is the address the phone coordinates pointed at. Look!'*

'Have you tried next door?'

'Give me a minute, Ash, I have to provide a modicum of encouragement and guidance to my team member here.' She cleared her throat. *'HOW THE HELL DID WE MANAGE TO COCK THIS UP SO BADLY?'*

'It wasn't me!'

My thumbs poked at the screen:

> The boy's name was David Quinn, he was
> only 16. He had parents and friends and a
> family who loved him.
> I need you to tell me where Gordon
> abducted him from.

Send.

'Maybe ... maybe, I don't know, but ... maybe they were here, but they've gone now? ... Or something?'

'AAAAAAAAAARGH!'

Leah MacNeil:

> Grandad drove 2 a graveyard up by the
> castle & I'm so so sorry I didn't want
> nothing 2 happen 2 David & I just want 2
> die ☹☹☹

'Or maybe the guy's lying and he knows Gordon Smith? Maybe he's ... an accomplice!'

'John, you know I mean this in the nicest possible way, but you should really shut up now, before I do something you'll regret!'

'No, look: I'll call her mobile. Hold on...'

The sound of some boy band burst into life in the background, getting louder.

'It's coming from downstairs!'

And they were off and running again.

31

Mother called me back, ten minutes later. *'You still there, Ash?'*

I hobbled on a couple of paces, Henry's lead and my walking stick in one hand, phone in the other. 'Just about.' The sun was a fierce yellow smear on the horizon, the sky above turning to ink. Stars struggling to shine through as the cloud thickened and the wind picked up again.

'We found Leah MacNeil's mobile. It was in the householder's jacket pocket.'

'So Watt was right for a change. They were co-conspirators?'

'Householder swears he doesn't know Gordon Smith, he's never met Gordon Smith, and he wouldn't recognise Gordon Smith if he got in the bath with him.' A pause. *'Which struck me as a rather strange metaphor, but there you go.'*

'And you believe him?'

'Says he was in Stirling for work, stopped at the petrol station this morning to fill up, and that was all he knew till we smashed his door down and caught his wife on the toilet. We checked with his work – he installs and maintains poles for pole dancing – he was at a pole-dancing-for-fitness-and-wellbeing place, which is apparently a thing now. Our hypothesis is that Smith must've slipped it into his pocket while he wasn't looking.'

'And let me guess, he bought petrol from the Sainsbury's supermarket.'

'Kept the receipt so he could claim it back on expenses.'

'Can you email me a photo? Well, two photos: one of the guy and one of the receipt?'

I'd got to the edge of the police cordon, where a bored PC in a fluorescent-yellow padded jacket stood, huffing warm breath into his hands and stomping his feet, behind the line of blue-and-white 'POLICE' tape.

And there was Helen MacNeil, standing at the open hatch to 'FIONA'S FANTASTIC FRIED-FOOD EMPORIUM!' clutching a polystyrene cup of something and a thing in a roll. Staring at me. No sign of her horrible companion, so I gave her a small wave and a tight smile. Then went back to the phone.

'I'm starting to think things might not be as straightforward as they seemed.'

A moment's silence. Followed by, '*Straightforward? Have you been working on a different case, because the one I'm investigating has been a great big bucket of slithering venomous snakes since the start!*'

'No, I meant…' Yeah. 'Look, I've got to go: Helen MacNeil's here.'

'*Have you told her about her granddaughter?*'

'Do you want me to?'

'*No.*' And with that, Mother hung up.

I thumbed out a reply to Leah's latest text.

> Where are you? How can you be texting
> me, when the police have got your phone?

SEND.

Helen MacNeil stomped over to the cordon, chewing on her butty. 'You found something.'

I nodded towards the manky yellow Golf. Couldn't tell if anyone was inside, the industrial estate's lights sucked the colour out of everything and the rusty hatchback's windscreen was opaque in the gloom. 'You didn't ditch Jennifer, then.'

'Is it Leah? Is she in there? Did he kill her?'

'She's using you, Helen. And once she's done, she'll dump you and move on to the next sucker.'

Helen's butty stabbed towards the warehouse. 'IS MY GRANDDAUGHTER IN THERE?'

'No, OK? She's not.' I closed my eyes for a second, took a breath, and tried for that reassuring-police-officer voice again. Maybe this time it'd work? 'Shouting the odds isn't helping you any, Helen. Go home. We'll be in touch if—'

'What home? You mean the one that'll fall into the North Sea, soon as the next storm front hits? The one I've been thrown out of by the bastarding council, who want sixteen grand to tear it down first? *That* home?'

Pop-ding.

'Investigations like this take time. We—'

'HE KILLED MY DAUGHTER!' Hurling her polystyrene cup to the ground, where it exploded in a spray of beige.

The PC shuffled over. 'All right, let's all calm down.'

'DON'T YOU TELL ME TO CALM DOWN!' Helen glared at him, hard enough to make him back off a pace.

'It's all right, Constable, she's with me.' I ducked under the cordon and grabbed her arm, pulling her along. 'Why don't we have a nice walk?'

Pop-ding.

Soon as we were out of listening range: 'Will you stop acting like a psycho for two sodding minutes?'

Helen shook her arm free. 'Gordon Smith killed my—'

'I know. And what do you think's going to help catch him: shouting the odds, or letting us do our jobs?'

'YOU'RE DOING BUGGER ALL!'

Henry hunkered down and growled at her.

'We're *working*. And you're not the only one who's lost a child.'

She scowled back at me. 'Six million.'

'It's not—'

'Don't pretend you've never taken a bung, because I *know* you have.'

'That wasn't—'

'Six million pounds and all you've got to do is give me an hour alone with him, somewhere out of the way. Somewhere no one can hear him screaming.' She stepped in closer, till our noses were almost touching. 'One parent to another. Because

305

the bastard killed my child, same as some bastard killed yours. And he deserves to *suffer*.'

Had to admit, she had a point...

The last glimmer of sun disappeared below the cold blue horizon. Clouds thickening overhead. Wind picking up enough to send a ceilidh of crisp packets whirling into a reel that swept across the road as I ducked back under the cordon of 'POLICE' tape again and pulled out my phone.

Checked the two text messages from Leah:

> U found my phone? Cool!!!!
> I lost it ages ago 6 weeks had 2 blagg
> this 1 off my mate coz she was getting a
> upgrade but it's knowhere near as good

And:

> I don't no how grandad knew David but
> they were all happy & friendly when he
> got in the car so I thought they was
> friends
> But they wasn't friends later

Bit of an understatement, given what Gordon Smith had done to him.

It explained Mother's phone cock-up, though. If Leah had lost it six weeks ago, that would be one week before she disappeared. Only she hadn't lost it at all – Smith had taken it. Planning ahead. Knowing we'd probably try to trace Leah through her phone, and that he could use that to throw us off track.

Like I told Franklin: you don't get away with killing people for fifty-six years by being an idiot.

Which meant we'd need a new warrant to track the phone she was actually using, and Watt was a complete and utter moron. And I'd take *great* pleasure pointing that out to him the next time we met.

Henry went back in the car, then I lumbered through the

prop warehouse to the scenery one. It looked as if Franklin had finished her statement, because DS Marland was getting her to sign it in his notebook.

Marland held up a finger. 'Ah, ex-DI Henderson, shall we...?' A frown. 'Er... Mr Henderson? Hello?'

But I didn't stop, I hobbled straight past, making for the heart of the huge open space, where the diesel generator's growl was the loudest.

Those two big work lights glared down on David Quinn's tattered remains, making every drop of scarlet sparkle as if it'd been wired up to the mains. It was impossible to tell which of the white SOC-suited figures was DCI Jopson – they all looked the same with their facemasks and safety goggles on.

But I was about a dozen feet away when one of them looked up at me and froze. Then hurried in my direction, arms held out trying to block my way:

A man's voice, so definitely not DCI Jopson, only slightly muffled by the facemask. 'WHAT THE *BLOODY* HELL DO YOU THINK YOU'RE DOING?'

'Where's Jopson?'

He kept coming. 'THIS IS A CRIME SCENE, YOU MORON! GET THE HELL OUT OF HERE!'

'Jopson, I've got—'

His hand slammed into my chest, forcing me back a step. 'BUGGER OFF OUT OF IT, YOU'RE CONTAMINATING—'

The SOC suit crinkled as I grabbed a fistful and hauled, pulling the dick off his feet and hurling him face-first into the rack containing Widow Twanky's laundry. He bounced off it, setting the metalwork ringing, then crashed backwards onto the concrete floor with a breath-robbing *whoomph*.

Looked as if he was about to struggle to his feet and have another go, so I thunked the rubber tip of my walking stick hard into his stomach, and, as he folded up, jabbed it into his chest and forced him down again.

'I discovered the body, you absolute muppet. My DNA and fibres are already all over the scene.' And limped on past. 'Which one of you is Jopson?'

The entire group had turned to gawp at me, but a figure over by the body raised a hand. 'Ex-DI Haroldson.'

Close enough.

'I've got an abduction point for you. And you'll want to pull the CCTV from the Sainsbury's petrol station as well.'

'Oh, will I now?' It sounded as if she was trying to hide the amusement in her voice, but not doing a very good job of it. 'And would you like me to do this *before* or *after* you've beaten up the rest of my team?'

Shrug. 'I'm easy.'

'Fair enough.' She pointed. 'But we're still going to need your shoes.'

'Ah, here you are.' DCI Jopson had changed out of her white SOC suit into something a bit less rustly: dark trousers and a black padded jacket that acted like camouflage in the graveyard's darkness, leaving her head to float, disembodied, five feet above the ground. 'How are the wellies?'

'Rubbish.' But at least it was better than being up here in nothing but my socks.

Most of Stirling was hidden from view: a wee chunk of the castle poking out on the left, a short line of houses – lights shining in their windows – the Church of the Holy Rood's dark medieval bulk on the right, bordered by a sliver of the town that was more rooftops than streets. A band of trees rustling in the groaning wind. Headlights on a distant road.

Five o'clock and the place was dead. Which was appropriate.

'We'll send your shoes back to Oldcastle when Forensics have finished with them. You can keep the wellies, though – souvenir of your time in beautiful Stirling.' Jopson turned and looked out over the graveyard, its headstones little more than indistinct lines in the gloom. 'I used to come here every lunchtime. Take Lottie for a walk. You know what cockapoos are like – adorable ninety percent of the time, but if they get bored it's like sharing an office with an extremely annoying toddler.'

'Why did you stop?'

'Turns out people don't like dogs weeing on their relatives' graves.'

'True.' It hadn't stopped Henry from cocking his leg on the odd Burgess of Trade on the way up here, though.

'If anyone asks, I gave you a proper bollocking for putting DI Erskine on his arse, back there. But, between you and me, he's a massive tosspot, so I quite enjoyed the floorshow.' She produced an iPad from a huge handbag and flipped open the cover. The light from its screen bloomed in the darkness, showing off another half-gum-half-tooth smile. 'Apparently he bruised his coccyx when he hit the floor. With any luck he won't be able to sit straight for a month.' She logged in and brought up a video. Passed the iPad to me as she dipped back into her bag again and emerged with a pre-wrapped sandwich. Tore her way into the cardboard triangle, setting free the sulphurous scent of eggs. 'Normally it takes hours and hours to work our way through CCTV footage, but as you had the time and date on the petrol receipt…'

The Sainsbury's petrol station filled the screen, taken from one of the cameras mounted on the awning that covered the forecourt. 'This is your man, here.' Pointing her sandwich at a long-limbed bloke in jeans and a thick sweater. He finished filling up an ugly four-by-four, hung the pump up, then set off towards the shop to pay. About eight foot from the door, someone bumped into him, then both did the standard I'm-so-sorry-no-my-fault-after-you dance, and disappeared inside.

Jopson chewed her way through one triangular, overstuffed half, getting mayonnaise on her cheek. 'Don't look at me like that, I skipped lunch. Some antisocial sod found a tortured teenager in a warehouse, remember?' Then she launched into the other half.

She was sooking her fingers clean by the time the man who'd bumped into Mother's householder emerged on screen again.

Jopson tapped the screen, freezing the image, then zoomed in. Leaving twin greasy smears on the glass.

Bit grainy, but the guy *did* look a lot like Gordon Smith – the same high forehead and Santa beard.

'Gets into a grey BMW and drives off towards the industrial estate next door.'

So he'd ditched the ancient Mercedes, because he knew we'd be looking for it.

She spooled the footage back to the two men bumping into each other, at the same increased magnification. 'Smith definitely slips something into your boy's jacket pocket.'

The phone he'd stolen from Leah.

Mother's householder was telling the truth.

I turned to Jopson. 'Can I ask a question?'

'You can try.'

'Why are you showing me this?'

A shrug. 'You could call it my kind and generous nature, or you could call it your boss's boss's boss calling *my* boss and asking us to play nice and coordinate our inquiries. Seeing as we're both after the same killer.' Jopson shut that video and started another one. This time it was a narrow cobbled road, the colours turned monochrome in the streetlights. A BMW came chuntering up the street. 'This is from a CCTV camera, outside the Old Town Jail. About a two-minute walk, that way.' Pointing in the vague direction of the medieval steeple.

The footage was grainy and badly lit. Impossible to tell if there was anyone but the driver in the car.

'There's meant to be cameras in the church grounds, but they got vandalised in September and they've still not fixed them. But half an hour later...'

The footage jumped under her sooked finger, and there was the same BMW heading off down another cobbled street, past an old-fashioned-looking building with a saltire flag flying above its front door. Again, no way to tell if Gordon Smith had passengers or not.

'We've got his car at the roundabout before Sainsbury's, then on CCTV inside the industrial estate. Got some bodies going around to see if any of the businesses in the area caught it on the way in or out, but I'm not holding my breath.'

'What about David Quinn?'

Jopson shook her head. 'Too dark. There's a few possibles,

310

but they're all wearing hoodies, so they could be Lord Lucan, for all we know.' A shrug. 'Far as we can tell, the last person to see David alive, other than Gordon Smith, was the friend he'd gone round to study with.' She hooked a thumb over her shoulder, away from the graveyard and towards those narrow cobbled streets. 'Shall we go pay the young man a visit?'

'I don't really know.' Bailey White's cheeks flushed even darker as he sneaked glances at Franklin's chest. 'It... We never... I don't know...' Somehow, blushing made the pimples that speckled his face look even angrier.

It was your standard teenaged boy's bedroom, small and cramped, with piles of clothes in the corners and posters of bands you've never heard of on the walls. That funky feet-and-armpit smell. A carpet that would probably light up like a Jackson Pollock painting under a UV lamp.

Crowded too, what with Bailey, DCI Jopson, Franklin, and me, all squeezed in here. But at least Henry had elected to stay in the car.

Jopson had draped her padded jacket over the back of a dining chair, brought through from the flat's tiny dining kitchen, revealing a stripy red-and-blue top. 'Think carefully, Bailey, it's important.'

His eyes drifted to her chest, then on to Franklin's again. He blinked a couple of times, cheeks going nuclear, before looking away. 'I ... don't know.'

I leaned back against the built-in wardrobe. 'Maybe it'd help if we all had a nice cup of tea? Help jog the old grey cells.' Jerking my head towards the door. 'Think you and the Detective Chief Inspector could sort something out, DS Franklin?'

The pair of them turned to stare at me.

'You know, a nice cup of tea?' Doing the whole raised eyebrows thing as I mouthed, 'Go away!' at them.

Then the penny must have dropped, because they both stood and bustled out of the room. 'Yes, good idea.' 'Everything's better with a cup of tea.' Leaving me and Bailey alone in his smelly teenager's den.

Soon as the door shut he hissed out a breath and sagged, eyes wide. 'Wow.' Then up at me. 'You work with her all the time? Detective Sergeant Franklin? She's *gorgeous*! Could be on *Love Island*, or a porn star, or anything!'

The dining chair creaked as I settled into it. 'Right, now the women aren't here whipping up your hormonal porridge, you can tell me why you're lying.'

That blush was back. 'I'm not.'

'Come on, Bailey, it's just us in here. When David left your house, he went up to the graveyard. We both know it's not on his way home.'

'I...' Bailey shrugged one shoulder. 'He...' Deep breath, staring down at his bitten fingernails. 'He was really excited about meeting someone. Someone he fancied.' The blush deepened. 'David's been...' He cleared his throat. 'David's mum and dad think he's like this straight-A student and totally normal and everything, but they don't know he's bi.' Another lopsided shrug. 'Bisexual. He told me last year.' Bailey held up a hand. 'I mean, I'm not, you know, gay or anything like that, I definitely like women, with boobs and stuff. But David fancies men *and* women.'

'And that's who he was going up to the graveyard to meet? A man?'

'Didn't say, but he had that ... *spark* in his eyes, you know?' Bailey raised his head and stared out of the bedroom window at the darkness beyond. 'We've been best friends since primary two. We're doing the same exams so we can go to Art School together. Study drama and filmmaking.'

'I'm sorry.'

His shoulders curled forwards and he nodded. Wiped a hand across his eyes. 'You won't tell anyone, will you? About David being bi? He never came out, because it'd kill his mum and dad.'

Poor wee sod.

Both of them.

David wouldn't get to be himself, not even in death. And Bailey?

I levered myself out of the chair. 'My best friend's gay; he told me *years* before he finally came out and left his wife. It's not easy, being responsible for someone else's secrets.' I gave Bailey's hunched shoulder a squeeze. 'You've been a good friend to David. Don't let it eat you.'

Then let myself out.

32

'…*really love that song. Kar Stanton and "She Can". Think that's got a real chance of being Christmas number one, this year…*'

The A90 thrummed beneath the pool car's tyres, oncoming headlights gleaming in the darkness.

'*We've got the news and weather coming up in twenty minutes, but first here's Closed for Refurbishment and "Whatever She Wants" brackets, "She Can't Have"!*'

We'd not long passed the sign for Glendoick Garden Centre when my phone *pop-ding*ed again.

LEAH MACNEIL:

> I'm sorry I can't leave my phone on it sets
> off the car speakers & grandad would no I
> had it & he will punish me
> I don't want 2 end up like David

Pop-ding.
LEAH MACNEIL:

> We've stopped somewhere I think its the
> countryside coz there's no lights we've
> been driving 4 ever I have to do what he
> says & behave or he will punish me

Pop-ding.
LEAH MACNEIL:

> Tell granny I love her & I'm sorry I wasn't
> a better granddaughter but I was selfish &
> stupid & she was always there for me
> when she wasn't in prison

Pop-ding.
Leah MacNeil:

> I don't think grandad will ever let me go
> home
> One day I'll make him angry & he will cut
> me in2 tiny bits like all the others
> I'm sorry 4 everything

I picked out a reply.

> We'll find you before he can hurt you,
> Leah. You have to hold on and not give
> up.
> We WILL find you.

Send.
And, hopefully, she'd still be in one piece when we did.

The song on the radio crash-bang-walloped to a halt, then
was replaced by something equally shouty. I turned it down
and called Mother.

'Have you kicked Watt's backside into orbit yet?'

A pause. *'Ash, how nice to hear from you. Again.'* Didn't sound
like it.

'How did he manage to get a trace set up on the wrong
bloody mobile?'

*'Is there a point to this call? Because I've already had words with
John and he's getting a new warrant sorted out.'*

'I even forwarded you Leah MacNeil's texts! How could
anyone not spot they weren't from the same phone number?'

*'This isn't helping. Now do you have anything constructive to add
to the investigation, or can I get back to slowly working on a stress-
related aneurism?'*

'Has anyone looked into Gordon Smith's sexuality?'

315

Franklin overtook a Luton Transit van, with 'SAMMY'S MIDNIGHT FLIT ~ YOU'D BE NUTS TO TRUST ANYONE ELSE!!!' and a grinning thumbs-up squirrel on the side.

Then, finally, Mother was back, voice cold and clipped. *'Does it matter?'*

'Probably not, but our latest victim: David Quinn. He was bisexual and excited about meeting someone the night he died, which turned out to be Gordon Smith. Of course, he also wanted to study drama and filmmaking at university, so that might be how Smith manipulated him into going to the scenery warehouse. But if you're looking for a mentor, would you *really* set up a meeting, at night, in a graveyard?'

'Gordon Smith's sexuality is immaterial. You want to know what is material? Catching him. Now how about trying to do that instead of casting aspersions on the LGBTQI community!' Then complete silence from the phone. She'd hung up.

Lovely.

I looked across the car at Franklin, partially lit by the dashboard's glow, and partially by the oncoming headlights. 'Did *any* of what I said sound homophobic to you?'

'Wasn't paying attention. Now any chance we can have the radio up again? It's been a long couple of days and I'd rather not fall asleep at the wheel on the way home.'

Franklin pulled in to the kerb on Guild Street, spitting distance from Divisional Headquarters. Cracked a yawn that showed off loads of perfect teeth with only a couple of fillings at the back. Then blinked a few times and slumped in her seat. 'Right: what time tomorrow?'

'Nine. Mother owes us a long lie-in after all that.'

A hollow laugh. 'Yeah, right.'

I climbed out and collected Henry from the back seat. 'Go home, clamber into a hot bath, and get some sleep. Get out of the bath first, though, unless you fancy drowning.'

She rolled her eyes and I thumped the car door shut. Waved as Franklin performed a three-point turn and headed off towards the town centre.

Wind chased the wee lad and me as we ducked around the corner onto Doyle Lane, borrowed wellies going *week-wonk* as I limped past two closed charity shops and a chipper with a bored-looking man slumped behind the counter. Then in through the hallowed portal of The Tartan Bunnet Café.

Condensation pewtered the windows, greasy with the scent of hot chip fat and generations-worth of fried bacon. The twin red lights atop Castle Hill Infirmary's incinerator chimneys glowing like a pair of eyes through the misty glass. Small square tables draped with red-and-white checked plastic cloths; the squeezy kind of condiment containers that no one ever had in their home; and a TV on a shelf, up above the counter, the picture as indistinct as the outside world, obscured by its own patina of grease.

An old-fashioned bell tinkled, announcing our arrival to the gathered masses. Which, this evening, consisted of a fat man frowning away at the *Castle News and Post*'s crossword, a uniformed PC with a squint face and a side parting, and Alice.

She looked up as I closed the door behind us, a large mug cradled in her hands. Smiled a thin, sad smile. Then she caught sight of Henry and scooted out of her chair, dropping to one knee and holding her arms out towards him. 'Oh, I've missed you!'

'Thanks a bunch.' But I let go of the wee lad's lead anyway and he scurried across the scarred lino to her, tail whumping away so hard his back end wasn't really under control.

Sitting in the corner, the PC raised an eyebrow and his tea in salute, the crime-scene smears of a long-dead fry-up on the empty plate in front of him. Fiddling one-handed with his phone. He'd dumped his stabproof vest on the seat next to him, like a hollow companion keeping him company while he finished his dinner and wanked about on Facebook. What was his name again: MacAskill? MacAllister? Something like that. He hadn't been around when I'd been a DI, anyway. Or even after they demoted me. Maybe he was one of Shifty's team?

I gave him a nod in return and settled into the seat opposite Alice as she finished giving Henry the prodigal Scottie dog's reception. Which genuinely took about five minutes – oohing and aahing over him while I sat there ignored like a boiled jobbie.

Finally, she surfaced from beneath the table. 'Sorry, but I really have missed him.'

Her mug was warm to the touch, and when I gave it a sniff: coffee, without even a whiff of booze. It went back on the table. 'And sober too?'

'I listened to what you said, and I'm giving it a go.' That sad smile again. 'It's that or retire. Pack in the behavioural evidence analysis game and go be…' Her shoulders sagged. 'I don't know what I could be. I've never done anything else.'

A woman scuffed out from the back, her face as lined and saggy as an elephant's scrotum, thin white hairs poking out from her chin and cheeks. A headscarf with wisps of grey escaping from underneath to stick to her shiny forehead. She thumped a mug down in front of me then cleared her throat – like someone rattling a tin can half-full of gravel. Her voice wasn't much better. 'Decaf tea, milk, no sugar.'

'Thanks, Effie.'

'You wanting food? Course you are, look at you, you need feeding up. I'll do you some chips.' Then turned and scuffed off back the way she'd come.

The tea was hot and bland and milky. 'So how did you get on with your child-killer?'

Alice pulled a face. 'Profiling sober isn't the same at all. I miss the feeling of … I don't know, invulnerability? Omnipotence? Instead I spent half the time second-guessing everything I'd done. Urgh…'

'Couples who kill.'

'And Bear's *still* convinced that Gòrach's someone on the Sex Offenders' Register, so what's the point of me even bothering? Could've spent the day reading a book instead.'

'Say you weren't very bright, and you fell in with a dominant personality who wanted to go out murdering people. And wanted you to go with him.'

'Doesn't matter how many ways I twist it, I can't get the

profile to match someone who's already offended. It doesn't fit. This is him trying things out, he's never done that before, I *know* he hasn't.'

'How long would it take before you started *wanting* to join in?'

'A little boy's life is at stake and they're not listening to me, Ash. No one's listening to me!' Alice sagged a bit, then took a slurp of her un-Irish coffee. 'And it's not so much "wanting" to kill people as it is wanting to please your new partner. The subservient one in the relationship usually has very low self-esteem, which makes it much easier for the dominant one to ... let's call it *shape* them. After a while you might think you were really into it, but if the dominant partner goes to prison, or gets ill, or dies, the subservient one soon gives up offending. They don't crave the kill, they crave the approval it gets them.'

Which would make sod-all difference to anyone unlucky enough to come across them in the meantime.

Alice looked at me over the rim of her mug. 'You think Leah MacNeil helped Smith kill your young man in Stirling?'

'Don't know. Maybe. Difficult to tell when we can only communicate via the odd text, but she's certainly not telling us everything. She's hiding stuff.'

'Wouldn't you? Imagine being an eighteen-year-old girl and the man you've called "Grandad" your entire life – the man who raised you, because your mum's dead and your real gran's in prison – *makes* you watch him torture a sixteen-year-old boy to death. How much would you tell the police after that?'

'Fair enough. But the—'

'Here you go.' A heaped plate of chips appeared in front of me, and when I looked up, there was Effie. 'Did you some fish fingers as well. Eat. Eat.'

Soon as she was gone, I slipped Henry one of Captain Birds Eye's finest breadcrumbed digits.

Over in the corner PC MacAskill / McAllister was looking over my shoulder as he dug about in his Police Scotland fleece pocket. Dumping a clattering handful of change on the chequered tablecloth. Stood. And wriggled his way into his stabproof vest. Going at a fair clip, too. As if he'd suddenly realised he was due back on patrol five minutes ago.

Then the door dinged behind me, letting in a howl of cold air.

He hurried past our table, not making eye contact – because why be normal when you could be a freak? – then *clunk*, the door shut again.

I nodded at Alice and squirted a dollop of mayonnaise onto the side of my plate. 'You can help yourself to a chip, if you like.'

She didn't move. Just sat there, staring over my shoulder, like the PC had. Eyes getting wider. Mouth trembling.

Then a high-pitched breathy voice scratched through the café's muggy air. 'A most generous offer, Mr Henderson, and one I shall be delighted to profit from.'

Oh. Cock.

I slid my right hand across the sticky plastic tablecloth, making for the knife and fork that had arrived with my chips.

'Now, now, Mr Henderson. I assure you that any attempt to deploy cutlery as a weapon at this juncture would be counter-productive to the good doctor's wellbeing. And I'm sure none of us would want that.' He made his way around the table till he was standing behind Alice. Put his hands on her shoulders.

She flinched.

Beneath the table, Henry growled.

I stayed perfectly still. 'Joseph. Get your hands off her. *Now.*'

He did, then smiled. He'd had his teeth done since we'd last met – veneers, crowns, and implants replacing the damage I'd caused. It didn't help any, though, he was still an ugly wee bastard. Short; ears sticking out like the handles on a funeral urn; Neanderthal forehead; jutting chin; hair shorn to barely more than stubble, showing off the extensive collection of scars that crowned his misshapen head. A blue DIY tattoo of a swallow staining his wrist where it jutted out of his shirt sleeve. Black suit. Leather gloves. 'How delightful to make your acquaintance again, Mr Henderson, though I'm despondent that it couldn't be under more opportune circumstances.'

I risked a glance over my shoulder, and there was the other half. I nodded. 'Francis.'

He nodded back. "'Spector.' His John Lennon glasses had steamed up in the Tartan Bunnet's chip-fat air. A big droopy Irn-Bru moustache beneath his twisted and flattened nose, the soul patch under his bottom lip already going grey. His curly red hair was streaked with it too, pulled back in a ponytail, the hairline ragged around a line of scar tissue where I'd tried to cave his skull in with an unopened tin of beans. Black leather jacket, black shirt, black jeans, heavy black boots.

I scooted my chair sideways, so I could keep an eye on him and the brains of the operation at the same time. 'I thought you two were banished from Oldcastle on pain of dismemberment.'

'Ah, yes, after that unfortunate misunderstanding about Mrs Kerrigan. Well, it's to our benefit that those who once governed the more … *nefarious* aspects of this great city have retired to what I understand is a rather splendid private island in the Caribbean. Meaning that Francis and myself have been able to return and take up a more entrepreneurial role.' He pulled out a small metal wallet and slid free a white rectangle. Placed it on the tabletop. 'Our card.'

'J&F ~ Freelance Consultants' and a mobile number. No names, no address, no details.

'What do you want, Joseph?'

'Me?' He sighed. 'Alas, it is with a heavy heart that I stand before you today.' He put his hand back on Alice's shoulder and gave it a squeeze. 'We have—'

'Do you remember what I said I'd do to you if you ever touched her again?'

The growling got louder, darker.

'Now, let me think…' A frown pulled at that scarred dome. Then the smile was back. 'Ah yes, you said you would, and I hope I'm quoting this correctly, "break every one of my fingers then make me eat them"? A tad macabre and melodramatic, but then tempers were rather heated at the time, as I recall. Sadly, they seem destined to be that way again.'

Francis took off his steamed-up glasses and slipped them into his jacket pocket. No emotion at all in his small pink eyes. 'Yup.'

Joseph clasped his hands together and turned to face the fat man, who seemed to have developed an all-consuming interest in his crossword. 'Sir, I believe the most efficacious way for you to ensure your continued wellbeing is to exit with the *utmost* alacrity. There we go.' Giving a muted round of applause as the man grabbed his newspaper and coat, then scrambled for the door, nearly tripping over a chair in his rush to get out of there.

The bell dinged as he disappeared into the night.

'And Doctor McDonald, it would be best if you could control your canine companion. I would hate for something untoward to occur to it. Veterinarian treatment can prove *very* expensive when a pet has suffered serious injury.'

Alice snatched Henry up and clasped him against her chest as the wee lad snarled.

'Thank you. Now, where were we?' Joseph clapped his gloved hands together. 'Ah yes: you see, Mr Henderson, a mutual … well I can hardly call her a "friend" in the circumstances, but I imagine "acquaintance" shall suffice, has commissioned the services of myself and my esteemed colleague to, as she put it, "beat the living shit" out of you. Apparently you threw her mobile phone off a ferry, and said certain things that caused her great consternation and personal distress.' He took his hand off Alice's shoulder to hold it up, palm out. 'Now, I can assure you that this assignment will give neither Francis nor myself anything but displeasure to perform, especially given our shared history, however a contractual obligation *is* a contractual obligation.' A what-can-one-do shrug. 'But it is within our gift to keep said beating as brief as is humanly, if not humanely, possible. So, if you would care to accompany my associate to the exterior of this fine establishment, he will perform the unpleasant task before us, while I keep the good doctor here company to ensure any thoughts of noncompliance are furthest from your mind.'

If he thought I was going to meekly stand outside and take a kicking, he was in for a nasty shock. 'How did you know I was here?'

'Ah, Mr Henderson, ever the inquiring mind, I do so admire that about you. Let us simply say that gentlemen in our position

322

may obtain information to our advantage from those prepared to divulge things they perhaps shouldn't in exchange for financial gain or the diminution of certain debts.'

AKA: some bastard ratted me out.

I cricked my neck to one side, then the other. Rolled my shoulders.

I'd taken Francis before and I could do it again.

As long as I made sure he—

The world snapped back through ninety degrees as Francis's fist slammed into my face.

33

A high-pitched whine burst across the café, accompanied by a swarm of wasps – making fierce yellow circles in the corner of my eyes. And then the pain hit. Slicing through my sinuses, digging its claws into the back of my eyes and my skull. The world stinking of hot iron and cracked pepper as my head rocked forward again and scarlet spurted down across my shirt.

'Gnnn...'

'Now, Francis! That was hardly sporting, was it? You didn't even allow Mr Henderson the opportunity to stand up.'

'Sorry.'

Hands took hold of my jacket's lapels, hauling me out of my chair as the room waltzed one way then the other, the wasps getting louder. Scarlet droplets bursting against the linoleum at my feet.

Henry's barks rang out like a shotgun.

Alice joined them: 'GET OFF HIM, YOU BASTARD!'

'Now, now, dear Doctor, let's not escalate this situation unnecessarily. Control that animal, before it gets hurt.'

I blinked away the tears. Brought my fists up.

Francis's head got smaller for a heartbeat, then swelled up like a meteorite, slamming into the bridge of my nose with the crack and pop of a thousand fireworks. Filling the world with the stench of raw meat. My right leg stopped working, the knee refusing to hold my weight as the café's waltz turned

324

into a polka and boiling petrol washed through my face. Bursting into flame as it touched whatever was left of my nasal cartilage. I grabbed a handful of table, keeping myself upright. But only just.

FIGHT BACK!

I swung. Missed.

'That's the spirit, Mr Henderson! Do not go quietly into that dark night!'

That was the trouble with gobby bastards – too much time spent on word-of-the-day calendars and not enough learning the proper bloody quotes.

More barking.

I spat out a mouthful of copper pennies. 'Come on then. That all you've got?'

Effie emerged from the kitchen, teeth bared, a frying pan clutched in one hand like a mallet. 'What the *hell* do youse bastards think you're doing in my café?'

'How unfortunate.' Joseph raised his eyes to the grubby ceiling as if the answer to Effie's question was written there. Then turned his cold hard smile on her. 'I take it you are the proprietor of this fine establishment? Well, if you'd be so kind as to take a seat and remain silent, we shall try to conduct our business here with the minimum of disruption to your premises. It would be a matter of personal regret if we were forced to cause damage to your fixtures, fittings, and limbs.'

Alice's voice slashed through the muggy air: 'EFFIE, CALL THE POLICE! CALL—Ulk…!'

The clatter and scrabble of dog claws on the linoleum.

'Now, dear Doctor, I do believe I counselled against interfering.'

Alice.

I turned, teeth bared and there was Joseph, standing behind her, with his right arm around her throat, left arm locking her head in and forcing it forward. Chokehold. Shutting off the blood to her brain.

Henry charged at Joseph, jaws snapping, barks ringing out.

Then a whimpering yelp as Joseph lashed out with a foot,

sending the brave wee lad flying as Alice's face darkened. 'I *warned* you!'

Right, that bastard—

Francis's left fist cracked upwards into my ribs, nearly lifting me off my one good foot. Taking all the breath in my lungs with it. And the other knee gave way.

This was it.

The scarlet-spattered linoleum rushed up to meet me. Now the kicking would start. The stamping. The broken bones and fractured skull. The internal bleeding.

Clutching at the table didn't help – it dragged the checked plastic cloth off, taking the sauces and salt and mugs and plate and chips and fish fingers with it. A shattering of crockery, the ping and clang of cheap cutlery bouncing.

Then *BOOM*.

The Tartan Bunnet's front door burst open and Helen MacNeil charged over the threshold, screaming something without words in it, mouth wide, teeth flashing, all the cords in her neck standing out like the cables on a suspension bridge.

Francis got as far as, 'Naw—' before she crashed into him, knocking him off his feet and sending him flying into the nearest table with a crunch of buckling chipboard. He was bent backwards over it, hips jutting, arms flailing as Helen leapt on him – one knee slamming down into his groin. And that was it for the table. The entire thing collapsed and Francis thumped into the floor with Helen still on top as she grabbed his ponytail and battered her other fist off his face five or six times in rapid succession, like a jackhammer, sending up tiny spurts of scarlet with every impact. Re-breaking that squint nose, shutting his eye.

Then twisting around and onto her feet again.

Can't have taken her more than a dozen seconds, and Francis was a groaning mess of battered skin, blood frothing at the side of his mouth and dribbling down his cheek.

Joseph swivelled, putting Alice between Helen and himself. Partially releasing his chokehold to dig a hand into his jacket pocket. 'Now I know we haven't been properly introduced, but

I can assure you that this encounter will *not* go well for you if you don't turn around and leave right now.'

She kept her eyes on him as she picked up one of the broken table's metal legs, holding it like a baseball bat, slapping the other end against her palm. 'You know who I am?'

'I haven't had the pleasure.'

'Oh, it's no pleasure, I'm pretty sure of that.' Stepping closer. 'See, I know who *you* are.'

'Then you know that, much though it may pain me, I shall not hesitate to do the good doctor here serious harm if you don't depart as requested.'

Helen shrugged. 'Go on, then. She's nothing to me. But *this* one?' Pointing the table leg in my direction. 'He's mine. And you better pray he's still useful to me, because see if he's not?'

'Unnnnnngh...' Francis rolled over onto his front. Struggled up to his hands and knees. Blood dripping onto the linoleum beneath his face. Another grunt and he was sitting back on his haunches, face already swelling up. Wobbling in a circle, as if the whole café was swaying.

Welcome to the dance.

Helen didn't even look at him. Instead she swung the table leg in a fast, flat arc behind her.

A muffled *clang* as the metal cracked off Francis's head, and gravity reclaimed him. On his side, lying there, mouth open, eyes closed.

But at least he was still breathing.

Alice, on the other hand, was going a darker shade of red, hands scratching at Joseph's arm, mouth opening and closing on nothing. Feet scratching across the linoleum. One arm wasn't enough to cut off the blood flow, but plenty to make sure she couldn't breathe.

I hauled myself up the nearest chair. 'LET HER GO!'

'Going to give you a choice, Joseph. Either you take your boyfriend and you run away, or I do the same thing to you that I did to Neil Stringer.' The table leg slapped into her open palm again. 'Five. ... Four.'

He licked his lips. Looked from Helen, to the length of metal in her hands, to Francis, then back again. Then closed his eyes and nodded. 'I suppose there's only one course of action open to me.'

'Three. … Two.'

Joseph's left hand flashed up from his pocket, an old-fashioned cutthroat razor snapping open. Blade gleaming as he hurled Alice to one side. 'You'll regret your—'

'One.' The table leg rose, then fell, sharp and hard across the scarred crown of Joseph's head. Enough weight behind it to bend the metal.

Joseph staggered back, thumping into the wall. Spitting out a gobbet of scarlet. Then lunged, cutthroat razor hissing through the air. Might have got her too, if she hadn't leapt out of the way.

The table leg came crashing down again, on his left forearm, and this time that metal-tube noise was joined by a muffled pop and Joseph's cutthroat razor skittered off across the linoleum, to thunk against a skirting board. The hand that'd held it hung at a very unnatural angle, as if his wrist started halfway up his arm now.

He sank down to one knee, grimacing as he clutched those shattered bones to his chest. 'GRRRRRRRRRRRRRRAAAAAARGH!' Lurching to his feet again. Standing there, hissing breath in and out between his gritted teeth, red bubbles popping around those perfect veneers.

Alice scrabbled back against the wall, hands rubbing at her throat as she wheezed in ragged lungfuls of air.

A thump, and the kitchen door swung open. Effie, standing there, holding an old-fashioned beige phone to her ear, its curly flex festooned with greasy fluff. 'The police'll be here any minute!'

Helen nodded. 'You're lucky Mr Henderson and these women are here, Joseph. Otherwise you'd both be dead by now.' A cruel smile. 'You should say "thank you" to them. Or shall I batter your boyfriend's brains out?' Resting the tip of the table leg against Francis's forehead. 'Go on: *say* it.'

'Gnnn…' Joseph swallowed whatever it was down. Then forced the words out. 'Thank you.'

'Now, like I said: take your boyfriend and bugger off. Before I change my mind.'

'Here.' Alice wriggled back into the booth next to me, holding out a tea towel full of ice. Voice trembling and a lot higher than normal. 'Are you sure you don't want to go to the hospital, because I really think you should go to the hospital.' Pressing the cold damp towel against my forehead.

I tried for: 'Give me that.' But what actually came out was a nasal mushy: 'Gibbee dat.' I held the icepack over as much of my face as possible. Breathing hot peppery breaths into the clammy fabric while my head throbbed like a monstrous heart. Every time I inhaled it was like being punched in the ribs again. Knowing my luck, Francis had broken a few of them. But I wasn't all that keen on prodding the things to find out.

The Monk and Casket wasn't the fanciest pub in Oldcastle, or the nicest, or most hygienic. But it was dark and relatively quiet, nestled down at the bottom of Jamesmuir Road. The kind of place that had mock-Tudor nonsense on the outside; scarred wooden tables, red vinyl upholstery, and sticky wooden floors on the inside. A couple of puggy machines flashed and dinged in one corner, a pub quiz one over by the toilets. As if anyone in the Monk and Casket gave a toss what the capital of Paraguay was, as long as the booze was cheap. Not that it was busy in here: a couple of elderly prostitutes with bottles of extra-strong cider, a pair of miserable middle-aged men hunched over pints of Export, and an old wifie nursing a port-and-lemon while feeding Bacon Frazzles to the wee Westie poking out of her tartan shopping trolley. Alice. Henry. And me.

Oh, and Hairy Joe, currently serving Helen MacNeil with his usual grudging and surly approach to the hospitality industry.

I ruffled the hair between Henry's ears. 'How you holding up, teeny man?'

He gazed up at me with big sad dark eyes. Because no one was feeding *him* Bacon Frazzles. But, thankfully, Joseph didn't appear to have caused Henry any permanent damage.

Alice pawed at me again, all fussing and jittery. 'It wouldn't take long to go to the hospital. It's—'

'I'm *not* going to the hospital!' Let's face it, I'd had worse beatings in the past. Lots and lots of them. This one barely made the top fifty...

Helen returned to the table, hands wrapped around two pint glasses of something pale, two shorts, a tin of Diet Coke and a packet of cheese-and-onion. A pint and a nip went in front of me. Then she settled into the other side of the booth and slid the Diet Coke in front of Alice. Who slid it back again and helped herself to one of the whiskies, knocking it back in one. Then gulping down about half the pint before Helen could open her mouth to complain.

'I don't drink.' The Coke tin *tisssshhh*ed at me as I clicked the ring-pull back. 'Pills.'

She watched, mouth pursed as Alice polished off the last of the pint.

A burp. 'I needed that, does anyone else feel like another drink, I think we deserve another drink, I'll get a round in shall I, yes, a drink's exactly what the doctor ordered, or what the doctor's about to order, I mean I *am* a doctor, so technically it's not really drinking it's medicinal.' A cold metallic bark of a laugh. Then she hurried over to the bar.

Helen took a sip of whisky, rolling it around her mouth. Then, 'She's kind of ... jumpy.'

'Last time we had a proper run-in with Joseph and Francis, it didn't end well for a friend of ours.' I closed my right eye and pointed at it. 'Alice had to watch.'

'Not everyone's got the guts for it, I suppose.' The last of the whisky disappeared. 'What happened to you? Used to be a safe bet at the Westing – don't remember anyone even making it to the second round against Ash Henderson.'

'Yeah, my bare-knuckle days are long gone.' I puffed out a breath. 'Thought you were still palling around with Jennifer Prentice?'

'Needed a lift back to Oldcastle, didn't I? Besides, she wants to drive me about, following you, *and* pay for the petrol – like

I'm going to turn that down?' A smile. 'Soon as your DS friend dropped you off, I told Jennifer where she could stuff her book. And when I saw that pair of freaks going into the Tartan Bunnet...?' Helen shrugged, then started in on her pint. 'You owe me, now. Big time.'

'Francis sucker-punched me, OK?' I dabbed the icepack against my face, going delicate around the nose and eyes. 'How bad does it look?'

'You really want to know?'

'That bad?'

'Worse. Hold still.' Then she reached across the table and placed her palms against my cheeks. 'This is going to hurt.' Her thumbs jabbed into the sides of my nose and twisted.

A crunching noise filled the world and molten glass exploded between my eyes, rushing out across my cheeks, nostrils and sinuses catching light. Scalding liquid pouring down my top lip and spattering onto the tabletop. '*Fuck!*'

'Don't be such a baby.' She pressed the icepack against my face again. 'You're getting blood everywhere.'

'Son of a bitch...'

She pushed every beermat on the table into the spreading pool of bright scarlet. Leaned back in her seat, took a bite out of her pint – giving herself a pale froth moustache in the process. 'Way I see it, I saved your life. And Dr Whatsit, too. And probably your mutt as well.' Another mouthful. 'So yes, you *owe* me.'

Yeah, I probably did.

Someone else I owed was Jennifer Bloody Prentice. All I did was chuck her phone into the sea, and she pays Joseph and Francis to 'beat the living shit' out of me? No way I was letting her get away with that. She could—

'Oh my God, what happened?'

When I looked up, there was Alice, staring, drinks wobbling on a round brown tray.

'Fixed his nose.' Helen toasted her with the pint. 'You're welcome.'

'I'll get a cloth...' And she was gone again.

'The exchange rate is: your life, Dr Weirdo's, and the dog's for Gordon Smith's. I think that's fair, don't you?'

The throbbing was settling into a dull ache – as if someone was squatting inside my skull trying to shove my eyeballs out of their sockets with hobnail boots on. 'What happened to the six million?'

'That's gone down to two again.'

Not to be sniffed at – assuming my nose ever worked again. Two million would set us up somewhere new. Somewhere that wasn't Oldcastle. Somewhere Alice could retire and maybe we could open up a bookshop or a pub or a wee hotel or something. Somewhere no one would come looking for us after I skinned Joseph alive.

— sauf', und würg' dich zu todt! —

(drink, and choke yourself to death)

34

'...afraid you're right, Jane. We've barely caught our breath from Storm Trevor and here comes Storm Victoria...'

'Gah!' Fumbling for the alarm-clock radio, mashing the button to make the idiots shut the hell up.

'...have to batten down the hatches for the next three, maybe four days as this area of low pressure—'

Blessed silence.

And then the *real* pressure kicked in – as if someone had jammed a bicycle pump into my sinuses and was ramming the piston home with every beat of my heart. Mouth, sandpaper dry. That's what happened when you couldn't breathe through your nose.

Probably didn't help that I'd packed it full of cotton wool to stop the bleeding.

And *still* the world stank of burning bees.

Getting back to sleep wasn't going to be an option, was it? At least not without a shedload of painkillers and a big glass of water.

I struggled out of bed, ribs screaming like a slaughterhouse, grimaced and winced my way into the tartan dressing gown hanging on the back of the door, and hobbled into the corridor.

Clicking the lights on sent frozen daggers stabbing through my retinas, so I switched them off again. Limped through the gloom.

No sign of Henry in the living room. Probably curled up at the foot of Alice's bed.

Which was good, because no way in hell could I face any sort of enthusiasm this early in the morning. 06:25 according to the microwave clock.

Two amitriptyline got washed down with a glug of water, followed by a tramadol for good measure.

Getting old, Ash. Used to be a time you'd shake something like this off, and be up and doing the next day ready for anything. But now?

Two punches and a head-butt, and it was as if I'd been run over by a tank.

Outside the floor-to-ceiling windows, the city was a shroud of faded streetlights, draped over the valley's corpse. But the glass was cool against my forehead.

Question was, what was I going to do about it?

How about arranging a small accident for Jennifer Prentice? The kind that ended up with her missing a limb or two... Or was that OTT? Didn't feel like it, going by the rusty sawblades hacking their way through my head and ribs, right now. *Something* had to happen, though: she wasn't getting away with it.

And she wasn't the only one.

No prizes for guessing how Joseph and Francis had found me – that would be PC MacAskill / McAllister. Sitting there fiddling with his phone. Texting them to say I was in the Tartan Bunnet Café. 'COME GET HIM! LOL! XXX!' And probably some sort of thumbs-up emoji. Hanging about in the café, till they turned up to take over.

And if he was taking money from 'J&F ~ FREELANCE CONSULTANTS' chances were he was doing favours for other scumbags too. Have to add *him* to the list.

My phone was where I'd left it: plugged into the wall, recharging. When I picked the thing up, the screen came to life, displaying the icon that meant a text message had come in while I'd been asleep / unconscious.

More than one message, as it turned out.

336

LEAH MACNEIL:

When I was little I wanted 2 B a princess
then I grew up & then I wanted 2 B a vet
and work with all the lovely animals but
I'm 2 stupid 2 get in2 university

LEAH MACNEIL:

It doesn't matter now because I'll be dead
& no one will ever find me & that's
probably OK because I don't deserve 2 live
no more because of David

LEAH MACNEIL:

I keep thinking about how I could have
saved him how I maybe could have
stopped grandad before he did what he did
but I didn't & I no its 2 late 2 change it

LEAH MACNEIL:

I hope you told my gran that I love her
and I'm sorry
It's so cold and dark here
I think I will be dead soon
Thank you 4 trying
Goodbye ❤ ❤ ❤

The texts had been sent over the space of fifteen minutes, at around three o'clock this morning. Should've been plenty of time for RoboSabir to track down where Leah's texts were coming from. So why wasn't there a single message from the damn thing giving me coordinates?

Well, don't see why I should be the only one awake and worrying about it.

I called Sabir.

He answered on the second ring. *'Not youse again! I'm werking on it, OK? Jesus. Hold on.'* Then the clickity rattle of a keyboard getting punished. *'There.'*

My phone ding-buzzed in my hand. An email, from Sabir, with three names and locations in it:

- TROY CULLEN [MALAGA]
- CHRISTOPHER MULVANEY [NEWCASTLE]
- KERRY DRYBURGH [FOCHABERS]

'What the hell is this?'

'What do you think it is? It's three of yer unknown victims, all right? Thank you, Sabir, well done you true and trusty IT demigod. Have you got any idea how much digging I had to do to get them for ye?'

'OK, OK. Thank you, Sabir. Now, can you please tell me why your stupid half-arsed phone trace thing doesn't work any more? Leah MacNeil sent me a bunch of texts at three this morning and I've had no notifications about her location at all!'

'Oh, for the love of Anfield... Hold on.' More keyboard noises. *'According to this, her phone's sitting in your bloody Divisional Headquarters.'*

Her phone was *what*?

I scrunched my eyes shut, making the stabbing pain behind them even worse. 'That's her old phone. It's supposed to be tracing her new one!'

'Well, how am I meant to know that? You buncha knobs never tell us anything, I'm not Fox Mulder here, Ash, you do have to actually tell us stuff!'

The window *boing*ed as I thumped my forehead off it. 'DC Watt got a new warrant.'

'Good for DC Watt. But I'm still not feckin' psychic.'

'All right, all right, sorry. I'll text you the number.'

'Jesus, it's like amateur hour at the clown college.'

'Thanks, Sabir, I really...' Silence from the other end: he'd hung up. 'Appreciate it.'

At least the tramadol had started to kick in, that nice warm feeling dampening down the burning ache. Enough to try going back to bed, anyway.

*   *   *

The phone's anonymous ringtone dragged me from one of those bad dreams that wasn't so much scary as crushingly depressing. Any last wisps of it were battered into oblivion as the thumping headache started up again.

I fumbled my phone from the bedside table. Lay back with the other hand cupped over my throbbing eyes. 'What?'

'Ash? It's Rosalind. I'm downstairs. Are we going to morning prayers or not?'

Oh, for God's sake...

'Thought we agreed on a lie-in?'

'Are you OK? You sound all bunged up.'

Suppose there was no point fighting it.

'Give me ten minutes.'

'Rough night?' The smile was loud and clear in her voice.

'Like you wouldn't believe.'

By the time I'd made it into some clothes, an old pair of trainers, and through to the living room, Alice was sitting on the couch, knees up to her chest, staring at the TV, thick black bags under her eyes.

'...continues for missing five-year-old, Toby Macmillan. DI David Morrow says it's too early to give up hope yet.' And the screen cut to Shifty, in his best suit, standing in front of DHQ, caught in the flickering light of what had to be at least two dozen camera flashguns. Eyepatch giving him a slightly rakish air.

Putting on his serious voice: *'We know Toby Macmillan is out there, and we will find him.'*

Sooner or later.

And we knew from the first three victims what 'later' would look like.

I kissed Alice on top of the head, which was a stupid idea, because bending forward made my brain inflate like a balloon – slamming against the inside of my skull. 'Ow...'

She looked up at me, grimaced. 'You look *terrible*!'

Staying perfectly still till the room stopped lurching. 'I have to go, Franklin's outside.'

'...*vitally important anyone with information that might lead to us finding Toby Macmillan comes forward as soon as possible...*'

'You should be in bed.' Rising up from the couch. 'Don't go. Call in sick. You *are* sick!' Pointing at our reflections in the windows. 'Look at yourself.'

'No.' Didn't need to – I'd seen it in the bathroom mirror: the lines of sticking plaster across my nose, the cotton wadding jammed up both nostrils to keep it from setting even squinter than it already was. The map of blues, greens, and purples that covered my face from eyebrows to cheeks like a mask. Never mind that my ribs were one big bruise, all down the right-hand side. I winced my way into my jacket. 'What are you up to today?'

'Ash, *please*.'

'Look, I'm going to morning prayers, and I'm going to try catching Gordon Smith before he kills Leah MacNeil. Poor cow's convinced she's already dead. How do I turn my back on that?'

Alice sagged. 'Fine. I'm ... I don't know. Maybe I'll go talk to some of the people Bear thinks aren't worth interviewing. Maybe I'll...' A thin trembling groan wobbled its way out between her lips, then she curled forward, cradling her forehead. 'Ash, I can't stop thinking of what they did to Shifty. Every time I close my eyes, I see it...'

The man himself disappeared from the screen, replaced by the newsreader again.

'*Sport now, and the Scottish Premier League doping scandal has claimed another three clubs—*'

I killed the TV. 'Look, I'm sorry about last night. You shouldn't have had to... I'm going to take care of it. I promise.' Gave her a hug. 'Still thinking about retiring?'

'Actually,' she let her head fall onto my shoulder, 'I've been thinking about Gordon Smith.'

'Because maybe going off and doing something else wouldn't be a bad idea?'

'The boy he killed in Stirling. I think he left the body in that warehouse because he didn't have access to his usual disposal methods. Couldn't bury him somewhere private. Somewhere ... intimate. Couldn't start a new collection.'

'We could get ourselves a wee hotel on the west coast, with a cosy bar and a view of the sea.' Or we could if I took Helen MacNeil's two million.

'What worries me is that he couldn't wait. If he'd waited till he was somewhere he could safely kill and dispose of the body, we'd never have found out, would we? Everyone would've thought David Quinn had disappeared.'

'Would you like that? Just you, me, and Henry? No more murderers and thugs and dead bodies.'

Alice gave my ribs a squeeze, sending icy knives slicing through the muscles. But the tramadol blunted their blades a bit. 'I'd like that very, very, very much indeed.' She huffed out a breath, then rested her head against my shoulder. 'Gordon Smith's been murdering people without a single slip-up for fifty-six years – we only discovered what he's been up to because his garden fell into the sea. He knows he doesn't have to hide it any more. Time's running out, we'll catch him eventually, so why not go out with a bang?'

God, that was comforting. 'Maybe you're the one who should stay home? Get some proper sleep instead of passing out after too much booze?'

'He's escalating.'

'I know.' I kissed her on the head again. And this time my brain didn't *quite* feel as if it was about to burst out through my shattered skull. 'Stay here. Keep Henry company.'

'You've got Leah MacNeil to save, I've got Toby Macmillan.' Another deep breath. 'Anyway: better get going, that pretty DS will be waiting for you.'

'Ten minutes, my arse. I've been waiting here for...' Franklin stared, mouth hanging open, as I grimaced my way into the passenger seat. 'What the *hell* happened to you?'

The streetlight's jaundiced glow probably wasn't helping any. 'Henry's spending the day with Alice.'

'No, seriously, you look like someone threw you off the top of a tower block!'

Felt like it too.

341

'Are we going or not?'

She shook her head. 'What kind of person beats up an old man with a walking stick?'

An old man? I slumped back in my seat. Oh, today had got off to a *flying* start. 'Just … drive.'

35

Mother stared at me in much the same way Franklin had. 'No.'

'What do you mean—'

'I mean no! "N", "O", spells "no".' She pulled her chin up and in, eyebrows raised. 'Bad enough you look more like a violent criminal than a police officer at the best of times, but now? There's not a chance in hell I'm letting you loose on the public like that.'

The front room she'd commandeered to run the investigation had earned itself five or six more desks since Sunday morning, complete with cheap office chairs. The mildewed wallpaper almost completely hidden behind a plethora of printouts, maps, and actions. Including a brand-new section devoted to what was left of David Quinn. It was a safe bet that the team had grown too, but right now, it was only the three of us in here: Mother, Franklin, and me. So at least *someone* was out there getting on with catching Gordon Smith.

'We're supposed to be—'

'How many different ways do I have to say this? No. *Nein.* Not in this life or the next.' She folded her arms beneath her bosom and hiked it up about six inches. 'And Rosalind, what were you *thinking*? You were meant to be in charge!'

Franklin shrugged. 'Not my fault. He was like that when I picked him up this morning.'

'Oh, for God's sake. This is—'

'Well you should've thought of that *before* you did whatever it was you did to end up looking like Mr Blobby's punchbag. And you're hereby banned from taking a public-facing role till you stop looking like it. End - of - argument.' She pointed at a subset of actions, pinned up on their own as if they'd got something infectious. 'You can pick a task off the background-work list, and like it.'

Bloody hell.

'Sorry.' Franklin shrugged. 'I'd fight your corner, but you don't have Henry with you, so…' And with that she swept out of the room.

'I bought you a sausage and a go on the carousel!' But the door closed without an answer.

Mother was staring at me again.

'What?'

'I *really* hope that wasn't a euphemism…'

I limped over to the crap-jobs list. A bunch of them involved grubbing about in the Oldcastle Police archives, so no thank you. I'd been down there often enough and the entire system was a shambles. Another was chasing up every cast member who'd ever done a pantomime with a set designed by Gordon Smith – which I'm fairly certain was supposed to be DC Watt's job. Another couple would mean spending the day chasing up other forces and lab results. And last but not least: 'CHECK ON PETER SMITH'S FARM ~ BLACK ISLE (LEEAZE N DIVISION).'

What on earth did, 'Leeaze' mean?

And then it dawned – Watt's spelling really was atrocious.

I ripped the sheet of paper from its thumbtacks, folded it, and stuck it in my pocket. Then turned to Mother. 'OK, make-work it is. But I'll need a pool car.'

It wasn't a *bad* car. And at least it was an automatic. But the Misfit Mob's ancient Ford Mondeo had the same funky smell that all pool cars got after a few years. The upholstery absorbing the kebab, burger, fish-and-chips, KFC, coffee, and BO of so many thousand hours of stakeouts and general wear – the rubbish and discarded wrappers only shovelled out when it officially constituted a public health hazard, or no one could see out the windscreen any more. The carpet mats were stickier than the Monk and Casket's floorboards.

Alice's voice crackled out through the car's speakers. *'Wait, you're going* where?'

'Well, I didn't have any choice, did I? It was this or sit on the phone all day, talking to morons.'

'You could've stayed at home!'

'So could you.'

'Urgh...'

I took the turning for Tomintoul, abandoning the throbbing highway that was the A93 for the even more backwater A939 – according to the road sign, anyway. Scenery wasn't bad. Nothing special, but there were hills and fields and trees and things, glowing in the morning light. A big green tractor thundered along the road ahead of me, great gobbets of mud flying from its oversized wheels. Might as well live dangerously...

Put my foot down as hard as its bullet hole would allow, and eased out onto the other side of the road.

'Ash, are you driving? Are you talking to me on your phone and driving?'

'Relax, bought one of those cheap hands-free kits from Tesco on the way out of town. Got about another two hours to go and the radio's broken. Only entertainment I have is talking to you and trying to lose my tail.'

Past the tractor, back in again.

Clusters of long-dead ragwort peppered the fields to either side of the road, poisonous dark heads rattling atop poisonous grey stems.

'You still there? Hello?'

Her voice was up nearly an octave, the words fast and shrill as a dentist's drill: *'Who's following you? Is it them? Is it Joseph and Francis? Oh my God, they're going to kill you! You have to lose them, Ash, you have to—'*

'Relax: it's not them. Deep breaths. Calm.' A quick glance in the rear-view mirror confirmed that the rusty blue Renault was still there, overtaking the tractor now. 'It's Helen MacNeil. So even if the pair of them *did* show up, they'd be the ones needing help.'

'Oh.'

'What about you? Anything exciting happening?'

'Not really. Been speaking to Andrew Brennan's mum's social worker. Thought maybe there'd be a connection buried somewhere. Gòrach's not been in trouble with the police, but he's got to have had problems in childhood, you don't wake up one morning and decide you're going to start strangling small children, that kind of thing takes years, decades to work up to. And he's got to be local too, otherwise he wouldn't have seen Andrew playing under the railway line.'

'So no joy.'

'Not yet, but I've made a list. I'm positive someone knows something, they just don't know that they know it. But maybe I'll be able to draw it out of them? And we'll find Toby Macmillan before Gòrach kills him and everyone will be happy and no one will have to die and I'll not feel like such a useless failure.'

Not this again. 'You aren't a failure! You've put loads and loads of monsters behind bars, saved countless lives because of it.'

'I couldn't even last two nights sober, Ash.'

True. 'You had a nasty shock last night, that's all. Stop bashing yourself in the head with a mallet the whole time.'

The trees on either side of the road were sticks and bones, naked of leaves. More ragwort, standing guard along the banks of a swollen grey river.

Still nothing back from Alice.

'Have another night off the booze tonight. Maybe see if you can last till Friday?'

'I… I like the idea of running a hotel on the west coast. With a nice view. We could do writing and painting retreats and cookery courses and wine tasting, well maybe not wine tasting, and I could learn to bake bread and we'd be happy and away from all this … shite.'

There was Helen's fusty blue Renault in the rear-view mirror again.

'You're sure that's what you want?'

'It has to be better than this, doesn't it?'

Two million pounds.

346

'OK. If you're *positive*. That's what we'll do.'

'We could call it Henry's Hotel, and the sign would be a Scottie dog that looked exactly like him and we'd let people bring their pets when they visit!'

All I had to do was catch Gordon Smith, and let Helen MacNeil kill him.

A smear of snow coated the hills on either side of the Lecht, not enough to make the ski slopes useable, but Storm Victoria would probably take care of that.

I pulled off the road and onto the gravel parking area. Clambered out into the blustery morning and the *whomp-whomp-whomp* of the resident wind turbine. Held a hand up as Helen MacNeil's rusty Renault puttered into view. Don't think it enjoyed the long twisting slog up the hill as much my manky Mondeo had.

She frowned through the windscreen, then parked next to me. Stepped out, shoulders back, chin up, as if expecting a fight. Old denim jacket on over a Cannibal Death Ray T-shirt. 'You look like shit.'

'Nice to see you too.' Stuck my hands in my pockets. Turned to face the hills, with their lines of pylons marching off into the distance – the chairlift's hanging seats swaying as the wind howled down the hill. 'Used to come here when I was a kid. My dad thought everyone should know how to ski.'

'You're going north.'

'There's this old cine footage of us, in our really horrible brightly coloured ski suit things. Green and orange and white. Must've looked like a right bunch of numpties.'

'Has someone spotted him?'

'Snowploughing down that teeny Robin run, squealing with excitement.'

Helen narrowed her eyes. 'Where's your copper friend, the young black one with the big boobs?'

'Oh, to be a wee kid again...'

'Answer the bloody question! What – are – you – doing – here?'

The Mondeo's roof was cold beneath my shirt sleeves. 'I'm not allowed to go out and do official police things, today. Apparently I'd scare the natives, what with all the bruises. So I'm off to search Gordon Smith's brother's farm.'

'We should be rattling people's teeth! Some bastard knows where he is.'

'Course, N Division have already searched it, but if there's one thing I learned from all my years on the force: never trust a police officer you can't look in the eye or kick in the arse.'

She banged her fist down on the car's roof. 'You're not helping!'

A pair of ravens scudded sideways across the car park, wings shuddering with the effort of holding on. A minibus grumbled up to the ski resort lodge, a gaggle of schoolgirls avalanching out of the doors soon as it came to a halt. Shouts and laughter whipped away by the wind.

'This security van full of cash, art, and jewellery: how easy is it to get to? Assuming someone had to make themselves scarce before the police started sniffing around. Hypothetically speaking.'

Helen turned and leaned back against the Mondeo. 'So you *are* interested.'

'Let's pretend I am. How easy is this stuff going to be to shift?'

'The thing about prison is you get to meet a lot of people who're up to their ears in dodgy stuff. And it's quality stuff.'

The squealing horde battered into the lodge, out of the wind, leaving a ragged man in a corduroy jacket to lock up and follow them in. Leather patches on his elbows, so I'm guessing geography teacher.

'Cash has to be clean. Nothing sketchy or traceable.'

'Do I look like an amateur to you?'

'And in case you're in *any* way unclear on this: I'm not the forgiving kind when it comes to being screwed over.'

She leaned in closer. 'Neither am I.'

Fair enough.

Helen plipped the locks on her Renault, then marched around the Mondeo and got into the passenger seat.

I opened the driver's door and stuck my head in. 'What do you think you're doing?'

She hauled on her seatbelt. 'Why follow you all the way to the Black Isle, in my own car, when Police Scotland's paying for *your* petrol?'

Great. A passenger.

I climbed in behind the wheel. 'Radio doesn't work.'

Helen reached into her jacket and pulled out a business card. 'Got you a souvenir from last night.'

'J&F ~ Freelance Consultants.' The bottom half of the card was stained with dark brown smears. Could've been Francis's blood, but it was probably mine.

'Why the hell would I want that.' Tossing it back to her.

She dipped into her jacket again, only this time it was Joseph's cutthroat razor that appeared. 'Thought you might want to give that mobile number a call.' A flick of the wrist and the blade clacked out of the handle, shining and sharp. 'You could set up a meeting. And make sure neither of them survives it.'

Can't say it wasn't tempting...

Sunshine washed across the patchwork of grey and brown on both sides of the single-track road, a sliver of the Cromarty Firth sparkling between the fields and the next set of hills. Land rising on the right of the car, speckled with more dead ragwort, and falling away on the left. Small jagged flashes of white marking the end gables of tiny farmhouses.

Sky the colour of wet slate.

Helen curled her top lip. 'Why are we stopping?'

'Because N Division should have someone watching the place, in case Gordon Smith decides to use it as a bolthole. And I *kinda* think whoever's on guard duty will want to ask a load of questions about why I've got one of the victims' mothers in my car.'

She turned and scowled at the back seat and the drifts of litter in the footwell. 'How big's the boot?'

Big enough.

We both got out and she clambered into the Mondeo's boot, lying on her side – knees drawn up to her chest.

'Make yourself comfy, might be in there for a while.'

'This better be worth it.'

'Hey, you could've stayed at the Lecht, or headed back to Oldcastle. Cadging a lift was *your* idea, remember?' I clunked the boot shut again, before she could say anything. Got back behind the wheel.

Half a mile further on, a sign sat at the side of the road, the post knocked squint, the paint peeling, but the name was still visible: 'WESTER BRAE OF KINBEACHIE FARM' pointing to a rutted track with grass growing up the middle.

Don't know what Peter Smith had been complaining about: the fields on either side looked solid and well drained, without the usual bouquets of weeds and rushes. And then I got to the brow of the hill.

Only it wasn't really the top. The hill continued on up, but between here and there was a depression – like some vast rusty spoon had scooped out a hollow that stretched from left to right, leaving a smear of mist lying in the dip. It cast a veil over water-puddled fields thick with the pale-beige spines of dead reeds. A huge clump of gorse spread out from the edge of what looked like forestry commission pines. But while the pines were up on the lip of the crater, the heavy dark-green gorse reached *way* down into it, covering a good five or six acres. And right in the middle, where the sun probably never shone, sulked a farmhouse that would've fit right into a low-budget horror story. The corrugated roof was corroded and saggy, one wall bulging out around a cracked windowsill. It might have been white once, but now what little paint remained was flaking off, the colour of ancient bones. One storey of misery, with two dormer windows that made angry eyes on its miserable face. It sat, surrounded by a collection of farm buildings, some of which still had functional roofs. Just about.

And no sign of a patrol car.

Because, hey, we're only trying to catch someone who's been

350

murdering people for fifty-six years, right? Why expend any bloody effort at all?

I followed the track down into the mist, potholes making the Mondeo lurch no matter how hard I tried to steer around the damn things. Which wouldn't be doing Helen many favours, stuck in the boot.

A flat area sat at the track's end – grass and weeds flattened in ragged circles that expanded and spawned tangents off to the house and every outbuilding. That would be the N Division search team, then.

Going by the tracks they'd trampled, they'd been pretty thorough, but that was still no excuse for leaving the place unwatched. Unless they had someone lurking in one of the outbuildings?

I pulled on the handbrake. 'Stay here, and keep quiet. I'm going to check.'

Nothing back from Helen.

Good.

Nice to know *someone* could do as they were told.

I climbed out into the gloom.

36

Up on the ridge, those forestry commission pines shuddered in the wind, but down here it was still as a shallow grave. The bushes and trees undisturbed. My breath added to the fog, drifting away into the pale grey air. It was thicker down here that it'd looked coming down the hill, softening the edges and draining the colour out of everything.

God it was bleak. No wonder Peter Smith abandoned the place.

'Hello? Anyone here?'

Silence. Not even an echo.

'HELLO? POLICE!'

Took out my phone and called Mother as I followed the track over to the miserable farmhouse. 'I'm at Peter Smith's farm – drove right in, not so much as a tape cordon. Highlands and Islands have left the place completely unprotected.'

'Oh, in the name of...' A pause. *'Are you sure?'*

'No patrol car. And no answer when I shout, either.'

'Hold on.' Her voice went all muffled. *'John? ... John! Get in touch with N Division and ask, politely, why the hell they don't have anyone watching Peter Smith's farm.'*

All the way around the farmhouse, peering in through the windows. Looked as if no one had lived there in years – everything was covered in grime and mould. The door wasn't even locked. It swung open with a push.

Couldn't smell anything, what with the wadding stuffed up my nostrils, but the air in here was ripe with the gritty bitter taste of mildew and mice.

Unlike Gordon Smith's house, the furniture hadn't been gathered together into one big unlit bonfire. Instead it'd been abandoned to rot.

Kitchen: empty. Living room: empty. Bathroom: empty. Storage room: empty.

The stairs creaked and groaned as I climbed up to the narrow landing. Bookshelves lined the small recess opposite, the paperbacks all bloated and speckled.

'*Ash, you still there?*'

'Maybe.' Door number one opened on a small grubby bedroom barely tall enough to stand up in: empty.

'*N Division say they haven't got the resources to mount a twenty-four-hour watch on Peter Smith's farm. Only they used slightly more colourful language than that and implied if we'd wanted such a thing we should've said so and paid for it.*'

The joys of modern policing.

'Well, don't look at me. Sooner I'm out of this hellhole the better.'

Door number two opened on the mirror image of door number one: empty.

So much for that.

Back downstairs and out into the mist again. 'Don't think anyone's been here since Peter Smith got done for murder.'

'*Well, have a look round then come back. We'll find you something else to do, where no one's going to see your battered face and run screaming for the hills.*'

'As my dear departed granny used to say: awa an' boil yer heid.' I hung up, went back to the Mondeo and popped the boot. 'Might as well stretch your legs, there's no one here.'

Helen climbed out and turned on the spot, grimacing at the dilapidated buildings and crappy fields lurking in the mist. 'Gordon used to tell me stories about coming up here as a wee boy. Summers spent digging ditches and fixing fences. Couldn't stand the place.'

No wonder, if his uncle was abusing him.

I headed over to the nearest outbuilding – a cattle byre, going by the concrete floor and barred central walkway. Half the roof was crumpled on the ground, water dripping from the twisted sheeting.

'So where's this security van hidden?'

She didn't even look at me, just stepped through an open doorway, voice echoing against concrete walls. 'Somewhere no one's going to find it.'

Ah well, it'd been worth a go.

I followed her through into what looked as if it might have been a feed room at some point. The roof was all in one piece, though the metal rafters must've been used by generations of pigeons as a roosting spot, the floor beneath them streaked and spattered with mounds of droppings. Another load of guano speckling a long metal ladder, mounted sideways on hooks. Yet more crusting the upturned corpse of a long-dead wheelbarrow. 'Did Gordon Smith ever mention anywhere else he went as a kid? Anywhere he might've felt safe?'

'Caravan park near Oban. B-and-B in Carlisle. Some sort of old hotel near Pitlochry? Hated the lot of them.'

Across a courtyard littered with rusting hulks of farm machinery. In through the open double doors to a steading with no roof left at all, and a big pile of broken sheets that may or not have been asbestos. 'But the security van's in Oldcastle?'

'You'll find out when I get my hands on the bastard who killed my Sophie.'

'Because I've only got your word that you know where it is.'

'Trust is a wonderful thing, isn't it?'

Back out into the mist – getting even thicker now, oozing around the grey buildings' edges. As if it was searching for us.

A big metal shed, three sides open to the gloomy air. Two ancient tractors that would probably be worth a few quid if they weren't nearly solid rust, sagged on deflated crumbling tyres. Black plastic covered a crumpled pyramid of haylage that probably hadn't seen the light of day for a decade.

Three more buildings to go.

The first one was a huge chicken shed, still full of the eye-watering spikey ammonia reek of hen piss, strong enough to stab its way through the packing in my nose. But now the shed was home to stacks and stacks of rubbish – bin bags, baling plastic, feed bags, plastic tubs... As if someone had found a nice safe place to fly-tip their commercial waste without having to pay any landfill charges.

My phone did its *buzz-ding* thing. I left it in my pocket.

'Is there anywhere else you can think of? Anywhere Gordon Smith might be hiding?'

She stared at me. 'If there *was*, why would I need you?' She spat a gobbet of phlegm out onto one of the few clear patches of floor. Then stepped outside again. 'And if you expect a cut of my six million, you'd—'

A scream cut through the mist, high-pitched, young, and female. Coming from somewhere close.

Helen's eyes widened. She spun around. 'LEAH? LEAH!' Then charged off towards the biggest of the two remaining buildings: a barn with crumbling walls. 'GET YOUR HANDS OFF HER, YOU BASTARD!'

I lumbered after her.

The barn was breeze-blocks for the bottom eight feet, above that it was all corrugated concrete panels topped by rusted metal roofing. The only door, on this side anyway, was one of those oversized metal sliding jobs – big enough to drive a tractor and bogey through.

Helen grabbed the handle and hauled, grunting with the effort.

I thumped my shoulder into the edge and shoved.

Between the pair of us, we got the ancient runners squealing, the door juddering open inch by inch, until the gap was big enough to squeeze through: Helen first, then me.

Inside, two thirds of the space was taken up with more fly-tipped agricultural rubbish, bags and baling plastic mounded nearly to the rafters. A chunk of the roof sheets had caved in, lying in a crumpled metal heap on the filthy concrete floor.

Sickly yellow-green weeds growing up through the cracks. What looked like an inspection pit off to one side.

And there, in the corner – between a smaller, human-sized door and a dilapidated tractor bogey – was a young woman. The bastard had tied her to a set of metal bars that poked out of the breeze-blocks, spreadeagled like a hunting trophy waiting to be skinned. Sobbing and thrashing against the dirty-brown rope that held her wrists and ankles. Grubby jeans, a stained hoodie open over a once-white T-shirt. The bright-violet hair had turned into out-of-a-bottle blonde, but it was *definitely* her.

'LEAH!' Helen sprinted.

'GRANNY!' Tears streaked her face, cheeks and nose hot pink. Every inch of her trembling. 'OH GOD, GRANNY, HELP ME! HELP ME!' Jagged, shrill, terrified.

Helen skidded to a halt in front of her. 'Where is he? Where's the *dead* man that did this to you?'

'YOU HAVE TO GET ME OUT OF HERE!'

'Where – *is* – he?'

Leah glanced towards the smaller door. 'He… He didn't… I'm so scared, Granny, I can't—'

'Shhh… It's OK, baby, I swear. It'll all be OK.' She turned as I hobbled the last few yards. 'You: get her out of here.' Helen pulled the cutthroat razor from her pocket and tossed it to me. 'I'm going after him.' Then she kissed Leah on the cheek. 'It's OK, Ash is a friend. He'll look after you.' Then she was off, battering through the door and out into the mist again.

Right.

I pulled out the blade and grabbed the rope holding Leah's left wrist to the nearest bar. The blocks' pitted surfaces were stained with brown-black splotches and smears, lots more on the concrete floor at her feet. 'Told you we'd find you.'

Joseph's cutthroat razor hissed through the old rope in four or five slices. Say this for the ugly, psychotic little git, he kept his weapons sharp.

'Ash? Ash Henderson?' Leah blinked at me, as if finally recognising me from the Edinburgh Christmas Market, then curled her now free hand against her chest. 'I've been so scared…'

'I know, but it's over now.' The rope holding her right wrist parted even easier. 'You're going home. He can't hurt you any more.'

'There was so much blood…'

My knees creaked as I winced my way down to tackle the rope around her right ankle. 'We're going to get you into—'

'LOOK OUT!'

A noise behind me, like a careful footstep on the gritty dusty floor.

Sod.

Before I could turn something thin and white flashed downwards in front of my eyes, then pulled tight around my throat, digging into the skin, burning, crushing. 'Ulk…'

Heat rushed up my neck and face, bringing with it the stings of a thousand angry wasps, pressure building behind my eyes. Fingers scrabbling at the plastic cable where it dug into my flesh.

No air. No air. Can't…

I tried a reverse head-butt, but Gordon Smith's face wasn't there to slam into, and the cable buried itself deeper into my neck.

He'd used Leah as bait, and I'd taken it.

Stupid. Bloody. *Idiot.*

Slammed my left heel backwards, but all I got was a grunt in return. Glancing blow. Not hard enough to break his shin.

The barn went dim and dark at the edges, the middle filling with starbursts.

A trap. And you fell for it.

Darker.

The razor.

USE THE RAZOR!

I brought it up, blade shining like neon – leaving a swirling trail behind it as it cut through the air – but fire seared through my wrist and the cutthroat disappeared from my numb fingers. Clatter, thump, scrape.

Barely even felt the concrete floor cracking into my knees as my legs gave way.

So much pressure, my skull was going to burst.

Arms hanging limp now.

No fight left.

Let everyone down.

I'm sorry…

Darkness.

'AAAARGH!' My eyes snapped open, then the pain hit, as if someone had stuffed my throat with scalding gravel, making every breath a stinging struggle.

Gordon Smith lowered the bucket, filthy water dripping from it. A smile pulling at his Santa Claus beard. 'Hello. I don't think we've met. I'd shake hands, but as you can see, mine are full and yours are tied.' He tossed the bucket away to *bing* and *whoom* against the concrete floor.

He had his other arm around Leah's throat, pinning her to his chest. Her eyes wide as she stared at me. Then he dipped his free hand into a pocket and came out with a four-inch kitchen knife. Pressed it against her throat. 'Isn't this fun, boys and girls?'

I let my head fall forward, tried to drag in something deeper than a thin tortured wheeze. More filthy water cascaded from my hair, running down my face, pooling at my feet as I hung there, rough rope around my wrists, more around my ankles, fixed to the same bars set into the breeze-blocks.

So much pain and struggling and all I'd managed to achieve was swapping places with Leah MacNeil. And that was hardly an improvement, was it?

What a bloody idiot.

Franklin was right, I *was* an old man. A stupid, useless, old man.

Who was about to die. Probably in screaming agony, going by what Gordon Smith had done to David Quinn in that Stirling warehouse.

Unless I could get him mad enough to lose control and make it quick. Or the cavalry arrived in the nick of time?

Now would be good.

Any minute now.

Please.

Smith raised his big bushy eyebrows and beamed, as if he was performing for a crowd of small children. 'I understand from my dear friend, Leah, that you're a *police* officer. Isn't that interesting? Now, I wonder how we can turn that to our—'

'GET AWAY FROM HER, YOU FUCKING PRICK!' Helen.

Oh thank *God*.

She'd squeezed herself through the gap between the big door and the wall again. Standing there, holding a dirty-big dod of wood with a lump of rusted metal on the end. Not quite a pickaxe handle, but it'd been something similar before the years had got to it. Sledgehammer? Splitting maul? Whatever it was, in her hands it looked deadly.

Smith backed away a couple of paces, turning so he was facing Helen and me at the same time. Still with that kids' TV presenter smile. Which turned into a pantomime frown. 'Now, now, we shouldn't use naughty language like that. Have to set a good example for the younger generation, don't we?' Tightening his arm around Leah's throat.

'Let her go, Gordon. Let her go and you and me can talk about this like adults.'

'Oh no. Why would I abandon lovely Leah? She's been such a *good* girl, haven't you, Leah?'

'I swear to God, Gordon, if you don't let her go I'll—'

'Threats don't help anything, do they, Leah?'

She made a high-pitched yelping noise as the knife twisted against her throat and a thin line of blood trickled its way down into her T-shirt where it spread like a poppy blooming.

'All right! All right.' Helen lowered her weapon. 'Let her go. Take me, and let her go.'

'Well, that doesn't sound very—' Smith's face creased and his head drooped. A deep breath, hissed out between pursed lips. 'I know, Caroline, but I'm *dealing* with it. ... Because I'm dealing with it! You can *see* me dealing with it!' He raised his eyes to the corrugated roofing. 'I know! Please, for once in your bloody life, can you—' A pause, then Smith's shoulders curled

359

inwards. 'I'm sorry. You're right, you're right: there's no need for that kind of language.' He glanced towards the corner of the barn. 'I apologise.'

There was something there – lurking in the gap between the tractor bogey and the wall. Like a granite thermos flask with silver handles fixed to it. That's what Gordon Smith was talking to. And apparently, it was answering back.

Helen stared at him, mouth hanging open. 'What the hell are you on?'

Talking to his long-dead wife, presumably, because this whole situation wasn't buggered up enough as it was.

'Now, if you don't mind, Caroline, I'm trying to— ... Yes. ... I know. ... I *know*! For goodness' sake, woman, can you not let me—' A longsuffering sigh. 'Fine. But for the record I think this is a terrible idea for everyone concerned, OK? But if *you* think *you* know best, we'll do it *your* way, shall we? As usual.'

He lowered the knife and took his arm from around Leah's throat. 'Go on, then. Off you go and be with your granny.'

Surely it couldn't be that easy, could it?

Now all we had to do was get Smith's dead wife to put in a good word for me and we could all go home.

After Helen had bashed his brains in, of course...

37

Leah ran into her grandmother's arms, burying herself in a fierce hug. Voice a muffled sob. 'It's all been so horrible!'

'I know, sweetheart, but it's over now.' Stroking Leah's hair. 'Shhh... Shhh... It'll be OK, I promise.' Then Helen stepped back, breaking the embrace. 'I need you to go wait outside for me.' Kissing her forehead. 'Granny has something she has to take care of.'

Leah scrubbed a hand across her eyes. 'You're going to hurt Grandad.'

'He's *not* your grandad. He never was.' She raised the rusted sledgehammer / splitting maul again. 'Now go wait outside.'

'No.' Leah retreated towards us, feet scuffing through the dust. 'You can't hurt him.'

'Please, sweetheart, you don't—'

'He's my grandad!'

'HE KILLED YOUR MOTHER!' Helen's eyes shone in the dim light, face darkening as she followed Leah further into the barn. 'He tied her to the wall in his basement and he tortured her to death!'

Still backing away. 'That isn't—'

'HE TOOK PHOTOGRAPHS! I've seen them.' A sniff and Helen shook her head. Pulled out her phone and held it up. 'I've *seen* what he did to her.'

'What *he* did to her? How about what *you* did to her? You never loved her!'

'Of course I loved her!' Tears glistening on Helen's cheeks now. 'She was my baby, and—'

'Then why were you never there for her?' Voice sharp and cruel, circling Helen, spitting it out. 'If you loved Mum you wouldn't have spent half her life in prison! And even when you weren't, Caroline told me all about the drinking and the drugs and your dodgy criminal mates coming to the house at all hours. Police kicking down the door every other day.'

Gordon Smith stepped towards them.

But when I opened my mouth to warn Helen, all that came out was a barbed-wire wheeze.

'Leah, that's not... I made some mistakes, but—'

'Mum *hated* you. You poison everything you touch. She was better off *dead* than being with you.'

Helen wiped the tears away, but more spilled down her cheeks. 'I didn't—'

'Granny and Grandad looked after me, because you weren't there! You weren't there for Mum and you weren't there for me, because you're a selfish cow!

'Leah, it's not—'

'I *HATE* YOU!' Leah's hand flashed out, the slap ringing in the barn's cold air.

Helen's phone flew, bounced once off the concrete floor, then skittered over the edge of the pit and disappeared. She turned back to face Leah, a scarlet weal already starting to swell up on her cheek. Muscles cording in her neck like guy ropes. Empty hand clenched tight into a fist. Body trembling.

Deep breath. Force it out. Warn her. A barely audible, 'Look out!' crackled from my ruined throat. Ropes biting into my wrists and ankles as I thrashed against the restraints. Getting nowhere.

And Helen didn't move. She stood there staring at Leah's twisted flushed face.

Gordon was behind Helen now, the kitchen knife clutched in his right hand as he snatched his left arm around her throat, just like he had Leah. Helen stiffened, but the blade was already streaking down towards her stomach.

A *thunk*, a grunt, then another and another and another, the knife punching its way into Helen's T-shirt, over and over. *Thunk, thunk, thunk, thunk, thunk, thunk, thunk, thunk, thunk, thunk…*

The rusty splitting maul / sledgehammer clattered to the barn floor and Helen's knees gave way. Then Gordon Smith let go and she slumped beside it. Dark red spreading out into the grey concrete.

He stepped back, arms outstretched, standing perfectly still for a moment. 'And: scene.' He gave Leah a deep bow. Turned and did the same to me.

Leah bit her lips together. Then wiped a hand across her tear-stained cheeks. Shuddered out a breath. Raised her eyes from her murdered grandmother, to Smith. Voice small and hesitant. 'Did I… Did I do it right?'

'You did it perfectly, Pickle Pudding Pie!' He swept her up in a hug, lifting her off the ground and spinning around a couple of times, before depositing her back on her feet again. 'You're the best granddaughter an old man could ever have. Yes you are.' Booping her on the nose. 'I'm proud of you.'

Oh, for God's sake…

Looked as if we knew what happened when a couple-that-kills loses one half. It recruits another.

'You pair of bastards.' A sandpaper whisper, that probably didn't travel more than a couple of feet.

Leah skipped over, grinning. 'I can't *believe* you fell for all that text nonsense. "Oh, I'm so scared!", "I don't know where I am!", "Please come rescue me, because I'm a weak and feeble woman and you're a big strong man!"' A mocking pout. 'Bit of a sexist bastard, aren't you?'

'Language!' Smith glowered at her. 'We've talked about this, Leah.'

'Sorry, Grandad.' She lowered her eyes, all scrunched up with deference. Then reached for my jacket. 'And speaking of phones.' Going through my pockets till she pulled mine free.

Leah gave it a quick once-over, then turned and handed it to Gordon Smith. 'Here you go.'

'Thank you kindly.' He flipped the case open and poked at the screen. 'What's the passcode?'

Wasn't easy, with my throat like scorched gravel, but I managed to force it out: 'Go fuck yourself.'

'What did I say about bad language? Leah?'

She curled a hand into a fist and slammed it into my stomach. Only she wasn't used to punching people, and I was far too used to being punched. She'd telegraphed it badly enough I had plenty of time to clench all the muscles and be ready for it.

'Now, Mr...?' he looked at Leah, eyebrows raised.

She smiled back. 'Henderson.'

'Ah yes, Mr *Henderson*, don't you think it'd be fun if we sent your "guvnor" a series of texts saying you've searched the family farm and moved on to greener pastures? Maybe you're having a long dark night of the soul? After all, there's lots of places a poor depressed policeman can throw himself off the cliffs and into the sea around here.'

'It won't work.' Starting to get a hint of my old voice back.

'It did with Leah's mum, Sophie. I was *particularly* proud of that suicide note; six pages of tortured angst, and they believed every single word. Took sixteen years for you to come sniffing about like Dixon of Dock Green. Now can I please have the passcode for your phone, or would you rather play Spanish Inquisition? I have lots of lovely toys in the car: all sharp and spikey and *so* full of screams.'

'You can't trust him, Leah. You were right – sooner or later he's going to turn on you.'

'No, he won't.' She took his hand. 'Grandad's been there for me my entire life. We're family.'

'He's *insane*! He's talking to his dead wife, Leah! You can't trust...'

Wait a minute.

Her grin was huge, eyebrows up. 'That was *my* idea. We rehearsed it all the way up in the car.'

'Isn't she clever?' Smith pursed his lips together, nodding as if he was accepting an award. 'People like a compelling narrative, Mr Henderson. The dotty old man talking to his dead wife. It's a standard enough trope – so far, so pedestrian – but what if she answers back? Oooh, he must be dangerous and deranged! A wild and crazy man!'

'And you fell for *that* too.' Leah gazed up at him. 'Grandad won't hurt me, because he loves me and I love him.'

Time to start on plan B.

I stared at Smith. 'You're shagging her? What, your real wife dies of bowel cancer and you take up with the girl who thinks you're her *grandfather*?'

The smile slipped from his face. 'You watch your mouth.'

'Moved her right into the bedroom and let her take your dead wife's place, didn't you?'

'I'm warning you, Mr Henderson.' Teeth bared, knife clutched in his blood-dripping hand.

'Did you bother waiting till she was sixteen, or did you come back from the funeral and screw her on the kitchen counter? What was she, fourteen? Because we know you like them young, don't we?'

'YOU SHUT YOUR FILTHY MOUTH!' Moving fast, knife flashing upwards.

'No!' Leah got in between us, arms out, blocking the way. 'He's doing it on purpose, Grandad! Trying to get you mad. Shh... It's OK. Shh...' Sounding exactly like her grandmother. 'He *wants* you to kill him quickly. And we want access to his phone, right?'

Gordon Smith lowered the knife. 'You're right, you're right.' And the smile was back. 'You're a good girl, Leah.' He placed the blade's tip against my chest, Helen MacNeil's blood seeping into my shirt. 'I don't know what sort of perversions you get up to in your family, Mr Henderson, but Leah is my grand-daughter. We don't do that sort of thing.' He put a bit of pressure on the knife.

It was like being scalded, waves of burning heat radiating out across my chest. Breath hissing out between my clenched teeth. Fresh scarlet joining Helen's blood on my shirt.

'Now, I'm going to ask you very nicely for the passcode to your phone, and you're going to give it to me, or we won't be friends any more. And you *really* won't like that.'

'Go – to – Hell.'

'Think this is bad?' Twisting the knife, sending a fresh wave searing through the skin. 'Not even gone in a half-inch, yet. Now, give me the passcode.'

'Actually,' Leah put a hand on his arm, 'there might be a better way. Can I have his phone back?'

'Of course you can, sweetie.'

She turned the thing over. Held it up so he could see the back. 'See this round thing here? It's a fingerprint reader, so you don't have to keep putting your code in to unlock the phone.' Leah reached up and grabbed my left wrist. 'Open your hand.'

'Get stuffed.'

Smith twisted the knife again. 'Let's not be rude to the young lady.'

'ARRRRGH!' Couldn't help it. My fingers uncurled on their own, going from a fist to a claw as a fresh wave blistered out.

She grabbed the middle finger – yanked it back hard enough to make a dull *pop* sound deep inside my hand and red-hot glass exploded all the way up my arm.

'*Jesus…*'

Leah pressed my dislocated finger's tip to the phone's sensor. 'This little piggy isn't working.'

Arthritis screamed through the twisted joint. Then she grabbed my index finger and hauled that one back too. More broken glass, lancing deep into the flesh.

The phone buzzed in her hands as she stuck the finger against the sensor. 'And we're in!' Leaning back against the tractor bogey. 'Now, texts, texts, text, texts…' Poking at the screen while my hand burned. 'Here we go. Oh, look, you've got a new one from someone called "Dr McFruitLoop". Let's see… "Ash, Mother has shown me some of Leah's messages. They worry me. Something about them seems staged. As if she's faking speaking like someone else."' Leah nodded. 'You see, men aren't bright enough to spot that kind of thing. Do you have *any* idea how much of a hassle it is to jump from the text keyboard to the numerical one and back again to write "into" with a number two instead of "T.O."? Anyway, let's see… What shall we say, Grandad?'

Smith pulled the knifepoint out of my chest. 'How about we text whoever's in charge first?'

'Erm…' Creases bloomed between her eyebrows as she prodded the screen. 'We've got a DI Malcolmson and a DCI Jacobson. Ha! Henderson, Malcolmson, Jacobson – looks like Oldcastle Police hire a lot of wannabe Vikings, doesn't it?' More prodding. 'He's got lots more recent texts from the Malcolmson number.'

'Then let's start there. "I have searched the farm and there is no one there. No signs of habitation at all."'

'Good. Then, how about… "I don't know what to do next. I'm sorry. I've failed you all." Send.'

'Do another one: "I am going to drive down the coast and try to think. There has to be a way I can make it up to everyone. I do not think I can live with myself if there is not."'

'Hold on.' Head down over the phone, fingers going. 'Have to trim nine characters off, so it'll fit… And: send.' A grin. 'This is fun.'

Gordon Smith turned to me. 'Aren't you going to say, "You'll never get away with this?"'

'You're going to kill Leah, and she knows it. Sooner or later, whatever the hell is wrong with your twisted bastard brain will snap, and you'll carve her up into little pieces.'

'Dear, oh dear, your language really is atrocious. And you're missing your *cue*.' He stuck his feet together, arms outstretched, chin up, like a circus ringmaster about to announce the next act. 'This is the part of the pantomime when Evil Uncle Abanazar explains his wicked plan to poor hapless Aladdin. You're a police officer, surely you're *dying* to know what my motivation is? When did Caroline and I start killing people and why? How did we ensnare darling Leah in our web of *depravity*? What we're going to do next?' Smith gave a lopsided shrug. 'To be honest, I never really like those Bond villain moments. Always seem rather staged, don't they? Best to leave some things to the audience's imagination.'

Shoulders back, Ash. Chin up. 'The police are on their way. I called them before we came in here.'

'Good job we're not doing *Pinocchio*, or your nose would be three-foot long.' He pulled a length of white electrical cable from his pocket. 'Did you like being garrotted? I've never tried it before, but it was all over the papers this weekend, wasn't it? "The Oldcastle Child-Strangler strikes again", and I do so like to be "down with the cool kids".' That indulgent Santa smile spread across his face. 'Apparently it's all the rage.'

Don't flinch. Don't move at all.

'Now, normally I'd take my time – get to know you better over the next three or four hours – but while I'm sure you're lying about calling the cops, it would be silly to take the risk.' He held up the electrical cable again. 'Still, sometimes the important thing is to do your best and hope it'll all turn out OK, don't you think?' He looped the cable over my head, wrapped the ends around his hands. Pulled till it bit into my neck again, not hard enough to choke off the air or blood. Not yet.

Deep breaths.

Stay calm.

Stay still.

This was a better, quicker end than his torture toys.

Be a man.

Don't beg.

Don't cry.

Don't scream.

Don't give the bastard the satisfaction.

'Hold on a minute, Grandad.' Leah frowned at my phone's screen. 'It's locked itself again.' A tut. 'Going to keep doing that, I suppose.' She wandered across to where the cutthroat razor had fallen and picked it up. 'Still, as long as we've got his fingerprint, we don't really need the rest of him, do we?' Her grin was even more unhinged than Smith's was as she twisted the blade, making it glitter. 'We should take the whole finger, though. Better safe than sorry.'

Oh Christ.

So much for not screaming…

38

Cold. Cold and dark. And numb…

I hauled in a gritty breath, throat like a tombola full of razor blades.

Everything else, though: numb.

Then pins and needles.

Then the world burst into full-strength agony.

Clenched my teeth together. Hissing those razor-blade breaths in and out.

Something pressing down on my back.

I forced myself over and whatever it was shifted. Not *heavy*, but everywhere. A blanket of rustling plastic that slithered and clunked. Bin bags?

Shoving them aside revealed a square of grey corrugated roofing, far, far overhead, surrounded by a tunnel of black that narrowed away from me.

Still alive.

Then a coughing fit grabbed hold, slashing through my throat and battering my ribs, each convulsion like being stamped on by a horse.

And then the *real* pain set in. Someone had dipped my left hand in a bucket of petrol and set fire to it – flames searing the flesh all the way up to my elbow. 'AAAAAAAAAAAAAAAAAAAAAAAAAARGH!'

Squeezing my scalded hand in the other one didn't make things any better.

It was too dark down here to pick out any details, but when I held my aching hand up it made an imperfect silhouette against that grey patch of roof. One thumb, three fingers – one poking out at an unnatural angle – and a ragged stump marking the first joint past the knuckle where my index finger used to be.

Closed my eyes and tried not to see the cutthroat razor hacking through the skin and cartilage. Block out the sound of snapping tendons. Bile rising…

God knows how, but I shoved it all down. Then wriggled backwards, till I bumped into the wall, worked my way up so I was sitting with my back against it. Legs splayed out in front. Breath hard and ragged, throat like I'd gargled boiling drain cleaner.

OK, she dislocated your middle finger. You're going to have to reset it. You can do that, right?

What choice did I have?

Deep breath.

I wrapped my right hand around the thing and pulled – out and down, making the joint crackle and *scream* – and let go. My finger popped back into place. Teeth gritted, air hissing in and out through them, trying to keep everything inside. This time, when I held the hand up, the silhouette looked more hand-shaped, but the relocated knuckle was the size of a squash ball.

Another coughing fit left me slumped against the wall, blinking the tears from my eyes.

Still alive.

That was something, right?

Still alive.

Bit by bit, details emerged from the darkness. I was surrounded – no, *part-buried* under more of that agricultural waste: feedbags and tubs of supplement, the huge tough cobwebs that big round bales of haylage and the like got wrapped in before the plastic went on top.

They must've dumped me in the barn's inspection pit. Only from down here it was clearly a lot deeper than you'd need to get underneath and fix a tractor.

Come on, Ash: up.

Clutching my ruined hand to my chest, I hauled myself upright with the other, the pit's brick walls rough against my fingertips. But at least I still had all of them on that side.

Still alive and with *most* of my fingers.

No doubt about it, I was a lucky, lucky man.

Jesus…

The inspection pit's lip was a good dozen feet above my head.

Thrown into my own private oubliette and left for dead.

Wait a minute…

A noise coming from deeper into the darkness: scrabbling. Scratching.

Rats?

Oh, getting luckier by the bastarding minutc.

And then what might have been a gasp.

My voice sounded as if I'd stolen it off a very old man: 'Helen?'

Swallowing to try again felt like gulping down a deep-fried hedgehog, spines-first. 'Helen, is that you?' Wasn't much of an improvement, to be honest.

I grabbed the nearest chunk of rubbish and hurled it behind me, did the same with the next one. 'Helen! Where the hell are you?'

She was over in the opposite corner, on her side, knees curled up, arms wrapped around her stomach. Skin pale as moonlight against the black-plastic bale wrapping. Breath coming in shallow huffing breaths. 'Mr … Mr … Henderson…'

'It's going to be OK.' I half knelt, half collapsed beside her, trying to inject some sort of jollity into my broken-gravel voice. 'Going to take more than this to stop Hardcase Helen MacNeil.'

No reply.

'I'm going to look through your pockets. You'll be fine.' I searched her denim jacket: wallet, some chewing gum, a pack of cigarettes, and her car keys. Where was her phone?

Oh, bloody hell…

When Leah slapped her – she dropped the damn thing and it ended up in the pit.

'Bastard.' OK, this wasn't impossible. Her phone was down

371

here somewhere. All I had to do was rummage through the four billion tons of crap till I found it.

How hard could it be?

'About bloody time!' A small Samsung, with a cracked screen, tucked in next to the inspection pit's wall, buried under a mound of festering black-plastic bin bags. With any luck they'd broken its fall, and Christ knew I was overdue some luck.

My fingers fumbled around the rim, searching for the power button. The time glowed across the middle of the black screen. '14:10'

Damn thing was locked, though.

I scrambled back through the bin bags to Helen. 'What's your passcode?'

It took three goes to get the words out of her. 'Two … zero … zero … two.'

The screen bloomed in the darkness. The backdrop was that photo of Leah as a toddler, held in her mother's arms, at Balmedie Beach – Helen had arranged all her app icons so they framed, rather than obscured the pair of them.

'I'm going to disable your lock screen…' Only took a handful of pokes and swipes. 'Then let's get the torch up and see what we're dealing with.' All happy, nothing to worry about at all.

Cold white LED light slashed out from the phone's flash, pulling bin bags and rubbish into sharp relief.

I peeled Helen's arms away from her stomach – getting a sticky *skreltch*ing noise as the T-shirt stretched up with them, then tore free of the skin. When I lifted the tattered fabric, everything underneath was dark and slick, individual stab wounds still visible through the caked blood. Had to be a dozen of them. Probably more. Only a couple were still oozing.

Yeah, this wasn't good.

Wriggling out of my jacket brought a fresh round of missing-finger agony, but I managed. Folded the thing into a rectangle of wadding with an arm sticking out both sides. Then slipped it around her middle and tied it tight. Or as tight as I could with my left hand screaming at me.

Helen didn't make a single sound. She lay there, panting out thin shallow breaths.

'I'm going to call nine-nine-nine.'

'D... Don't.'

'Helen, you're—'

'I'm ... I'm already ... dead.'

Time to force that jolly tone again: 'Don't be a moron, it's—'

'I'm ... sorry.'

'This wasn't your fault, it's—'

'I was ... I was in ... the car ... when the ... Prentice bitch called ... them. I knew...' A small pained smile. The blood-smeared lips dark against her ghost-pale face. 'Thought I ... could ... rescue you ... and you'd ... you'd have to ... help me.'

Oh well, that was sodding *great*. 'You could've told me they were going to have a go! I would've still—'

'Shut up ... and ... *listen*. ... The security ... security van ... is buried ... under a pile ... of washing ... machines ... in Wee Free ... McFee's ... scrapyard ... he ... he doesn't ... know ... it's there.'

Wee Free McFee?

Might as well stick my head in that car crusher of his and save everyone the bother.

'You ... you can ... have ... the lot.'

'Thanks, but he'll—'

'*If* you ... promise...' Helen's head fell back against the plastic. 'Promise ... you'll kill ... Gordon ... Smith for ... for me.'

'I'll kill the bloody pair of them.'

'It's not... It's not ... Leah's ... fault. ... She's weak. ... Gordon ... Gordon twisted ... her.' Helen's hand trembled its way into mine. 'Make ... make the ... bastard ... *suffer*. ... Make him...' One last breath wheezed out between her bloodied lips, and that was it. She was gone.

I sat back on my haunches.

Nothing to stop me calling 999 now, was there?

But what good would that do?

They'd get me out of this sodding pit, for a start.

And then what? They cart Helen off to the mortuary; open an investigation; have some meetings; argue about budgets and resource allocations; draw up a list of actions; and achieve sod all.

Yes, but—

Wasn't as if we didn't know who killed her, was it? Or who helped.

But the pit—

Helen didn't want Gordon Smith arrested and prosecuted, did she: she wanted him dead.

And so did I.

Besides, what was I supposed to do: call 999 and explain how I'd ended up stuck in an inspection pit, in the middle of nowhere, with the dead body of a civilian. A civilian I *really* shouldn't have smuggled into a potential crime scene. Suppose I could claim she'd been here when I arrived, but they'd know that was a lie, soon as they questioned Gordon Smith or Leah MacNeil. Or found her car, parked at the Lecht, seventy miles away. At which point I'd be looking at a charge of perverting the course of justice, reckless endangerment, and anything else they could throw at me. Which meant at least eight years back in Glenochil Prison.

Sod that.

So no: no 999.

Time to call Shifty. He'd help. The keypad buttons glowed beneath my grubby fingertip: 'Zero, seven, eight, four...?' What the hell was the rest of his mobile number?

Well, it wasn't as if I had it memorised, was it? I always pulled it up on my contacts list, same as everyone else.

Bastard.

Could always call control – had the station number off by heart – get them to put me through to him... And then there'd be an official record of the call. It'd be on tape. They'd know the number *I'd* been calling from, they could triangulate it via the base stations. And I'd be screwed again.

Couldn't even call Alice. No idea what her mobile...

Wait a minute.

I fumbled in my pocket and dug out one of the business cards I'd liberated from Alice's handbag.

You wee *beauty*!

All her contact details were there. I punched in her number and listened to it ring and ring and ring, then finally go through to voicemail. 'Alice? It's Ash. I need you to call me back on this number ASAP, OK? It's really, really important!' And in case she didn't bother listening to her voice mail:

> Alice – I'm in BIG trouble. I need your
> help.
> Call me back on this number!

SEND.

Oh for... She'd have no idea who sent it, would she.

> It's Ash – I'm on someone else's phone and
> I need you to call me soon as you can!

SEND.

Now all I had to do was sit here and wait till she got back to me. Which could take minutes, or hours, knowing Alice. Hours sat here, in the cold and dark, like a useless lump of skin. Because it wasn't as if the stump where my finger used to be was going to get infected or anything, surrounded by all the crap that'd been dumped in here.

God's sake.

OK, so all I had to do was get myself out of an eighteen-foot-deep brick-lined pit with no ladder and a buggered hand.

Yeah ... Alice was right: I should've stayed at home.

The last chunk of agricultural rubbish went on the pile in the corner. That was pretty much all of it, leaving the inspection pit's dirt floor bare. Had to be nearly seven feet between the top of the heap and the barn floor above. Reaching distance.

Assuming my ruined hand held out. The fire had settled to a dull throbbing ache, but knowing my luck, the slightest knock would set it alight again. But it was too late to worry about that now.

375

I backed off to the opposite corner.

Helen lay flat on her back, arms crossed over her chest, eyes pulled closed. And yes, I know it didn't make any difference to her – she was dead. Still...

I turned off the phone's torch again.

Up above, that rectangle of concrete roofing had darkened a couple of shades. The sun wouldn't have to sink very far to plunge Wester Brae of Kinbeachie's ninety-three awful acres into darkness. And there was only so long a mobile phone's battery would last.

Right.

Let's do this.

Took off at a lumbering run, across the narrow space, and leapt, my bad foot scrunching into the pile, pushing off, left foot sinking, push off again, right foot—

The entire thing collapsed, bags and tubs and folded sheets of binding and wrapping slithering off each other in a dusty avalanche. Stumbling. Falling. Arms and legs flailing. Then BANG, smashing into the dirt floor as crap tumbled over me, left hand bouncing off the—

'AAAAAAAAAAAAAAAAAAAAAARGH!'

Like someone was holding a lit blowtorch to it, the skin blackening and curling, smoke rising from the hacked stump where my first finger used to be, spreading through my hand and up my arm until the world roared and crackled and...

Darkness.

My eyes flickered open, and there was that patch of roofing again, every inch as far above me as it'd been the first time. Only now it was the colour of ancient tarmac. Digging Helen's phone from my pocket explained why – five minutes to three. I'd been out for about half an hour.

Just enough time for that bastarding missing finger to settle into pulsing waves of heat and pressure. Each one breaking against my forearm. Probably infected.

Still no reply from Alice.

> Where the hell are you? I need you to call
> me back! This is serious and urgent, Alice,
> I'm not kidding about here.
> CALL ME ASAP!

SEND.

A shiver rattled its way through me. Lying down here, in the cold and damp – it'd seeped its way deep into my bones. Wonder if it was bad enough to cause hypothermia? Maybe not now, but by about three in the morning? In November. In the wilds of Scotland?

Wonderful.

I switched on the torch app again. This time the light was slightly less bright than before – the battery showing twenty percent as I drifted the beam around the pit. Brick walls, streaked with mould and glistening with moisture. Patches of greasy white fungus, growing out of the mortar.

Why the hell wasn't there a ladder?

There should've been a bloody ladder…

But there wasn't, so no point moaning about it, was there? *Think.*

OK, so piling the crap up didn't work.

What else?

I shoved a chunk of that spider's web stuff off my legs and sat up. Then frowned at it. There was a good chunk of it down here – thin plastic netting. Thin, but tough. Robust enough to wind around a four-foot bale of hay to keep it all in place while it got shifted about by tractors and forklifts. Maybe even robust enough to take my weight?

One way to find out.

Twenty-two past three, according to Helen's phone, and the corrugated roofing was nothing but a patch of slightly lighter black overhead.

Still nothing from Alice.

I wrapped the end of my makeshift rope around the middle of my walking stick and tied it off with a couple of clove hitches.

Mostly by touch – which wasn't easy with frozen numb fingers – because the mobile's battery was down to five percent. Half a dozen chunks of webbing, all twisted and tied into a lumpen cord with big knots every twelve inches or so. Seemed solid enough.

Hopefully…

Now all I had to do was chuck the walking stick up into the barn above, and it'd catch on something and I'd haul myself out. Easy. Nothing to worry about.

I rested my forehead against the damp brick wall.

It was about time my luck turned, right?

Please.

I wrapped the loose end of the netting rope around my right wrist, then javelined the walking stick up over the lip of the pit – hard as I could. Clunks and clatters as it bounced off the concrete floor. Then silence.

OK.

I pulled on the rope, reeling it back in.

Come on, come on, catch on something you rotten…

'Bastard!'

The stick came rattling back over the edge and thumped down into the pit again.

Another go – trying a different side this time.

Clunk, clatter.

Pulled on the rope again…

And there was the stick again, falling into the pit.

Again. And again. And again. With exactly the same result every time.

I was going to die in this *bloody* pit and all because Alice wouldn't ANSWER HER BLOODY PHONE.

'AAAAAAAAAAAAAAAAAAAAAAARGH!' Kicking a tub of supplement, sending it bouncing off the bricks to *BOOM* and splinter.

Slumped back against the wall.

This was impossible.

So call 999 while you've still got some battery left, you idiot. Or are you *actually* planning on dying from sheer pig-headed obstinacy.

Eight years in prison.

Damned if you do, dead if you don't…

One more go.

Maybe if I could get the stick to catch across the corner of the pit?

It'd break. The plastic webbing might be strong enough to take my weight, but I doubt a wooden walking stick would. Needed something a bit more solid…

I risked another chunk of the phone's battery, turning the torch on again as I dug through the rubbish Gordon and Leah had dumped in on top of us. They'd chucked Helen's rusty sledgehammer-thing into the pit too – I'd *definitely* seen it when I was searching for her phone.

There you go: it was under a pile of slithery bin bags.

The thing was solid and heavy in my hand. OK, so trying to batter my way out wasn't going to work, but that thick wooden shaft would hold my weight.

It got lashed to the end of the rope, at right angles to my walking stick. A clawless grappling hook.

Four percent battery left. Turning the torch off plunged the pit into darkness so thick you could almost taste it.

Last chance, Ash. Don't cock this one up.

I hurled the grappling end up and over the lip, where two of the walls met. Pulled back on the rope, slow and steady.

Come on, come on…

Oh, thank Christ – the sledgehammer wedged into the corner. Probably wasn't very stable, but it was this or admit defeat, call the cops, and wave goodbye to seeing the outside world again before my sixtieth birthday.

Deep breath.

I reached up as far as I could and took hold with my good hand. Wrapped the injured one around the rope below it – only gripping with the thumb and bottom two fingers – and pulled myself up, bent my knees, clamped my feet together above one of the many, many knots, and used my legs to push. Inching closer to the lip. The sledgehammer shifted a couple of inches, but not too much. Pull, push. Pull, push.

Closer and closer.

Please let this work.

Pull, push. Pull, push.

Come on.

Sweat trickling into my eyes, more between my shoulder blades.

Pull, push. Pull, push.

Nearly there...

Come on, come on, come on...

And finally I got my left arm over the lip of the pit, three working fingers scrabbling at the dusty concrete barn floor.

DO NOT FALL!

One more push with my legs and both arms were out, the sledgehammer's shaft pressing against my chest as I did my best to push it further into the corner.

Oh God, it was slipping.

The bloody thing was slipping sideways as I struggled to get out. Any minute now one end was going over the lip and I'd be right back where I started.

No, no, no, no, no...

39

A final push, clambering over the sledgehammer, legs kicking out over empty air as it spiralled away into the darkness below, crashing into the brick walls, then the *whooooomph* of it hitting part-filled bin bags.

I heaved … and at last my top half was out on the concrete. Far enough that I could swing my left leg up and roll onto the surface.

Lay there, on my back, blinking up at the vast expanse of corrugated roofing as it faded to black. Breath heaving in and out in huge broken-glass lungfuls. Sweat cooling on my face, clammy on my back and chest.

Free…

Oh, thank God.

Pfff…

Took a while, but finally my heart stopped doing its belt-fed mortar impersonation, the breaths less like I was being suffocated. Throat still ached like a bastard, though. That throbbing razor-wire feeling pulsing up and down my left arm.

But I was out and I was alive. Which was one step closer to getting my now imperfect hands on Gordon Smith and his vile protégée.

The floor lurched as I struggled to my feet, so I moved away from the inspection pit – wouldn't do to go plummeting down there again – and pulled out Helen's phone.

Still nothing from Alice.

I called her anyway. Listened to it ring through to voicemail.

'Alice, it's Ash. Call me back!'

END.

So much for that.

Took a while, what with my walking stick being at the bottom of the pit, tied to the sledgehammer, but I limped out of the barn and into the courtyard.

Darkness filled the hollow, turning the mist into an almost solid thing, but up above, the sky was fading to a rich deep purple, fringed with neon-pink clouds, a crescent moon hanging low in the sky – tainted, yellow, and septic.

No sign of my pool car. The bastards had taken it.

So all that effort and I was still stuck.

Somewhere off in the distance, a fox screamed.

Could take Helen's rusty blue Renault, I suppose, but I'd have to get back to the Lecht first...

Oh, *bloody* hell.

Curled up, good hand clasped to my face. Muffling the scream.

Her car keys were back in the pit with her body.

'BASTARD!' Bellowing it out didn't help any, all it achieved was making my throat hurt even more.

Well, what were you going to do, leave her down there to rot? Sooner or later someone would come back here and find the corpse, with *my* DNA and fingerprints all over it. Ash Henderson, I'm arresting you on suspicion of murdering Helen MacNeil...

And how was I supposed to get about without my walking stick? Plus, I needed those car keys.

Fine.

I limped back to the cattle byre and through into the pigeon-smeared feed room. Took that long, shit-speckled ladder off the wall, and hobbled back to the barn. It clanged and rattled into the pit and I winced my way down into the dark again. Doing my best to keep the severed stump of my missing finger away from the bird crap as I climbed.

The phone's torch was barely bright enough to make Helen out by. Battery: three percent.

I grabbed my improvised grappling hook and hurled it out of the pit.

Then bent and took hold of her jacket. Heaved her up into a sitting position, hunkered down and wrestled her over my left shoulder in a half-arsed fireman's lift. Struggled upright again, hissing breaths out between gritted teeth.

'Why'd you have to be so damn … *heavy*?'

The ladder's rungs creaked beneath my trainers as I wobbled my way out of there.

OK, decision time: put her down, untie my walking stick, and get her back over my shoulder; or keep going. Should've got that bloody wheelbarrow when I took the ladder. Even a knackered wheelbarrow would be better than no wheelbarrow at all.

Too late for that now, though.

Keep going it was, because, honestly, if I put Helen down, no way I'd be able to pick her up again. Out into the cold night air, hobbling towards the farmhouse. Getting slower and slower. Every other step sending frozen needles slamming through my right foot. Breathing like the little train who couldn't.

This was a stupid idea.

Shut up.

Should've left her at the bottom of that bloody pit.

No.

I shouldered the farmhouse door open and paused on the threshold – letting the doorframe take some of Helen's weight while I huffed and puffed and my foot and hand screamed at me.

Come on. Nearly there.

At least the stairs had a handrail I could lean on.

Up into the gloom.

Ducking to get her through the doorway and into one of the bedrooms. Dumped her on the ancient bed, sending up a huge *whumph* of dust, the springs and mildewed mattress sagging under her. Some people looked peaceful in death – that cliché about 'not dead, only sleeping' existed for a reason – but Helen MacNeil wasn't one of them. She looked like what she was: a woman in her mid-fifties who'd been stabbed to death.

I untied my jacket from her middle – no point leaving it there, wasn't doing her any good now – then went through her pockets again. Car keys and sugar-free chewing gum; the wallet had twenty quid and some credit cards in it; a lighter tucked into the half-empty crumpled pack of Embassy Regals; and there, in her back pocket, the business card with 'J&F ~ FREELANCE CONSULTANTS' on it. That dark smear of dried blood had been joined by fresh red.

Stood there, staring at it for a bit.

Then unfolded my jacket. It crackled, shedding flakes of brown-black as I hauled it on, gathered up Helen's things and stuffed them into my jacket pockets. Got her straightened up, hands crossed over her chest again.

Should probably say something, but what was the point? Dead was dead. Flowery words weren't going to change that.

Besides, she knew Jennifer Prentice had hired Francis and Joseph to beat the crap out of me. Helen should count herself lucky I wasn't leaving her for the rats.

Someone had painted the window shut, but the bedside cabinet smashed through the single glazing easily enough. It landed with a splintering *crump* in the front garden.

Good enough.

The bed's legs squealed across the lino floor as I dragged the thing as close to the door as I could get. One last look at the hollow body lying on the bed. And it was time to get a move on.

Back downstairs I gathered all the furniture that I could and heaped it up in the living room, directly under Helen's final resting place, like the pile in Gordon Smith's house. Tore down the mildewed curtains – bit damp, but they probably had enough polyester in them to counteract that. I heaped them onto the crumpled remains of the bedside cabinet I'd thrown through the window, and tucked both under the dining room table, arranging the splintered chipboard into a rough pyramid. Then pulled out Helen's lighter and turned the cigarettes and their

384

packet into a fire starter. Coaxing the flame as it licked its way across the chipboard to reach the mouldy curtains.

One minute it looked as if the damned thing was going out, but the next the curtains let loose a muffled *fwoom*, and blue light burst into the room, black smoke curling up to stain the yellowed ceiling.

I backed out of there as steam rose from the dining table, the ancient varnish blistering. Then one side of it burst into flames, catching the chairs I'd piled on top of it. Didn't take long before they were ablaze too and it was getting difficult to breathe.

No way my bonfire was putting itself out anytime soon.

Down the hall and out into the front garden – leaving the door open for a good through draught. Flickering yellow light spilled out of the uncurtained lounge window as the flames grew.

Maybe a neighbour would wonder about the strange glow coming from the abandoned farm next door, and call the fire brigade, but it wasn't likely. Helen's funeral pyre would burn till there was nothing left of her but ash and a few tiny fragments of blackened bone. No DNA, no fingerprints, no dental records.

A Viking funeral.

Of sorts.

I pulled out her phone: two percent battery, complete with a warning that all unsaved data would be lost. Might as well give Alice another go.

Voicemail.

Didn't bother leaving a message.

Why could no bastard answer their bloody phone?

There was *one* other option…

I pulled out the business card for J&F ~ Freelance Consultants. The mobile number was almost invisible in the firelight, but twisting it made the black ink shine against the bloodstains. Not exactly ideal, but what else was I supposed to do?

Joseph picked up on the third ring. *'Salutations, caller, you have reached the offices of J-and-F—'*

'Joseph, it's me: Ash Henderson.' Hurpling my way to the barn as the farmhouse crackled and popped behind me, heat washing against my back. 'Hello? You still there?'

'Ah, my apologies, Mr Henderson, your call took me aback somewhat. On account of our last meeting coming to a … less than optimal conclusion for all parties concerned.'

'You said it was only business. That true?'

'Of course it's true, I know I speak for my associate and myself when I say that we have nothing but respect and admiration for you, despite our occasionally adversarial encounters at the instigation of embittered third parties.'

The sledgehammer-grappling-hook lay where I'd chucked it. 'I need a lift, no questions asked. And I need it now.'

'Intriguing… Very well. Let me know where from and where to, and I shall see to it that you are conveyed from the former to the latter with all possible alacrity.'

Good enough.

I fumbled at the knotted baler netting with my good hand.

No point hanging around here – it might be unlikely that the next-door farm would call the fire brigade, but it was by no means impossible. And it would *probably* be a bad idea to still be standing here, basking in the heat of the burning building, when they arrived.

'Mr Henderson?'

'Going to the Lecht. Coming from Wester Brae of Kinbeachie on the Black Isle, or as far down the road as I can limp away from it.' My walking stick came free and the sledgehammer clattered down to the concrete again. My fingerprints would be all over it, and the baler netting too. They'd need to go in the fire. Should've worn gloves…

Cock.

There was a packet of blue nitrile gloves in my pocket. Could've pulled them on over my ruined hand to keep the stump clean. *Bloody* idiot. Probably too late now.

I dug the pack out anyway, ripped it open with my teeth. 'And I'll need a doctor when I get back to Oldcastle. Stitches, antibiotics, probably a tetanus booster too.'

'I'm sure we can facilitate such a thing. In pursuance of which, I believe it would be efficacious to text you an address where—'

Silence.

'Hello?' When I checked the screen it was black. The thing had finally died.

I struggled my left hand into the glove, hissing and wincing and swearing, until the bloody stump was safely cocooned in blue nitrile. Then chucked the sledgehammer and my baler-netting-rope in through the farmhouse window, one arm shielding my face from the scorching heat. Then did the same with that long stepladder. It wouldn't burn, but hopefully, by the time they dug it out of the rubble, any forensic trace evidence would be so deteriorated it'd be sod-all use to anyone.

Course, there'd be all the bin bags and bits of plastic in the inspection pit...

I hobbled back into the barn. A wide patch of darkness marred the concrete where Helen had been stabbed. Yeah, forensics were *definitely* going to search this place. Maybe the bin bags would catch? I dragged a couple off the big pile at the end of the barn and ran Helen's lighter beneath them. Took a while, but finally one caught, dripping burning tears of melted plastic as whatever it was inside burst into flame. I pitched it into the pit, then set fire to the other bag and stuck that one against the bottom of the heap where it'd come from.

Didn't take long before the inspection pit was popping and crackling, spewing out noxious stinking clouds of grey smoke, lit from below. Two minutes later the big pile was doing the same.

Back outside, into the clean damp air.

Looked as if Peter Smith had got his wish. He'd said the place needed burning down. Writhing orange light spilled out of the barn, and the farmhouse was well on its way – now the upper floor was ablaze, flames crackling out through the broken bedroom window.

Bye, Helen.

Then I turned around and limped away into the mist.

*   *   *

That septic moon was a faint rancid sliver on the horizon as I hobbled along the road, in the dark, and the frigid wind. Sweat trickling between my shoulder blades. Ears like two stinging lumps of ice. Moving with an awkward rolling gait, to the constant *thunk scuff, thunk scuff, thunk scuff*, of my walking stick's rubber end hitting the tarmac.

Would be easier if I could hold the bloody thing in my left hand, as usual, but no way I was risking it. Not with the whole hand throbbing like I'd battered half a dozen nails into it, then stuck it in the microwave. So instead the stick hit the ground on the same side as my bad foot.

Half an hour of this and my back was joining the chorus of aches and pains.

The sky above was awash with stars, gleaming and indifferent in the ink-black sky. The landscape rendered in shades of dark, dark grey. The yellowy lights of cottages and farmhouses in the distance.

Thunk scuff, thunk scuff, thunk scuff...

Keep moving.

Imagine all the horrible things you're going to do to Gordon Smith when you catch him. How many different ways you can make him—

Light bloomed in the darkness ahead, getting closer, bringing with it the growl of a diesel engine as the greeny-yellow grass verges glowed in the approaching headlights. I hobbled off the road, but the big four-by-four didn't drive on past. Instead it pulled to a halt when I was level with the passenger window.

A proper teuchtermobile: one of those flatbed trucks with mud streaked up from the wheel arches, tree rash turning the dark-blue paint matt along the sides. The passenger window buzzed down and a man scowled across the car at me – over-weight and balding; one eye narrowed, the other all puffy and bruised; a line of sticking plaster across the bridge of his nose; two of the fingers on his right hand taped together. The thick Highlands accent wasn't helped by the nasal twang. 'You Henderson?'

'Might be.'

'You look like shit.' He pointed. 'Get in.'

Inside, the cab was covered in a layer of dust, the rubber floor mats nearly invisible under all the dried mud and wee stones. Probably stank as well, going by the mangy collie sitting on the back seat, but with my nose packed with cotton wool, I'd just have to imagine the smell.

My driver didn't wait for me to fasten my seatbelt before grinding the truck into gear again and lurching off down the road.

I stretched my gammy leg out in the footwell. 'You got a name?'

'No.' Then he clicked on the radio and that was it as far as conversation went for the next hour and a half.

Some sort of crappy country and western drivelled away as we pulled off the tarmac onto the gravel car park. The ski lodge sat in darkness, not a soul to be seen as my driver came to a halt beside Helen MacNeil's mouldy old Renault.

My driver hauled on the handbrake. 'Out.' Bringing the total number of words he'd spoken to ten.

'Thanks, it's been a *real* pleasure.'

Another my-dang-dawg-done-died-and-my-cheatin'-wife-done-left-me lament started up in a blizzard of banjos and wailing. I climbed out and watched him swing his truck around and back onto the road. Heading north again, red tail-lights disappearing into the darkness.

Tosser.

Sweat chilled on my forehead.

Probably got a touch of a fever. That would be the infection spreading. The wind turbine's *whoomp, whoomp, whoomp,* marking time with my pulse. Mouth dry as cornflour.

I unlocked Helen's car and collapsed in behind the wheel.

Slipped the key into the ignition and turned it, getting a low guttering *chud-chud-chud* in return. 'Come on you rusty piece of shite...' *Chud-chud-chud* – then finally it caught and a rattling gurgle burst free from the engine.

A cable poked out of the cigarette lighter, and a minute's

389

fiddling plugged it into the bottom of Helen's phone. The light came on – charging. First piece of luck I'd had all sodding day. Which didn't even vaguely make up for the Renault being a manual.

My blue-nitriled left hand squeaked against the gearstick, missing finger radiating snarls of heat all the way up my arm as I put the thing in first and hauled the wheel around, making a wide circle in the car park until the Renault was pointing the right way. Bumping up onto the tarmac.

An hour and forty minutes back to Oldcastle.

At least I wouldn't have to listen to any more country and bloody western: I could drive south in silence. Plotting my revenge.

40

I checked the phone again:

Unit 6,
Haversham Industrial Estate,
Shortstaine,
OC19 3FG

It was a manky cluster of corrugated lockups and warehouses, lurking behind barbed wire and chain-link, the signage faded. The road more pothole than tarmac. I parked in front of Unit Six – painted an unappealing shade of khaki, washed in the sodium glow of a lonely streetlight – next to the shiny black Transit van that sat outside it.

Killed the engine.

Curled forward until my forehead rested against the steering wheel's rough plastic.

Let the breath trickle out of me.

Hand: on fire. Bullet-hole foot: ablaze. Back: made of roasted gravel. Head: thumping like a drum solo.

Come on, Ash. Up.

What if it's a trap?

Then Joseph and Francis kill you. Which, to be honest, would be an improvement right now.

OK.

Out into the night, letting the wind slam the car door for me.

Unit Six was locked, but I leaned on the bell with my gloved thumb anyway. If this really *was* the headquarters of J&F ~ Freelance Consultants, probably best not to leave any fingerprints.

Two minutes later, the door swung open, and there was Joseph. A large wad of cotton padding made a lopsided hat, secured to the crown of his scarred head by strips of white tape. Left arm encased in a fibreglass cast from elbow to palm – pale stubby fingers poking out of the end. Big smile. Which slipped as he looked me up and down. No doubt taking in all the bloodstains and dirt. Then the smile was back again. 'Ah, Mr Henderson, you appear to have made excellent time. Do come in, do come in.' Stepping backwards and ushering me through into a large-ish open space, big enough to fit a two-up two-down semi. Workbenches ran along the back, with a pair of big stainless-steel sinks set into them. A small office area was walled off on one side, its flat roof covered with stacks of cardboard boxes. But what really drew the eye lay in the middle of the concrete floor. Literally.

A young man, couldn't have been much over twenty-five, lay on his front, his thin face turned towards us – streaked with tears and dust and snot. Denim jacket, stone-washed jeans. Wrists fastened behind his back with cable ties. Ankles held together the same way. Francis stood over him, one booted foot between the guy's shoulder blades, leaning on a golf club. Sand wedge, going by the steeply angled head.

'Francis, look who's joined us, it's Mr Henderson.'

He nodded in my direction. ''Spector.' His face was a swollen mess of puffy purple-and-blue skin, fading to yellow at the edges. He sported a wad of cotton too, only his was taped to the side of his forehead, above a thick black eye.

The three of us must've looked a proper sight.

Francis pulled a golf ball from his pocket and placed it into the cup of the young man's ear.

When I looked at Joseph, he shrugged.

'I'm sorry to say that Albert here has breached his employer's terms and conditions regarding the organisation's sales and accounting practices. To wit: skimming ten percent off both the merchandise and monies received. Luckily, Francis is fully qualified to supply a remedial training course on retail ethics.'

A high-pitched, 'Please! Please, I won't do it again, I *swear*!' burst out of Albert's mouth.

'Do you like golf, Mr Henderson?'

'No.'

'Oh, that *is* a shame. What could be finer than a good-natured sporting contest, with hearty companions, out in the glory of nature's bounty?'

Pretty much anything.

Francis lined up the sand wedge, tapping it against the back of Albert's skull. 'Better hold *real* still.'

'Please! I didn't mean it! I'll give it all back!'

'This way, Mr Henderson.' Joseph walked past as Francis teed up, and I followed him into the small office. He turned and shut the door behind us, as a bellowed, *'FORE!'* belted out, followed by a *crack*.

Then the screaming started.

Inside, the office didn't really look like the kind of place a pair of gangland thugs would operate out of. It was far too … ordinary, with a whiteboard, shift rota, and nudie calendar on the walls. Two filing cabinets; two desks; a pair of office chairs; and a woman in her mid-thirties, staring wide-eyed at the window through to the big room. Mouth hanging open. One of those sensible mumsy haircuts, framing an oval Asian face. Trouser suit. Floral blouse.

'Mr Henderson, allow me to introduce Dr Fotheringham. She'll be taking care of whatever your unspecified medical emergency is.'

'FORE!'

Crack.

The screaming got louder.

Dr Fotheringham's hand came up to cover her mouth. 'I'm… It…'

'Nothing to worry about.' Joseph lowered the blinds, shutting out the view. 'Now, in the interest of doctor-patient

393

confidentiality, I'll leave you two alone. Should you need anything, I shall be outside assisting my colleague; do not hesitate to call.' He slipped from the room.

She blinked at me a couple of times, mouth working on something sour. Couldn't blame her, I probably looked pretty terrible, what with the two black eyes, broken nose, neck wrapped in stripes of dark-purple bruising, blood-caked jacket, and one blue nitrile glove. Then a deep breath and she sat down on one of the office chairs, keeping her eyes away from mine. 'I've … I've never done this kind of thing before.'

Not exactly reassuring.

'So what are you, a vet or something?'

'What? No, I mean I've never,' deep breath, 'worked for gangsters before.'

'Ah.' I lowered myself into the other chair and stretched out my aching leg. 'Not here by choice then?'

'Hardly! That…' she jabbed a finger at the door, '*person* dragged me here, soon as my shift was over.'

Oh, for God's sake. 'He kidnapped you?'

Her cheeks darkened. 'Not, *kidnapped*, kidnapped, I mean I came of my own free will, but it wasn't as if I had any option, did I?' She cleared her throat. Brought her chin up. 'Now, what seems to be the trouble?'

I peeled off my filthy jacket and dumped it on the desk. 'Why didn't you have any option?'

'Have you been stabbed? That's a lot of blood. If you've been stabbed, you need to go to hospital. I can't treat you if you've been stabbed.'

'He's got something on you, hasn't he?'

'And why are you only wearing one surgical glove?'

'Must be something pretty serious.'

'Can we get this over with as quickly as possible, please? I'd like to get home to my husband, child, and Labrador, before anyone finds out I've been here.'

Fair enough.

I winced my way out of my shirt, exposing the shallow twisted stab wound in the middle of my chest, then peeled the blue nitrile glove off – biting my top lip as the rubbery skin tugged at what remained of my index finger. It was enough to rip off a chunk of soft yellow scab, setting it bleeding again.

'Oh my God.' Fotheringham blinked at my ruined hand. Nodded. 'Right, we'll need to clean that up. And...' Huffed out a breath. 'Christ.' She produced a holdall from beneath the desk and rummaged through it, pulling on a pair of latex gloves. Placed a stainless-steel kidney dish on the worktop, lining it up with a half-litre bottle of saline, a couple of vials of something clear, two syringes in sterile packaging, a thing of stitching needles, and some thin twine.

Then removed a scalpel handle from its pack and clicked an individually wrapped blade into place.

Took a couple of deep breaths. 'In order to stitch the skin together, to make a proper seal, I'm going to have to...' She swallowed. 'I'm going to have to shorten the bone.'

Of course she was. Because clearly I hadn't suffered enough, today.

'I can give you some antibiotics and a local anaesthetic.'

Thank Christ for that.

'Are you allergic to Levobupivacaine or Amoxicillin? Hope not, because they're the only things I could get at short notice.' One of the syringes got unwrapped and filled from a vial. 'You may feel a small scratch.' As she slid the needle into what was left of my index finger. Then did the same thing four more times at various points across the stump and hand. 'That'll take a couple of minutes to start working.'

It was like plunging a red-hot sword, fresh from the forge, straight into a trough of icy water. My shoulders sagged as the pain hissed away in clouds of blessed steam. Didn't even know I'd been holding them in so tight. 'Thank you.'

Fotheringham soaked a wad of cotton wool with saline and dabbed at the ruined finger. Keeping her eyes on her work. 'What was it, some sort of gangland punishment? The Yakuza do that, don't they? When you've done something wrong and you need to atone.'

'It wasn't the Yakuza. And I'm not a gangster: I was trying to catch a serial killer.'

'Oh.'

'It didn't exactly go well.'

She nodded. 'Nothing ever does.' Then picked up the scalpel. 'You probably want to look away at this point.'

Damn right I did: staring at the nudie calendar instead. An oiled-up woman, infeasibly over-endowed in the breast department, was helping an equally glistening musclebound man to change the carburettor in some sort of sports car. Though if anyone from the Health and Safety Executive had seen them doing it in the nip, they would've shut the garage down in a heartbeat. Which *almost* managed to take my mind off the pulling and pushing happening in my hand as Fotheringham sliced away.

'You want to know what kind of hold they have on me?' Sounding brisk and professional as she reached for what looked horribly like a mini-hacksaw. 'The trouble with having a small gambling problem is that it can sometimes turn into a *big* one. And apparently I can either "lend medical assistance from time to time" or the one with the ponytail breaks my arms and legs.'

Don't think about the rocking motion, or the hissing-grate of metal teeth cutting through numb bone.

'So this is my life, now. At least – hold still, please – until I've paid off my debt. There.' A half-inch lump of something pink clanged into the kidney dish, setting it ringing like a bell. 'Now I need to flush out the wound and we can get you stitched up. Then we'll do the wound on your chest, the lump on your head, and, if there's time after that, I'll take a look at your nose…'

A huge wodge of white bandage turned my left hand into something out of a Boris Karloff film, but at least it didn't hurt any more. Not after the anaesthetics and painkillers. And I could breathe properly again, too. Which was a shame, as the stench rising off Albert wasn't exactly the freshest.

He was curled up on his side, one bloody hand clutched over

his ear, knees up to his chest, sobbing. His jacket was gone, revealing a SpongeBob SquarePants T-shirt turned scarlet around the shoulders with blood. A big damp stain darkened his tatty jeans, the sharp-yellow smell of urine mingling with the deep-brown stink of emptied bowels and bile-green BO.

Joseph clapped his hands together. 'Mr Henderson! I trust Dr Fotheringham has earned her fee this fine evening? Oh, and I thought, given your current state of … let us describe it as sartorial deficit, you might appreciate a change of coat.' He whipped out a denim jacket, which looked a *lot* like the one Albert had been wearing when Francis teed off the first time. 'I know it's not up to your usual standard, but I hope it might pass muster until something better, and less tarnished with haemoglobin, comes along.'

The thing stank of weed, but it was better than what I had on. 'Thanks.' Bit tight, though. I tucked my gore-soaked jacket under one arm.

'Excellent.' He clapped his hands. 'Now, shall we—'

'How much for a gun?'

A moment's silence as Joseph looked at me, head on one side, a faint smile on the edge of his lips. 'Francis?'

The big man was over by the sinks, washing the head of his golf club. A nod.

'Would you be so kind as to escort Albert here from the premises? Maybe drop him off somewhere inconvenient so he can find his own way home? Mr Henderson and I have business to discuss that would benefit from the utmost discretion, and I hesitate to burden Albert with a secret he may have difficulty keeping. Especially as I'll wager he's *quite* keen to stay firmly attached to his remaining ear.'

A nod, then Francis limped across the concrete floor, grabbed Albert by the scruff of the neck, and dragged him out through the unit's door, into the night.

Joseph's expression softened. 'Poor Francis. I know it might seem difficult to tell the difference, what with his taciturn nature, but your friend's knee did him a significant damage last night. There's talk of a surgical intervention being required.'

397

Good.

'Gun: how much?'

'May one enquire to what employment you propose to deploy this firearm? Only, these days being what they are, it behoves the responsible businessman to ensure that such an item does not contribute to unnecessary scrutiny or offences of a terrorist nature.'

'I'm going to kill someone with it. *Slowly.*'

'Ah, in that case I would recommend staying away from the larger end of the munitions spectrum, lest the trauma of a single usage prove too deleterious to the recipient's continued survival. A shotgun, or a forty-five, for example. No, I think what might suit your purpose best is a point two-two, and, by cheery happenstance, I *do* happen to have such an item available.'

'When?'

'Normally we like three to five business days, but as I sense an urgency to your request, shall we call it ...' he checked his watch, 'eleven tonight? And, as a conciliatory gesture, I shall offer you a substantial discount on your medical attention, transportation, and firearm. Shall we say, a thousand pounds for all three?'

A grand. The price of black-market guns had gone up since last time I'd bought one. 'Deal.'

'Wonderful. Then I shall see you this evening at eleven. Please do ensure you have sufficient funds with you at the handover, the rate of interest on overdue accounts can be quite ...' he glanced back towards the office, where Dr Fotheringham was framed in the window, watching us, 'crippling'.

Outside, the shiny black Transit had gone, leaving Helen's mouldy Renault alone in the car park. Well, *my* mouldy Renault now, I suppose. My phone too.

I pulled it out and checked, but there was still nothing from Alice.

Where the hell was she?

One more go.

But when I called Alice, it rang through to voicemail. Again. 'Alice, it's Ash. Call – me – back!'

398

Probably lying face down on a conference-room table some-where, surrounded by empty vodka bottles. *Oh, I can't* possibly *profile sober.*

Which meant she'd be sod-all use. And as I still hadn't got a clue what Shifty's number was, I'd have to track him down the old-fashioned way. After all, it was only about ten minutes from here to Divisional Headquarters and I had two hours to kill before guntime.

I got in the car.

No sign of Shifty, but I tracked Rhona down in the DHQ canteen, wrapping herself around what looked like a chip-and-sausage butty, tomato sauce dribbling down her chin. She'd had her hair done in a Fleabag bob, exposing a pale swathe of neck at the back and a pale swathe of forehead at the front. Which didn't do much to distract attention from the saggy purple bags under her eyes, or the off-yellow circles of ancient sweat staining her shirt's armpits.

She looked up as I thumped down in the plastic chair oppo-site and helped myself to her coffee. Which had too many sugars in it.

Her eyes widened, staring at me with her mouth hanging open, showing off those grey tombstone teeth of hers. 'Ash? We thought you were dead! How did... What happened?' Her nose wrinkled. 'And what is that *horrible* smell?'

'Shifty about?'

'You sent all those texts to Mother: how you were really depressed and going to end it all!' Then Rhona stood and thumped her fist into my shoulder. 'You worried the living shit out of us!'

'Ow!' Had to give it to her, she could punch with the best of them. 'Someone stole my phone.'

'And you look like you've been run over by a combine harvester!' Pink flushed her milk-bottle cheeks. 'Sorry. Poor choice of words. I mean...' An embarrassed cough. 'You know, in the circumstances.'

Nope, no idea.

'You didn't answer the question: where's Shifty?'

'What?' Tiny creases lined up between her plucked-and-drawn-in eyebrows. 'No, yeah, he's up the hospital?'

'You're not making any sense, Rhona. And you need to stop taking sugar in your coffee, this is bogging.'

She put her butty down. 'Ash, he's at the hospital waiting for word on Dr McDonald.'

'Alice? Why would he—'

'Someone hit her with a car. She's in intensive care.'

Jesus…

41

The double doors banged against the wall as I lurched through into the High Dependency Ward. Posters covered its institution-green walls, rows of machinery lined up on their wheelie trolleys. Outside, in the corridor, the strip lighting pinged and flickered, but in here it was turned down to a twilight glow.

A small round woman in green hospital scrubs with a black cardigan pulled on over the top emerged from the nurses' station. Frowning as she sniffed the Albert-scented air. 'Can I help you?'

'Alice McDonald.'

'And are you family?'

'Is she OK?' Stepping closer. Please let her be OK. *Please.*

'They operated for four hours, but she's stable now.'

'Where...?'

'Come on.' The nurse turned and lumbered away down a corridor lined with shared rooms, their inhabitants barely visible in the gloom – lying still as the dead. 'You look like you need to see a doctor, yourself.'

'What happened?'

We turned a corner into a row of private rooms.

'Here we go.' She pointed.

'Ash?' Shifty jumped to his feet, sending the plastic chair he'd been sitting on bashing into the wall. His one remaining eye was bloodshot and watery. 'What the hell happened? We thought you'd topped yourself! You sent all those—'

'Who was it?' I lumbered over to the observation window.

Alice lay pale and broken, like a dropped china doll, flat on her back with wires and tubes going in and out of her – connected to a bank of monitoring equipment and drips. Winking red and green lights in the darkness. Bandages covered half her face, the first stains of bruising leeching out from underneath.

Something tied a ragged knot in my chest.

The nurse picked a clipboard from the rack by the room's door. 'They managed to put her left leg back together, and she'll probably lose some function in her right arm, but the big thing was the ruptured spleen and liver damage. We'll have to wait till she wakes up to find out if the fractured skull has caused any … complications.' She patted my arm. 'Alice is getting the best possible care, I promise.'

'Thank you.' It came out strangled.

'Give me a shout if you need anything, OK?' And with that she was gone.

Shifty joined me at the window, hissing it out: 'Where the buggering *wank* have you been?'

'Who did it?'

'We thought you were dead: they fished your car out the Cromarty Firth!'

'Shifty, I swear to God, either you tell me who hit her, or I'll—'

'We don't know, OK? An auld wifie found her lying at the side of Glensheilth Crescent in Kingsmeath and called it in.' He rested his forehead against the glass. 'I've got people going through every piece of CCTV footage in the area, but there's no cameras where it happened.'

'Why the hell did you let her go out there on her own?'

'I didn't "let her" anything! She's on *your* LIRU, team; you think I'd have let this happen if I was in charge?'

No. This was Superintendent Jacobson's fault.

Kingsmeath. She was knocked down in Kingsmeath – where she'd said the child murderer, Gòrach, came from. Where he felt comfortable. And she was off interviewing possible witnesses

402

that Jacobson had either ignored or discounted. What if one of *them* was Gòrach? What if he'd run her over, because she'd got too close?

'Ash, are you OK? Only you look—'

'Where are her things?'

It took some doing, Shifty's warrant card, and a couple of threats, but finally the hospital handed over the big plastic bag containing everything Alice had on her when she arrived.

The scent of sandalwood and disinfectant mingled with the flat, slightly *plasticy* taint of recycled hospital air.

They'd cut her clothes off, most of them stained almost black with blood. Those little red trainers of hers torn along one side. I went through her pockets, slow and careful, like I'd done with Helen. Car keys; wallet; the Danger Mouse watch I'd given her for Christmas two years ago; a crumpled bunch of receipts, the print almost impossible to read in the low light; three pounds seventy-five in change, a wodged-up paper hanky; a small packet of dog treats; lipstick, mascara, and a tube of foundation; and last, but not least – her official LIRU-issue mobile phone.

Same kind that I'd been given.

Meaning that unlocking it was as easy as holding her cold pale index finger to the sensor on the back.

It buzzed and let me in.

Alice's app management wasn't nearly as tidy as Helen's – about two dozen filled the screen, almost totally obscuring the backdrop. Alice and Henry and me, at the Sands of Forvie, all three of us grinning away at the camera, as if nothing bad ever happened and no one had to die...

I swiped through to the security settings and added my right index fingerprint to the authorised list. Tapping the sensor till the light went green.

A knock at the window.

It was the nurse who'd shown me where Alice was, pointing at her watch and mouthing *'Time!'* at me through the glass.

The phone went in my pocket. Then I leant forward, brushed

a stray lock of hair from the unbandaged half of Alice's fore-head, and placed a kiss on her brow – soft and gentle, the skin so cold and clammy against my lips. The lingering taste of iodine and salt. 'I'll find who did this to you, I promise. I'll find them, and I'll make them wish they'd never slithered down their mother's leg.' One more kiss, and I stood. Nodded. Turned. And hobbled from the room.

The nurse closed the door, soon as I was outside. 'We'll be in touch if there's any change.'

'Thank you.' I thrust the plastic bag into Shifty's arms. 'Get the car. We've got work to do.'

Shifty steered with his left shoulder up, head tilted to the side, pinning his mobile to his ear as he drove the pool car along Kings Drive, heading for the Calderwell Bridge. 'Uh-huh. Soon as you can. ... Yup.'

Outside, the traffic puttered along, cars and buses, taxis and lorries, people staggering by in the ten o'clock haze of an evening's alcohol. Happy and ignorant.

'Yeah. ... Think so. ... OK, I'll tell him. ... OK, thanks, bye. ... Bye.' Shifty straightened his head, left hand disengaging from the gearstick and popping back in time to catch the phone before it hit his lap. Slick and practised. 'Voodoo's going through all the ANPR footage for Kingsmeath, including all routes in and out. Maybe we'll get the bastard coming or going?' He nodded to himself. 'And I've stuck a lookout request on Alice's wee jeep. Mind you, if it's been parked in Kingsmeath since lunchtime, might've been nicked and broken down for parts by now. Or joyridden and torched.' He loosened his tie another couple of inches. 'So, are you going to tell me what happened to you, or not?'

'Long story.'

'And does it explain why you're wearing that denim-jacket abomination and smell like a hippy's squat on bong night?'

We passed a man being taken for a drag by an Alsatian nearly twice as big as he was.

Oh no...

'Where's Henry?' Can't believe I'd forgotten all about the little lad. 'Is he OK? Who's got him?'

'Can we not worry about your bloody dog right now? We need—'

'What if he got run down too? If Alice wakes up and he's dead, it'll break her heart.'

'Well … maybe he's back at the flat? Maybe she didn't take him with her, today?'

Not likely. Worth checking, though. 'Can you send someone round?'

Shifty's mouth clamped shut. Hopefully to stop him saying something stupid that would get his jaw broken. Then a sigh. 'I'll give Rhona a call.' Scrolling through his contacts as we wheeched through a pedestrian crossing.

Not exactly safe driving for a man with only one eye.

He did the shoulder-ear pinning thing again. 'Rhona? It's me. … No, no change. Listen, I need a favour – you know the flat on Shand Street, Ash and Alice are staying in? … Yeah. … Shut up for a minute, OK? I need you to get the keys from whoever's got them, go round and check if Henry's there. … Yes, Henry the dog. … Just *do* it, Rhona. Please. … Thank you.' He dropped the phone from his shoulder, caught it, and slipped it back into his jacket. 'You happy now?'

'Not even vaguely.' I scrolled through the calendar on Alice's mobile. 'She's got a bunch of appointments down for today. When did the call come in?'

'Now you're asking.' Shifty pouted, frowning. 'Half past one, twenty to two, maybe? Have to check my notes to be sure.' Up ahead, the 142 to Blackwall Hill pulled out without indicating and Shifty slammed on the brakes, leaning on the horn – long and hard. 'ARSEHOLE!'

Half one. So while I was lying at the bottom of that bloody pit, garrotted and left for dead…

The bus driver stuck his hand out the window in what started as a cheery wave, and ended with nothing but the middle finger extended.

'Cheeky bastard.' Shifty followed the bus through a pedestrian crossing. 'Got a good mind to stick on the lights and music. Pull him over. See how he likes that.'

There were four appointments in Alice's calendar before noon. Half a dozen after it.

09:00 ● **David REes – ABM's SocWok**
30m ☉ Council offices Sadler Cres

09:30 ● **Ann Tweedale – LTM's SocWok**
30m ☉ Council offices Sadler Cres

10:30 ● **KAren Kennedy – OH's Teach**
30m ☉ Marshal School Burns Road

11:00 ● **Dr Lochridge – OH's Sch Therap**
30m ☉ Marshal School Burns Road

12:00 ● **K Dewar – TMM's Law**
30m ☉ SG&B Rainburgh Lane

13:00 ● **Chris McHale – TM's CAM**
30m ☉ F4 16 Greenview Dr

14:00 ● **LYdia McNaught – TM's SocWok**
30m ☉ Burgh Lib – Cafe

No point looking at anything after two o'clock.

Pretty certain that 'TM's SocWok' stood for 'Toby Macmillan's Social Worker'. There wasn't a phone number attached to the diary entry, but it'd be easy enough to find. I called the Council's out-of-hours switchboard, pulled rank, and demanded to be put through. Two minutes of hideous hold music later, and Lydia McNaught was on the line.

'Is this a joke? Have you any *idea what time it is? It's after ten! I'm at home! Can't this wait till—'*

'Police. You had an appointment with Dr Alice McDonald this afternoon.'

'*Dr McDonald?*' A revolted snorting noise. '*In that case you can sod right off, too. I wasted my whole lunch hour hanging around the library café waiting for her. You can tell that rude bitch: I don't care how busy she is, common courtesy would've been a phone call to cancel and apologise! I've got too much on my plate as it is, without some ignorant—*'

I hung up on Lydia McNaught. Prodded Shifty's shoulder as he took us over the Calderwell Bridge, the Kings River a slab of black marble below. 'Any idea what "C.A.M." stands for?'

'Do I look like a sodding...' A frown. 'Actually, now you mention it: Court-Appointed Mentor. They do it for toerags who won't pay any attention to their social worker. Think of it like a big brother who gets paid to give you a hard time.'

OK, well at least that gave me somewhere to start. If Chris McHale was court appointed, his phone number would be on file. I gave Sabir a ring.

It barely rang before his voice boomed in my ear: '*Alice? Are you OK?*'

'We don't know yet.'

'*Bastard. ... Ash? That you? Where the hell you been? Bear's at DEFCON One, what with all them creepy texts you been sending about doin' yerself in.*'

Not me: Leah MacNeil.

On the other side of the bridge, Shifty threw the car right at the roundabout. Into Kingsmeath.

'Sabir, can you access Alice's calendar?'

'*Two seconds.*' Some clacking. '*In. What do you need?*'

'Can you text me phone numbers for everyone she had an appointment with today? But send them to *her* mobile, not mine.'

'*See if you catch the tosser what done it? Fuckin' do* him, *right?*'

'Thanks, Sabir.'

That's exactly what I was going to do.

A patch of what was probably supposed to be parkland broke up one side of Glensheilth Crescent. Clearly no one had bothered looking after it for years, leaving the place overgrown and thick with gorse, brambles, and dead nettles. The trees drooping and twisted. At one point, there would have been winding paths and play areas, now the only sign left was the line of concrete lamp-posts, all of them broken, leaving the place shrouded in darkness.

The seven tower blocks that wrapped around this side of the huge Blackburgh Roundabout hulked in the middle distance, welcoming as tombstones. Somehow all the lights being on made them look even less friendly, while Glensheilth Crescent itself had all the charm of a council estate that'd been designed to make sure the working classes knew their place. Boxy grey-and-brown terraces next to boxy grey-and-brown semis and a boxy grey-and-brown community centre with boarded-up windows.

A square of blue-and-white 'POLICE' tape sat at the edge of the 'park', the colour leeched from it by the guttering sodium glow of a nearby streetlight. Shifty parked next to it. 'That's where they found her.'

I climbed out into the wind. Turned, frowning at the curving line of neglected houses. 'No witnesses?'

Shifty lumbered after me. 'None that'll talk to the police. You know what Kingsmeath is like.'

Should do: lived here long enough.

If it wasn't for the tape cordon, that square of rough ground probably would've blended into the rest of the park. Yes, the overgrown grass had been flattened, but it wasn't until I played my … *Alice's* phone's torch over it that a big patch glistened a stomach-clenching shade of burgundy.

Shifty's hand thumped against my shoulder and squeezed. 'I know.'

Took some doing, but I nodded. Huffed out a breath. Cleared the knotted barbed wire out of my throat. 'You search the street for her car?'

'No sign.'

Sod. 'So what was she doing here, then?'

The phone ding-buzzed. A text from Sabir with names, addresses, and numbers for everyone Alice had in her calendar today.

I tried the one for Chris McHale, the Court-Appointed Mentor. Listened to it ring and ring. 'What about the surrounding streets?'

Shifty shrugged.

'OK, we'll start there, then.' Limping across the road to Glensheilth Place, a short street with only a handful of terraced houses on either side.

Then, at last, *'If this is a marketing call, you can shove your—'*

'Mr McHale. Police.'

A groan. *'Let me guess, Tracy Fordyce has tried burning the school down, again? That wee horror needs locking up, she's got "future serial killer" written* all *over her. Tenner says—'*

'You had a meeting with Dr Alice McDonald this afternoon.'

No sign of Alice's Suzuki Jimny on Glensheilth Place, so I kept going, round onto Forbes Drive, where the houses were slightly more upmarket, but not by much.

'You cheapskate bastards should be paying me a lot more to mentor horrible shites like Tracy Flipping Fordyce! I tell you, it's—'

'Mr McHale!' Putting some menace behind it: 'Did you meet with Dr McDonald, or not?'

'Weird bint: curly hair and verbal diarrhoea? Wanted to talk about Toby Macmillan? Yeah, I met her.'

I checked my watch. Quarter past ten. Forty-five minutes to guntime. 'Can you come past the station tomorrow and give a statement about what happened to Toby?'

'What, another *one? You better be paying me for this. I'm not running a charity here, you want my time you have to pay for it.'*

'Yes, of course. We'll sort all that out when you come in tomorrow morning.'

'Should think so too.' He hung up.

Prick.

Shifty was staring at me. 'What was that all about?'

'Chris McHale was the last person to see Alice. Ten minutes after meeting him, she's found by the side of the road. You think that's a coincidence?'

'Then why did you tell him to come into the station tomorrow—'

'Because I don't want him spooked and buggering off before we go over there and break his legs.' I turned and headed back towards the car. 'You coming?'

'Hell yeah.'

42

Ten minutes later we were parked outside 16 Greenview Drive, which didn't have a single scrap of green in sight. It was a four-storey grey-brick tenement that stretched the length of the road, mean little windows scowling out over the rutted tarmac to an ugly boxy building that looked more like a Victorian prison than a synagogue. They'd mounted a handful of fixed security cameras high up on the walls, but that hadn't stopped some moron spraying anti-Semitic graffiti across the front door. Because why live-and-let-live when you could make a bigoted wanker of yourself?

None of the cameras were turned in our direction. Which meant we couldn't use them to catch Chris McHale following Alice from here to where he ran her over. But it also meant no one could prove Shifty and I had paid him an extremely painful off-the-books visit.

I held up Alice's phone in my bandaged hand, screen filled with the map of Kingsmeath. 'Way I see it, she could go two ways to her appointment at Burgh Library,' pointing at the massive roundabout it sat in the middle of, 'one: you go down to Montrose Road, back to the bridge, then up King's Drive. Two: you cut through Kingsmeath. Banks Road, straight through to McNamara Row, then left onto Glensheilth Crescent.'

Shifty pulled a face. 'What about Denmuir Gardens?'

'They've dug it all up in front of the primary school, after that sewage-pipe leak.'

'Still doesn't explain where her car is. She'd—' His phone launched into the theme tune from *Mastermind*, and he pulled it out. Checked the caller ID. Answered it. 'Rhona? … Uh-huh. … Uh-huh. … OK. … No, thanks anyway. … Yeah, I will. Thanks. Bye. … OK, bye.' Puffing out a breath as he slid the phone back in his pocket. 'Henry's not at your flat.'

Maybe he was still in the car? Because the alternative didn't really bear thinking about.

But one thing was certain, Chris McHale was about to have a very bad evening.

I struggled my right hand into a nitrile glove – not easy with the left all clarted in bandages, climbed out of the car, and limped over to number sixteen. No names on the intercom. The services button had been taped over, so I tried 'FLAT ONE' instead, leaning on the buzzer until an irritated voice crackled out of the speaker.

'What? Jesus. I was on the bog!'

'Got a chicken vindaloo, lamb biryani, steamed rice—'

'I didn't order a curry. You've got the wrong flat, muppet.'

'Yeah, but the guy's buzzer isn't working, and if I don't deliver his meal they're going to take it out my wages. Come on, be a mensch.'

'Gah… Fine.' A grumbling metal noise, then *click*, the door was unlocked.

Worked every time. Well, almost.

I pushed inside, Shifty following me up the dark winding stairs to the first floor.

Flat Four had a bicycle chained up outside it, seat and handle-bars removed. A small plastic plaque on the scuffed brown door: 'C McHale Esq' so an even bigger prick than he'd sounded on the phone.

Shifty pulled on his own pair of nitrile gloves. 'What if he's got someone living with him, or a visitor?'

'Then they get to have a horrible evening too.'

'Fair enough.' Shifty put one fat thumb over the spyhole

and knocked with his other hand. Raised his voice for, 'Deliveroo!' Knocked again. 'I wasn't kidding, by the way, that jacket's hideous and it stinks of weed.'

'My own coat's covered in blood, OK? It was this or looking like something off the *Texas Chainsaw Massacre*.'

Shifty gave the door another knock, louder and harder this time. 'Not sure it's much of an improvement.' Deep breath, another thumping knock. 'DELIVEROO!'

A thin metallic rattling noise, then the door popped open a crack and a sliver of puffy face glowered out at us. 'You've got the wrong—'

Shifty rammed his shoulder into the door, ripping the security chain from its moorings, as he lumbered in over the threshold.

The man stumbled back, one hand clutching his face. A short bloke, pale and overweight, hair swept up at the front into a greying quiff, wearing tartan lounging trousers and a faded 'Steampunk Sex Toy ~ World Tour 2013!' T-shirt. 'You can't—'

A right hook to the uncovered side of his head sent him crashing against the wall, then slithering down till he was slumped against the skirting board. Shifty stood over him, flexing that big fist.

'Chris McHale?'

He wobbled where he sat. No reply.

'Fine.' Shifty grabbed him by the lapels and hauled him upright. 'Let's find your bathroom, shall we? See if you float.' Opening doors at random, then shoving McHale inside.

While the sound of water splashing into the bath echoed out into the hall, I checked the rest of the flat. It had the clinical tidiness of a neat-freak who lived alone and didn't get out much. A big collection of vinyl records, all in alphabetically labelled shelving. The same with DVDs. Widescreen TV and a turntable. Bedroom was every bit as neat, and so was the kitchen. A selection of coats and jackets on hangers in a hallway alcove, shoes and boots lined up in pairs beneath them. Which only left the bathroom.

Not quite so tidy in here. Not with Chris McHale cowering next to the toilet, while Shifty filled the bath.

I leaned against the doorframe. 'You've been a naughty boy, haven't you, Chris?'

'You can't... I didn't...' Deep breath. 'Please! This isn't—'

'Going to give you one chance, then it's face down in the bath you go.'

'*Please!* I don't know what she's told you, but I never touched her, I swear! She's a lying bitch, you know that. All she ever does is lie!'

'You greasy bastard.' A nearly-full bottle of Alberto Balsam Sunkissed Raspberry shampoo didn't weigh all that much, but if you hurled it with enough force, at someone's face...

McHale shrieked, flinching back against the cistern, hand coming up to cover his left eye. 'I didn't touch her! She was playing on the swings and she fell off and I helped her up, that's all! I didn't mean to see her knickers.'

Ah. So he *wasn't* talking about Alice, then?

The matching raspberry conditioner felt as if it had a bit more heft to it. 'Dr McDonald. She interviewed you this morning: one o'clock.'

'Doctor...? This isn't about Tracy Fordyce?' A small laugh. 'It's not about her. I didn't—'

The conditioner battered into his forehead, hard enough to split the plastic and send a gush of sweet-smelling pink out across his chest and the wall behind.

'Aaaaaaaargh!'

'You followed Alice after she left here, didn't you, Chris?'

'Please, please I don't—'

'You followed her and somehow you got her out of her car, and then you ran her over.'

'That's not—'

'She's in *Intensive Care*, you little shite!'

Shifty turned off the taps and hauled Chris McHale from his hiding place. 'Time for swimming.' Then whacked him against the side of the bath and shoved his head under the steaming water.

Arms and legs thrashing, or at least until Shifty knelt one leg across the guy's calves.

'Think that's enough?'

I held out my good hand, fingers counting down to a clenched fist.

McHale surfaced, bringing an arc of raspberry-scented water with him. Coughing and spluttering between the sobs.

'What did you do with her car, Chris?'

'I … I didn't … didn't do … anything … to her! I … I swear! On … my mother's … *grave* … I never … touched her.'

'Under you go.' Shifty put his weight behind it this time, grinding McHale's face into the bottom of the tub. 'What if the wee shite's telling the truth?'

'Alice said there might be a paedophile ring operating in Kingsmeath. Can you think of a better cover than being a Court-Appointed Mentor? Your charges come pre-messed-up, who's going to notice them going slightly further off the deep end, because you're fiddling with them too?'

'And he's seen this Tracy girl's knickers.' A frown. 'That's probably enough.' Shifty hauled him back above the waterline.

'AAAAAARGH!' More coughing, followed by a *lot* of retching.

'*Quiet!*' Shifty slapped him, hard. 'Want me to give you something to scream about?'

'Please! … I swear … she … she came and … and asked her … questions … and wrote it all down … then … then she left!'

I picked up a pumice stone – that would do a fair chunk of damage at high velocity. 'What did she ask you?'

'I don't… I think it was … mostly stuff about Toby Macmillan and did … did he have any friends and … what was his family really like. … Because they all pretend they love him when the cameras are on, don't they? But his stepdad liked to … to use the top of his head as an … ashtray, didn't he? And they broke … broke his arm when … when he was three. And … and his mum's … doing eighteen months … for neglect.'

Poor wee sod.

'What else?'

McHale blinked at me, tears and snot mingling with the water running from his flattened quiff. 'I don't *know*.'

'Time for another dunk?' Shifty tightened his grip. 'In you—'

'No! I…' Biting his lip. 'I don't… She went really weird and quiet … towards the end. Kept flipping back through her notes and staring at something. Underlining bits.'

'Why?'

'I don't know! Please, I promise you, I don't. I was telling her about Toby's mum appealing against her sentence, and that's when she stopped paying attention. Said she had to go walk her dog. Then she left. I *swear* that's all that happened!'

Shifty raised the eyebrow above his eyepatch. 'Once more for luck?'

Shook my head. 'No. I think he's telling the truth.'

'Oh, thank God…' It was as if all the bones had been removed from McHale's body, leaving nothing but a soggy limp slough of skin behind. 'I never touched her.'

'Now then,' Shifty's massive paw wrapped itself around McHale's face, thumb and fingers digging into the cheeks, forcing the lips out into a chicken's-bum pout, 'just so we're clear, I ever hear that you've been looking funny at a wee girl you're supposed to be mentoring? I'm going to come back here and they're going to find what's left of you floating in this bathtub. Am I clear?'

McHale nodded – not easy with his face in the vice of Shifty's grip, but he did it.

'And see if you think you'll get any help from the police about our wee visit tonight?' Shifty reached his free hand into his jacket and produced his warrant card. Shoved it against McHale's eye. 'I *am* the police. And we're gonna be watching you.'

'Got you a present.' Shifty tossed a black leather jacket at me as we marched out the main door and back onto the street. 'Chris McHale decided he didn't need it any more.'

Bit old-fashioned, but had to admit: it smelled a lot better than Albert's stinky denim job.

I transferred the contents of my pockets and climbed back into the pool car. Clicked the seatbelt on as Helen's phone *ding-buzz*ed at me.

UNKNOWN NUMBER:

> Salutations, Mr Henderson. I am pleased
> to confirm that your appointment has been
> arranged for 23:00 at Rushworth House, in
> Camburn Woods.

Damn it.

According to my watch, that was only ten minutes from now, and while it wasn't *impossible* to make it all the way across the river and through town to Camburn Woods in time, we'd need lights and music on to do it. Which wasn't exactly low-profile when it came to buying a black-market handgun.

Shifty started the engine. 'Where to?'

And I still hadn't got my hands on Joseph's thousand pounds.

'How much cash have you got on you?'

'Dunno.' He pulled out his wallet and checked. 'Sixty-two quid and some smush. Why?'

Mine held the twenty I'd taken off Helen's body, three ten-pound notes of my own, and that fifteen-quid gift voucher from Winslow's. Doubt Joseph would accept it, though.

'We need to stop at the nearest cash machine.'

Shifty did a three-point turn, then took a right at the round-about – up over the bridge that crossed the railway line, Saint Damon of the Green Wood lurking in the darkness below. 'What are we buying?'

'Gun.'

'Ah...' Silence as we headed up Banks Road. 'Only – and don't take this the wrong way – your luck with guns is *not* great.'

'If I take the maximum cash out on my debit card, and you do the same, and we use Alice's too, plus all the cash we've got on us, that'll cover it.'

'You sure we wouldn't be better off with something like a machete, or a baseball bat? Something cheaper and less ... disastrous?'

'I've got three people to kill, Shifty. Maybe four.' Because Wee Free McFee wasn't likely to stand back and let me go rummaging through his scrapyard, looking for a buried security van full of stolen jewellery and artwork.

'OK. *Four* people?' Shifty puffed out his cheeks. 'That's a lot of people.'

The streets of Kingsmeath drifted by the car windows. Dark and miserable.

I picked out a reply to Joseph:

> Change of plans. I need you to meet me
> at the Burgh Library. Make it quarter past.
> I have business here I can't put off.

Send.

They probably wouldn't like that, but tough.

The phone went back in my new jacket's inside pocket. 'Where's her notebook? McHale said she was making notes and looking back at them. It wasn't with her things at the hospital.'

'You *sure* these four people have to die? We couldn't, you know, rough them up instead?'

'One of them's the bastard who put Alice in Intensive Care.'

'Assuming we can catch him.' Shifty parked outside the Post Office on Greenhorn Place. 'Cash machine.'

I sat there, looking out of the passenger window, but barely registering the small row of rundown shops. 'McHale said Alice told him she had to walk Henry. On her way to the library, she sees that chunk of parkland on Glensheilth Crescent, pulls in, gets out of the car, and this Gòrach bastard runs her over. Which means he was following her.'

Wind scrabbled at my back as I climbed out of the car, stuffed Albert's stinking denim jacket into the nearest bin, then limped over to the cash machine. Took out the maximum daily allowance, then did the same with Alice's card – easy enough as she used the same pin number on everything, including the TV's parental lock at home: 3825, which, apparently, spelled a very rude word in predictive text on the old flip phones.

'Bloody freezing out here.' Shifty shuffled past as I stepped away to count my cash. Then he swore, nearly dropping his debit card as his phone launched into the *Mastermind* theme again.

Pinning the thing between his ear and shoulder as he slipped the card into the machine and punched in his pin. 'Rhona? ... Uh-huh. ... Uh-huh. ... They did? Where?' Turning to me. 'They've found Alice's jeep.' Then back to the phone. 'Yeah. ... OK. ... Uh-huh. ... OK, look, is the dog there? ... Damn it.'

No Henry.

'Where's the car?'

He took his banknotes from the machine and handed them over. 'Halfway through the front window of that Cash Converters on Brokemere Street. Pair of wee scroats used it as a battering ram. Made off with a bunch of crap jewellery and some electric guitars. Last seen legging it down McLaren Avenue, heading for Camburn Woods.'

'Get them to search the car for Alice's notebook. See if we can figure out what she saw that tipped her off.'

'Rhona? I want that vehicle searched. We're looking for a notebook. ... Uh-huh. ... Uh-huh...'

Shifty's cash went on the pile, bringing our grand total to one thousand and ten pounds.

'Well get them to look again! ... Uh-huh. ... You're sure? ... Bugger. ... No, if it's not there, it's not there. ... Yeah, thanks, Rhona.' Shifty put his phone away. 'Take it you got the gist?'

'If it's not on her, and it's not in the car, then *he* took it.'

'Doesn't help us any, though, does it?'

We got back in the car. Sat there with the engine running and the blowers roaring.

'So we look at who she'd already seen. One of the people Alice interviewed said something important about Gòrach.'

'Yeah.' Shifty bit his top lip and frowned. 'Ash, you know I'm your best friend, right? And I'd go through ... have *gone* through some pretty rough shit because you needed me.' A finger came up and pointed at his eyepatch. 'But tonight you're talking about killing four people. I'm not going through everyone Alice saw today and torturing the living hell out of them. Chris McHale was different, he's definitely dodgy...' Shifty pulled his shoulders in and looked out the driver's window. 'I gotta live and work in this town, afterwards.'

419

'How about—'

'And these people you want to kill: I get the bastard who hurt Alice deserves everything he's got coming, but who are the other three? Why am I making myself complicit in their murder?'

'They're...' Deep breath. 'I made a promise to Helen MacNeil.' Pulled down my collar and showed off the necklace of bruises. 'Gordon Smith killed her. Then he strangled me, dumped me in a pit, and left me for dead.' I held up what was left of my butchered hand. 'Leah MacNeil hacked my finger off with a cutthroat razor. She's been in on it all along.'

He stared at me. 'So they're the ones who gave you the black eyes.'

'No, that was ... someone else.' No point naming names. Joseph and Francis were kind of a sore spot where Shifty was concerned. 'Jennifer Prentice paid a couple of thugs to jump me. Didn't go well for them.'

'Oh, for God's sake.' Shifty sagged in his seat. 'So, let me guess: she's the fourth person who needs murdering?'

'No. I haven't quite figured out what I'm going to do there.'

'Who's number four, then?'

'If it helps, there's a cut of six million in it for you, when this is all over.'

That got his attention. 'Six *million*?'

'Security van, stolen from Steve Jericho. Remember him? Owned Hallelujah Bingo? Twenty K in cash, the rest in half-inched artwork and jewellery. It's buried under a stack of washing machines at Wee Free McFee's place.'

'Wee Free McFee?' Shifty covered his face with his hands. 'No...'

'I'm going to buy a family hotel out on the west coast, and Alice is going to run retreats and things.'

'Yeah, but *Wee Free McFee*!'

'He's the possible fourth person.'

An old woman clumped past the car, dragging a big fat Yorkshire terrier behind her. Pausing only to make 'wanking' gestures through the windscreen at us.

Off in the distance, a small motorbike revved and revved and revved its engine.

The streetlight we were parked under flickered off and on.

Shifty's hands fell from his face. 'You do know this plan is totally insane, don't you?'

'How about we *don't* torture the people on Alice's list, then? How about we interview them, like Alice did. Would that make you feel any better?'

'You want to break into Wee Free McFee's scrapyard and steal six million quid's worth of swag from right under his nose, but you think not *torturing* people's going to make me feel better?' He stared up at the car's roof. 'I must be off my bloody head.' But he put the car into gear anyway. 'Where next?'

43

Meathmill House and Meathmill Park stood sentry on either side of the road, eighteen-storey tower blocks, with lights glittering in nearly every window. Monolithic and ugly, even in the darkness. The pool car slipped down the ramp between them, disappearing into the curved embankment and an underpass that was almost solid graffiti. Not the artistic kind, either – the concrete walls were caked in decades of tags and swearing and claims that X loves / shags / 'takes it up the arse' from Z, Y, and their own dad. Had to be a foot thick in places.

We emerged out the other side and there was the huge architectural monstrosity masquerading as Burgh Library, perched on top of its dumpy hill. All curved concrete walls and ceramic tiles and weird rooflines that dipped and rose like a sales graph. Far too much glass on show, and not enough taste. Most of the lights were off, leaving nothing but a faint orange glow on the ground floor.

Shifty pulled into the car park, and I pointed towards the far corner, where the CCTV cameras dangled from their mounts like rabbits hanging in a butcher's shop window. That was the joy of the Kingsmeath side of things, anything designed to help law enforcement didn't usually last long.

I undid my seatbelt. 'Stay in the car.'

'Humph.' Shifty killed the engine. 'That'll be shining.'

'And before you get all stroppy it's for your own good.'

A small laugh. 'Ash, there's no way—'

'I'm serious. In – the – car.' The wind wasn't bad down here, but the roar of traffic, wheeching its way around the top of the steep embankment, was pretty much constant. That's what happened when you built your library right in the middle of a massive great roundabout. 'And stay here till I get back.'

I thunked the door closed and hobbled off to stand with my back against a sign advertising upcoming author events and computer classes for the over-sixties. My breath plumed in the sharp peppery air.

Hand was starting to throb. That would be the local anaesthetic wearing off.

Come on, Joseph, finger out.

At least he had all of his.

Good job I'd scored a blister pack of Naproxen from Dr Fotheringham when she'd finished stitching me up. Two got forced down, dry. Could've gone for something stronger, but being semi-stoned was probably not the best idea for tonight.

Not given what I had planned for whoever put Alice in Intensive Care.

Her phone buzzed as I unlocked it: bang on quarter past eleven, according to the screen.

No text from Joseph or Francis, saying they'd be late.

You'd think gun-peddling-thugs-for-hire would have better manners than that.

There, nestled amongst the rows of apps that covered Alice's screen, was one with a bullseye target and a big arrow pointing at the middle. It sat above Henry's left ear, the wee lad grinning, tongue dangling out the side of his mouth like a big pink sock. Couldn't remember what the app was called, probably something spelled with 'Z's instead of 'S's and a couple of numbers or unnecessary asterisks replacing random letters. The tracker app she'd installed on my phone.

Meaning there was no need to sod about with official channels to find Leah MacNeil and Gordon Smith. Assuming they hadn't ditched my mobile somewhere.

My finger hovered over the icon.

423

Of course, what I really *should* do is call Mother. Find out where the app said my phone was and let her send in the heavy mob. An end to Gordon Smith's fifty-six-year reign of horror. Picture in all the papers, commendation from the top brass. Closure for Smith's victims' families. And he'd spend the rest of his life in a padded cell with no hope of ever seeing the outside world again.

Yeah, but you promised Helen, didn't you? As she died.

You *promised* her.

What about Leah? She'd probably get off on a diminished-responsibility plea: eight years, tops. Bet she'd be out in four. If that. And if I brought her in, she'd tell everyone what I'd done to Gordon Smith. And that would be me screwed, because there was no way I could let him live. He had to die, which meant she did too.

I'd made a promise.

And soon as I'd sorted out whoever it was that'd hurt Alice, I'd keep that promise.

Because what was the point of a man if he didn't keep his—

Here we go.

A shiny black Range Rover growled its way up the ramp from the Blackwall Hill side, headlights sweeping the car park as it turned. I stepped out into the glow of a lamppost and raised a hand. The Range Rover swung towards me. Came to a halt, when I was level with the passenger window.

It buzzed down and Joseph smiled out, that lump of cotton wadding looking more than a bit ridiculous, perched at a jaunty angle on top of his scarred head, as he leaned on the sill. 'Mr Henderson, while your choice of location is perhaps a touch less suitable for clandestine exchanges than the one proposed, I have to express my approbation for choosing a library. Bravo.'

Francis leaned over from the driver's seat and gave me a nod. ''Spector.'

The thousand pounds made a disappointingly thin slab of slithery plastic and paper as I handed it over. 'Count it.'

'Oh, I trust you, Mr Henderson.' Joseph slipped it into an inside pocket. 'After all, we're both gentlemen, are we not?

Our word has value beyond the mere pursuit of Mammon's favours. And in exchange, I give you this.' He held out a small yellow-and-blue backpack, done up to look like a Minion, complete with one 3D eye-goggle and a big cheesy grin. 'In case you're interested in the details of such things, it contains a Walther P-Twenty-Two Q.D. renowned for its tactical styling, exquisite trigger, and second-strike capability. Holds ten rounds in the magazine, one in the breach, and the slide is textured – making it easier for someone with restricted hand mobility to "rack in a round" as our American cousins would say.'

Wouldn't be surprised if he was sporting an erection at this point, going by the expression on his face.

'I have furnished you with twenty-five rounds, which I believe should be sufficient for all but the most prolonged gun battles. Somehow I think you're more inclined to precision than the "spray and pray" approach, but if you require an additional stock, please don't hesitate to get in touch as our customer loyalty scheme is most generous.'

I lowered the rucksack. 'Is it clean?'

'As a nun's conscience, Mr Henderson.' He gave me a wave, then faced front again. 'Francis, it's time we were away. I believe Mr Henderson is most eager to be about whatever business instigated his purchase from us this blustery night.'

Another nod from Frances. ''Spector.'

'Oh, one more thing.' Joseph held out a crisp white business card. 'If the occasion arises, Mr Henderson, when you feel you might benefit from the assistance of two *very* capable gentlemen who possess those most admirable of traits: determination, dedication, and a somewhat *laissez-faire* attitude to other people's physical wellbeing, I do hope you'll think of us.'

Well, you never knew. I accepted the card and tucked it away.

'Excellent. Oh, and I like your new jacket.' Then the window buzzed up, the Range Rover swung around and disappeared off down the ramp to the Blackwall Hill side of Blackburgh Roundabout again.

Twenty-five rounds would be plenty for what I had in mind.

I took my new Minion back to the pool car.

Shifty glowered at me, from behind the wheel. 'Tell me that wasn't who I think it was!'

'Who we going to interview first?'

'Ash, I'm serious – that better not've been Joseph and bloody Francis!'

My seatbelt clicked into place. 'Why do you think I made you wait in the car?'

'OH, FOR FUCK'S SAKE!' Battering a fist off the steering wheel. 'How could... Have you forgotten what they did? To me?' Pointing at his eyepatch again. 'HOW COULD YOU?'

I sat there in silence and let him seethe at me while I struggled my right hand into another nitrile glove.

Then unzipped the Minion's head and pulled out a clear-plastic Ziploc bag with the gun in it. Stubby and black, almost invisible in the gloom. Didn't weigh much, probably not even half a kilo, but that was without the magazine or bullets, of course.

'You want to know how I could?' The gun swung in the bottom of the bag as I held it up. 'This is how.'

Shifty's shoulders curled inwards as his scowl turned away from me and out of the windscreen instead. 'I *hate* those guys.'

'You don't have to go through with this, Shifty. You can drop me back at the hospital and walk away. I'll take care of it.' I dipped into the rucksack again. Two more Ziploc bags: one with the empty magazine in it, the other containing a drift of small brass-cased bullets with grey tips. Like tiny metallic lipsticks, not much bigger than a finger bone. Assuming you still had all of yours. 'But if you *are* walking away, I need another favour before you go.'

He didn't look at me. 'What?'

'Can you load the bullets into the magazine for me? My hands don't work properly any more.'

'Should never have let you talk me into this.' Shifty pulled up at the kerb, outside a classic seventies bungalow on Muchan Road. Grey harling and brown pantiles. A second-hand Audi in the driveway and a well-manicured garden out front, turned monochrome in the pale-yellow glow of the lamppost two houses down.

'I *told* you, you didn't have to come.' The Minion joined me from the rear footwell. 'I can do this on my own.'

'Bloody reverse psychology.' But he undid his seatbelt and climbed out of the car anyway.

I joined him, and we hobbled up to the front door. Leaned on the doorbell.

'But we're only questioning them, OK?' Shifty jerked his chin out. 'No violence, or shooting anyone.' Pointing at my Minion. 'Not unless we're one hundred percent *positive* they're the one who tried to kill Alice.'

Deep inside the house, the ringing went on and on and on and on.

'I said that, didn't I? God, you don't half whinge.' Nudging him with my shoulder and smiling to let him know I didn't really mean it. In that manly, non-communicative way.

And still the bell rang.

'Maybe this Dr Lochridge's not in?'

Beginning to look like it. But of all the addresses Sabir texted me, this was the one closest to the library. Alice's eleven o'clock appointment – Oscar Harris's school therapist.

'OK, who's next on the—'

A clunk and the door swung open, revealing a middle-aged woman in a silk kimono, eyes bloodshot and unfocused, not exactly steady on her pins. Bottle-blonde hair frizzy and down past her shoulders. Orange dust on her fingertips. She licked her lips a couple of times. Sounding as if she was trying to keep the Aberdonian twang out of her slurry voice. 'Hello? Can I … help?' The words rode out on the sweaty-armpit stink of fresh weed, tempered with tangy cheese.

'Dr Lochridge?' Shifty showed her his warrant card. 'Police. Can we come in, please?'

Her bloodshot eyes drooped a little and so did her shoulders, then she turned around and scuffed away down the hall.

We followed her in, down a tidy corridor lined with framed children's drawings, and into a living room dominated by a saggy leather couch, covered in throws and cat hair. A big ginger tabby, sat on the coffee table, paused in the middle of cleaning itself to glare at us.

Dr Lochridge collapsed into the couch and helped herself to a fresh bag of Wotsits. Eyes drifting to the half-smoked joint perched on the edge of a handmade ashtray. 'It's only for personal use. And I never do anything around the children.'

Couldn't care less.

I took the matching saggy leather armchair. 'You met with Dr Alice McDonald earlier today.'

'Did I?' A frown. 'Suppose I did. She talks … a *lot*. And really quickly. How does she manage it? It's like she never even breathes.'

'What did you talk about?'

A loose-limbed shrug. 'Oscar Harris, I think. How was he, did he seem upset or troubled by anything before he went missing?' More Wotsits disappeared. 'Course he was. Between you, me, and Sigmund, I think someone was *abusing* him. Only he was too scared to admit it, even to me. People think that kind of thing doesn't happen to kids who attend a good school, but it does.' She chewed, face sagging. 'Poor tiny soul.'

I looked at Shifty.

He grimaced. Sucked air in through his teeth. 'Yeah, we got a distinctly greasy vibe off … someone we interviewed, but they had an alibi for when Oscar went missing. Even so, they clammed up and set their lawyer on us.' Not like Shifty to be so careful about not giving out any hints.

'So did Alice say anything before she left?'

Dr Lochridge squinted at her cat for a while. Then nodded. 'She said she liked Sigmund. Which is good, because he's the loveliest cat in the world.'

Ann Tweedale blinked at us with bleary eyes, voice a clipped whisper. '*No.* Of course I don't.' Soon as we'd appeared on her doorstep, she'd hissed us to silence and escorted us into the kitchen of her tiny mid-terrace house, on Blackwall Hill, right next to the railway line. It ran on a cutting along the end of her back garden, twelve feet higher than the ground her home was built on. Be amazed if much natural light ever made its way in through the windows.

Tweedale was a sporty type, with bags under her eyes and an oversized 'Donald Trump Est Un Branleur Massif!' T-shirt that hung down to the knees of her penguin pyjama bottoms. Furry slippers on her feet. Curly hair yanked back in a messy comet-tail.

Shifty leaned against the worktop and folded his arms. 'And there was nothing else?'

'Shhhh!' Tweedale pointed up towards the ceiling. 'You wake Charlene up, I'll bloody throttle you.' She gave him a good glower. 'Your doctor woman turned up, asked a load of questions about Lewis Talbot – all of which I'd already answered for your idiot police mates, by the way – then went away again. I helped all I could, but I was his social worker, not his mother. Lewis had a shitty life, his mum battered the hell out of him, his grandad abused her, and so on and so forth, yeah unto the tenth generation. Then some bastard throttles Lewis to death.' She wrapped her arms around herself. 'And I know I shouldn't, but sometimes I wonder if it wasn't for the best.'

She must've clocked the expression on my face because she rolled her eyes, arms hanging loose at her sides. 'I said "sometimes", OK? You don't know what it's like down in the trenches. You police kick in their doors, seize their property, and cart off their relatives – it's us poor sods that have to try and stitch them back together. You know what Lewis had to look forward to? Poverty and abuse and no opportunities.' Voice getting louder and more bitter with every word. 'They wouldn't let me put him into care because *apparently* there's bugger all left in the budget this financial year. Who'd be a bloody social worker?'

The wail of a small child boomed out through the ceiling above.

Ann Tweedale glared at me, voice back to a harsh whisper again. 'Now look what you've done!'

* * *

429

'So what do you think?' Shifty took us back under the railway bridge. 'We any nearer to catching this bastard?'

'Don't know.' I checked the list again. 'What's closest: Ditchburn Road, or Corriemuir Place?'

'From here?' His top lip curled. 'Six of one.' He reached out and clicked on the radio, landing us halfway through a song where some popstar tosser moaned about how unfair life was.

Take a number, mate, and get to the back of the queue.

'Your choice, then.' I pulled out Alice's phone and called the hospital as Shifty headed east, back towards Kingsmeath, rather than Castleview. 'Hello? I'm calling about Alice McDonald.'

The switchboard put me through to a woman with a lisp and a Geordie accent. *'There's no change at the moment, pet, but it's early days. We'll give you a call if anything happens, and you've got me word on that.'*

'Thanks.'

A glance from Shifty when I put my phone away. 'No change?'

'No change.' My head fell back against the rest. For some reason, there were footprints on the inside of the pool car's roof. Not shoeprints – bare feet. 'Tell me about this "greasy vibe" you got, when you were interviewing someone about Oscar Harris?'

'Hmmph. His uncle's a DJ, does club nights at Bang-dot-Bang-dot-Cheese and the House of Ultimate Ding. Bloody places these days, whatever happened to sensible names? He's one of those … neckbeard types, you know? The ones who don't grow a moustache to go with it.'

'Doesn't make him a paedo.'

We drifted down Hillside Drive, past all the peaceful side streets with their trees and working streetlights.

'Never trust anyone who doesn't grow a moustache to go with their beard – man or woman. It's a sign something's very badly wrong in their heads. And you didn't hear the way he talked about Oscar. Like the kid was a family pet.' Shifty put on a faux-posh Oldcastle accent, stressing the vowels in all the wrong places. '"Such a clever boy.", "He's a good boy, yes he is. Very good." And, like I said, soon as he trotted out his alibi he lawyered up. That says "dodgy bastard" to me.' A small smile. 'Even if his lawyer *was* a total shag.'

But then Shifty always did have terrible taste in men.

Left at the roundabout, onto Blackwall Avenue, heading back towards the library.

'Think we should put some lost-dog posters up around Glensheilth Crescent? If Alice stopped to let the wee man have a pee, he might've run off.'

Shifty raised one big rounded shoulder. 'Suppose it wouldn't hurt.'

And then we sat in silence, all the way up Blackburgh Road, over the railway bridge. Nothing but the radio to cut through the disinterested growl of the pool car's engine. One miserable song following another.

The DJ faded down the latest parade of whining as we pulled across the central reservation, turning right across the dual carriageway and into Kingsmeath again.

'There we go, The Mighty Beetroot and "The Day My Heart Stopped Beating", taking us up to the news and weather. It's twenty past midnight and you're listening to The Witching Hour with me, Lucy Robotham, on Castlewave FM.'

I cleared my throat. 'You know, you could come with us, if you like? When we open this hotel. Get away from ...' indicating the rows of small houses on either side of the road, 'all this.'

'...seventy-year-old man has died as Storm Victoria works its way up through Great Yarmouth, creating havoc with high winds and heavy rain...'

Shifty's voice was flat as an ironing board. 'What, and throw away my stellar career with Police Scotland?'

'...seen up to ten centimetres of rain in the space of two hours, and now severe weather warnings are in place for northeast England, the Central Belt, and eastern Scotland...'

'You could take people shooting? Or do murder mystery weekends, ABBA tribute nights, Eurovision parties – you like that kind of thing, don't you?'

'What, because I'm gay?'

'...hit Oldcastle at some point this morning. Bob Eason has had a setback in his bid to resurrect the Warriors, as council safety officers refuse him permission to reopen City Stadium for a charity concert. Local rap star Donny "Sick Dawg" McRoberts was rumoured to be headlining...'

I stared at him. 'No, because you've got terrible taste. And it's not just in men, you like all sorts of stuff that's either crap or not good for you.'

'...later this year. Police are appealing for witnesses, following a hit-and-run on Glensheilth Crescent earlier today. The victim, said to be—' I switched off the radio.

Shifty nodded. 'Alice is going to be OK, you know that, don't you? She'll pull through.' His hand left the steering wheel to clamp down on my shoulder, voice going for cheery optimism and not exactly making it: 'Besides, after all that booze, bet she's pickled enough inside to last for generations.' A sad smile. 'You and me will be a thousand years dead, in our graves, and she'll still be bumbling about, annoying everyone.'

Yeah...

Then why did I have this gaping hollow in the middle of my chest, that kept filling with scalding concrete?

— in the darkness, bleeding . . . —

44

Shifty took a right, onto a street with loads of tiny roads leading off both sides of it – each one only big enough for a dozen tiny houses and their tiny gardens. He pulled up about two thirds of the way along. 'Number fifty-four.'

It wasn't much to look at: a modest semi, the mirror image of the house it was attached to. No garage, just an empty off-road parking bay. Two windows downstairs, three up. Wooden cladding on the upper storey, as if someone had tried to make this part of the street look less depressing. And failed.

We climbed out.

He gave my shoulder another thump. 'She'll be OK.'

I pulled out Alice's phone and checked her calendar again: 'K Dewar – TMM's Law' which had to mean 'Toby Macmillan's Mother's lawyer.' The mother who broke her wee boy's arm, invited an abusive stepdad into his life, and was currently appealing against her conviction for neglect.

And Ann Tweedale thought we didn't know what it was like down in the trenches, as if we didn't wade through them every single day.

Shifty sniffed as we made our way up to the front door of number fifty-four. 'Any chance we can grab a bite to eat after this one? Haven't had anything since lunchtime.'

Right on cue, my stomach growled like an angry bear. Had

I eaten since breakfast? Don't think so. And that was a *long* time ago. 'Who's still serving, after midnight?'

He leaned on the bell. 'That chippy on Shand Street will be open. Or the Kebab shops down Holland Street.' No sign of life from inside, so Shifty had another go on the bell. 'Shawarma-Llama-Ding-Dong's meant to be good and they don't shut till the clubs turf out at three.' The bell rang again. 'Or we could get something from the big Winslow's and take it back to—'

The door opened and a blurry figure stood there, blinking out at us. Oily coils of whisky oozed out with him, leaving one of his knees locked and the other one wobbly. Wrapped in a towelling dressing gown, brawny arms poking out of the short sleeves. 'What?' Voice all slurred. 'I was … was in the bath …'

Broad shoulders. Thinning hair, swept back from a tanned scalp. Strong jaw and muscular neck. But it was the eyes that gave it away: bright sapphire, with a dark border.

He was the solicitor I'd met at HMP Oldcastle: the one having a weep, round the side, by the bins; the one who said we could probably buy Steven Kirk off with eight to ten grand, so he wouldn't press charges.

Shifty gave him a goooood long look up and down. A half smile. 'Kenny.'

Kenneth Dewar's bottom lip wobbled for a moment, then tears spilled out of those wolf's eyes. 'I'm sorry.'

I banged the tip of my cane on the door. 'Much though I hate to break the sexual tension, you had an appointment with Dr Alice McDonald at noon.'

He nodded. Palmed the tears from his eyes. 'I heard on the news. I'm so, so sorry.'

Shifty rubbed his hands together. 'Look, can we come in? It's Baltic out here.'

Another nod, then he turned and led the way into a living room festooned with old magazines and empty takeaway containers. Many of which harboured things well on the evolutionary route to sentience. The whole place smelled like a bin bag that'd been left in the sun.

436

So much for 'completely shaggable' – Kenneth Dewar was a slob.

He scooped armfuls of yellowed newspapers off a cheap couch and waved us to sit. Wiped away the tears again. 'How can I help?' Sounding slightly more sober now.

When he dumped his hoarded newspapers behind the couch there was a Father Jack clatter of empty bottles.

A quick peek over the back revealed that most of them were supermarket own-brand whisky. So not *just* a slob, a functioning-alcoholic slob.

Given the state of the place, it was probably more hygienic to stay standing. 'We need to know what you and Alice talked about.'

'Yes. Of course.' Dewar gave a deep, shuddering breath, looking at the floor beneath his wet feet – drips of soapy water soaking into newsprint, turning it a darker shade of grey. 'She was lovely. She really was. Wanted to know all about Oscar and Lewis and Toby and Andrew. And … she was so easy to talk to, you know?' Dewar folded his thick arms around himself, muscles rippling beneath the hairy skin. 'I've never met anyone so sympathetic to other people's problems.'

'And what problems were those, Mr Dewar?'

His shoulders came up. 'Sheriff, Gerrard, and Butler do mostly corporate work, but the partners think it's important to have a presence in the courts as well. And I'm always the one who ends up lumbered with the scumbag defendants – the wife beaters and the sex offenders.'

Sounded familiar. 'Because there are enough fascist states in the world without us being one of them?'

Another nod. 'You think it's easy? Walking into those inter-view rooms, knowing your client is a rancid piece of shit who ruins everything, every *life*, they touch? Dr McDonald *under-stood*.' Dewar bit his bottom lip, those wolf's eyes spilling tears down his cheeks. 'She gave me her card, for… She said I might benefit from therapy. And now…'

That was Alice, always trying to help the broken and the lonely.

Shifty pulled a face, raising his eyebrows as Dewar stood there and sobbed.

Well what the hell was I supposed to do about it?

I cleared my throat. 'Do you need us to call someone?'

Dewar scrubbed at his face again. 'Sorry. You don't need to see this.'

'It's OK.'

Another shuddering breath, then what was probably meant to be a smile. 'Sorry. I'd better get dressed. Standing here like an idiot. Please,' pointing at the tip he lived in, 'make yourselves at home. I'll only be a minute.'

Then he turned and slumped from the room, one hand over his face, shoulders trembling. Then the heavy damp *slap-slap-slap* of his feet, climbing the stairs.

'Jesus.' Shifty puffed out his cheeks. 'What a mess.'

Difficult to tell if he was talking about the house or the man.

'Think you dodged a bullet, there.'

'Yeah, probably.'

Upstairs, a door clunked shut.

I leaned back against the wall – it was the only clean surface in the room. 'So Alice comes here, she asks Dewar about all the victims, offers him therapy, then heads off to her next appointment: Chris McHale.'

Shifty checked his watch. 'Maybe we should've tried Ditchburn Road, instead?'

Outside, the first spots of rain clicked against the living room window.

A big tabby cat slunk its way through the front garden, across the empty parking bay, then up the waist-height brick wall and down into next door's.

Empty parking bay.

Surely someone working for a hotshot corporate law firm would have a car? So where was it? And back at the prison, he'd said he was working on an appeal by a prisoner who'd beaten up the mother of his child, and now wanted access to the kid. Bet that kid was Andrew Brennan's baby brother.

438

Alice said there was a paedophile ring operating in Kingsmeath, but what if it wasn't a ring? What if it was *one* man?

'Shifty?'

He puffed his cheeks out at me. 'I think we should go eat before we interview anyone else.'

'Oscar Harris's uncle, the DJ with the neckbeard – you said he gave you an alibi then got his lawyer involved. Who was the lawyer?'

Shifty's finger came up to point to the ceiling above our heads. 'Like he said, he has to represent all the dodgy scumbags, so...' Shifty's eyes widened.

I followed his gaze to the light fitting. Water oozed out around where the thing fixed to the plasterboard, trickled down the plastic cable and dripped off the lightbulb. Pattering down on the already wet newspapers where Dewar had been standing.

'Move!'

Out the living room door, lumbering up the stairs, Shifty hard on my heels.

The landing handrail was festooned with clothes, the carpet sticky as I lurched past an open bedroom door – another tip – to the closed bathroom. The handle rattled as I gripped and twisted, but didn't open.

Locked.

'Shifty!'

He barged past and slammed his shoulder into the door. It boomed and rattled. So he did it again, only this time the thing smashed inwards, the lock ripping from the doorframe, bottom hinges giving way so the door sagged like a twisted sail.

Water covered the bathroom floor, spilling out over the sides of an overfilled bath.

And there was Kenneth Dewar, lying naked in it, both arms stretched out in front of him, slashed from elbow to wrist the flesh inside dark – pulsing deep-red swirls out into the tub. A serene smile on his face. 'I'm sorry...' as his head fell back to thunk against the mould-blackened tiles.

'Bastard!' I grabbed him by the shoulders and shoved his head under the water.

'What the hell are you playing at?' Shifty tugged at my arms. 'Get off him!'

I let go with my bad hand and threw an elbow backwards. It thumped into something solid, but Shifty didn't let go.

'It was *him*! He hit Alice with his car – that's why it's not parked outside! Hiding the evidence. He's Gòrach.'

'If he's Gòrach, he's the only one who knows where Toby Macmillan is, you idiot!'

Oh for…

Shifty was right.

I hauled Dewar out of the bath and onto the bathroom floor, bringing a tidal wave of pink-tinged water with him. 'We need tourniquets!'

'On it.' Shifty lurched out to the landing and returned seconds later with a T-shirt from the railing and a pair of jeans. He twisted the T-shirt into a thick cord and tied it around Dewar's upper arm, as close to the elbow as possible, tendons straining in his neck as he pulled it tight enough to make the stitches creak. 'Come on, come on, come on. Stop bleeding, you wanker…'

It was the jeans next: twisting one leg then tying it around Dewar's other arm.

Sat back on his haunches. 'Not great, but it'll have to do.'

I curled a hand into a fist. 'Only needs to last till he tells us where Toby Macmillan is. Then he dies.'

Shifty shook his head. 'Are you off your head? If he dies *now*, he dies pissed on whisky – anaesthetised, feeling no pain, and by his own hand. Thought you wanted to make him suffer?'

My mouth opened, then closed again.

Had to admit it: Shifty had a point.

He took hold of Dewar's ankles and dragged him out onto the landing, making for the stairs. 'This bastard's going to hospital, and when he gets better, he's going to prison, where we'll make sure every single day is like the Marquis de Sade's worst nightmare.' Shifty paused, frowning down at the pale naked body – the lolling head, open mouth, and closed eyes. 'Well, as long as he doesn't die on the way to A-and-E.'

'We need to question him *before* we call an ambulance.' Not that he looked in any fit state to be interviewed. Better get his attention first – wake him up a bit. I limped forward onto my bullet-holed right foot, took the weight, then smashed my left heel down on the bastard's balls.

He sat upright, howling, elbows coming in towards his groin – the arms and hands dangling from them already going a blueish grey.

I squatted down beside him. Slapped him hard enough to shut him up.

He blinked back at me, mouth a trembling wet line. 'I'm sorry…'

'It was you, wasn't it? You killed Andrew Brennan and Oscar Harris and Lewis Talbot and Toby Macmillan. It wasn't a paedophile ring, it was *you*. You had access to every one of those little boys, because you represented their abusers, didn't you?'

'I…'

'But Alice was on to you, wasn't she? So you tried to kill her.' I grabbed a handful of that thinning hair and yanked his head back, glared down into his bloodshot eyes. 'Two questions. One: where's Toby Macmillan? And two: WHERE'S MY FUCKING DOG?'

The paramedic hissed out a breath, shook her head, then tutted. Clunked the ambulance's back door shut. 'He's made a right mess of himself, hasn't he?' A nod set bright ginger curls bobbing. 'Still, he was lucky you were here! Be dead otherwise.'

We stood back as the ambulance pulled away, lights flickering blue-and-white, siren rising in harsh electronic pulses that faded into the distance.

Two patrol cars sat outside the house, parked half on the kerb.

Our backup.

One pair of PCs, in the full high-viz kit, were out setting up a cordon of 'POLICE' tape big enough to take in Kenneth Dewar's semi and the house next door too. Struggling as the wind tried to snatch the tape from their hands, setting it *burrrring* and *whirring*.

The second pair of uniforms were on the other side of the road, getting stuck into the door-to-doors, dragging people out of bed at quarter to one in the morning.

Wouldn't be long before some concerned householder got in touch with the media and the street would be swarming with outside broadcast vans and cameras and microphones and reporters. Doing bits to camera. Asking the neighbours what Kenneth Dewar was like, and had they any idea he was a child-murdering bastard? Oh no, he was always so quiet and polite, kept himself to himself. Same thing *everyone* said when they lived next to a monster, because if they admitted knowing he was a wrong-un all along, that made them guilty of keeping quiet about it and letting four little boys die.

Shifty stepped back into the doorway, out of the wind and rain. 'Absolutely starving.'

'Not much we can do about that now.'

His big round shoulders drooped. 'Probably not.'

A boxy Range Rover growled its way along Corriemuir Place, parking outside the cordon. Wouldn't have thought journalists would've got here so fast... But it wasn't a journalist who climbed out of the big ugly car, it was Detective Superintendent Jacobson, wearing his trademark brown leather jacket and pelt-like hair. Holding a hand above his eyes, like the bill on a baseball cap, to keep the rain off his glasses.

He flashed his ID at one of the uniforms and ducked under the cordon. Marched over to us, trying to look stern and serious, while the corners of his mouth twitched. 'DI Morrow, Ash, you got him?'

Shifty pointed at me. 'Figured it out.'

All pretence at hiding the smile vanished and Jacobson play-punched me on the arm. 'Knew there was a reason I keep you on the books! You look like crap, by the way.' Beaming as he stared up at Dewar's house. 'What about Toby—'

'He buried Toby Macmillan in Camburn Woods, round the back of those abandoned World War Two barracks.' I tucked my throbbing left hand into my pocket before Jacobson could

442

see it and start asking awkward questions. 'Doesn't know exactly which one, but won't be hard to find with a dog unit.'

'Oh...' Jacobson's smile disappeared, a pained expression blossoming like a gunshot wound. 'Poor wee sod. Thought we might actually manage to save this one.' A nod, trying to sound upbeat again: 'Still, at least we got the guy, right? He won't be hurting anyone else.'

Shifty jerked his chin up, setting his jowls wobbling. 'He's the one who tried to kill Alice.'

'Is he now.' Jacobson's face pinched. 'Well, I think he's going to find his time inside *very* uncomfortable indeed. If I've got anything to say about it, anyway.'

Sounded as if torturing Kenneth Dewar was going to be a team sport and, while I wasn't normally a team player, that sounded like something I could definitely get behind.

Jacobson nodded. 'Speaking of Alice, any more news?'

Shifty shook his head. 'No change. They have to wait till she wakes up.'

'Damn it. Well, if there's anything I can do, you...' He raised an eyebrow as a dark Fiat Panda rattled its way up the street towards us. 'Ash, you might want to brace yourself.'

The Panda screeched to a halt outside the cordon and one of the PCs hurried over, holding his arms out to block the way.

Mother scrambled from the car, leaving the engine running as she marched for the 'POLICE' tape. She didn't bother flashing her ID, instead Mother stuck two hands against the PC's high-viz chest and shoved him into next door's garden. Flat on his back in the rose bushes as she ducked under the barrier, stormed right up to me, eyes hard and round, mouth a small tight circle with gritted teeth in the middle. Her right hand flashed up, the slap hard enough to snap my head to the left, leaving the skin hot and stinging as she grabbed me by the lapels. 'WHAT THE *HELL* DO YOU THINK YOU WERE PLAYING AT?' Then let go and wrapped me in a serious bearhug, setting the ribs squealing all down one side where Francis punched me last night. 'We were worried sick!'

'It wasn't—'

'You've got some explaining to do, young man!'

'Yes, but—'

'Sending all those, "life can't go on" texts – you said you were going to kill yourself! What were we supposed to think when your pool car turned up in the Cromarty Firth?'

Sod.

So much for sneaking back to Oldcastle and keeping everything secret.

45

Well, Mother didn't need the *whole* truth, did she? Just the bits that wouldn't get me arrested.

'Gordon Smith attacked me at the farm, after I called you.' Unzipping my new leather jacket to show off the bloodstained shirt, and neck covered in bruises. Then pulling my bandaged hand from my pocket. 'He set fire to the place. I barely got out alive. Smith must've taken my phone and my pool car.'

She pulled her chin in, doubling, then tripling it. 'But how did you get back to Oldcastle?'

Good question.

Come on then, *answer* it.

'I'm … not entirely sure, I've been kind of disorientated. Probably in shock from being strangled and all the blood loss.' Holding up my bandages again. 'He cut my finger off.'

That should hold her.

And not a single mention of Helen or Leah MacNeil.

Mother's face softened and she gave me another hug – not so rib-crushing this time. 'Go home. You look exhausted. It's—'

'Sir? Ma'am?' One of the PCs came huffing up the pavement at a run, face red above her fluorescent-yellow padded jacket, one hand holding the bowler hat on her head. Stopping in front of us with her back to the wind. 'I've found Dewar's car!' Pointing over her shoulder. 'Bonnet's all dented and there's

445

what looks like blood in the wheel arch. Silly bugger didn't even put it through the carwash, ma'am.'

'Good work.' Mother patted her on the shoulder. 'Now off you go and call for a full SOC team, I want this place—'

Jacobson cleared his throat. 'As *senior* officer, and someone who's actually *on* the Gòrach investigation, perhaps you'd let me be in charge of my own crime scene? After all, DI Malcolmson, I believe you've still got a killer of your own to catch?'

Pink flushed Mother's cheeks. 'Only trying to help.' She stuck her nose in the air. 'And as Ash is seconded to *my* team, I'm sending him home.' She made shooing gestures at me. 'Go on, off you go.'

'While Mr Henderson is indeed seconded to *your* team, he remains an active member of *mine*. And as he's now caught the man who abducted and killed four children, I'm going to need him to give a statement before he goes anywhere.'

How lovely, two bosses fighting over me. Be still, my girlish heart.

Didn't matter anyway, whatever happened here, I wasn't done for the night. Not by a long way.

Sitting on the other side of the interview table, Rhona opened her mouth wide in a jaw-cracking yawn that was disturbingly infectious. Hers finished with a small burp and a shudder. Then she turned her notebook around and pushed it across the table towards me. 'Sign and date it at the bottom there.'

Soon as I'd done that, she clicked off the recording equipment.

They'd done up Interview Room Three at some point, replaced the sagging stained ceiling tiles with fresh white ones; swapped the tatty blue carpet tiles for hardwearing grey; given it a fresh lick of magnolia and a new Formica table – still bolted to the floor; but they hadn't managed to shift the lingering scent of sweaty feet and boiled cabbage.

She took her notebook back, pursed her pale lips at it for a moment, then flipped it shut and slipped it into her pocket. 'And that's *everything* that happened, is it?'

'Scout's honour.'

Well, I might have left a couple of bits out. Like torturing Chris McHale. And trying to drown Kenneth Dewar as he lay there bleeding to death. And buying a black-market handgun with the intention of blowing lots and lots of holes in the aforementioned Kenneth Dewar's face, Your Honour. But other than that, my statement was *more-or-less* the truth.

Oh, and I *might* have left out the fact that I had an app on Alice's phone that could locate Leah MacNeil and Gordon Smith, but that was understandable, wasn't it? What with being in shock because of all the strangling and blood loss I'd suffered.

Amazing I'd managed to make a statement at all...

Rhona stared at me in silence. Letting it stretch long beyond the point where it became uncomfortable.

She was getting better at this interviewing game, but I'd taught her all the tricks she was currently using, so it was easy enough to sit here looking open and innocent.

At last, she nodded. 'I take it you and Shifty worked this story out between you?'

'*Story*, Detective Sergeant Massie? I have no idea what you mean.'

'Right then. As long as you both stick to it, you'll be fine.' She stood. 'You did a good thing tonight, Ash. Dewar would've kept on killing kids if you hadn't stopped him.' Rhona placed a hand on my shoulder, on the way past. 'However you did it.' Then walked out of the room and closed the door behind her.

I let out a long dry breath.

Got away with it.

I pulled out Alice's phone and opened the tracking app. The 'word' 'FonezFindr!' flashed up on the screen – so I'd been right about the awful spelling – with a couple of setting options and three numbers listed under the heading 'Phones You Are Tracking'. No idea who the other two were, but my mobile was top of the list.

When I selected it, a stopwatch appeared, the hands turning in one direction while a progress bar rotated around it going the other way.

Please don't be switched off.

Please don't be dumped in a bin or some sucker's pocket.

Please be—

WE'VE FOUND YOUR PHONE!
Click on the link below to view on a map!

Here we go.

It brought up a map of Scotland, then zoomed in on a red arrow pointing at the east coast, Oldcastle getting bigger on the left of the screen, then disappearing as Clachmara filled its centre. The map wasn't quite up-to-date – it still included the houses that'd fallen into the sea because of Storm Trevor – but if the arrow wasn't pointing directly at Helen MacNeil's house, I'd buy a hat and eat it.

Maybe this was Gordon Smith sending a message? Dumping my phone back where it all began. Showing off for the dress circle.

Or maybe he really *was* arrogant enough to think he could go back there and we wouldn't notice?

Suppose I'd find out soon enough.

But, in the meantime, probably best to throw some blood in the water, see if I could distract the sharks. A quick text should do it.

And soon as it was sent, I gathered up my stuff and left.

Shifty was waiting for me when I stepped out of the interview room, leaning back against the wall and playing something on his phone. He barely looked up. 'Give your statement?'

I hauled on my new jacket. 'Where's the rucksack?'

'In my locker.' His eyes narrowed. 'Why?'

'Because I know where Leah MacNeil is. Or, at least, I know where she *might* be.' I held up my unruined hand. 'And before you say anything: yes, I know, I should tell Mother so she can get the heavy mob sent in. But we spent all that money on a gun...'

Shifty nodded. 'Shame to let it go to waste. We'll need a vehicle too. Something we can burn afterwards.'

'Helen MacNeil's Renault's still parked up the Hospital. No one'll miss it.'

'Works for me.' He pushed off the wall. 'You want—'

A voice boomed down the corridor. 'Gentlemen!' And there was Chief Superintendent McEwan, marching towards us with his sidekick, Samson, scurrying along behind him. They were both in civvies – jeans and a sweatshirt for Samson, tan chinos and blue polo shirt for McEwan. As if he'd only ever seen people wearing casual clothes in eighties catalogues.

McEwan stopped right in front of us and patted Shifty on the shoulder. 'DI Morrow! David. Excellent work, really *excellent*.' I got a pat too. 'And you, of course, Ash. Well done. This is magnificent news: the Oldcastle Child-Strangler in custody!' A frown clouded his features. 'Of course, it's a shame you couldn't save Toby Macmillan, but the important thing is our man's off the streets. Isn't that right, Alan?'

Samson nodded. 'Yes, sir.'

'We're arranging a press conference for first thing tomorrow – want to stay ahead of the news cycle, don't we? Yes. It's going to be good to stand up there and rub all their noses in it. O Division's full of useless tossers, is it? Ha! And there'll be a commendation going into your file, DI Morrow, don't you worry about that.' Another pat on the shoulder. 'So, I want you in here, booted and suited, and ready for the cameras by half seven.' Then McEwan's eyes drifted back to me. Taking it all in: the black eyes, the bruised throat, the bandaged hand... He bit his top lip and furrowed his brow. 'Actually, Ash, maybe you should sit this one out and get some rest. Might not be the best optics, you sitting there looking as if you've gone the wrong way through a threshing machine. Got Police Scotland's reputation to think about, after all.'

Like I gave a toss about its reputation or his press conference.

'Anyway, I want to congratulate you both again for the sterling work you've done!' Then he turned on his heel and marched off.

Samson hesitated a moment, his granite slab of a face working its way into a smile. 'That was some serious coppering you two did tonight. The boss is right, you—'

McEwan's voice boomed down the corridor again. 'Oh, do

keep up, Alan. And make sure my dress uniform is cleaned and pressed for tomorrow's briefing!'

'Wonderful.' Samson sagged, stared at the ceiling, took a deep breath, then turned and hurried after the Chief Super. 'Yes, sir.'

Poor sod.

Soon as they were gone, Shifty cricked his head from side to side. 'Where we off to? And can we *please* get something to eat on the way? I'm not—' His phone rang, getting louder and louder in the corridor. 'Sorry.' He pulled it out and answered. 'DI Morrow.' Scrunched his forehead up and closed his eyes, listening. Then, 'No, Russell, I don't. ... Are you *deaf* as well as Hobbit sized? I'm not commenting on an ongoing— ... I don't care what the rumour mill says, "no comment" ... OK, I'm hanging up now.' He did, then hissed out a breath. 'Bloody journalists. Someone's leaked we caught the Oldcastle Child-Strangler.'

I checked my watch. 'Didn't take them long.'

'Bet it's that moron Blakey. Wouldn't trust him to—' Shifty's phone went again and he peered at the screen with his one good eye. 'Jennifer Prentice? Don't think so. Decline.' Poking the button. 'They're going to be at this all night, aren't they?'

'Probably.' The frenzy would be gathering outside Kenneth Dewar's house, cameras focused on his front door, working out how much moral outrage they could whip up. Or doorstepping Dewar's victims' parents, milking their grief for a ninety-second slot on the morning news.

On the plus side, it meant that they'd abandon Clachmara for a while. Leaving it all nice and quiet for Shifty and me to rock up and make sure Gordon Smith and Leah MacNeil got exactly what was coming to them.

Strange what one little text can do.

Shifty switched his phone off and put it away. 'OK. Food first, then murder. Can't be killing people on an empty stomach.'

The scent of onions, garlic, and slow-cooked lamb mince filled Helen's manky Renault as Shifty finished his extra-large doner with yoghurt *and* chilli sauce. Parked here, at the brow of the wee hill, headlights off, engine running, looking down over what was left of Clachmara as Storm Victoria hammered into it. Rain clattering against the car's roof.

Helen's street shivered in the darkness, bushes whipping back and forth, lampposts swaying. And not a single press vehicle to be seen.

Even the Mobile Incident Unit had been pulled back, away from the advancing cliff edge. The safety barrier had retreated with it. Now the sections of temporary fencing didn't cut through the garden between Helen's house and the one next door – both had been placed on the sacrificial altar of coastal erosion. An offering to the howling gods of wind and rain.

Shifty smacked his lips and sooked the milky-pink juices from his fingers, before scrunching up the waxy paper his kebab came in and chucking it in over his shoulder.

Well, we were going to burn the car anyway, what was the point keeping it tidy?

He scrubbed his face with a napkin. 'Any joy?'

I put Alice's phone back in my pocket. 'No change. Doctor says she's stable.'

Shifty nodded. 'But that's good, right? Stable? Means nothing's gone wrong.'

'Yeah...'

Wind tore at the car, rocking it on its springs, screaming around the doorframes, groaning through the gap between the chassis and the potholed road. As if the dying town was crying out in pain.

Shifty's napkin joined the kebab wrapper. 'You *sure* they're here?'

'Nope. But my phone is.'

He nodded. 'Maybe it's a trap?'

'How could it be a trap? They think I'm dead. And they don't know about the tracker app.' I pulled my new Minion rucksack through from the back, unzipped it, and pulled out the gun. Small and black against the pale grey shape of my gloved hand. The nitrile surface sticky and squeaking against the grip as I held the .22 up. 'Besides, we've got this.'

451

'Still think we'd be better with baseball bats.' But he put the Renault in gear anyway, drifting down the hill, nice and slow. Shame we couldn't have the headlights on: it might have meant not crunching and lurching through every single sodding pothole on the way down. 'Can't see another car, can you?'

Apart from the MIU, the road was empty. Even Helen's caravan was gone.

'Maybe they parked somewhere else and walked?'

'In *this*?' Shifty peered out through the rain-lashed windscreen. 'You'd have to be off your bloody head.' He slowed to a halt, two houses back from the new fence line. 'And so do we.'

The safety notice had broken loose from its bottom moorings, leaving the sign to hinge up and clang back down against the chain-link, setting the metal rattling. 'WARNING! ~ COASTAL EROSION ZONE ~ NO ENTRY ~ DANGER OF DEATH'

'You ready?'

He reached behind his seat and came out with an extendable baton, then into his jacket for a palm-sized can of pepper spray. Flicked the cover off, gave the thing a shake, then flicked the cover back on again. 'Ash?'

'Shifty.' I pulled the gun's slide back, racking a round into the breech. Joseph was right – it was easy enough for someone with 'restricted hand mobility'.

'It's … you know?' Shifty wriggled in his seat. 'We've never killed anyone before. Not *killed*, killed. Pretty much everything, but.' A long breath. 'I guess I'm a bit—'

'So give me the keys and stay in the car.'

'Really?' Looking at me, face sagging at the edges. 'And let you walk in there, alone? With no backup?' He turned the engine off. 'How's the saying go? A friend will help you move house; a *real* friend will help you kill a pair of murdering scumbags, dispose of their bodies, and wheech a security van full of stolen artworks out from under the nose of a psychotic religious nutjob.' A nod, then he opened his car door, letting in the outraged bellowing of Storm Victoria.

I struggled out the other side, clutching onto the car door as the wind tried to tear it from my bandaged fingers. Struggling to hold it and the gun and my walking stick all at the same time. Might be better to stick the safety on again and put the .22 in my pocket. At least till we were inside. Rain battered its frozen nails into my face, sparking like fireworks against my jacket as I lurch-staggered my way along the wet pavement to the security fence.

Shifty got there first, huge round shoulders turned against the storm, water running off his big bald head. He grabbed the two nearest sections of fence and pulled at them – the padlocked chain held them too close to get through.

OK, so Gordon and Leah wouldn't have cut the chain somewhere obvious, like here, they would've done it somewhere out of the way, somewhere less easily spotted.

I worked my way left, along the line, testing as I went. Through the gap between the two houses – caught in a sudden and blissful stillness as they acted as a windbreak – still nothing. Then along the waist-high wall separating their back gardens. Curling forwards into the wind again.

The cut section was at the far end, where the gardens of Helen's street butted onto those of the next street over. Just as dark and deserted. Which explained how they'd got in without anyone noticing. Have to hope they hadn't got out the same way.

We slipped between the unchained sections, over the boundary wall, and into the back garden of the house next to Helen's. Sticking as close to the building as possible for shelter. One more short wall and we were on Helen's property.

The wind was stronger here, punching into my chest, trying to steal my legs out from underneath me. And oh, how the sea *roared*.

A huge chunk of the garden had already surrendered to the waves, leaving the far edge of the house sticking out into the void. Only by three or four foot, but still... Wouldn't take much for the entire thing to go crashing over the edge.

Yeah, this was a *really* stupid idea.

Maybe we should keep an eye on the place instead? Hang back and wait to see if Gordon and Leah came out? Jump on them then?

And give up the cover of night, the element of surprise, and any chance of killing the pair of them. There'd be a police presence back here by seven, doubt whoever got the early shift would look the other way while we did what needed to be done.

So it was this, or nothing.

And with any luck, the house would stay in one piece till we'd got out of there.

Shifty pointed at the kitchen door, and I nodded.

He took Helen's car keys, then worked his way through the bunch till one slid home into the lock and turned. We crept inside. Closed the door, nice and gentle, behind us.

Stood there, dripping on the linoleum. Trying not to breathe too loudly.

46

The outline of work surfaces and kitchen units lurked in the gloom, not enough light filtering in through the window to make out any detail. Breath a dark grey fog, cold biting at my wet skin.

All around us the house creaked and groaned in the wind. That sizzling hiss of rain smashing itself against the kitchen window.

I slipped the gun from my pocket, gloved fingertips exploring the metal above the handle, till the safety catch clicked off. Keeping my voice barely audible. 'OK. We search each room, slow and careful.'

Shifty's reply was equally quiet: 'Why are they lurking in the dark if this isn't a trap?'

Now *that* was a very good question.

'Well … it's what, half two in the morning? Maybe they're asleep.' In a house that could fall into the North Sea at any minute? Not exactly likely. 'Look, just be careful, OK?'

I crept out of the kitchen into the hallway. It was even darker – not so much as a sliver of natural light to chisel shapes out of the blackness. Inching forwards, using the walking stick to find the edges of obstacles before I barged into them.

The first door opened on a smallish room with tiled walls, going by the way my scuffing feet echoed back at me. A rectangle of dark grey against the black was probably a bathroom window…

This was stupid. How were we supposed to search the place if we couldn't *see* anything? 'Shifty, where are you?'

His voice was a whisper at my back. 'Here.'

'Can you turn the torch down on your phone, or is it full pelt or nothing?'

'Don't know...' Some fumbling noises, then a hard white light lanced out, pulling a circle of detail from Helen's bathroom. Black and white tiles, a shower curtain with cartoon characters on it, a neat array of shampoo and conditioner bottles along the edge of a salmon-pink bathroom suite. Then the beam faded to a soft yellowish glow, and darkness reclaimed most of the room.

We tried the next door: a faded bedroom, the double bed rumpled and unmade. No sign of personal items or touches in here. Helen's prison cell was probably more homely than this.

The room next to that was another, smaller, bedroom. But where Helen's was bare, this one was festooned with posters – boybands and popstars I'd never heard of, for the most part, with the occasional kitten-and-inspirational-quote to break up the monotony. A row of kids' and YA books. A wicker hamper overflowing with mildewed dirty washing. A single bed with a unicorn bedspread, the sheets cold and damp to the touch. Didn't look as if anyone had stayed here for months.

So much for catching Gordon Smith and Leah MacNeil asleep.

That left the lounge.

I crept after Shifty, following the thin waxy beam of torch-light.

The multigym's stainless-steel framework glinted in the dark, still huge and taking up a third of the room. The same ratty furniture lurking around it. The only thing different was the living room rug. It'd been draped over the top of Helen's coffee table, exposing the edges of a trapdoor.

Bet all the houses round here had one. Oh, some homes might be bigger than others, some might be semidetached, some might have an attic conversion, but in the end they all shared the same DNA. And that DNA included genes for a basement...

456

Shifty whispered out a cloudy breath. 'Sod.' He pulled his shoulders in. 'We gotta go down there, don't we?'

'Yeah. We do.'

He turned on the spot, sweeping the torch's beam around the room again. 'Be the perfect place for an ambush. Soon as we're in the basement, the trapdoor's nailed shut and we're stuck there while the whole place collapses.'

Right on cue, the roof growled above our heads, followed by the rattling clatter of what was probably a roof tile coming loose and being swept away.

'OK.' I tightened my grip on the gun, took a deep breath, and nodded.

'Off our bloody heads...' Shifty bent down, grabbed the ring set into the trapdoor, and pulled. The thing hinged open with a Hammer-House-of-Horror creak. He pointed the torch beam, illuminating a steep flight of wooden steps. 'Try and not get me killed, OK?'

'Do my best.' The steps moaned beneath my feet as I edged my way down into the darkness.

The musty scent of a long-abandoned room mingled with sour dampness and something sharp and metallic. The air tasted of it too.

Impossible to see anything in here, but swinging my walking stick from side to side drew a hollow thunk from something on either side. Cardboard boxes?

Could *really* do with a light down here.

Sod.

One barely functioning hand for the walking stick, one hand for the gun. How was I supposed to work the torch on Alice's phone at the same time?

Unless...

I unzipped my jacket, put the .22 away, then started up the torch app on Alice's phone. Slipped it into the top pocket of my blood-stained shirt. A good inch protruded from the top, letting LED light spill out onto stacks and stacks of sagging boxes. The gun came out to play again, my breath steaming out around my head, caught in the harsh white glow.

Everything the torch beam touched jumped into focus, but everything else was completely and utterly swallowed by the dark. Inky black and impenetrable. Where the light was bright enough to see by, the beam was no wider than a beachball, but anything more than six feet away stubbornly refused to emerge from the gloom.

Still, it was enough to get a feel for the place, and where Gordon Smith's basement had been empty – except for his killing apparatus – Helen MacNeil's was littered with the debris of three lives. Kids' bikes rusted away alongside collapsed boxes of plastic toys. The remains of a teddy bear going mouldy where it poked out the top of a box full of vinyl records.

No point sneaking around now – if they didn't know we were in here, they never would.

Deep breath. 'GORDON SMITH! ARMED POLICE! COME OUT WITH YOUR HANDS ON YOUR HEAD!'

The only sound was my breath and the distant mourning gale.

Then Shifty's voice hissed down from the living room. 'Anything?'

Back to normal volume: 'Don't think they're here.'

'Bugger.' His heavy feet thumped down the stairs. 'We're too late, then. It's…'

When I turned, he was standing with one foot on the bottom step, chin up, nostrils flaring.

'Can you smell that? Sort of … butcher's shoppy.'

Which probably meant Gordon Smith and Leah MacNeil had got their hands on another victim. Shifty was right: we were too late.

'BASTARD!' Bellowing it out, eyes screwed shut, knees bent, walking stick and gun clenched in aching fists.

And now we had yet another crime scene to manage before the damn thing fell into the North Sea.

'Great.' Shifty scuffed a toe through the dust. 'You want to call it in, or sod off out of it? Either way, they're not here.'

The rubbish didn't fill the entire basement, Helen had left a meandering path through the boxes. Tempting though it was to get the hell out of here, it meant we'd never know who they'd killed. More importantly, the *family* would never know what'd happened to their child / brother / sister / parent. So I hobbled along the path, taking my little ball of bright-white light with me. Past rows and rows of long-forgotten crap, the top surface of everything clarted in a thick layer of gritty brown dirt – probably drifted down from the floorboards upstairs.

The basement opened out at the final turn. Not into a wide-open space, but a hollow, not much bigger than a double bed.

I stopped where I was and stared.

The rear wall, the one closest to the devouring waves, the one that stuck about four feet out from the crumbling headland, had a body spread-eagled against it. Her arms were tied to the floor joists of the room above; legs more than shoulder-width apart, ankles tied to the barbell from Helen's multigym. Head hanging forward, blood … *everywhere*.

'Jesus…'

Strips of skin hung from long ragged wounds, showing off the dark glistening muscle beneath, the occasional flash of bone where they'd dug deeper. A wide pool of shining burgundy seeping across the concrete floor.

I stepped closer, and slow-motion ripples spread out from my boot.

David Quinn, back in Stirling, had been bad enough, but this was much, much worse.

A muffled rumbling shook the basement and fresh dust drifted down from the floor above, shining like dying stars in the torchlight.

Cut her down. Cut her down and get her out of here.

With what? They took Joseph's cutthroat razor off you, remember?

'Shifty, you got a knife?'

No answer.

'Shifty!'

Still nothing.

I jammed the gun in my pocket, reached forward, took a handful of dyed-blonde hair and pulled her head up. Nothing but hollow sockets stared back at me, but there was no mistaking that heart-shaped face, the long sharp nose, or the broad forehead.

Just like her grandmother's.

Leah MacNeil.

47

I huffed out a breath and stepped back, letting her chin fall against her chest again.

How could Smith...? She was like a *granddaughter* to him. OK, so Leah was a monster, but she didn't deserve *that*.

'Shifty?'

Another rumble, and this time the floor trembled beneath my feet, sending slow sticky ripples spreading across the bloody pool.

I turned, but there was no sign of him. Nothing but darkness where the torch's beam couldn't reach. 'SHIFTY: STOP SODDING ABOUT!'

Maybe he'd done the sensible thing and buggered off out of here, before everything collapsed into the sea? Maybe that wasn't a daft idea at—

Alice's phone rang in my top pocket: David Bowie's 'Ashes to Ashes'. The ringtone she'd set so she'd know it was me calling.

Which could only mean one thing.

I pulled out her mobile and answered it. 'Gordon Smith.'

'*Ah, Mr Henderson, I'm so glad to hear your voice again!*' It was little more than a whisper, barely audible over the creaks and groans of the storm-battered house. I turned the phone's volume up full. '*You're not a man who likes to stay dead, I like that about you.*'

'You killed Leah.'

'Yes, well...' He cleared his throat. *'Turns out you were right about that, so credit where it's due. You tried to tell her, remember? But would she listen? Teenagers, eh?'* Putting on a singsong voice for, *'What ya gonna do?'*

Another rumble, and this time a sound like ice cracking on the surface of a very deep dark lake joined it. The torch hadn't switched off as the call came through, so I held the phone in front of my face, swinging it around. That pool of blood had got a lot shallower around my trainers.

'Where are you?'

'You see, I know a lot of people look at someone my age and they think, "He can't be any good with modern technology and stuff; dinosaurs were roaming the earth when he was a wee boy, for goodness' sakes!" But you can't be a Luddite and work in the theatre these days, it's all electronics and software.'

That cracking noise sounded again.

I backed away from the end wall.

Actually, *sod* backing away, I turned and hurried through the maze of boxes and family crap. 'She looked up to you like a grandfather, Gordon. She loved you!'

'So I had a dig through your phone and discovered the tracker app. Did you know, if you agree to be traced, you automatically get to see where the phone tracing you is? It's rather sweet, really. An exercise in trust and mutual surveillance.' Still no louder than a whisper. *'At first I thought you were this Alice woman, but then I saw you and your fat friend creeping into Helen's house and I have to admit, it was quite the shocker. I could've sworn you were dead when we dropped you in that inspection pit. I clearly need to work on my garrotting skills.'*

I turned the last corner, before the stairs, and stumbled to a halt.

'Anyway, as you've come all this way, it would've been rude of me not to pop in and say hello.'

Shifty lay facedown on the concrete, one arm twisted beneath him, the other hand still clutching his collapsible baton. The back of his bald pink head was stained, wet scarlet.

'And I'm sorry Leah couldn't be with us – not in spirit anyway – but I simply couldn't cope with her foul language any longer.'

I spun around, torch brushing the nearest boxes with its narrow beam of cold white light. 'If you've killed Shifty, I'm going to tear you to pieces.'

'So I gave Leah the starring role in her own production: A Delicate and Terrible Death. She was excellent, Mr Henderson, screamed like a professional. Her mother would've been so proud.'

I hunkered down beside Shifty, dropped my walking stick and felt for a pulse. Still there. As I stood, something glittered in the torchlight – halfway up the wooden steps to the trapdoor. Like a granite thermos flask with silver handles fixed to it.

The funeral urn from the barn. The one Gordon Smith had been talking to.

That's why he was whispering down the phone at me: he was *in* the basement. I swapped the mobile into my bandaged hand and yanked the .22 out again.

'Do you ever go to the pantomime, Mr Henderson? You should: it's one of the finest theatrical traditions we have in this country, certainly the purest. People think it's silly, with its dames and its principal boys and its call-and-response, but it has rules and conventions, traditions and truths that stretch back into antiquity. They connect us with the fairy tales our ancestors told as they cowered in their caves in the night.'

'Where are you?'

'After all, what is life if not a pantomime?'

I hung up and turned again, torch sweeping around like a lighthouse. The gun following it. 'COME ON YOU BASTARD, LET'S SEE IF YOU'VE GOT THE BALLS!'

A laugh slithered out in the basement. 'He's behiiiiiiiiiiind you!'

48

Something hard and heavy cracked across my shoulders. I staggered forwards, stumbling over Shifty, the phone flying out of my ruined hand to bounce against the nearest boxes. Its torch-light swinging and tumbling – then thump, it hit the floor, beam shining straight up into the dusty air.

A line of sharp-edged grey whistled towards my head, shining bright as it passed through the LED beam – hooked, like a hockey stick, but longer. More solid looking. And coming in fast.

I got my arms up just in time for it to crack across them instead of my face. Sending me crashing over backwards against the stairs.

The gun hit the ground and skittered away, came to rest with a dull metallic clank.

'Don't you play shinty, Mr Henderson? It's a great game. Very physical. Keeps you fit!'

Another whistling crack and the stick battered into my arms again, hot and numb at the same time, the muscles howling, bones creaking. Wooden steps groaning against my spine.

DO SOMETHING!

Smith loomed out of the darkness, pausing above Alice's phone so the torch caught him from below. Lit like a monster in an ancient film – his lined face slashed with shadows, eyes glittering in the hollow of their sockets, Santa beard turned into something a lot less wholesome. 'It's a shame we don't have more time, Mr Henderson, I'd love to stay and play, but the house is *hungry*.'

Another rumble, and this time the cracking noise didn't stop, it built and grew, thin and cold, snapping and pinging. Concrete and brick giving way, then: *WHOOOOOM...*

The back wall disappeared. One moment everything beyond the torch's beam was utter darkness, and the next a pale grey light snarled into the basement – borne on the wings of a howling wind. Sucking the air from the room, sending it spiralling out into the night, as what was left of Leah MacNeil vanished into the North Sea.

Waves booming and roaring right outside that ragged patch of grey.

Gordon Smith leered in his DIY monster-light. As if he wasn't already horrific enough. 'Time to say goodnight, children.' Edging closer, shiny stick in one hand, Joseph's cutthroat razor in the other.

I scrabbled backwards, up the bottom couple of steps. And something bumped against my shoulder. Something about the size of a thermos flask with silver handles. Cold and smooth against my palm as I grabbed it. 'Oh no it isn't.'

'That's the *spirit*!' The razor's blade glinted in the narrow torch beam. 'OH YES IT IS!' Lunging for me, cutthroat sizzling through the angry air.

I lunged too – left arm up to block it, right swinging hard.

It was like being punched in the bicep. And then the impact of Caroline's urn, smashing into his head, shuddered up my arm.

'Ungh...' Smith reared away from me, a silhouette against the angry storm. 'Don't...'

Another push, swinging the urn like a baseball bat.
Thunk.

The crunching thump of old cardboard boxes collapsing under someone's weight.

Bouncing the urn off Smith's head must've loosened the lid, because it popped off, and a vortex of gritty grey swirled its way through the torchlight, en route to the gaping hole at the end of the basement.

'CAROLINE!' Banging and crashing through the junk.

I snatched up the phone and swung the torch around.

There was Smith, on his hands and knees, scraping dirt and ashes from the concrete floor. 'No!'

Where are you, you rotten...?

There – lying on its back, against the leg of a mouldy old teddy bear. Matt, black, and deadly. The phone went back in my bandaged hand and I snatched the gun up again.

Let's see how Evil Uncle Abanazar did with a couple of bullets in him.

The basement shook and that ragged slab of grey got bigger. Chunks of the upper floor raining down at the far end, tumbling away into the hungry waves.

'What have you done?' He was still on his knees, scooping up handfuls of dust.

I tossed the urn to him. It hit the concrete and bounced with a hollow ringing *poonk*.

'WHAT HAVE YOU DONE?' Reaching for it.

Three limping steps and I was close enough to jam the .22's barrel into the back of his right knee. 'It's after midnight, Smith. Time to turn back into a pumpkin.' And pulled the trigger.

It was as if someone had slammed a claw-hammer down on a sheet of metal, the sound echoing off the roof before being swallowed by the howling wind.

Must've come as a shock, because Smith didn't start screaming till I stuck the barrel into the back of his left knee.

Another hammer blow.

The room rumbled. The ice cracked. Another chunk of basement vanished.

Definitely time to go.

Gordon Smith stared back at me in the thin beam of the phone's torch, eyes wide, mouth wide – full of teeth and agony. Both hands wrapped around his knees, blood pulsing out between his pale fingers. Tears streaming down his face. He was saying something, but whatever it was, the storm was louder.

Back to Shifty.

'God's sake, man, you weigh a bloody ton...' But I got my shoulder under him, hauling and shoving and struggling his fat bloody arse up the wooden steps, heaving him onto the living room floor. Rolling him clear of the trapdoor, so I could slam it shut. Wind whistling through the gaps – pulled down by the air roaring out through the basement.

Probably gilding the lily, but in case a double kneecapping wasn't enough to keep Gordon Smith where I'd left him, I put my shoulder to Helen's multigym and *pushed*.

Teeth gritted, putting my back into it...

The entire thing crashed into the floorboards with a wood-splintering crunch, completely covering the trapdoor with about a ton of metal.

Yeah, Smith was going nowhere.

I grabbed a handful of Shifty's collar and dragged him backwards out of the room, legs aching from the effort, along the hall and out the front—

Bloody thing was *locked*.

Another booming rumble and the sound of rending beams and cracking mortar drowned out the wind.

Was there time to get him all the way down the hall and out through the kitchen?

He had the keys on him.

Great – why don't I stand here like a bloody moron, going through Shifty's pockets WHILE THE BASTARDING HOUSE FALLS DOWN!

'AAAAAAARGH!' I turned him around and hauled his lardy backside down the hall, sweat prickling in the cold air, breath huffing out great plumes of steam. 'If we get out of this alive, you're going on a *massive* diet.'

His body slid better on the kitchen linoleum.

Out the kitchen door, and into the thundering rain and screeching storm.

My trainers dug into the wet grass, slipping and skidding through mud, pulling with both hands now. Fire and broken bottles slashing through the severed joint where my finger used to be, scarring their way up my arm. Every single step setting off a fresh explosion of flame in my bullet-hole foot.

We'd almost made it to the garden wall when Helen's house gave one final groan of pain, then thundered in on itself as the storm ate it whole.

49

The doctor stepped back to admire her handiwork. 'Not bad. You'll have a scar, but it could've been worse.'

I turned my elbow out ninety degrees. A neat line of small black stitches ran along a dark puckered ridge of skin halfway up my bicep – stained dark orange with antiseptic. That 'punch' had been the cutthroat razor. Good job Gordon Smith hadn't kept it sharp or the thing would've chopped its way right down to the bone. 'Thanks.'

A blush darkened her cheeks. 'Twice in one day. We must stop meeting like this.' Dr Fotheringham put the forceps and needle holder back on the tray. 'If anyone asks, I gave you amoxicillin.' Pocketing a couple of small boxes. 'Obviously I'm not going to really give you *more* antibiotics, because, well, you know.'

'Don't worry, your secret's safe with me.'

Outside the curtained cubicle, the sounds of Castle Hill Infirmary A-and-E thrummed and bustled all around us. Moaning, crying, someone singing a sectarian song while someone else screamed at them to shut their orange-bastard mouth.

Fotheringham wrapped the wound in gauze, then cotton wool, then crisp white bandages. Pulling them tight and tying them off. She didn't look me in the eye once. 'Well, that's us all done. You'll need to get those stitches out in about a fortnight: better safe than sorry.'

The sound of someone being copiously sick echoed through from the next-door cubicle, but Fotheringham didn't even flinch. 'Can I ask,' she pointed at my arm, 'was this the same "serial killer"?'

I pulled my bloodstained shirt back on and hopped off the trolley. 'Not any more.'

Fotheringham wrestled me into a bulky black padded sling, adjusting the straps and Velcro till the entire arm was immobile. Then helped me drape my 'borrowed' leather jacket over my shoulders. 'It'll take a while to heal, so make sure you rest it.'

'Want to take a little advice from someone who's been where you are? Once people like Joseph and Francis get their hooks in you, it's not so easy to wriggle free. Stop the gambling, get help, or you'll be gutted and filleted by the time they're done.'

She gave me a small sad smile. 'Oh, how I *wish* it was that easy...'

They'd moved Kenneth Dewar out of the High Dependency ward into a private room on the sixth floor, with a uniformed PC sitting guard outside, reading a Hamish Macbeth novel: *Death of a Crime Writer.* She looked up as I hobbled over on a borrowed NHS walking stick. 'Guv.'

So, one of the old guard, before my demotion.

I nodded at the observation window. 'He say anything yet?'

'Came round about two hours ago. Since then it's been mostly sobbing and sleeping. Think they've got him on some *pretty* strong meds.' She put a marker in her book. 'Mother ... I mean, DI Malcolmson's been looking for you. Says you're not answering your phone.'

Maybe because I hadn't actually worked out what, or how much, to tell her yet.

'Any chance...?' I pointed at the door.

The PC raised an eyebrow. 'On your own? Sod all, Guv. Orders from the Chief Super, in triplicate: Dewar goes to trial, dirty wee child-murdering bastard that he is.'

'Wouldn't have it any other way.' After all, we needed him to get all better so he could enjoy his daily torture. I opened the door and stepped into the familiar disinfectant-and-misery-scented air.

They'd hooked him up to a drip and a heart monitor, but other than that, he was machinery-free. Lying there, on his back, with his mouth hanging open, chest rising and falling in time to a deep rumbling snore.

Probably loud enough to disturb the other patients. That wasn't fair, was it? Someone should do something about that.

So I pinched his nose shut, the palm of my hand covering his mouth.

'Guv!'

Dewar spluttered his way into consciousness, a small scream muffled by my hand.

I let go and gave the PC a smile. 'Oh look, he's awake.'

Dewar blinked at me, then around at the room – as if taking it in for the first time. 'How…?'

The chair's rubber feet squealed across the green-terrazzo floor as I pulled it closer to the bed. Thumped down in it. 'Not going to kid you, Kenny, I'm tired, I'm sore, and I've had a *bastard* of a day.' Pointing at the PC. 'She's here to make sure I don't strangle you, like you strangled Andrew Brennan, Oscar Harris, Lewis Talbot, and Toby Macmillan.'

He closed his eyes and nodded, mouth a tight squirming line as tears squeezed out. 'I'm sorry.'

'So you keep saying.' I leaned forward. 'You thought you'd fooled everyone, didn't you? But you didn't fool Alice.'

'She … she'd been so *nice* to me … and then … then she called and said … and said she wanted to talk to me again.' Big fat tears plopped onto the sheet, turning the fabric the colour of spoiled milk. 'And I knew she'd … she'd worked it out.'

'So you tried to kill her.'

'I didn't want… I need you to understand … understand why—'

'Kenny, Kenny, Kenny: I don't care.' I tilted my head back and winked at our uniformed friend. 'You might want to cover your ears for this part: plausible deniability.'

She shifted her feet, hands opening and closing. 'You're not going to *hurt* him, are you?'

'Me? Hurt *him*? Why on earth would I do that? Now Simon says: cover your ears.'

She did.

'Remember when you said I should find the bastard who killed all those little boys, and make him *pay*?' I leaned in. 'This is for Andrew, Oscar, Lewis, and Toby. But it's *especially* for what you did to Alice.' Had to be quick, before the PC could stop me – standing and slamming my right fist into his face. Putting some weight behind it. Driving his head back into the pillows.

'GUV!' She lunged, but I backed away from the bed, hand up.

'All finished.' Arthritis howled its way through my knuckles, but it was worth it.

'What the *hell* have you done?' Staring at Dewar as scarlet gushed out of his newly squint nose.

'I didn't do anything, Constable. Kenneth Dewar became distressed – probably the guilt of strangling four wee boys – and tried to injure himself. I saw you rush to his aid and save the day. You should get some sort of commendation for that.'

She licked her lips. Looked from Dewar's sobbing, blood-dripping face, to me, then back again. 'I saved the day?'

'Like a pro. Very proud of you.'

A nod. 'Cool.'

Kenneth Dewar: welcome to the rest of your life.

Shifty threw back his blankets and sat bolt upright in his hospital bed. 'Come on, time to go home.'

I put a hand against his chest and pushed him back into the crinkled sheets. 'You've got concussion, you silly bugger.' Pulled the blankets over him again. 'You're going nowhere.'

Someone had removed his eyepatch, so instead of a jaunty-big-fat-bald-pirate, he looked more like a confused hairless middle-aged man with a weight problem and a clenched fist of scar tissue where his right eye should have been. He squinted the other one at me. 'What happened in the basement?'

A voice behind me: 'Yes, Ash, what *did* happen in that basement?'

Ah...

'Mother, I hear you've been looking for me?'

When I turned, she was standing in the doorway, a bit on the rumpled side, heavy bags under her eyes, thick brown overcoat flapped open to reveal a pair of jeans and a sweatshirt with a grinning cat on it. Not quite 'I got dressed in the dark', but close enough.

Mind you, it wasn't as if I was going to win any prizes for sartorial elegance – done up in the same clothes I'd gone to work in yesterday morning. All covered in dried blood and dirt and dust.

She looked me up and down, drinking it all in. 'You smell like a fight in an abattoir.'

I pointed at Shifty. 'DI Morrow got a tipoff that Gordon Smith had been seen in Oldcastle. We thought he might go back to Clachmara, so we headed over there. Turned out we were right.'

'And?'

'He resisted arrest. DI Morrow and I barely managed to get out before the house fell into the sea. Gordon Smith didn't.' Not sure if it was worth complicating things, but if the bodies washed up somewhere any half-decent pathologist *might* just notice someone had blown both of Smith's kneecaps off: 'When we got there he was fighting with Leah MacNeil, she managed to wrestle the gun off him.'

'There was a *gun*?'

I shrugged. 'She didn't get out either. Shifty and I tried, but...' A long weary sigh. 'She kept screaming about how he'd killed her mother and she was going to make him pay.'

That should cover it. And with any luck, by the time Leah's body turned up – if it ever did – it would've been battered about enough by the storm, collapsing headland, and waves to obscure any signs she'd been tortured. Wouldn't hurt if the fish and crabs ate most of the evidence, either.

'Oh Christ.' Mother covered her face with her hands. 'Helen MacNeil will go berserk when she finds out we let her grand-daughter die.'

'Maybe not. Leah did avenge her mother, after all. Old-school gangsters like Helen would've appreciated that.' Sod it: wrong tense. Should've been, *will appreciate* that. But hopefully Mother wouldn't notice.

She lowered her hands and narrowed her eyes. 'Why do I get the feeling you're not telling me everything?'

'No idea. But you should be putting Shifty forward for a Queen's Medal.' I patted him on the arm. 'He was a brave little soldier and a credit to the force. I couldn't have got out of there, without him.' Which had the benefit of not actually being a lie – there was no way I'd leave Shifty in a collapsing building.

The sounds of a busy hospital, chuntering away in the wee small hours, throbbed through the floor and air conditioning.

Eventually Mother nodded. 'I can't remember, were you always this much of a pain in the backside?'

'Probably.'

'Ow...' I creaked and groaned my way into the high-backed chair beside Alice's bed. 'What a sodding day.' Wasn't a single inch of me that didn't ache. And that was *after* taking a double dose of Dr Fotheringham's painkillers.

Alice hadn't moved since I'd last seen her – still lying there, hooked up to her bank of machinery, one arm in a cast from shoulder to fingertips, one leg from hip to toes, bandages and cannulas and drips and wires and a bag dangling from the bedframe.

I struggled out of my jacket and draped it over my chest.

Should probably have gone home first for a shower and a change of clothes, but the last faint wisps of adrenaline had gone, leaving nothing but the inevitable crash into unconsciousness. And if I was going to fall asleep for eighteen hours, I'd much rather do it here.

In case she woke up.

Eyelids were getting almost as heavy as my head.

A jaw-cracking yawn.

I let my head fall back. Up above, the ceiling tiles made a moonscape of tiny pocks and craters. Nearly died *twice* today, something of a record, even for me.

Tomorrow: going to have a long lie-in, nice big breakfast – sod salted porridge and decaf tea, it was time for a proper fry-up at that greasy spoon down Tollbooth Row – then take the wee man for a hobble in Kings Park. Throw some bread at the...

Oh bugger.

I sat up and fumbled Alice's phone from my pocket. Unlocked it. Then went searching for that business card. Dialled the number.

A mumbled voice. *'Hello?'* The sound of lips smacking on sleep-sticky breath. *'I mean, J-and-F Freelance Consultants, how can—'*

'Joseph, I know it's late, but I need your help.'

Because sometimes you really did need the assistance of two *very* capable gentlemen with a somewhat *laissez-faire* attitude to other people's physical wellbeing.

— time, gentlemen, please —

50

'Well?'

I let the blind fall back. 'All gone.'

The private room was festooned with Mylar balloons, some at full bobbing strength, others at half-mast, all covered in slogans like 'Get Well Soon!', 'You're A STAR!', and for some bizarre reason, 'HAPPY BIRTHDAY!'

'Three days.' Sitting in the visitor's chair, Shifty curled his lip. 'You'd think catching two massive serial killers would hold their attention for *at least* a week. Four dead wee boys and … how many victims for Gordon Smith?'

'No way of knowing.' Even if Alice and Franklin were right about Smith keeping all his homemade torture porn on his phone, it got wheeched out into the North Sea – along with the man himself, Leah's body, and Helen's house. '*At least* thirty-six, if you count the panto cast and crew that went missing from productions he worked on, plus the basement Polaroids. And we've only got IDs for about a dozen of those.'

Shifty scratched at the wadding taped to the back of his head. 'Bloody media.'

'Didn't you hear? Train crash at Waverley Station this morning: thirteen dead, eighty-seven injured. Suspected terrorism.'

A grimace. 'Fair enough. But they could—'

My new phone blared out its anonymous ringtone. 'Hold

that thought.' I pulled it out and checked the screen. Not a number I recognised. Pressed the button anyway. 'Hello?'

'*ASH, YOU UTTER BASTARD!*' For some strange reason, Jennifer Prentice sounded upset. Poor thing. '*WHAT THE BUGGERING HELL DID YOU DO?*'

'Me? Why do you think I did anything?'

'*Because I've had four parking tickets since Wednesday, two on-the-spot fines, AND MY BLOODY BOSS JUST SACKED ME FROM THE BLOODY PAPER!*'

'Oh dear, that *does* sound terrible.' Doing my best not to grin. 'Bye, Jennifer.' I hung up.

Shifty beamed back at me. 'She like her present?'

'Loving it.' Amazing what could be achieved if you had dirt on the right kind of people.

The room's door opened and a nurse nodded at us, dressed in pale-green scrubs and white oversized trainers, hair pulled up in a bun, a piercing in each of his nostrils. 'Did anyone order a forensic psychologist?'

Shifty's eyebrows went up. 'With extra cheese?'

The nurse ducked out again, then reappeared wheeling Alice into the room. 'Ta-daaa...'

She'd put on the baggy blue tracksuit I'd bought her at Abdel's Bargain Warehouse – roomy enough to fit over the cast on her left leg and the one on her right arm – with 'Unicornicopia' picked out in pink sequins across the chest.

One look, and Shifty burst out laughing.

'What?' Her voice slightly muzzy. They'd scaled back on the bandages, but most of her face was stained navy and yellow. No white at all in her left eye, only red. 'What's so funny?'

'Without meaning to come off as a complete gay stereotype: Girlfriend, you should *not* go out dressed like that.'

'Ash?'

'You do look a teeny bit like a Smurf with jaundice.'

She stared down at herself. 'Oh, Ash!'

'It fits OK? That's all that matters.' I took hold of the wheel-chair's handles.

The nurse flipped off the brake. 'Once round the block, then I want her back in bed, understand?'

'Yeah, we'll see how we go.'

'So Dorothy says, "Don't look at me, I'm vegetarian: I had the falafel for lunch," and she's in getting her hip resurfaced because apparently they didn't put it in properly the first time, which isn't exactly great, is it, you come in here you think they know what they're doing, but she'd had the falafel which meant—'

An electronic voice crackled out in the lift. 'Ground floor. Doors opening.'

'—had to be someone *else* who'd nabbed the packet of Peperami off Rosemary's bedside cabinet and it can't have been Jeanette, because they took her dentures out before they did her colonoscopy and lost them.'

Shifty pulled a face over Alice's head, rolling his eyes and sticking his tongue out.

I wheeled her out into the hospital's reception area – a wide expanse of brown tiles with steel benches painted in primary colours to match the various wards and lines set into the floor.

'That's when I had my revelation, you see... Ash? Are you listening?'

There – over in the pink section with 'Maternity' in big white letters on the wall behind her. It was thingy, the pregnant almost-qualified forensic anthropologist from Clachmara. The one who'd spotted the bones sticking out of the crumbling headland. Which meant, technically, a lot of this was all her fault.

She must've sensed me staring, because she looked up from whatever newspaper she was reading and waved.

Sod.

Suppose I should really go say hello.

'Stay here a minute, OK?' I abandoned the wheelchair and limped over there.

She had her kid with her, but he was hunched over a colouring-in book, probably making a dog's arse of another paleontologically inaccurate rendering.

481

She smiled and levered herself out of the metal seat, one hand cupping the underside of her bulge. 'Mr Henderson.' Face flushed, neck too – the skin bright pink as it disappeared into her stripy top. 'What are you doing here? Are you here to see me?'

'No, it's...' Pointing back towards Alice and Shifty.

'Oh, right. Yes.' Sounding disappointed. 'Anyway, I wanted to say, thank you. DI Malcolmson said it was your idea to get me involved in that post mortem? Of the remains you found buried in Gordon Smith's garden?' She pulled a quick frog face and shrugged, eyes getting wider with every word: 'Best – day – at – work – *ever*. We even got an ID! And Professor Twining was so impressed he offered me a job on the spot. Well, soon as I evict this teeny monster.' Patting her swollen stomach. 'I can even go back and finish my degree part-time.'

'Good. I'm glad.'

Her smile slipped. 'Of course, the council came round the next day and condemned my house, so Alfie and me will be homeless in two weeks, but there you go. At least I got to tell them to shove their sixteen-grand demolition-and-recycling fee up their landfill site. I only rent the thing, not own it.'

'Well, I thought I should come over and, you know...' Backing away.

'If you hear about a council house going spare or anything, let me know, OK?'

'Will do.'

'Thanks again.' Grinning and waving at me as I limped back to Alice and Shifty. 'Maybe we'll get to work together, catch more killers! How cool will that be?'

Yeah, she was probably nutty enough to fit right in.

'Where was I?' Alice frowned up at me as I took hold of the wheelchair's handles again. 'Oh, yes: so that's when I had my revelation, you see Phyllis was on the ward because they were digging out an ingrowing toenail which is meant to be a day procedure, but she's got cystitis and kidney stones the size of—'

'Speaking of revelations,' heading for the main exit in a last-ditch attempt to derail *Dr Alice McDonald and the Mysterious Case*

482

of the Disappearing Peperami, 'Bear interviewed Kenneth Dewar yesterday. Dewar says he killed the boys to "break the cycle".'

Alice looked up at me. 'Cycle?'

'Says he knew most of his clients were abused as children and that turned them into people who abused children. And he knew his clients had abused these little boys, so killing them was breaking the cycle. Thinks he's a hero for saving all the children they'd have grown up to abuse.'

The doors hissed open and we emerged into the glowing golden light of a sun-drenched Friday morning. Not a cloud in the sky, not a hint of wind.

'Well that's...' Alice shook her head. 'Hold on, he says he took no sexual pleasure from killing them? He didn't go home and fantasise about it, while he played with himself?'

'Purely a selfless act, apparently.'

A large shiny black Range Rover sat at the edge of the turning circle, in defiance of the hospital's no-entry policy for anything other than ambulances and buses. I aimed for it.

'If he was doing it for the good of the community, why did he strangle and revive Lewis Talbot over and over again for an hour and a half?'

'That's what I asked.'

Shifty sniffed. 'Because he's a lying scumbag?'

'Maybe he believes it himself? Or he needs to.' Alice tilted her head back, eyes closed, sunning her bruises. 'After all, he doesn't *want* to be a monster, does he? He wants to be the hero of his own story. So he can fantasise and masturbate and think he's doing the world a good turn all at the same time.'

Soon as we got within six feet of the Range Rover, the passenger door popped open and Joseph stepped out – dressed in a sharp black suit with a white shirt and red tie. Greying fibreglass cast poking out the end of his left sleeve. The wad of padding had gone from his head, leaving a small white square dressing behind. He smiled and performed a small bow. 'Dr McDonald, how delightful to see you up and about, even if it's in a non-ambulatory capacity.'

Alice stiffened in the wheelchair.

I put a hand on her shoulder. 'It's OK.'

'And Detective Inspector Morrow, I trust you're enjoying this fine morning and your well-earned veneration for capturing both the Oldcastle Child-Strangler *and* the Coffinmaker. Bravo!'

Shifty didn't move. Barely even breathed.

I nodded at the car. 'You managed?'

'Oh, indubitably, my dear Mr Henderson, we did indeed manage.' He turned. 'Francis, can you bring our guest out, please?'

A thunk from the other side of the huge car, then another one, and Francis emerged, boasting a face that was even more bruised than Alice's. And there, trotting along behind him, was—

'Henry!' Alice threw her working arm out. 'Oh my lovely hairy man!'

The wee lad scrabbled at the end of his lead, pulling to get to her, but Francis held on tight till Henry jumped up into Alice's lap, then handed the leash to me with a nod. ''Spector.'

Lots of wriggling and giggling as Henry slathered Alice with his big pink tongue.

'It really was quite a remarkable hunt, Mr Henderson! At first, my plan of attack was to knock on doors and … *encourage* people to report their sightings of your canine companion, but then Francis came upon the undeniably ingenious idea of putting posters up all over the area and offering a small reward. Alcoholic, rather than monetary in nature, what with our target audience residing in Kingsmeath. Lo and behold, it did indeed garner the desired result.'

Shifty backed off a pace, fists curled, shoulders back, one remaining eye narrowed.

I took my hands off the wheelchair. 'Shifty, why don't you take Alice and Henry for a walk? I won't be long.'

Shifty didn't move.

'Please.'

An ambulance siren wailed into life, somewhere behind the main hospital building, grew louder, then dopplered off into the distance.

Finally, he took hold of the handles and Henry's lead, turned the wheelchair in a sharp one-eighty, and marched off, back stiff as an ironing board.

Joseph raised one eyebrow. 'DI Morrow seems rather tense to me. I fear he bears some degree of ill-feeling towards Francis and myself as a result of that somewhat unhappy incident involving Mrs Kerrigan.'

'What do I owe you for finding the dog?'

A quick look left and right, then Joseph dropped his voice to a whisper. 'Just between us, we rather enjoyed the experience, didn't we, Francis?'

That got him a short upward jerk of the chin.

'It's so nice to be involved in a commission that doesn't involve *breaking* anything or anyone, and the look on the good doctor's face when she was reunited with her boon companion… Ah.' He placed a hand over his heart. 'That, my dear Mr Henderson, is reward enough for us.'

Dear God, Joseph and Francis were human after all.

'Thank you.'

'It is, indeed, our pleasure, Mr Henderson.' A small bow, then he climbed back into the Range Rover. 'Francis?'

The big man nodded at me again. ''Spector.' He got in behind the wheel and the huge car drove off, the wrong way up a bus lane, before cutting the corner and heading away towards Logansferry.

So it wasn't just other people's physical wellbeing they had a *laissez-faire* attitude to – it was the Highway Code, too.

By the time I caught up with them, Alice and Shifty were in a patch of green, flanked on two sides by the maternity hospital and the old Victorian sanatorium. Henry charging round and round the wheelchair, legs and tail going like the clappers, mouth hanging open in small-dog joy.

Our small dysfunctional family, back together again.

Now all we had to do was break into Wee Free McFee's scrapyard and liberate a buried security van full of stolen artwork – without getting hacked to pieces and fed to the psychotic maniac's dogs – find a reliable fence to sell the stuff, launder the money so no one could trace it, buy a small hotel on the west coast, and retire to a life in the hospitality industry.

How hard could it be...?